KILEY KNOTT

A God of Man

For the storytellers.
AI can never replace us.

Contents

Preface

When writing stories already told, already written hundreds of different ways over millennia, people may tell you that you did X wrong, or Y character is not portrayed right. May I recommend to those people who are looking for the perfect Odyssey myth story that they check out Homer's *The Odyssey.*

It's, like, really good.

It has all the Telemachus and Odysseus attention to love, in the playground of Athena's battlefield.

But this story isn't their story — it's Hermes'.

Why Hermes?

Well, besides being Odysseus' great grandfather in a handful of sources, his role in Homer's Odyssey is rather interesting. He appears only twice to the central character and it is always for the hero's benefit. I found his secret motives intriguing; Hermes has always been my favorite Greek god — his stories lend him to feel very human amid his godliness, and any immortal with human qualities makes for a great novel protagonist.

I wanted to make a unique, Ancient Grecian world with the gods and heroes we all know, balancing the myths with inserting them into this timeline. The Multiverse of Myths, one could say. Interpreting gods sometimes, inadvertently falls into tropes, but fleshing each out to have multi-faceted personalities was very important to me. This story mostly has Hermes, Poseidon, Apollo, and Athena, but I hope that the others, even in their small moments, reveal to you that they are more than a single characteristic.

Acknowledgments

I would be amiss if I didn't immediately thank my alpha readers JJ and Lauren (and our production cats: Anne, Lilly, Jinx, and Garbanzo Bean) — as well as those who contributed to funding this story and my tear production: JJ, Zav, Carter, Tess, Ashley, Michael, Ellie, and Pupbee to bring it to life with illustrations by the infallible Alina Aleksanyan. He turned my passing wishful comment into a reality and I am so grateful for all the time he took out of his own busy schedule to deal with me and my silly ideas. Seriously — an incredible artist.

Cheers to my local library, who let me wander out with a stack of the Iliad and Odyssey and other Greek myths, and hold onto them well after the due dates. Thank you musicians for providing music to hyperfixate to while I wasn't writing, so that I never could rest from the characters in this story. I'd also like to thank the Hellenist worshipers out there on the clock app; as a Catholic, I enjoyed hearing the stories of your experiences with your gods. Your altars are always so beautiful. I hope you find my fictionalized portrayal of your pantheon honorable enough!

To my family who let me sit through the holiday season ignoring everyone as I wrote for seven hours of the day, thank you. To my friends who hyped me up in my ramblings, I love you dearly. It was insane that I wrote a debut, it's even more crazy that I kept going.

A post mortem thanks to Bartholomeus Spranger and his 1585 art *Hermes and Athena* which has been used for the cover.

Chapter 1

Hundreds of slain men watered the outskirts of Troy with their blood. Soldiers with their bowels strewn several yards away donned spears between their teeth — as if they were vipers frozen in strike, though tongues rotted far from their cracked heads. Officers lay bare, stripped of their glistening and hardened armor; breastplates of grime and mud settled over each broken chest. Ditches turned into deep bloody chasms as the rain continued to pelt down over the land.

In the darkness of night, the field of Anatolia did not creak nor moan. Those who survived the slaughter retreated to their camps.

Timely Thanatos had walked his path while the butchery occurred.

Bodies of the lucky warriors were already collected for proper funeral rites — none more grand to the Archaeans than Patroclus, and Hector to the Trojans. Those whose names would be remembered to history through bardic songs and epics were taken in turns from the field. Immense pyres were struck and tiresome games distracted soldiers, while mourning wails and prayers echoed from every mortal's throat in hopes to reach the warring gods who had all fallen back to their mighty palaces of Olympus.

Save for one.

That pitiful immortal floated through the wreckage of corpses with his cloak pulled high over his helmet, shielding his face from Zeus' unyielding rainstorm. The long, split cloak draping across his chest floated behind him like the tail of a swallow, shimmering like distant stars over every decaying body he hovered by. With an outstretched arm, he displayed a golden caduceus, and upon dipping the wand to a mortal, summoned the poor thing's soul to the surface.

An ugly ghostlike visage trembled, naked and confused, the same as so many others before him.

"Worry not for where you are," the god spoke plainly. "For I'll bring you to where your brothers-in-arms await the keen Charon and his boat on the River Styx. You will not be lost along the way while I'm your guide."

He extended his free hand, armored with a light silver bracer, his palm baring gentle skin, perfect and tempting to touch. The spectre examined it with the intrigue of a poor man.

"Come, you hesitant creature," he titted, "take my hand and you'll find no more suffering on this mortal plane."

The ghost finally nodded, reached up to trace his pallid fingers against warm skin, and the soul added more starlight to the lively cloak.

For over two-hundred souls, for men young and old, the growing weight of their sorrows and regrets pulled on his shoulders. But the buzzing wings on his sandals wouldn't let him be made any heavier for it, dashing over the bloody mounds and foul-smelling earth. He placed his caduceus in its loop behind his back and glanced once more across the land of waste and sorrow. A scrutinizing sweep to be sure he left no soul unattended, lest he'd be an awful psychopomp.

Choking silence and the blackness of death were the only two remaining on the field once teeming with rows of men and their chariots.

The god hovered for a moment longer; the tails of his cloak unbothered by the rain that sought to pull all warmth from his body. With a sigh, he breathed out the tainted air in his great lungs, and, in the breeze, disappeared from Troy.

His flight over Oceanus covered hundreds of miles. The kind, old Titan whose waters led to the Underworld knew this taken path by heart, and allowed the small psychopomp countless untroubled passages. He basked in the warm mist and gently swayed over rocking waves as the rain dispersed the further west he traveled. The cloak flew back off his head, caught by the wind as it cut around a sleek helmet crafted by Hephaestus himself, altered for the times of war. Wings unfurling from under the helm propelled him faster until he became a mirage on the ocean's surface, casting waves aside to bring rocking wakes for boats miles away.

He hoped that this journey was at least *entertaining* for the souls he carried with him. No mortal could ever say they traveled faster than this.

Intransigent, no matter how many times he was told by Thanatos that mortals feel very little once dead, he still insisted that under his guidance, the fun was untouched by the affliction of mere death.

A cave grand enough to house a fleet of ships sat jaggedly out of the water at the western-most edge of the world. Rocks of black kimberlite and volcanic slate, with terrifying rows of toothlike stalactites, foreshadowed the massive, black dog that guarded its inside. Immense pillars of carved silver towered upwards toward the heavens.

Horrifying as it appeared, the god flew right in — a twinkling aurora of a figure.

Down he plunged over the river rapids into the deep cavern that fell far beneath the earth. Humid gusts ruffled his curly hair and the strange light of the approaching river gave his usual rosy skin a green hue.

Here was Styx, daughter of Oceanus. Her river was calm and cold, swirling with the shimmer of millions of oaths and promises; the clarity of the water made the bottom appear within arms reach — a mistake for many who tried to cross it without the loyal ferryman.

The beaches between Styx and the Acheron River were lined with souls that awaited their journey to the Underworld. Those who were fortunate enough to be buried properly held their coins in hand. It was a fruitless task to ignore the wailing laments heard echoing through the cave. The psychopomp settled himself atop a flat stone that overlooked the queue of men and women, and his billowing cloak finally settled.

He removed his wand from the many belts about his waist and presented it in front of him. From the starlit cloak to the caduceus the souls ran out one by one. A dozen to a hundred, two-hundred and more added to the expansive shore until the cloak was still and left a simple teal. Several ghosts grasped at his legs and clothing. The touch was inconsequential to him — a weak, cool sensation — and he indulged some by letting their hands remain as he descended the rocky pedestal. His sandals rendered him so weightless that his feet left no prints in the sand.

These dead soldiers joined a line that wrapped and coiled like a snake. Among them was one soul that would need further guidance, and the poor god was happy to accommodate.

Reaching the center of the newly arrived, he crouched to the sand and rested his hand over the infant. Among the boy's wrappings were two gold coins to pay, for he was dearly loved. Minding his head, the god lifted the infant into his arms and continued on to the river's edge to wait among the dead.

Time was irrelevant down in the Underworld. He babbled away to the spectres next to him as they stared into the void. Too many hours had passed since he was able to speak to someone with working ears, to hear his own voice as he complained and jested and talked much about nothing as the back of his mind rattled with distant prayers and pleas.

They all waited for the toll, the deep resonating bell that rang in the ferryman's arrival.

Charon — that keen man, pulling his boat along the river with solid, sure strokes — approached the shore with his head dipped low, face half-obscured by the ragged birrus pulled up over him. He was delightfully melancholy, not much of a talker as he held out his hand the moment he stopped his boat for the payment from each ghost for safe passage.

The young god lifted his eyes from beneath his helmet and cocked his head as he waited for the souls to board. Charon's deep set, dark stare slowly shifted to look at him. A blink.

"Hermes," he muttered through a tired, gravely breath.

What joy! A true welcome this time.

"Fair and fierce Charon," Hermes said with a grandiose sweep of an arm. "I've come with the fallen warriors of Man's consequence of Troy. Mighty father Zeus is rather content with the realm's population and has called the gods to his halls." He paused only for a moment to regard Charon's apathetic brow, then added, "Lord Hades should expect no more great influx of souls for a few weeks, at least. I have yet to return home since being commanded out. You recall I've delivered Prince Hector in days past, and *now…*" He raised the infant. "Prince Astyanax, for you, my dear friend."

Charon's heavy gaze lowered to the babe.

"If you could deliver him to his father in Elysium; it'll please Lord Apollo immensely — after losing the city he championed over — to see the royal family reunited."

"There is no guarantee that he will be recognized," Charon said.

"So the infant is a little crushed from his deadly fall," Hermes shrugged, "but humans are clever and fathers know their sons. Take him to appease *me*, if not the sharpshooter, Apollo. He comes with payment."

Presenting Charon with the gold coins, the ferryman shifted his hardened jaw. Hermes sprinkled on extra shimmer to entice the avaricious quality that made him so compliant with his laborious job. With a silent sigh, Charon unfolded his left hand.

Hermes plopped the spirit right into the crook of his arm. "He's a baby, Charon," he exclaimed, sliding the coins into the psychopomp's pouch. "Can't expect him to get up, make a lyre and steal away with some cattle now, can we? I anticipate returning with a lighter load, if Zeus is merciful. I know how much you long to see me for some much needed conversation."

Charon's boat gently rocked as he adjusted his hold on the ghostly prince, his right hand gripping his pole. From under his hood, he shook his head with all the respect he certainly held for Hermes.

The continued line of lamenting spirits struck out their arms as they watched the ferry float away from shore again. The Guide of the Dead stood surrounded on the sandy beach, still being poked with tepid human fingers. He titted the impatient ones away, pointing to the line for them to stand and await their fate, and pulled loose the split-tailed cloak on his shoulders, no longer weighted with souls.

✳ ✳ ✳

Hermes hadn't slept a wink in five days.

Ascending from the rivers of the Underworld, his winged sandals pushed his strides and the feathers sprouting from under his helmet pulled him skyward out of the cave and back into the realm of Man. The air was crisp and calm of any storm. Resting the caduceus on his shoulder, Hermes peered to the distant shores of Troy.

Fires flickered on the shores where the Greeks docked their ships. They were to be on their *Nostoi* soon once the Fates' proclamation was played out. Every journey to be its own challenge, most definitely.

Prayers bubbled up as the mortals lay down for sleep and he contently granted them the rest and safe passages through their dreams. The nightmares that happened when their eyes were opened were gruesome enough.

Playing with them was one thing: stirring the pot when their society was too complacent and boring — but not war. He didn't take pleasure in fighting as Lord Ares did. It felt inappropriate; he was the last god these little humans prayed to in their short days before they laid in their most vulnerable state. He could lead a child or a cat to steal away with clothing or convince wives to shave away their kings' beards as they slept, but never would he ask for such violence.

With a long, grumbling yawn disguised as a song, Hermes tilted his head back and continued upwards. He climbed to Olympus, peeling through the layers of clouds that hid the top of the mountain from view. The hairs on his bare arm frosted, melted, and dried in an instant as he broke the surface; the moon was bright and the stars dazzled in the violet sky above palaces and grand gardens that rolled on for miles.

His sore knees bent more than usual as he landed on the stone courtyard and creaked to straighten. It was quiet for now — a rarity these years since quarreling and fighting split the Pantheon down the middle.

It was not Hermes' place to put the blame on anyone, but it was mostly Aphrodite's fault for blowing the petty mortal's gesture out of proportion and making a mockery of the holy Queen Hera and dutiful Athena.

That mortal, *Paris,* and his stealing away with a married woman sent the whole world crumbling in on itself. Olympus had never been so engorged with the drama of humanity. Even Hermes, who often saw himself as the curious one in human affairs, intended for the tryst to cause *some* mischief, but not a war. Mortals were waiting for an excuse to fight. Immortals too, for that matter. Yet for much of the infighting, he was ordered to sit back and await Zeus' commands like a meager cupbearer.

But he wasn't pointing fingers or anything.

Olympus was presently sleeping and Hermes yearned for the sensation of polite and temporary oblivion. He lumbered up winding staircases, through marble halls gilded with gold, and floated egregiously up another raised walkway to where the gods and goddesses' private homes were built. Beautiful and expertly crafted by Hephaestus, each was personalized to cater to the Olympian within.

Arms straining, he all but climbed up his own balcony to his chambers and fell through the open glass door.

Contrary to his love in taking up the entire sky with his flying, Hermes' abode was quite cozy. Perhaps being raised in a cave lent him the desire for comfort and quick access to anything he needed. The drapings along the wall and over his bed were a deep green, twisted with ivy carefully tended to by the mountain nymphs who lived within his palace.

He eyed the bed — softened with feathers and covered in silk — but his person was aptly *putrid.* Even his handmaidens' lips curled at the sight of him.

Hermes took to his chair instead, thumping into the cushions like a weary, old man. His girls wouldn't dare touch his Talaria without permission, but it took another moment for motivation to return, and he unlaced the leather sandals until his feet were freed and soaking in a large bowl. The wings poking out from gaps in his helmet folded so he could remove the metal as well, and the feathers happily fluffed up his own bronzed curls that lay just below his chin.

Off went his belts, sheath, and bags; maidens were very skilled with this. The caduceus was carefully placed on its pedestal near the bed. Hermes let the nymph undress him from the exomis he donned — the short, white tunic embroidered heavily along the edges with gold thread was like his uniform — and the cloak that slid from his shoulders.

No one was more content than him to be sitting naked knowing bathwater was being heated.

Immortal as they were, muscles still could ache and flesh could still be marred.

"Play a song for me," Hermes said, and two nymphs took up a flute. He felt no pity for the late hour — the staff of his household knew the time he worked was far more arbitrary than other gods. And he cared little if the noise from his walls disturbed his neighbors.

He rested his head back against the tub as his hair and feathers were gently washed, and his arms and legs firmly scrubbed and oiled. They presented him with a platter of ambrosia and a goblet filled to the brim with nectar.

Constant prayers continued to pour in, and he closed his eyes to grant as many as he could.

"My lord," his top handmaiden in pink said in her softest voice, "you have a visitor."

Hermes sipped at his goblet. "What madman has come to me at this late hour? They must be in terrible trouble or else they'd be at rest."

"The sun lord, my lord."

"Which one?"

"The pretty one, my lord."

Opening an eye, he glanced at the smiling nymph. "Which pretty one, Lyricaun?"

The nymph leaned on one foot. "My lord, it is your brother."

"Ah," Hermes said, sinking back into the water. "Madman indeed. Yes, let him in."

A chair draped with fur was brought next to the bath, a large, overflowing goblet set beside it. Through the large door that Hermes hardly ever used despite it leading to the rest of his home, entered Apollo. He was unarmored from his warring goldplate, wearing his golden, ankle-length chiton that glimmered in the candlelight, and a simple braided cord tied about his waist. An extra robe fell about loosely to his elbows and dragged behind him. The war had tired him too, if the weariness under his eyes that made the brown skin dull was any sign.

"Heard my arrival and had to climb from your bed, my dear Apollo?" Hermes asked, gesturing for him to sit.

Apollo worked at his lip and kept his amber eyes to the floor, but sat all the same. "I did hear you, yes. I haven't heard you in some time. Not since the gods faced each other in combat." He pinched the muscles of his hands. "I… did not see you amongst the violence."

"I was told you stood against Poseidon himself and declared you wouldn't fight him," Hermes said, swallowing the rest of his nectar. "Very honorable, much expected from our god of health not to bruise that old uncle of ours."

Apollo smiled, and nodded to the music that continued in the chamber. Hermes watched his thoughts tick through his head before arriving at his tongue. "My mother spoke to me not long after," he replied. "When *you* faced her, she spoke of — after Hera beat Artemis with her own bow and my mother was shaking with anguish for her."

Setting his cup atop his chest, Hermes pursed his lips. "Did she tell you of how immensely she kicked my ass? I nearly wept at her power, that amazing Leto. Sent me running to the hills!"

"She said you would not fight her."

He tsked and shook his head. "Pity. I would've loved to hear how she spun her story about my humiliating defeat. It would've been perfect. Tell Leto, if there's a next time, to make a lie as awesome and detailed as possible so I may laugh at myself more."

Apollo's warm hand fell atop Hermes' head. "Thank you, Brother, for not harming her. I am indebted to you."

"Oh, cease that nonsense. I doubt Lady Amphitrite would thank you for not blinding her husband. I could *never* bring myself to raise a hand to such an honorable and kind goddess. And as your mother, I wouldn't harm our friendship for which I so dearly cherish." Hermes picked at the platter of food as Apollo's fingers combed through his hair. "But you couldn't have just visited me in the middle of the night to offer your thanks. Your beauty sleep is needed."

"*Needed?* You rascal, I worried for you! So often I think Hades may keep you down there at work to grow his land and till them with souls."

"I'm a guide. It's my duty and I'm happy to do it," Hermes said, spinning his drink slowly. The nectar was too far gone to spill anywhere. "I *am* happy to do it."

His dear brother, the color gold itself personified, sang, "I do not believe that to be completely true." Propped against the back of the chair, he rested his chin on his arm. "At least not at this instant."

The bath was growing uncomfortable.

Setting his cup down, Hermes raised himself from the tub — the water splashing delicately back into its basin — and waited to be rushed and draped in soft linens. Apollo pulled his feet up onto his chair, patiently watching his little brother walk himself in circles with his handmaidens before ceremoniously collapsing back onto a divan. The wings sprouting from his head fluttered and spread themselves over his eyes.

"I haven't rested since I escorted Priam to his son's corpse and made sure he escaped. You'd have to tell me how many times Helios has pulled his chariot across the sky, I haven't had the time to look around myself. When I say I haven't felt the ground either in eons, Brother. Gaia may have forgotten about me —"

"Oh, Hermes," Apollo said.

"The mortals you've slain, that Ares and Athena slaughtered, those that drowned in a mere inch of the rain that Father sent over your city as they lay bleeding out… I've delivered countless souls to the shores of the Styx. And between these warriors, there are the little families that wait for them, passing in grief or taking their own lives." Clapping a hand to his ear, a heavy groan slipped through his defenses. "I can still hear them, you know, begging for me to bring their husbands, their sons, home. Yet they are *dead*, and I've already brought them to Charon."

Like a melting candle, Apollo drooped deeper into his chair. His long hair swayed in a phantom breeze. "It is a pity how fragile mortals are and how easily they bring about war. The prayers I have been receiving are from a captured and enslaved people now. I champion over a sacked city and yet those who have burned it sacrifice to me in their games. My heart grieves.

I could slay them all, but that would bring you more trouble."

"I wish to guide them home. As the Achaeans take to their ships to leave Troy's beaches, I can only plead to Father to send me to lead them to their people. I'd fill their sails and put strength into the arms of their rowers. When an assembly is called, I may find the courage. I heard the last one, but I was a thousand miles away."

Maybe it was a thousand and one. It was difficult to keep track of finite time in the span of forever.

Hermes opened his eyes. Apollo raised his brow.

"What is it?" he asked.

"My head's quiet," Hermes said.

"They have all fallen asleep."

"At last."

Stretching out one leg from his robes, Apollo rose and flicked his finger towards the nymphs in the corner, summoning his lyre. Or rather, what once was Hermes' lyre — the tortoise shell still polished and cared for. He danced his way over to the divan, throwing up Hermes' tired legs, and sat nimbly by his side. Hermes let them fall back onto Apollo's lap, staring at his elder brother with a growingly bemused smile.

"I get a song?" Hermes whispered, as if it were a secret to be spoiled by the god of music. "Something new?"

"Hush," Apollo said, strumming a note as he fiddled with the instrument the way Ares would with his swords, albeit far more gracefully. The god could compose as fast as the sun's rays reached the corners of Olympus.

"Are you not too tired? I'm pitied enough to receive a private concert?"

Apollo silenced the strings and turned his face to the young god who fussed with his belted cord like a babe would his mother's hair. "Shall I leave?" he asked.

"No, no!" Hermes smiled. "I've missed you too dearly to send you away. Tell me what this new song's name is."

With another gentle strum, Apollo sighed and shook his head. "I am calling it *The Infant and His Guide*. Be silent."

And he was.

Apollo started the song with quick tempered notes and carried it grandly and slowly, opening his arm to fill Hermes' halls with elegant, haunting tones. Hermes set his cheek upon a pillow. There must've been some tear in his eye, as his pink-clad nymph discreetly brushed a cloth over his lashes and shuffled the rest of her companions from the room.

No other god had unbound access to each other's palaces the way the two half-brothers allowed themselves. If Hephaestus was any wiser, he would have simply built a bridge between the neighbors.

Apollo's fingers moved as nimbly as Hermes' feet could, the tempo picking up again, echoing his quicksilver steps that danced on the wind. The song was his entire day, as if Apollo was by his side the whole time. When he roused to ask if his brother was watching him from his chariot, he received a wordless glare. Daring to interrupt Apollo's playing was akin to having Zeus toss them from the mountain heaven. So Hermes pressed his mouth to his pillow and ate his words.

They sat like that and lounged an hour more, filling each other's cups and laughing amongst one another. Hermes took up the flute, and together they composed a duet to amend the time they were separated through war.

"Helios will be upon us before you know it. I think you will find it best to sleep before the day stirs us to Zeus' great hall," Apollo said, picking up Hermes' warmed feet from beneath his robe. "And I'm content enough now to find rest. I wanted for my bed, but my mind would not let me until I knew you were back home."

"So kind of you," Hermes yawned from even deeper in his cushions.

"If you value yourself, you will float your little body over to *your* cushions and be one with the clouds."

"I cannot convince you to carry me there, can I?"

"I love you, dear brother, but not that much."

Hermes had to pull an eye open. "You said you're indebted to me."

"You wish to waste my favor on a two step journey to the bed that sits behind you?"

"It would be worth it," he grumbled, throwing his leg to the floor. "I shall see you soon to witness whatever drama remains between our family. I'll anticipate sitting by your side again. It felt wrong to have you across the table."

"I would like that very much. Though I cannot promise I won't also be part of the drama. It was, again, *my* city that lay under siege."

"There'll be no judgment from me."

They could have continued back-and-forth meaningless conversations for hours. Apollo pulled his robe up and tucked it around himself, picking up his goblet to finish what was there. He sauntered to the door and Hermes delicately leapt to his bed. They held their tongues and made sure not to turn to look the other way, lest the process would begin anew.

Ah, paradise! A bed and its pillows and soft blankets. Hermes rolled and slipped himself into the burrow of linens and silks. With his head quiet, he joined humanity in the peaceful slumber they now granted him.

But his dreams were warped. Too many melancholic journeys, too many pleas he could not grant. His sleep allowed his body to rest, but his mind brewed its own storm; and that issue itself was unlike any god's nature he knew of.

Chapter 2

There wasn't a soul on Olympus who ever found the need to rush. Gods, freshly anointed with oil, often walked their palaces barefoot, or donned slippers for their jaunts around their gardens and great city. There was no rain or snow to shield their faces from, nor cold to aggravate their skin. Olympus poured with grand misting waterfalls and glistened with the warmth of the sun. Along the perimeter of heaven, the strongest eagles from the earth rested their wings, Zeus' favorites.

Lesser gods and goddesses went about their promenades or basked on the fields among the flowers. A place with little cares and all the things they could entertain themselves with, the kingdom of Zeus was ripe with activity.

Yet Hermes ambled from his palace wanting only to fall back to his bed. His nymphs had followed him through the hallway, one attaching the golden brooch to his short tunic's shoulder, another combing his hair. Upon his head they placed a regal band to decorate his brow, tucking his curls and wings around the cord, then kissed his cheeks.

"Is he ill?" one whispered as he continued to saunter to the front corridor.

"No, he cannot be ill — he's just under immense stress," the other replied.

Was it so out of character that he did not kiss their cheeks in return?

Oh, it was the *silence*.

Picking his chin up, he quickly stole two kisses. "No illness, no stress," Hermes exclaimed with a careful wink. "The mortals have awoken and I feel Zeus has plotted his next move. This is practice so I can keep my comments in check. You know my habits. I fear now isn't the time for my clever quips, else I'll be tossed to tumble through the clouds."

Again.

He wasn't *thrown* exactly, but he was dangled over the edge as a punishment for slighting Hera. It wasn't even *his* intention — he was ordered to be sharp with his tongue. Zeus howled at the whole affair which meant the queen's wrath undoubtedly rose. And one can't punish the god king.

Needless to say, Hermes tried to avoid Hera as often as he could.

From the courtyard, it wasn't difficult to see the palace that overtook the sky. The stairs leading up to the central structure that hosted gilded feasts and important assemblies were lined with pillars of snaking bronze and marble, placed with expert calculation to humble any guest who wished to gaze upon the palace. Even Hermes bowed his head, not quite willing to be blinded by the sun that reflected off of each column, which always greatly amused Apollo, who, upon exiting his palace, merely directed the beams of light away from his eyes with a small wave of his hand.

His golden hair was plaited meticulously perfect out of his face; a simple shining cord tied the rest of the waves back. Descending the steps of his veranda, he idled for Hermes to catch up on the path.

"Perhaps you should dine with me tonight," Apollo said, looping his arm through Hermes'. "I will have a performance prepared for you and I can witness Sleep come to your eyes. It would make me the happiest god to know you cannot work all evening again with my invitation."

Hermes dragged two fingers across his eyelids and pinched the bridge of his nose as a breeze rushed down from Zeus' estate. "I believe I just need to go for a run after this. Perhaps chase a peregrine or tail after Iris if she is sent off. Not much opportunity to toy with Hera's herald as of late. She was far more useful than I in Troy — perhaps a good thing. Father was switching sides left and right after the Fates revealed how it all was to play out."

"He was useful at first," Apollo sighed, "before the Fates."

A thousand steps they climbed to the opulent palace, received by the king's servants and escorted to the central hall. Intricately carved marble and paintings from the time of the first immortals were all but covered by heavy tapestries commemorating Zeus' rule. The room carried the density of a storm cloud, dark at their feet, though light along its ceilings.

There they met Artemis in her silver and indigo attire, expertly sulking by her chair, which she placed as far from the queen as she could get away with without reproach. She wore her golden hair similar to her twin's, whether they intended to or not, but hers was firmly tied up with her diadem. Beneath the opalite brown skin of her back, there was still the discoloration of ichor running loose from Hera's wicked beating.

Hermes clicked his teeth.

"Do not speak to me," she commanded, holding her finger out to silence Hermes before he even had the chance to breathe. "I know every clever gibe you could conjure about it."

Apollo smacked it down. "He has not spoken."

"I could conjure quite a handful," Hermes replied. "But your mother truly obliterated me on the battlefield, it would be rude and unjust for me to mock your injuries when mine took long to heal as well."

"Mother told us you ceded the field," Artemis said bluntly.

Hermes threw up his hands. "I handed her the perfect moment! If it were Hera, she would've told everyone how she beat me blue with my own staff."

Apollo set his hands on his hips.

Hermes pursed his lips and a small, coy *whoops* slipped out between them.

As Artemis raised her fist, the pattering footsteps of Aphrodite entered in a twirling dance. The goddess stood with her back to them, her sheer gown presenting the full, round ass that mortals and immortals alike swore by. She waited with arms crossed for the heavier clicking behind her — Ares in half-plate, his short, dark hair still pressed down from the weight of the helmet which he hardly removed.

"Has his cock been healed since that Diomedes sent his spear through it at Lady Athena's behest?" Hermes popped onto his toes to ask Apollo. "I heard the cry from here. Your nymphs were ablaze with carrying linens. I *almost* volunteered to help."

"His cock should be healed, but perhaps not to Aphrodite's liking," Apollo said under his breath.

The two of them snickered.

"Her hand may still hurt." Hermes shrugged. "Too many men with too many spears."

"You two should be ashamed of yourselves. You most, Apollo. They were both our allies," Artemis huffed, shaking her head. She followed Hermes with her chin as he pulled out the chair next to her. "What are you doing?"

He gestured from himself to the chair.

Obviously sitting.

"You don't sit here."

"Someone has to be the better god and cross this petty boundary. The war is done, Huntress, and I miss my siblings. This is what I do. I have traveled from that seat," he said, pointing to the throne diagonally across, "to this seat. What a different view of the room you have."

Apollo sneaked a sip from the goblet by his station as the table finished its setting. "You force Ares to sit across from Athena," he noted.

Hermes beamed. "It'll be wonderful."

"The war is not done until it is long forgotten," Artemis said, kicking back on her throne. "When every mortal that has fought is dead and every hero that shed blood has been forgotten, *then* we may move on with normalcy. Until that day, none of this ridiculous squabbling changes."

The goddess Athena appeared in the room without a sound, her steps lighter than an owl's beating wing. Her brunette waves pulled into braids and sat lightly upon her bare shoulders. Despite being unarmed and free of her armor, it took very little for Ares to carry himself far away from the war maiden while she strode by. Both children of Leto drew their gazes towards the decorated walls, their jaws stiff as reeds.

Athena peered down her nose at the slight alteration in seating and hummed, but lowered herself to the spot she had occupied the last several weeks.

"Pleasure to have you back, Hermes," she said with a nod. Her voice was characteristically smooth and firm.

"Happy to be seen, Pallas Athena. You must be very pleased with the outcome — your warriors succeeded! I took note of the cunning gift given to the Trojans. Brought about laughter which I certainly needed after," he paused, and cracked a knuckle as it rested in his lap. "Well, before the Trojans *opened* that very fine wooden horse."

Athena's grey eyes crinkled in the corners, but her folded hands tensed. "Yes, it was a gracious offering to me. My warriors fought bravely."

Hermes cocked his head. "You're upset?"

She glanced at Apollo, returning her gaze to Hermes, piercing and strong. "A man committed sacrilege in my temple to a Trojan woman under my protection."

"The prophetess," Apollo replied through his teeth.

"I suppose I should be grateful you had cursed her," Athena said, shifting in her seat, "that no one would believe what she spoke. She had my schemes within her very grasp and yet was pulled away."

"And your very man raped her in your own temple," he spat.

Hermes retreated into his goblet.

"I intend to *strike* the son of Oileus down, believe me, Lord Apollo. There is no honor and life earned to mortals who defy *my* name in my temples. His hubris has condemned him and incompetence has damned the others." Athena's voice raised as if she was still on the field of battle. "Just because I fought with them does not mean they are perfect mortals. If they insult me, they are punished. And if they do not put the son of Oileus to death before departing in their boats, I will see that punishment delivered."

Almost unnoticed by all but Hermes, Hephaestus in his simpleness lumbered into the chamber, already agog at the volume the room had risen to.

Athena and her perfect posture never wavered as she held her cup and scrutinized the god of plagues who ripped so many of her mortal men from the world of the living. She took a sip, placed the goblet before her, and added, "Yet I have failed to see justice be done on your half of the field." Her gaze drifted over to Ares and Aphrodite who inched towards the table.

Apollo waved his hand. "When your generals prayed for true aim, it was still I who granted it. I cannot be blamed for defending my city and the citizens who revered me."

Unfortunately Hermes had run out of his nectar already, slinking deeper into his chair. Where were the cupbearers? He tried waving his cup around like a beggar pleading for coin. If he was to make it through a morning feast, he needed *at least* seven refills.

"As far as I'm concerned," Aphrodite said, draping her hair over one shoulder as she took her cushioned throne, "the Trojans have nothing to forgive. It was *your* Spartan who took the offensive."

He whistled down little Hebe with her large decanter of nectar. Seven refills indeed.

"Your precious mortal kidnapped his *wife*. A disrespectful smear to the laws of xenia," Athena argued and raised her finger to silence Aphrodite's retort. "And I do not care for the game proposed on Paris of Troy that you believe was anything more than a ploy to aggrieve the queen and me. To think a mortal man knows of the true beauty of women and goddesses. Your beauty is as stale as your vanity and you have reaped the death you hath sown."

A scarred fist rattled the table. "Bitch, how dare you!" Ares roared and promptly cracked. His voice was *still* hoarse from that infantile cry he gave upon being stabbed in the cock.

The young god chuckled to himself, spinning his fresh nectar by his nose. To witness that on the field would've made his day.

Heavy clacking echoes of metal journeyed into the Great Hall, with a lofty robe draped over a broad shoulder that cascaded like waves to the marble floors. Poseidon entered into an already roused party. His crown of shell and gold jutted out from under dark hair as if grown from his very skin. If he tapped his trident to the floor any longer, the quaking marble risked falling apart beneath it.

Quietly, though with steam still rising from Ares' battered head, the gods of Olympus nodded their acknowledgment of the king of the sea.

"Your prattle," he uttered, deep and annoyed, "could be heard for miles."

Hermes looked at Apollo. "If that's the case," he whispered, "then Father takes immense pleasure in letting us argue for his unseen entertainment." His brother fell back to his cushions with a fatiguing hum. With little effort,

Hermes sat up from his, and raised his goblet to his uncle. "Welcome, Lord Poseidon to our animated feast! We still await our King and Queen, but your presence loftfully fills us with the utmost joy."

As a supporter of the Achaeans, Poseidon took his throne by Athena. There was a special divot carved into his chair to hold his trident steady by his side. Its metal gleamed and rang like a distant rumbling avalanche. The old god was silvering within his beard and along the roots of his long hair, both hiding several braids donning cuffs and pearls. Poseidon took great satisfaction in sacrificial offerings made to him, and the most favored and fanciful found its way to his wardrobe or around his two palaces.

"*Argeiphontes*," Poseidon said once settled and reclined. "I am surprised you have joined us on Mount Olympus this day. Have my brothers no other tasks for you to perform? Perhaps I shall send you on my errands next should they have none."

Hermes smiled through a grimace, covering it quickly with a long quaff of nectar. "I delight for nothing more than to be useful. Father Zeus expects me to be among you and so here I am. If he wishes for me to aid in whatever it is you need, my Lord Uncle, then I'm at your service."

His timing was impeccable, if he said so himself, as resounding chorus calls signaled the arrival of the austere Hera with her shimmering crown and the teal train of a thousand eyes that blended in seamlessly to her peplos. She took long, slow strides, perfectly still, like she floated instead of walked. A foot or three behind her entered the god king, and the Olympians rose from their seats.

Zeus endeavored to make his entrances riddled with mystery for how he'd be playing out the Game of Man. Compared to the days prior, he too had disassembled his armor in favor of his bright himations. Gold threaded lightning bolts embroidered their way down the purple garment, and upon the left shoulder sat his great emblem of the gods, pinning the expert pleats together.

As peaceful as his clothing appeared, instead of a crown, upon his head remained his helm. Carved wings of eagles flushed from his face, the golden armor arching down his cheekbones. If it were not Zeus, the idea of only wearing faceplate would be ridiculous, for even Ares revealed his face when he found better comfort underneath his armor.

Standing at the head of the table, Zeus' cold eye quickly skimmed the gods and goddesses' faces before he gestured to an empty seat.

"Where is Demeter?" he asked plainly.

"She's elected not to attend," Hera replied, sitting down before anyone else had permission to. "You know she has remained a neutral party and I was not willing to force her attendance."

Plus, Hermes thought, she was enjoying what she could of her daughter's presence on the surface world. The time for Queen Persephone to return to Hades was rapidly approaching, as the leaves of the earth were already beginning to curl with the sorrow Demeter felt. Now she had lands watered with blood and coated with ashes to mend.

Or not… with dead crops to come, she may as well just leave the earth to soak up the ichor of mankind.

Zeus nodded and relaxed in his throne, took up his jeweled goblet, and raised it to the company. The Olympians returned to their seats and the previous arguments had ceased at once.

While the god king pondered the drink and the ambrosia carried out in droves, current arguments took place mentally. Several glares were thrown across the table between Aphrodite and Athena; Ares flinching when the goddess of wisdom moved her arm even slightly towards him.

Hermes propped his chin upon his palm and watched Hephaestus pick the soot from his short beard and return his bemused grin.

The morning feast was apt to take many different turns. If they were lucky, Apollo would summon servants from his palace to play a tune to accompany their meal and chatter. But the awkward atmosphere remained no less contentious now that the hall was full.

"Shall we look at how our game is playing out?" Zeus asked, though he meant not to get approval. He was going to summon the image of the human realm regardless.

A reflection formed in the empty rise above them: the beaches of sacked Troy where the tiny warriors of men were boarding their ships and casting off from the city. A bird's eye view — something Hermes would see, or from the vantage of Zeus' eagle form — they flew over the red-hulled fleet of Athena's favored, and the many pyres of fallen heroes on either side of the city walls.

It would be difficult for Apollo to seek any justice for the atrocities his people faced when so many of them were already dead. Hermes brought dozens of them to Styx on the daily.

He shook the images of their deformed bodies from his mind; the naturally short, fragile lives of humans mattered little to immortals like him, it was just how they were created.

Zeus was once very much on the side of the Trojans, sending countermeasures one after another against his wife's efforts to aid the Achaeans. How strange it was to see him concede to the Fates' message that Troy should fall and the princes slain, and pull his mighty chariot back to Mount Olympus. It forced Hera to return as well. The Fates were not goddesses to be argued with; they held the destiny of every man, woman, and child within their threads. Who was to say they didn't also hold the threads of every god in this room?

Hermes looked away from the scene. Athena's lip curled at her own champions.

"Father, my king," she said, and there bore a wisp of luck of her status as Zeus' favorite. He regarded her without annoyance of the interruption. "I bear a request that I beg you to grant me, and of it, that you lend me Lord Poseidon to assist in this immediate and urgent punishment."

Zeus' brow raised with a curious smile. "Dearest Daughter, what is it that you ask?"

"To carry one bolt of your power," she declared.

Apollo nearly choked on his drink. Hera's face swiveled.

"You beg to hold his lightning? What in Styx's name could have *possessed* you to concoct such an idea?" Hera exclaimed. Her nails dug into the table.

Athena kept her attention on Zeus. "I demanded the Achaeans amend their insults to me for committing sacrilege. They all let a man go unpunished, and so I require all of them to pay the price."

Zeus only smiled wider, looming in her direction. "Two of your Achaean ships have already departed with Diomedes and Nestor. What of them?"

"The commanders who remained behind in idle thought to appease me have had more time to undo their mistake. Let the warriors of Argos and Pylos return to their homes. Those who cast off now — they are the greater miscreants. With your permission and your power, Father, I will take Lord Poseidon with me to crush their fleet and disrupt their voyage with storms the likes no one has seen."

She stood, prepared to don her armor in an instant. The boats in the image above the gods had unfurled their sails and oars splashed silently into the water. Hermes picked his drink back up by the small of the stem and gave it a little spin. Human ships sank so easily — it would be a burial in the sea with the warriors lost. Quite *difficult* to pull souls from the dark depths unless they washed ashore.

"Brother," Zeus said, and Poseidon set down the ambrosia he was feasting on. "Does this satisfy you? Will you acquiesce to the goddess' demands?"

Poseidon glanced at Athena, then upwards to the scene playing out. The violence that swam inside his eyes churned.

"They are a cocky breed. I consent," he replied, and gripped his trident. "If you lend her your power, Zeus, I will see these ships ravaged."

"Outrageous," Hera hissed.

The more Hera protested, the more amusement Zeus saw in this arrangement. When Athena strode around the table, he grasped her hand, and her skin sparked with blinding power. It was just one strike she earned, but the goddess of wisdom did not miss; and Poseidon followed behind her as they made their way to the plane of humans.

Oh, why didn't the humans just kill that instigator? Hermes downed the rest of his nectar and pressed his face into his hand. So much trouble, and not even the fun kind.

"I cannot believe you would give that goddess your aegis just because she asked," Hera complained. She sat at Zeus' side and smacked his wrist.

"Were you not her ally *yesterday*, woman?" Zeus replied. "Alas, my dear *wife*, we cannot all get what we want when we want it, especially if we're to resort to petty tricks. Sit back, partake in the feast and let's wait to see how Pallas Athena and my brother strike these mortals on their nostoi."

The nostos is what mortals prayed to Hermes for. *Returning home a longer route by land would save them.*

Some troops had the foresight and lined up for a march through the country. Zeus sighed with lackluster disappointment, despite a few favorite mortals finding unknown mercy. Infighting spared some and cursed others, while the image followed the ships as they, by the dozen, dispersed into the Aegean Sea.

Black clouds roamed the corners of the ceiling's image when, at last, the god of tides made his presence known.

Morning dimmed to a horrible night when the sea rose with wakes as tall as mountains, and deposited heavy foam atop ships. As if they were front and center at a Spartan show, while several of the vessels were pushed sideways into the jagged rocks by the isle coasts, Ares pounded his fist on the arm of his throne, a wicked smile split across his face; Aphrodite tucked her feet up and rested a cheek on his arm; the twins and Hephaestus sat in silence, anticipating the arrival of Athena.

It was Hera who didn't bother, sitting straight in her seat to pick at the food laid out before them. She shook her head, indignant.

Prayers poured into Hermes' head while he watched between his fingers as two ships shattered against the stones and men fell into the ocean, swallowed up in the dark. The wings that curled behind his ears folded to cover them, as if that would make any difference to ignore the pleas for safety, for mercy in not having a proper burial to be brought to the Underworld. His toes curled under his chair at the cries no one else would have received; none but Athena and Poseidon, who had no intention to cease their retribution.

From Zeus' immense sight, Athena's chariot rode into view among the barrage of clouds. Her silver armor disappeared between the rain that pelted from the sky. She gripped her illustrious spear in her right hand. The weapon had ended many lives in the past decade, and was polished and sharpened daily by the Olympus forge. Athena lifted it up, lightning crackling down the polearm.

Hermes scanned the ships remaining. A few were thrown off course, disappearing from the image, likely sent far in opposite directions of their homelands. To his left, Apollo leaned over the table as Athena aimed true at the ship of Ajax the Lesser, hurling the great spear down to the boat. It ruptured and exploded — bits of wood and man scattering along sea and rock.

"The scoundrel lives!" Apollo cursed at the display. And truly, the warrior had crawled upon one bulging stone. They all heard the mortal's boast.

Ares shouted, "kill the rapist bastard!"

And Poseidon dipped his trident, summoning a quake that destroyed the rock under his feet faster than the mortal could blink. Another body sent to the ocean. The twins joined their allies in applause for the death of this one man.

Zeus' laugh was both infectious and alarming as the infliction of death and fear plagued the Achaean fleet. Very casually, he removed his helm — as if the war had completely come to an end right there on Olympus.

"Hermes, my herald," Zeus said, placating his hunger with ambrosia.

The young god stood before the king continued, poised to run and deliver as commanded. "Father?"

"Go down to survey the isles and along the wreckage," Zeus said. "If there are survivors there, or if any man tries to cling to breath he hasn't earned, slay them."

"Yes, my king," Hermes replied. He stepped back from the table, bowed his head, and exited the great palace.

He could only fly so fast without his sandals, and upon entering his home, his nymphs hurried to prepare him for his departure. They draped his cape around his shoulders as he propped his leg up to lace the talaria — their feathers fluttering like an excited hummingbird. His helmet returned for his wings to pull through, and he was presented his caduceus as a priestess would present a warrior his sword.

From his balcony, he flew. And he tried not to think; it wasn't his duty to think, it was just his duty to follow orders.

The descent from Mount Olympus was cold, and only grew colder as he entered the storm clouds, as if the earth couldn't be allowed one day of sunshine without havoc. With the point of his helmet arched down, he zipped past the returning god and goddess without acknowledging them — they'd done their task and were content to return home.

Hermes gritted his teeth and pulled back before a wake rolled up to greet him, the mist slapping his cheeks.

A desert of water.

Planks of wood drifted by his feet by the hundreds. He tapped one with his toe and moved another aside with the bottom tip of his staff.

This was not the first time Hermes was sent as an executioner by his father. In fact, he was the first of the young gods to draw the blood of an enemy. Nothing by force, of course, Hermes was not a god of strength nor of battle. He was a liar, and a kind liar at that — previously keeping the giant, Argus, company with conversation and music. The disgruntled guard was pleased for once, joyous for the companionship. Hermes sang him and his thousand eyes to sleep, pulled a blade from his satchel, and carved off his head.

Still, to slay Argus was to release a prisoner.

Standing above the sea in search of wide eyes and struggling hands wasn't the same.

He needn't remain in his thoughts for very long before wayward souls gravitated towards him of their own volition — the tips of his cloak were already awash with starlight and flew about with a life of their own. With his sandals' wings beating down on the water's surface, he skimmed the sea for survivors, collecting the souls that floundered, lost in the waves without a place to go.

A living hand gripped the leather cord of his sandal.

Hermes stopped and cast his eyes down at the young sailor who clung to two oars, his head dripping with the dark red of human blood. Too young to have a beard, just old enough to grow speckles of a shadow, the sailor squinted at Hermes through bruised, brown eyes.

Humans were so small. Hermes was the shortest of his Olympian brethren, and yet humans were *lucky* to come to his sternum. So he shrunk down to the height of Man, and the desperate hand fumbled to grip the god's ankle.

"P-please, Lord of Graciousness, lucky Hermes," the sailor begged in his language and Hermes understood. "Make steady my hands and point to the nearest shore so that I may swim to safety. I will g-give great sacrifice and pray to *you* alone for sixteen days." His urgent kicking struggled to keep his mouth above water as the oars rolled from under him. "Have pity, Conveyor of Dreams, I wish to see my brothers!"

"Human," Hermes spoke and the man's eyes widened at hearing his voice. "Your hands are strong, but you're mistaken." Lowering himself to the misty waters, Hermes touched the soaked hair that matted to the poor sailor's head. "To see me, you are *already* dreaming. You have a voyage to finish, though it isn't the one you expected. Close your eyes. Hear your brothers call for you."

From his hand, the snakes of the caduceus hissed a low tune. A melody to bring all mortals who heard to rest, to shut their eyes and relax, to slip gently from their makeshift rafts and into the abyss below.

"Forgive me," he whispered, another soul to his cloak.

Three hours of surveying the waters and jagged rocks, Hermes added only a dozen more men to the slaughter that his half-sister and uncle had begun. The other ships, it appeared, had gotten away from the brunt of the storm, whose clouds and waves still churned out deeper into the sea.

* * *

On the shores of the Styx, these men had less of a *proper* destination. Unless they were to wash ashore and receive burial rites, they'd remain on the beach for a century at least. As a guide, to inform them of this — they who hardly had a personality nor feelings to process such information until they were brought over — was a nuisance.

"*Weeks*," he heard Charon mutter, and if the ferryman's eyes were visible, there was no doubt they'd be rolling.

Hermes tucked his chin into the drape of his cloak. "I'm not to blame," he replied. "None yet are yours to handle. They'll walk until they are given their rites or they'll walk themselves into the Lethe or Acheron for all eternity. Whatever happens, some in here deserve the punishment; sent personally by Athena with the aid of the sea god." Sliding his caduceus into his belts, he crossed his arms like there was a chilled phantom breeze. "There'll be no more promises for how long it shall be before I return. I made an error, but, dear Charon, you must be glad I'm back after such a torturous fifteen hours! To be sure, my friend, to see *me* must bring you some light and joy."

Charon grumbled, taking coins from the line that was deemed never-ending during times of war. Hermes pressed his lips together and peered down the twisting queue of souls. Many of the spectres getting close to their journey were ones he brought just yesterday, and now procured coins from their surviving allies burying them honorably.

"Next time I come as an inconvenience, I shall bring you a gift," Hermes said. "The gift is more than myself, yes, although I know you'll protest — I'm the *greatest* gift that stands on your shores."

He continued to speak uncensored even as Charon pushed his ferry away, hovering over the mighty river.

"Now as to what signifies an inconvenience, I'll let you know, as it cannot be every time I guide humans here to add to your line. When you *receive* your gift, then you'll know you've been inconvenienced, and no sooner."

Blessed Charon was so easy to speak to, with replies so blunt that there was no worry for disagreements and arguments. Just two psychopomps continuing with their work.

Hermes stopped his following about halfway over the river, as the cave ceiling grew low and his Upperworld-white tunic began to shift Underworld-black, and Charon ferried the souls deeper into smaller passageways.

His crossed arms shifted into fidgeting fingers, pulling at each phalange until they cracked. Back to Olympus? He supposed so… Evening would be approaching and he had a dinner with Apollo scheduled, didn't he?

He flew over the beach to the dim light of the surface, avoiding the sailors' wandering hands as they lifted instinctively to the sky for him as they did before they died.

Chapter 3

There were several instances when Hermes joined Apollo in his palace where the two turned one hall that led to his conservatory into something of a *laboratory*. With nymphs at their service, the two gods picked apart herbs and flowers to experiment with their properties.

"And if we infuse it in wine?" Apollo asked, picking up a boiled lemon balm. He added the wine mixed by Dionysus before handing it to a nymph. They were the only ones capable of digesting the food and drink of Man.

"Calm as a butterfly in spring," the nymph mused, curling her legs up. She sipped the mulled wine again. "With some honey, I believe I wouldn't have a care in the world."

Hermes, sitting by the table full of bowls and boards, wafted the burning sage by his side. There were a dozen plants before him, grown within Olympus by Demeter and given to Apollo as gifts. Of her presents, there was one prickly flower that Hermes had buried deep in a pot and talked to for several candle-lengths of time. A twisting stem emerged from the soil, sprouting in six buds that flowered like six little mouths.

"Oh, feathers gleam down the mountain pass," he sang.

Their little faces turned up and hummed, *"down, down, down."*

Sprightly little creatures, Hermes thought, echoing their hums back.

Apollo, hands full of vials, turned his ear. "What is it you've created now? I leave you be for a moment and some magical species has burst under your watch."

"I've yet to name her," Hermes replied, dripping water on the dirt. "Consider her an apology gift for something I may do in the future to vex you; as impossible as that sounds, I know." Letting his chin rest on his hands, he glanced towards his brother and wiggled his nose. "Perhaps her humming nature may cure melancholia to bring us more hymns… *or* she may frighten mortals on their wild voyages — either way, great fun."

A sun-kissed finger poked the singing flower buds. "I think I will name her Theropes," he declared. They kissed his hand and sang their new name. "How charming your creations are, Brother. You are forgiven for whatever trick you play that riles me. Not very difficult for you to attain my forgiveness, however."

Surprising no one, Apollo's palace was warm, adorned with glass panes across the ceiling. When Helios carried the sun across the sky, the light would throw colors throughout the rooms, painting them blues and oranges and violets. The glass ran the length of his home, sometimes blown with intricate shapes. Hermes had broken one before, had it replaced right away, and Apollo still didn't notice the red phallus that projected onto the floor.

Just one nymph got sick from their playtime, which in all fairness was quite a *good* ratio considering the mixtures the two gods idled with. She was tended to by her sisters who patted her back and petted her hair while Apollo stuck his nose into the dish that made her woozy. Not the ointment to send down to the mortals unless they wished to vomit. Although a quick purge *could* be beneficial…

They both pursed their lips — *might as well offer it.*

Olympus furiously rumbled beneath their feet as if it were slipping from Atlas' hold, sending pottery rocking and crashing to the marble. Hermes lifted himself above the ground, his hands flat over Apollo's shoulders.

"Great Gaia, what is that?" Apollo called, hanging onto his brother in case the floor were to collapse from under them. "Surely not any games if we weren't invited."

"I can't say," Hermes replied, his mind already at work.

It could've been from Hephaestus' forge, there were times when he crafted their father's thunderbolts where the sheer power of them shook Olympus and Earth; or if Hera received unfortunate news, her anger was capable at times of being felt through the upper palaces of the kingdom…

"You didn't prophesize this?"

"You very well know my prophesies don't work like that."

To the doors of Apollo's palace they went, hugging the walls and clinging to his many gilded tables that were decorated with his favorite offerings from Man.

A cold wind whipped curling mist up the mountain of the kingdom, scattering dozens of minor gods from their leisurely promenades as clouds overwhelmed and crawled past the edges of Olympus.

The courtyard steps shook with Poseidon's every bound. Still seeping with ocean water that trickled down the marble, and draped in seaweed and foam, the god of the sea dragged his shrieking pronged spear in a white-knuckled grip.

What mortal rattled his foul temper enough to bring him from his own kingdom in the middle of the day?

"Zeus!" he shouted, and Apollo and Hermes aptly scrambled out the door, unwilling to miss whatever engagement was about to happen between the two kings. "I know he has given sacrifice to you," Poseidon continued. He slung the trident towards Zeus' palace. "If you have taken such disrespectful slaughter, I swear upon the Styx you will face my wrath!"

The god king presented himself in a sharp clap of light, already meeting Poseidon halfway down the stairs. Apollo and Hermes immediately hurled themselves behind a pillar.

"The ram," Zeus said with a laugh. "That's what burdens you, Brother? I know what he's wrought upon your son; I didn't care to hear the son of Laertes' prayers. He was lucky enough to escape the destruction of Troy's beaches, but *ah*, he's a favorite of my Athena — perhaps she wished for his survival. You know how few cunning mortals there are that she finds interest in."

"Cunning," he spat. "He has insulted me. Not only has he left my son alive after his act of cowardice, his hubris got the better of him, the incompetent *fool."* Poseidon's fist curled around his trident. "I care little for Athena's favorites. My kin has pleaded that the son of Laertes does not make it home,

so I will drown him and feed his flesh to Cerberus myself."

Zeus waved his hand. "Oh, calm yourself. Your storms have already made his struggles difficult. I know where he's heading: the island of our beloved Aeolus. Will it please you if I sowed distrust within his crew? Placate this anger so you'll join me for a game?"

The name Aeolus was known to all the gods, but to Hermes quite intimately. He was a minor king, keeper of the winds Hermes used to speed himself along his own journeys. For any mortal at sea to ask for his help was great thinking amidst a chaotic storm from Poseidon.

"I want him to suffer, Zeus. Suffer long so I can kill him when he believes it is over."

Hermes' jaw shifted. What did the poor human truly do to bring about *this* after surviving the war *and* Athena's punishment?

His winged foot was already starting to take a step back before the rest of him took notice, but Apollo's heated hand kept to his wrist, spellbound by the prospect that two of the most powerful gods were so hung up over one human. And they called *him* petty.

One of Athena's men. Hermes' thoughts drifted through the faces he had seen alive among the dead in the battlefield and city. The son of *Laertes...* A king of Ithaca whose paternal lineage Hermes did not care greatly for, but *oh! His wife* — the queen was named Anticlea, he knew this. She was the daughter of a renowned thief, the infamous Autolycus.

Hermes was very fond of Autolycus while he lived, witnessing the unconsidered trifles the man stole beneath people's very noses. He had a bias towards prayers sent against the thief, throwing them away in favor of letting Autolycus succeed with his more cunning feats.

He *was* Hermes' son after all.

The young god blinked several times.

The son of Laertes was his kin.

It shouldn't matter. Many of the gods lost kin of their own during the war — some were direct children, but if Poseidon was so rampant about his own...

Hermes' feathers flared.

Of all the people he guided to the Underworld, of the young and old faces of strange mortals who'd never see home, why not guide this one? Where was his ambition? To bring this man home to Ithaca after all the warrior had been through would cure the annoying ache in his heart and allow him true rest. It was a win-win scenario.

Odysseus.

He knew this name because Autolycus had named the infant himself, and the memory of the prayers of that day of his birth flooded Hermes' mind.

Damn it all, he thought, as Poseidon and Zeus reckoned that the mortal's fate deserved great anguish, and Hermes had little to do to contend with that. But nothing could stop him from checking in, per se, as discreetly as he could. He had unlimited and unquestioned access to all the realms.

His foot inched back more, the beats of his sandals' wings feeling all the curious motivation his heart stirred up.

"Hermes?" Apollo whispered. "You are shaking."

"Don't speak of it, dear brother, but I believe there is a prayer that I must answer in person."

"Now? I cannot think Father would wish you gone at this moment. *I* do not wish you gone at this moment. I'd worry for Athena if Poseidon is vengeful against one of her *own* mortals."

Athena, Athena, back to that goddess — yes, of course she had favored Odysseus, he was one of her best warriors. He recalled her being quick to answer his prayers during funeral games and protecting him on the field of battle. Would it be wise to discuss his intentions with Athena? She did destroy the fleet which Odysseus was a part of, so he must've done *something* to merit her anger, but nothing faulty enough if she allowed him to get away with an off-course ship.

Perhaps no discussion yet.

Hermes would hold his tongue.

"Hermes?"

The ship of his great grandson was headed to the wind keeper — fair enough. They would be safe there for as long as they stayed.

"I'll keep here for now, then, until things have calmed," Hermes replied. *Or when others are distracted.*

They remained pressed against the curve of the bronze pillar until Zeus put his large hand around Poseidon's shoulders and heaved him up to the grand palace.

* * *

Time moved differently in Olympus compared to the mortal realm, or rather, the gods felt time differently. Whether by the old Titan's hand or from the will of Zeus himself, what felt like days on Olympus could potentially be weeks on the Earth, regardless of the stable pull of the sun across the sky.

Was that a polite excuse for the gods' pitiful reason to hold grudges for an eternity, or to be idle within their palaces without leaving the heavens? *Yes, absolutely.*

But Hermes often ran by Man's concept of time. He was always busy, he argued, slipping away from arena games to throw himself down the mountain with his gear and a satchel of messages to run to their recipients.

In between, though, surely he could *make* time for his newly found interest.

The island of Aeolia was never meant to remain in one place. Drifting aimlessly along the ocean, carried by the breezes it garnered, it planted itself with giant columns to the seafloor and rested for several months at a time. Hermes easily came across it a dozen times on his trips, coasting around its cliffs and swooping under the island through its channels. The west wind was his favorite — making trips to the Underworld swift and steady.

And for a few days, that was the only wind he was enjoying.

But, as if no time had passed at all, the furious winds of Poseidon's storms returned with a vengeance. Hermes led with his staff and pushed against wayward whips of the monsoon as he quickly fought his way to the island sitting within the wind: the eye of a hurricane.

Two feet on the ground, he landed upright, just the way he intended — even if he ceremoniously tumbled over himself once or twice.

To his right, on the long grass with her handmaid, sat one of the daughters of the island, Eurygone. She plopped a strawberry in her mouth and nodded at Hermes with a small smile.

"Very nice entrance, my lord. I have seen nothing better," she said, sucking on the juice.

Hermes brushed his tunic and pushed his wings from his face. "Thank you," he replied, picking the fruit from her plate as soon as the maiden held it aloft. "You've quite the tempest stirring outside of your home. Have you noticed?"

Eurygone's smile waned. "Yes, my lord, though my father had believed it to be dealt with in the week past. I'm afraid the guests we have aided and sent on their way before had returned. They are cursed, he says! Releasing the scornful winds that my father had fought hard to seal for their journey."

Cursed, Hermes wiggled his nose. Yes, he supposed so.

"Are they still guests of your father?" he asked.

"Heavens no. It is unlawful to host those who are disliked by the gods… isn't it, my lord?"

She trembled at the look Hermes returned to her, and shifted her attention to the delicate and stained fingertips in her lap.

"Is the King of Ithaca someone you are searching for?"

Hermes sighed. "Silly question, girl. I must speak with your father; in his hall, I presume, if he's so swiftly sent the sailors away again."

Raising up the front of his helmet to the heights of Aeolia, the bronze wall that surrounded the island cast a heavenly glow upon the stone palace that sat high on its hill. Trees rustled lightly in a pleasant breeze, throwing shade upon the path that wound in circles to the great hall. He flew straight to the top and landed in the main courtyard, whose fresco walls were painted with immense color and illustrations. Each column had been detailed according to King Aeolus' twelve children. Halls to the west were spared no expense for hailing the gods, and to the east lay the family's private chambers; ahead of the courtyard, up a few wide steps, was the banquet hall — still bustling with the sound of men.

He leaned onto his caduceus like a cane, waiting to be greeted. Oh, the poor slave that jumped in her skin when she noticed him in his human-sized glory, no other disguise or form — too often he would visit the floating island that there was never a need to be coy. She shrieked and ran to her master's throne at the head of the table. Hermes swayed his cloak from side to side in the doorway.

They must've been dining on lamb and fish amongst the olives, figs, and cheeses spread over the table; the juices were potent under the heaping amounts of wine that wafted in the air. Being led in, he wished he could taste some of the savory meal, though he favored a sweet, but there was little time to spare with his tasks — and human food did nothing to aid a god's hunger.

King Aeolus, laughing with his neighboring friends and sons, looked up from his goblet only to sputter a curse of surprise from his lips. Hermes chuckled, not needing to say a word for the men nearest the old king to scramble from their low, cushioned chairs. One tossed his aside for another servant to bring in a throne that matched the king's. It was his eldest son, Hermes believed, though he couldn't be bothered to recall the name of that one; the more attractive was the second to youngest son, Xuthus.

"My lord," they said, presenting the cushioned seat. Hermes thought for a moment to simply take the floor for the laughs, but he relented, lounging back to face the keeper of the winds.

Aeolus balanced his goblet on the arm of his chair, the white of his beard by the curve of his lips was stained pink. "*Cyllenius* Hermes," he apologized, "we were not expecting you with Poseidon's wrath whirling about. What may we offer? Let us prepare you a sacrifice. Bask in comfort and we may bring you your favorite strawberries."

Tempting.

Hermes fluttered his wings and waved his fingers. "Remain steadfast, good Aeolus, I'm not to stay long… *but* should those berries be present at your table already, I'll partake in them while we speak." He set his staff aside. The king's wrinkled brow was always tense when Hermes was a guest, though tended to ease the longer he stayed.

"What does Mighty Zeus wish to tell me, divine messenger?" Taking the platter of strawberries from the servant, he handed them personally to Hermes.

"The visitor you had sent away," Hermes began, divulging in one before he spoke his lies, and Aeolus' beard crinkled into an awkward grimace. "The ruler of Ithaca and his crew, yes? Why was it that they returned to you and you've then refused to host them? As far as I know you, my dear little wind lord, *you* are most generous."

"O-odysseus," Aeolus said. He hastefully took a sip of his wine. "Yes, he and his fleet arrived to my island a month or so past, expressing their difficulties returning home from the war in Troy. Twelve ships, he had, though many were undermanned — I had my sons assist them in keeping the fleet moored while my daughters prepared a gracious and fine feast for them all. We were happy to have them at the time, and Odysseus is a talented storyteller! Filled the hall with their journey from Troy and Cicones, where they lost many men in their raid, to the land of Lotus Eaters. The king took tender care of his men to assure they all safely left that island — I am sure you have seen those poor things."

"Of course. Funny creatures, they are," Hermes replied, nibbling on another berry. "None of this seems like any reason to cut them from your shores."

Aeolus shifted in his seat. "Oh no, not this. The Royal son of Laertes went into some detail of his encounter with the savages on the Island of the Cyclopes. To expect hospitality and find oneself trapped in the lair of a murderer, well, I assured him on my island that we are heavenly hosts. But..."

Hermes clocked onto the Cyclopes — one of those was Poseidon's son, Polyphemus. The ugly beast was loud and unusual, but played a pretty tune when not shepherding his land. So Poseidon's son had trapped Odysseus and his crew in that cave of his and killed some of the Ithacan king's men. *Absolutely a means to kill the creature in return without hesitation.*

"Odysseus is a clever man, but has a human's ego, for certain," Aeolus continued. "He blinded the cyclops and stole away with the flock while taunting the thing."

An emphatic laugh echoed out from Hermes throat, unstoppable, and so contagious, the other men in the room couldn't help but laugh with him even if they didn't want to.

"He blinded his son, I see. Polyphemus assuredly *cannot* see that." Hermes cackled to himself, tapping his lips. "My, my, he let the thing live. What an unusually kind and cruel gesture. Full of mercy and yet a brutal punishment. Oh Odysseus, the man that you are."

Aeolus cocked his head. "Y-yes, he is very bold. The winds became rather tumultuous before he arrived and, after his story and polite pleading to help him and his men return home, I was willing to oblige them. It took much time, a *week's* worth, but I managed to capture the winds inside a bag for which I then gifted him. There came a warning with it, that if he opened the bag, the storm would be released. I did not realize he was to blame for the storm in the first place. If I knew he had such ill luck with the gods, I would not have given him the bag." If he could lean out of his chair any more, he'd be on the floor. "Believe me, gentle Hermes, forgive me!"

"My wind lord, hush," Hermes said, finishing off his strawberries. "The gods don't forgive, but trust that they're not angry with you. I wouldn't care if you hosted *all* of my enemies if I *had* any, as long as you had stories to tell me of their troubles. But I'm also not pleased that you sent him away the second time he arrived here."

"The bag was opened by one of his crewmen, though none would admit it. I did pity him, truly I did, but the storm — this storm — I cannot afford to be in Lord Poseidon's bad graces again."

"Let us not speak the sea god's name while I'm here, understand?" Hermes said, pressing a finger to his host's lips. "Humble as I am, I'm afraid in this storm I cannot find that son of Laertes, but it's very important I must. How long ago did he leave you? They must've tried to head towards Ithaca again."

Aeolus searched his drink. "The unlucky man was sent off a week and a day ago, my lord messenger."

Eight days, eight days… how far could a fleet get in eight days along the sea that hates them…?

"They had been following the coast of the Æthiopians," Aeolus exclaimed.

"Coming up from the Lotus Eaters is when they found us here."

"Ah, what a terrible idea," Hermes mumbled, letting his face disappear into the palm of his hand. The Æthiopians, so far away from the rest of the Greeks, were immensely fond of Poseidon. They made the most dazzling displays of sacrifice to him, it was almost like a third kingdom for the sea god. Dozens of his children and children's children lived there along the coastlines and cliffs.

If Odysseus was hugging the land in hopes not to find Hermes' vengeful uncle in the waters, he wasn't going to be greeted fondly. No one should make that foolish mistake, for Poseidon would use all his willpower to bring his ships to open water.

"Your goal is to find him," Aeolus said as he got to his feet. He approached the windows and looked out beyond his bronze walls. "The north wind blows strongest now. If I had your unstoppable sandals, I would search the Tyrrhenian Sea, my lord, up and around the islands of Sardinia and Sicily."

Curious, the young god thought hard. He was around there often and knew the lands and their people quite well as they explored their little mountain ranges and quaint stone temples. The Ithacans didn't feast again here, so they would have to *elsewhere*. Mortals became angry, little pests when they were hungry. More importantly, they needed a supply of fresh water.

Hermes filtered through the villages in his head. He could fly over them all in the span of a few hours.

Rising from the throne, Hermes took his staff. The company around him lowered their heads and raised their hands in prayer.

Cute.

They followed him like sheep down the steps to the courtyard. Likely would follow him over the wall if he kept going and didn't spin around to keep them in their painted pen. On any other day, he could play with these mortals for hours, running around their gardens and sweeping through the cave of winds, feeling human for just a little bit.

But no human could step up into the air like there were invisible stairs, and no human could look out on the horizon and see the land from across the world. Hermes licked his lips and politely thanked Aeolus for the treat and attention.

"Did Zeus have any other word for me?" the king asked, looking high above the columns.

Hermes thought quickly and smiled. "Do try and tame your winds the best you can without pulling them free from the ocean. Discretion, my lord keeper, is key."

* * *

The ocean gave him an uncomfortable bath for the next dozen miles as he ducked under leaping dolphins and over spouting whales around the Italian coast. The sun warmed his left cheek the further north he flew, and if he were a sailor, he'd look to moor his ships where the waters were calm. It was actually a little embarrassing though, Hermes hummed, of how long it was taking him to find twelve ships against the backdrop of a clear blue sea.

But he wasn't flying directionless. His eye locked upon a single ship far ahead that rowed with such lackluster speed, it must've been moving with no sense for some time. No prayers came from that ship, Hermes noted, at least not from the tired men who held onto the oars. The sail was battered and in need of mending and dared to drive the little crew into a knoll of rock.

They'd pray to him if he helped.

There was an island he knew well around these parts of the sea — quite a fiery island, but not because of any volcano or civilization. On pretty, luscious Aeaea were just a few young nymphs and their scarlet-haired guardian witch. Hermes knew it first for the many medicinal herbs that grew along the forest floors, and knew it second for the entertaining sex he was able to enjoy from time to time.

It wasn't the worst island to rest along its beaches compared to others that Poseidon's kin were rampant on. There were no immediate enemies unless the men aboard this lone ship fell for the Aeaean sorceress' trap.

Ignoring the fact that many mortals were absolute fools, Hermes eased the black ship into the island's cove with no trouble from the wind nor water. Private, silent thank you prayers popped like bubbles in his mind.

How wonderful. Don't go snooping too far, little humans.

The young god, hidden from Man's eye, rested himself atop the mast to watch the men collapse from exhaustion on the floor of the ship, their rugged hands rubbing circles into their sore eyes. Hermes felt two fall asleep at once. Some were in their late thirties, though many rose in age to forties and late fifties — it was difficult to tell with some men as their beards curled, and silver mixed with the many colors they came in.

And ah, did all of them aboard have some sort of beard now, and matted, unkempt hair to boot. *What a sad bunch.* Hermes sat and crossed his legs, peering over to the rear of the ship where the captain lay.

If Hermes' head could cock anymore than it did, he'd be scaring Apollo on the daily.

The captain had succumbed to the floor of his ship among his crew. His hair was loose and sat at his shoulders, dark brown with a sea-tossed curl. Still rather young, forty at best, but grey strands were taking root upon his head. He was short and broad, with an upper physique that would do well as an archer over all other weapons. Across his shoulders, now, *that* was what caught Hermes' attention: the fleece of a ram — what would be a prized ram, though now on its way to becoming quite weathered.

"Hermes, you lucky bastard," he whispered to himself, his wings fluttering with excitement. He floated right down next to the half-conscious man. It was bound to happen — he was simply an amazing god.

One ship.

There certainly was a reported *twelve* by King Aeolus just a few weeks ago.

Odysseus, there was no way you were this unlucky.

The men cared little to rouse themselves from their slumbering. Hermes imagined it would be tough to do so if he granted them the path to restful, gentle dreams. Those who held on to the strength to go below deck brought up what was left of their rations: a few soft pieces of fruit and damp bread swaddled like a babe that survived the journey. There wasn't enough food.

Barely enough to divide between forty-odd, overworked men.

Hermes glanced at the island. There was plenty roaming its forests, they didn't technically need to journey close to the protective *Circe,* who wouldn't be pleased to have men on her land.

"Captain!"

Hermes rolled himself back skyward before the king was confronted.

"Captain, these shores may be quiet for now, but who is to say what enemies lie in wait above the cliff or within the trees? Our men are exhausted, we have no food, and if we were attacked in the night then there is no doubt we will all die."

Hermes hummed, this one was a coward. *Go explore, coward. As if I would lead you straight to danger. Before the sun goes down, go and reassure you and your men.*

Odysseus rolled his head to the side until a crack resounded from his neck. "Eurylochus," he said, and his voice was bright and young like a song. "If it eases your nerves and prevents you from scaring my crew, I'll have a look around. But please, Brother, let the men rest. After the giants, they need the time to mourn; and I'll cry with them when I return. Dispense the bread, find what drink we have left. Pray I can source out a river or the home of someone *civilized.*"

He hailed for his spear and strapped it to his back once he rose to his feet. His hair desperately needed to be combed through; Hermes held back his hand to just fix it himself. It would be *easy.*

"What if something happens to you?" Eurylochus asked, following a step behind. He pushed his own unkempt hair behind his ears. "How will we know?"

"I won't go by the beach," Odysseus said. The rocks around them rose up to the clouds like a tidal wave. "I'll climb the crag. You can just watch and consider yourself entertained."

Tanned skin moved over muscle while he stretched out his arms and his joints continued to pop as if he were doing it on purpose. Hermes followed as he climbed over the side of the boat and dropped into the shallow water in case Poseidon found the little human and decided that a foot of water was enough to rip the poor man out to sea.

Climbing would be fun to witness; there was never a need for Hermes to really climb tall crags or cliffs. If he did, it was like climbing stairs. Gravity was more of a nuisance to mortals, but Odysseus nimbly picked himself up from the ground and onto the rockface.

His knuckles were red and curled harshly as he ascended, but the man's hands were large and sturdy. Hermes didn't *need* to hold out his arms right behind him like he were a mere infant trying to walk for the first time, but when they reached the height well above the sails of the ship, if Odysseus fell, he'd certainly die. The man had ill-luck radiating from his person; Hermes tried batting it away.

From going up to swinging sideways, the king of Ithaca battled the late evening breeze as the sun disappeared behind the tops of trees, shifting the sky a deep orange. Odysseus grunted and talking to the air. His fingers looked like they were going to simply pop off at any moment, and Hermes nearly exposed himself as the man leaned back to view the island's silhouette. No beasts or monsters lurking in the treeline above the ship, nor any immediate sources of food and water.

But there, just above in the distance!

A purple waving line of smoke.

"Oh gods," Odysseus muttered. He lowered himself to the rock and pressed his face into the stone. His arms shivered and only then were the tear stains on his dirty cheeks visible as he looked back at the sign of life. "I might as well be the one to investigate. My men are scared and tired — *I* am scared and tired. Please don't be more giants, I cannot bear to lose more of my friends to cannibals and clubs..."

A sniffle stopped a sob from rising. It was unexpected, the gentle consolations he whispered to himself, the desperate calls of "Penelope" that continued to bring him strength to move across the crag.

Hermes fiddled with his nails. *Go to the wood across the bend there*, he sent the thought to Odysseus' head. *Hunger is a heinous enemy.*

"A short search," Odysseus said. "Ten minutes and no more."

That would be plenty of time. Hermes darted off to the island's grassy earth, touching down on the blades sharp enough to cut ankles' skin. Pushing back his helmet, it remained strapped to his neck but out of his way as he walked through the trees. Cypress, pine, palm, and myrtle, the forest flourished in all shades of green. The approach of autumn didn't have any sway to their coloring; all was dictated by the Aeaean sorceress, and she preferred the comfort of warmth like her father, Helios.

Last time Hermes was here was *at* the behest of great Helios.

On his flights, the two of them would cross paths several times. Two of the busiest immortals were allowed a few ticks together. Helios radiated sunlight, difficult to look at directly, his halo burst with beams from his head — as opposed to Apollo, whose halo refracted light *around* his head, leaving his face still visible to kiss or mock or poke at. Helios had requested Hermes go down to all of his children and collect a small token of their love for him. The bag at the young god's side was full with pieces of spices or flowers, vials of oil, and short poetic hymns. A shame that many of these things burned up upon being delivered to the Hyperion god, but Hermes completed his job. Circe had offered up pork, which — Hermes thought now — was very dark of her indeed.

He listened for Odysseus to settle on the ground. With deep breaths, the human pulled out his bronze spear and held it carefully in front of him. Through the brush like a wolf, Odysseus crept, the hourglass ticking. He was going to find something to eat, or he and his men would die.

And Hermes couldn't have that happening. A journey to the Underworld now would put him and poor Charon in a sour mood, and Hermes gave himself one task to get his little great-grandson to his island kingdom.

With a wave of his hand, from the distant trees came a large stag, sniffing the low-hanging branches for berries to eat up. Its antlers curved high above its head, like wings of bone. A wondrous meal for any mortal feast, worthy of one of Artemis' hunts. Hermes patted himself on the back and rose up into the trees to watch the show.

Tension eased from Odysseus' muscles. A fresh wave of tears flooded silently from his eyes as the stag uncharacteristically ran right by him, so easy to slay with an aimed thrust of his spear. Prey rarely offered themselves to their hunter. The stag collapsed to the grass, huffing its last breaths while Odysseus crouched over it.

"Merciful god who watches," he said, and Hermes peeked over his branch. "Thank you for this gift. Tonight, we dine in your honor, for you have saved good men."

I look forward to it, Hermes thought, happily kicking his feet.

The tired king couldn't drag the beast behind him for it was so comically large. He squatted instead, and, with a painful grunt, heaved the stag over his shoulders. But he was laughing, quietly under his breath; Hermes heard it. He laughed as he stumbled and slid through the grass back to his ship, just as the sun dipped halfway beyond the horizon.

As most gods didn't eat human food, offerings at mortals' feasts were enjoyed through the scents and smoke and many prayers and praises sent up to them.

The men on the ship were overjoyed at their captain's return. Together, they laid the stag on a table to carve and separate the good flesh from the bad. Prometheus' gift to man roared up in the ship's fire pit, lighting the deck in warmth and some jovial spirit. They talked of home, of their families, and what would be the first thing they'd do upon reaching Ithaca's shores. In their wistful theoretical stories, as the meat roasted on the fire, Hermes stood like a shadow among them. He danced through the divine smelling fumes, churning the smoke in delightful little circles.

It was no altar or sanctuary, but their voyaging hearth was sacred enough for him.

"My brothers," Odysseus called. He didn't sit upon any throne, rather the skin of the ram acted as a mat to rest on and wait while his small crew grabbed their rations and huddled close to the fire as night overtook the sky. "We survived the beaches of Troy and the storms of Poseidon; we've escaped Cyclopes and Lotus Eaters; rejected by allies, and battled the Laestrygians… but most of our brothers, our friends, have departed from us to reside in the well of heroes, far beyond these shores. I grieve their loss — *our* loss — and will see them in every wave of the ocean and fall of a stone."

He stopped himself, watching the fire, then shook his head.

"There's been a rumor aboard this ship," Odysseus said, moving his grey eyes over every crying face that sat around him, "that the gods have abandoned us, left us with a curse to remain in exile from our home. But let me tell you now: we *have* friends on Olympus. When we pray, they listen. This stag is a gift! We may weep for our fallen, but in our remembrance, let's be reminded to not let their deaths be in vain. I know these eyes will see the beaches of Ithaca again. When our ship digs into her white sands, I'll be the first among us to kiss her earth."

"Captain, what god would possibly want to help us now?" Eurylochus said. He looked into the few cups of wine, each held only three sips a man.

"We'll offer to Zeus, the all knowing," Odysseus stood and said, pouring a libation to the god king. The crew bowed their heads and raised their drinks. "To Athena, who has always led in our cause and delivered us victory," he added, but sorrow seeped into his voice as he poured the next libation. Athena was his patroness, and she answered no man's prayers for some time. "And for this night and the next, wherever we are in the unknown, we know our guide, and offer the rest of this wine to Hermes."

Odysseus' cup was empty while his comrades drank and feasted. Hermes' enjoyable smile at being included in their toasts twitched into a chagrin scowl at the unhappy mood the king had left himself in. He sauntered over the deck, feet so light, his invisible form made no sound, and placed his finger into the cup. Into it poured the small dribble from the young god's libation.

It wasn't that Hermes didn't desire the sacrifice so normally reserved for Hestia; he just couldn't have Odysseus falling dead from thirst.

Odysseus startled quietly to himself, grasping his cup with both hands when he saw it swirling with liquid. The gesture was very well up Dionysus' alley, but Odysseus said nothing. He merely bowed his head and raised his cup once more.

"Let us rest peacefully tonight, Lord Hermes, wielder of the golden rod," the king prayed and Hermes' caduceus woke up from its slumber. The serpents twisted and rolled along the staff.

Hermes removed it and let it rest in his lap, placing himself just behind

Odysseus. A short, but thoughtful prayer; he'd be happy to oblige by it. And being so close, well, what a coincidence he may offer it immediately to the captain and crew of the *one* ship of Ithaca.

The cove of Aeaea was gentle and quiet. With the crag covering the ship on either side, the warm breeze only rolled off the shore, and never strong enough to overpower the fire in its central hearth. When the men had their fill of meat and the bones and intestines continued to burn into the night, Hermes let his caduceus lull them all to sleep on their mats, covered only by the linen clothes they arrived with.

Chapter 4

Hermes meant to return home to Olympus.

Really, he meant to and he tried. He'd leave humans without performing extra acts of kindness if he grew too bored. It wouldn't be unusual. *Staying* like this was unusual.

Hermes walked around the deck for hours until he roused to run to the deep harbor at the island of the Laestrygians — where pieces of bodies, few still intact, floated throughout a watery grave of the *eleven* lost ships of Odysseus' fleet.

Like fatigued butterflies, the lost souls wandering above the water fell at his feet. Hermes collected them all, taking their hands and adding the immense color back to his split-cloak. Some corporeal spectres pointed up to the cliffs above where the cannibals themselves lived — where the victims of their meals had bodies no more, but their battered and deformed souls waited, grief-stricken, by the ledge.

Charon would understand, Hermes thought, leading the way for these men. *What's a few more annoyances in the span of forever?*

His cloak grew so dense and blinding, he yelped when his feet tapped the water with how wildly it flowed. He was a beacon in the blackness of night, trudging swiftly over the ebb and flow of the waves. Nearly six-hundred men he guided, knowing fully well that, with no burial, there'd only be more wanderers for the beaches of Hades.

When he returned to Aeaea and shrank back down to mortal size, some of the sailors were awake, taking watch and sitting with their small hand-tools in silence.

Always working with the hands… one would think after gripping wet oars for hours at a time that these men would want their hands to rest.

Hermes settled himself in an oarsman thwart. *This couldn't have been comfortable.*

Pretending to take an oar, he pushed forward, practically bending over himself and heaved backward until he thumped his head on the thwart behind him.

And they did that all day? Being a sailor was monotonous! Oh no, no, he'd be happier as the captain, standing or sitting at the back of the ship with the nice chair of furs.

Their captain lay on his fur along the planks of the deck, curled up like a babe.

Odysseus slept as if he were a puzzle missing its pieces. His arms held out softly in front of him, a safe shelter empty of its inhabitants. Tears dried in the inner corners of his eyes and burned away the dirt and debris that wanted to settle on his skin.

"If I could bring you to Olympus," Hermes whispered, "you'd have the most grand bath. And won't stink as much as you and your dirty men do. I believe most animals are cleaner than your lot."

The human stirred, pulling his arms into his chest with a deep sigh. More sailors rose, groggy in the early hours of the morning. Eurylochus, the tall man with skin like jasper and a voice rather grating to Hermes' ears, strode by Odysseus without minding the sound of his footsteps to look out at the beach and the island beyond it. He stroked his face and twisted his fingers into a short beard that needed to be oiled.

"Captain," he called, stark over the laps of the ocean to the back of the ship. "We can start another fire for the rest of our meal, sir, but we are in want of water."

By Zeus, let this decrepit man sleep.

Odysseus pressed his fingers to his eyes and ripped the slumber right out of them, staring at the sky above as it shifted from pale pink to a paler blue. Painted clouds rolled by with the cold morning breeze off the ocean. Goosebumps ran over the men's bare arms and legs, bringing blankets, robes, and himations up over their shoulders.

"We'll have to secure the island, then," Odysseus said with a quick yawn. "Ask who among the crew would like to volunteer; then be prepared to split them between the two of us." He paused for a moment. "If there *are* no enthusiastic offers, we'll draw lots to see whose party explores and whose remain to guard and fix the ship."

"I'll ask them privately," Eurylochus replied. He shifted his jaw and turned to approach the largest of the men first who idled near the front of the ship.

Odysseus was already preparing sized lots. He pulled his hair back and knotted it behind his head before turning in his seat. "Polites," he said over his shoulder. "Would you mix these for me, away from my eyes so they can't call me biased?"

Polites was a few years younger than Odysseus, with fuzz that curled tightly around his jaw and dark eyes that held a gentleness saved for philosophers, not warriors. He looked like a mortal that Hades would take the visage of on his few visits to the world above — handsome yet unassuming.

"Of course, sir," Polites said, taking the lots. He cupped them in the loose fold of his tunic. "If it eases your conscience, Captain, I will offer to go with the drawn leader's party to explore the island."

"I don't know if anything will ease my conscience, Polites, but thank you. You're a good friend, and a brave man."

The jingling clack of wood sounded like paupers' music, and Polites dumped the lots into a bowl. Hermes watched from the boat's ledge, lounging while they decided amongst themselves who'd brave Circe's island and inevitably fall first to her clever and seductive ways. What a woman — if Hermes were any less of a sensational individual, she'd hate and curse him too just to protect her nymphs.

Lip-curling Eurylochus was picked to investigate, *how wonderful!* All the better for Odysseus to safely remain on the beach to mend the sails that would carry them east towards Ithaca. With the second-in-command went twenty-two men, Polites among them, with swords, spears, and bows strapped to their backs. Not a bad day to explore either. The sky was clear, though it rarely ever rained longer than an hour or two on this island and only when the witch willed it.

Hermes waved the rude man off into the forest. "Ta-ta," he said. "Have fun!"

Nothing should have surprised the young god; it was a rare feat to catch an Olympian off guard, but when Hermes looked back inside the boat where the remaining twenty-three men were, Odysseus was *staring* at him.

Or rather, in his direction.

But Hermes rolled right off the ship, clinging to its red and black sides like a spider in hiding. He was cloaked — there wasn't a practical reason why this human would notice he was there. His wings folded tightly against his hair; maybe they could be seen from his helmet? Not likely — but Odysseus was a favorite of Athena and she was very adept at invisibility. Maybe he was skilled enough to detect it.

His great grandson *would* be so talented, Hermes nodded to himself.

Not to be considered a coward if any of his family was watching, Hermes lifted his eyes above the bar. Odysseus was speaking with his men now, grasping their shoulders with his large hands, and working to bring down the torn sail above them.

Throwing ropes and untying impossibly tight knots, the canvas fluttered heavily to the deck, stirring the settled sand between each plank. Some men were ordered to the beach with spears to wrangle whatever fish happened to be swimming close to the rocks while the others restored the ship to something akin to its former glory. It wasn't perfect, but within the first hour of labor, they procured themselves a half-mended sail and six fish.

They needed music to work to or a song to sing, Hermes thought, something to replace the dour mood they sank so deep into.

Almost six-hundred loved men did die *horrible deaths just a few days prior, you fool*, Hermes mulled. Mortal lives were so fragile.

He ran the fabric of his cloak between his fingers and let his head rest again on the gunwale ledge. Those souls looked so heart-broken arriving on the beaches of the Styx.

If he couldn't sleep in his bed of silks and feathers, resting on the hard wood and the open air was fine. Better than nothing.

That annoying call of Odysseus' first mate woke him before the sun reached midday. Hermes sat up, swinging his legs outside of the ship as the man tumbled onto the beach, met with worried, steady hands of the crew. He pushed them aside, scrambling to reach Odysseus up top.

"Eurylochus, what's wrong? Where're the rest of your men?" he asked, the panic rising in his voice. He thrust his hand down and took Eurylochus by the arm to heave him on board. "Eurylochus?"

The man's pupils were blown, his skin pale and slick with sweat. Odysseus followed his arm down to his hand, which shook with all the ferocity of an earthquake. Eurylochus' speech was so enamored with the concept of a stutter that it was impossible to decode what he was saying. Odysseus tugged him to the ground and spoke like a parent would to a child.

"What. Happened."

"I knew there was something wrong when we came upon the palace. It gave off an aura of malice, of deceit, and I knew if we were to enter then it would be the end of us. But no one believed me, sir!"

"Palace? Whose palace?"

"The one lays central on this island. We could smell the hearth cooking and it appeared in a clearing, blooming with flowers of all sorts. Flowers of spring and summer, like Demeter herself could have planted them there."

"And the crew? Polites? They just broke in?" Odysseus asked.

"No, we were invited in at the door, but I didn't trust it. I said we should decline, but Polites led them all inside."

Odysseus' brow creased. "Speak plainly, Eurylochus. Where are the men now? Whose palace did they enter? Some barbarian?"

"A woman's, sir."

"I'm... sorry?"

"She opened the door and seduced the party with a cunning tongue and sweet words, but I didn't fall for it. When the men went in, I remained outside and listened," Eurylochus said and his cries escalated. "I heard toasting, but then their shouts overwhelmed all. She's a witch! The shouting turned to shrieks — cries of swine! I swear she turned them, slowly and agonizing, into hogs and took them away. Captain, if you'd have seen them, how they all still look like themselves in such a cursed way —"

"Where did you find the palace?" Odysseus stood up, but Eurylochus grabbed at his leg.

"Please, Ody, let us cut our losses! Tie back up the sail and leave this place; it's not safe. If you try to find them, then we will all perish as swine!"

Odysseus tore his leg from Eurylochus' grasp. "I refuse to have come this far and lose more of my friends. Brother, if it were me in there, would you leave me behind too? We're not foolish enough to be tricked by a woman, and now that I know she weaves magic, I'll be better prepared for it."

He left Eurylochus weeping and rushed to the chest keeping his military equipment and weaponry. Digging up his bow and sword, he left behind all else that would protect him, no helmet nor cuirass or greaves, just the chiton he wore and the sandals on his feet.

"Are you coming?" he asked, ready to throw himself onto the beach.

The man shook his head, hiding his face within his lap. Odysseus didn't argue or shame him for being a coward. With a simple sigh, the king of Ithaca left his ship and hurried up the sand.

"If I don't return by sundown," he told the rest of his crew, "set fire to these trees."

Hermes followed from above. Circe's palace was a thirty minute trek inland straight through the forest. He'd be lying to himself if he didn't admit he was curious of the outcome of wits between Circe and Odysseus. Circe was a smart woman because she had to be — men besides Hermes never made it off of this island if they dared to near her home.

Odysseus... Well, Hermes didn't know Odysseus too well yet. He was sort of fathering his way with the crew under him, and if a goddess like Hestia ever cared to show up to gatherings of the Olympians, she'd surely be rooting for him. If Athena once mentored him, then he had something more going on.

He did live *this* long, after all.

But Hermes didn't want to risk it; the man needed to succeed for Hermes' own sake, it was so pathetic to watch.

He could break the rules every now and then without much notice from Olympus. It wasn't like it was really *divine intervention.*

Arguably.

For debate.

Descending down to the outskirts of Circe's palace where those flowers bloomed, Hermes took his mortal form. Not very different than how he always looked — he was still beardless, his bronze hair sans wings curled around his ears and tickled the curve of his neck. His talaria appeared just as normal sandals, but all else remained the same.

He weaved through the trees, keeping a steady eye on the deep blue of Odysseus' tunic. Odysseus pushed aside vine and twig, his frown dug a crevice in his brow so deep one could fall in it. The edges of the clearing came into view and the human's shoulders rose with immense adrenaline. *Oh boy —*

Hermes reached out from beyond a tree and grasped Odysseus by the hand. It was a rough palm, scarred and blistered from war and ocean-faring; Hermes' was soft and inhuman, like it never touched work before in its existence. "Where do you think you're going, my unlucky friend, trekking through wood alone on unfamiliar land?" he said, a smile manifesting on his face.

The king of Ithaca whirled around, sword ready to pierce skin before it fell sideways. A smart man, those who knew the custom of xenia abided by it for their fear of strangers. Anyone could be a god; and sometimes that god could grab you in the middle of the woods to deliver you aid. His gray eyes blinked thrice, gazing at Hermes with quaking lips.

"Your men," Hermes continued, "are in Circe's palace cooped up like swine amidst the sties, and you've come alone to set them free? I'll warn you, good king, you won't get home if you continue like this. You'd remain there, trapped with all the rest of them."

Odysseus found his tongue. "I must try," he replied. "I will not leave them behind."

"I can save you from the great danger Circe presents," Hermes said, still holding onto his hand. He gestured to the flower field. "Will you follow me?"

"You…" Odysseus blinked once more. "You are the Olympian herald — you are Lord Hermes in the flesh, aren't you?"

Hermes' smile never waned. "Very perceptive. Does me being so entice you to follow me now, or should I be more persuasive? I'll admit, not many people refuse my offerings of aid. It would be the first time I had to beg a mortal to allow me to help them."

"I will follow," he said with a firm nod. "Forgive me, I thought I had displeased Olympus so greatly, I didn't expect… Was — was the gift yesterday from you? The stag couldn't be a mere coincidence."

Walking with him between the wild gardens, the young god pursed his lips. "Coincidences *seldom* happen."

An agreeable silence settled, but only for another minute. Upon the ground speckled spots of empty soil, seemingly where no flower wished to grow. Hermes sat and so did Odysseus.

"There is a drug to take," Hermes explained. "Like an antidote of sorts, to the poisons that Circe hides within the wine and food she serves any unwelcome guests. If you take it before you enter her palace, you'll have the upperhand for a moment, though not for longer than that. You must convince her that her attacks are worthless. Be sure to draw your blade before she does hers."

Odysseus watched Hermes' hands as he dipped them under the topsoil and pushed a few inches of dirt away to reveal a flower. White as snow, it grew brighter when revealed to the sun, and the petals unfurled themselves to bask in it.

"This herb grew when Helios slayed the giant, Picolus, to protect his daughter. It's of his blood — do *not* touch it directly!" Hermes said, smacking Odysseus' knuckles. "Mortals will rot should they touch godlike blood. I'll do it. Sit and be good."

"Sorry."

Hermes dug a little deeper, weaving his fingers through the soil until he felt the bulb of the root, and gave it a firm pull. The white of the flower oozed black, as the string roots were forever stained by the old ichor. Summoning a pestle and mortar, he ripped the roots from the flower and mashed them together until it became a powdery, tealike texture.

"Lord Hermes," Odysseus said, scrutinizing the process. "I don't mean to question your methods, but how do I not touch the herb, yet be expected to take it?"

Hermes glanced up from under his lashes. "Son of Laertes, you are so observant." He pulled a goblet from his bag and spun it until wine splashed up from its rim. With a quick flick of the mortar, the herb tumbled in. "You can consume Moly if you chug this and not let your tongue be curious about its taste. You'll find it disgusting, trust me."

"It won't rot out my insides?"

"I don't think so," Hermes replied, giving it a sniff. "I've never seen it happen to any mortal who consumed it, but I don't offer Moly to just anyone. I think you'll be fine. Not my intention to kill you, but if I accidentally do, I have an *in* with the honorable ferryman and perhaps we could cheat the process." He smiled and handed the goblet to Odysseus, whose concern didn't waver. "You will not survive *Circe*, I tell you that."

Worn hands reached out to take the cup. It was easy to see the thoughts whirling through the man's mind, his worry and sorrow were upon his face like a scroll to read. "This Circe," he said, staring at the liquid. "Is she truly as ruthless as you say? There's no hope to speak sense to her?"

Transactions on Aeaea were just that whenever Hermes stopped by: transactional. He didn't think to ever sit and get to know the sorceress any more than surface and the shallow level of personality that was seen through her father, Helios. "She's what she's had to be," Hermes replied. "Zeus once said when immortals stay amongst the humans, therein lies a weakness towards acts of panic and emotion. Hurry now. If you don't take the Moly, you'll never see your home."

Odysseus breathed heavily, looked Hermes in the eye, and raised the cup. With a nod, he tilted the wine straight back. His nose wrinkled and he brought his lips to his sleeved shoulder to wipe away the moisture that held onto the rancid taste. But he didn't scream and there was no rapid deterioration of the flesh.

Hooray!

"I won't be following you inside," Hermes said. "But I'll give you one last warning before I take my leave. The moment she draws her wand, take your sword and rush her like you mean to run her through. She'll fall to her knees and beg for her life, try to coax you to her bed with some sweet words and the like. Don't refuse immediately if you wish her to release your friends. Have her swear the binding oath of us gods that she won't ever plot some new scheme to cause you harm."

"And when she swears?" Odysseus asked.

Hermes pursed his lips. "Well then, my good king, I suppose you may have some fun."

The man's face grew red and so ridiculous that Hermes couldn't help but laugh at it. He leapt to his feet, the human visage slipping away with the breeze; Odysseus bowed his head at once.

"Thank you, kind Hermes, for your aid," Odysseus said.

"Thank me when you have a crew back. Less for my conscience should you fail and die."

"I will not fail."

Hermes hummed. He knew the king wouldn't. Better to leave with an air of mystery, though.

But he still didn't return to Mount Olympus — he wanted to see the action. In Circe's grand courtyards where the nymphs tended to plants and the livestock that freely roam, away from the sty of crying pigs, Hermes fluttered back to the ground as a rooster: a lovely golden one with a bright comb and a grand ass of teal and green feathers. Stepping with confidence over the stone walkway, he propped himself upon a railing overlooking Circe's marvelous hall.

Every long table had several stools, silver-studded and carved with delicate motifs to the sun god. The table itself was draped in white linen, covered in the island's fruits and flowers, with golden bowls waiting to be filled. Along the walls were glittering ornaments, a delightful feast for the eyes should they ever wander away from the food she always had prepared — a meal frozen in time, waiting for the next victim.

Where was she, where was she...

Ah!

Hair like wine, braided and bound down her back, it dribbled with gold right to her thigh and swung like a cat's tail. A girdle emblazoned with precious gems supported her gown, whose sleeves attached with delicate pins at the elbow and wrist. Raising her hand, she merely pulled a wand from the air, as if an invisible pocket followed her around. She swayed between her fixings, adjusting where dirty men had previously touched her home.

"CIRCE!"

Odysseus' voice rang loud and clear. Circe spun in her hall towards the gleaming doors, motioning to the other nymphs in the room to depart immediately. Out they ran, giggling softly to each other as they appeared in the gardens and courtyards right behind Hermes. One even daintily pet his feathered ass.

"Dearest stranger, god or man, please," Circe declared, opening the way to the heavyhearted king, "come inside. Your journey must have gone so off course if you wound up on my humble island. You look absolutely parched. Come rest. Allow me to take care of you." She gestured to her hall and Odysseus, bearing a brave face, entered.

She brought him to one of the stools and presented a cushion to rest his feet on. Speaking useless tales of nothing to a man who knew her scheming, she stirred up her potion under the guise of a wine, so willing and happy to give it to the guest who nary said a word to her.

"This will liven your spirit," Circe said, holding out the drink.

As Odysseus took it and gulped it down, Hermes' heart thumped too hard for the little body he was in — a small *doot* hiccuped from his beak.

What shouldn't have surprised at least two members of the party involved, Odysseus remained completely himself after Circe revealed her wand and awaited the squeal of a newly transformed pig.

She stuttered, her brow twitched. The son of Laertes wasted no time in unsheathing his blade. He ran at her with a cry worthy of Ares and she screamed at the sight of him, dodging under the blade as it thrust where her belly once was. The nymphs outside heard the panic and disappeared in a hurry to separate halls.

Scrambling on the floor, Circle hugged Odysseus' legs.

"What is this? Who are you and why have you come here? No one has ever drank from my cup and avoided my poisons —" Circe cut herself off, voice lowering as tears slid silently down her cheeks. "Hermes warned the coming of a man whose mind was immune to charm, can this be you? Oh, *sir*, please have mercy. Let me show you to my bed where we may build trust between each other. With our bodies in plain sight, you will see I have nothing more to hide."

Odysseus was fighting his instincts with shaking hands. He lowered his sword and looked to the inner chamber doorway for longer than any man ought to when asked by a woman to sleep with her.

"Circe, how dare you," he said.

Hermes mentally slapped himself.

The witch slowly picked up her head from his knees.

"You tell me to treat *you* with kindness when you've turned my men into swine and hold me here in your palace. Your amorous words drip with cunning deceit, but I'm not so easily persuaded."

Circe was on her feet in an instant, her long arms wrapped around the king in a soft embrace. "No, my lord, I do not hold you here," she replied. "And you wish for your friends back, that's *very* noble of you. You see, I am very protective of the nymphs under my care on this island. I only changed the men into their true forms to protect my girls."

"Release them to me as they were, Circe. I'll take them and leave this island for good. You have my word."

She titted, her lips poised in a full pout as she tapped Odysseus on the chin. "Words mean so little in terms of honesty, do they not? Actions, now, reveal the truest of us," she exclaimed, and gave his arm a little tug. "My chambers, sir? I insist."

How the young god wished to get inside Odysseus' head as he glowered at the witch. The two of them were practically equal in height, spinning around each other in a predators' dance.

She tugged again and Odysseus relented, and Hermes had to find another railing a few hallways down to perch himself up on. Circe's bedroom was draped in silks and finery too, with incense burning between curtains. She leapt upon her bed cushions, soft with feathers, bringing Odysseus along with her. But only one hand lay flat on the blankets, the other donned his blade, and he pressed it harshly against her neck.

"You think me so gullible?" Odysseus said. "Mount your bed? Not for all the world. You couldn't have picked a worse victim — I have a wife at home in Ithaca: a worthy queen, a princess of Sparta. Do you know the customs of Sparta that I had to abide by? My wife and I ceremoniously fought each other for *three* days until I could best her and declared she was finally mine." His nostrils flared. "And you believe I'd simply lay with you, Circe, because you think *this* is the way to understand each other? No. I won't even *touch* you unless you swear the gods' oath that you'll do nothing to harm me."

Circe laid wonderstruck. Never had she been so speechless at the behest of a man. Though she remained in silence, she pulled a dagger that she kept under a pillow, presented it to Odysseus' attention, and dissolved it from existence. Clearly and wearisome, she spoke the oath required for Odysseus to remove his sword from her throat, and she pushed back to sit upon her bed with a very unhappy frown.

"Of Ithaca, you say?" she said, bringing her hair over her shoulder. "You are King Odysseus, then, if the wife you speak of is a Spartan princess. What brings you halfway across the world? Weren't you and the gods all fighting in Troy? Cannot wring the bloodlust from your mind?"

Odysseus let his feet fall back to the floor. A groan carried out all the anxieties he brought into her house. His face hid in his hands. "We've been victims of Poseidon's wrath," he muttered. "On our route home, we were sent off course by a storm and struggled to find food. One island was flourishing with sheep, but they were guarded by a Cyclops. He didn't abide by Zeus' laws, though we didn't know it at the time."

He took a shaken breath.

"He killed several of my men and kept us trapped within his cave. I thought of a plan to trick him, to blind him and allow us escape. But after doing so and returning to our fleet, I was overcome with self-righteousness and revealed my name to that monster. And in turn he told me his. He is Poseidon's son. I blinded and mocked a *wrathful* god's son."

Circe cleared her throat, reached her hands out of her wide window, and clapped before returning to the bedding. "Poseidon," she repeated. "Yes, certainly not the one you would wish to be the enemy of. I have heard he holds the longest grudges; his temper is as unstable as the earth itself. But you are here in Aeaea; and the only goddess you need to know the name of is *me*."

Nymphs poured into the palace from every entrance, carrying with them all the necessities to make up the chambers required for true guests. Astonished at their beauty and speed — the nymphs were of the spring flowers and flowing rivers of the isle.

A bath was made up from a boiling cauldron and a bowl from the river; a nymph gently eased Odysseus off of Circe's bed, undressed him, and led him to the tub while the goddess supervised. He gasped in the comfort of being showered in warm water until all the exhaustion in his soul and body left him. The grime of the ocean voyage and the dried blood of his friends were scrubbed off his skin, his hair was soaped and combed through — no longer mousy, but full and long enough to be loosely braided as the handmaid saw fit. Circe returned with a lekythos of oil. From his temples to his wrists, his neck to his feet, they rubbed Odysseus down, dressed him in a very fine shirt, and cloaked him with a warm fleece.

To Hermes' eye, it seemed like the proper way a mortal king should be treated by his hosts at every point. He dooted — a prance back to that original hall, newly made up with real food and drink, where Odysseus was sat again. He washed his hands, and they presented him with real meat fresh from their fires.

But he just stared at the window, his mind elsewhere, and didn't lay a finger on the feast.

Circe strolled into the room, ready to take her chair when she saw him sitting like a dumb man. "Odysseus," she said, leaning into his view. "Why do you not nourish yourself? I have sworn to you on Styx that you will come under no harm here. No man has enjoyed a feast from me in centuries."

Odysseus shook his head. "How could any man in his right mind tolerate the taste of food before he's freed his brothers and looked them all in the eyes? If you truly want me to eat, then please, Circe, have mercy. I love them too dearly to be happy without knowing they're safe. Let me feast my eyes upon their faces. Show me that *actions* do indeed reveal the truest of ourselves."

She sat on the balcony's railing, next to Hermes as he patted his four-toed feet on the marble, being very much a grand rooster and not an eavesdropping god. Just over the bushes and hedges laid the pen of twenty-odd pigs, oinking and snorting, running in circles or nervously hiding in the shadows. Circe turned back to Odysseus, summoned her wand, and with a motion of her chin, strode outside with the king right at her heel.

With a wave, the pen opened up, and the swine shrieked and cowered together before being forced to line up like a row of soldiers. Odysseus slowed behind her, watching the fully sized pigs quiver and shake. Circe went along to each one and anointed them with a gold-tinted oil.

They began to shift with a startling painful *crack!* Bristles grew and coiled to short beards, leathery hides softened to fleshy, tall, youthful men once more. They bore recognition in their eyes, all turning towards Odysseus with tears overflowing, running to take his hands, sobbing in each other's arms.

A terrible and ugly and moving festival of weeping if Hermes ever saw one. Even Circe took a handkerchief from her nymphs and blotted her eyes. She sent them off to prepare more hot water for many a bath to be had this day.

"Odysseus," she called, and the king of Ithaca, a warm smile on his face, answered her sweetly with soft thank yous. "Go down at once to your ship at my shores and haul her fully up onto the beach. There are caves nearby to store your cargo and whatever gear you have remaining; then back here you are to come, and bring with you the remainder of your crew. I will have your men washed and dressed, truly feasting when you return."

"Dear goddess," he said, holding onto his friends' shoulders. "We'll be your most gracious guests."

"Yes, I would hope so," she replied, crossing her arms. "I do not get to host very often, you will find yourselves spoiled."

Her teasing was very persuasive for the lot of the crew despite their fear of her moments earlier. But for men to be doted upon by pretty, young-looking women, it didn't take much prodding. Odysseus ran off with newfound energy, and the crew was taken inside to be properly cleaned.

Circe remained in the courtyard, studying the empty pigsty she so often ignored. Over the hedges, the sound of splashing and deep, relaxed laughter echoed through the palace.

She sighed, tapping her wand to her crossed arm, and looked down at the rooster that pecked at some stray seeds.

"Hermes," she said. "What a pleasant surprise if it was one."

"I thought I was a fine looking rooster," he replied, shifting back. "Circe, *love*, it has been some time since we've chatted. What a fun new story you get to share with your next round of guests."

Circe curled her lip upward to something close to a smirk. "Aren't you cute? The cock suits you well. Why are you here? Did my father send you or has Zeus something to say to me?"

"Funny enough, neither," Hermes said. "I'm not here for you, as a matter of fact."

"Odysseus, then? Thought it was suspicious he was immune to my drug. The whole affair had your sticky, little hands all over it."

"Affair! I am astounded that there was *none!* You didn't lose your charm, did you, my dear Circe? Cannot sway a married man between your legs like you used to." Hermes leapt up before the witch struck the ground with a sparking blast of her wand. "Peace, peace, I jest of course. Yes, I'm here for the son of Laertes. He doesn't quite know that yet. You heard part of his tale; of all the generals who left Troy and are journeying home, there are few who are terribly off course. This man of Ithaca is one I have a keen interest in."

She looked him up and down and sauntered over to the pathway that led back her to luscious halls. "I can see why," she said, twisting a finger through her braids. "He is safe while he is here; I find he spins his stories very well. Must be a familial trait."

"You'll summon me when he's to leave," Hermes said bluntly. "And he *is* to leave, Circe."

"Why do you look at me with such distrust?" Circe covered her mouth with the back of her hand as it slipped into a genuine smile. "I could not possibly keep men on my island for longer than necessary."

Two liars laughed together.

"Burn a palm frond when they first speak of home and I'll be here," Hermes said. "Circe."

"Yes, yes. A palm when they long for Ithaca." Circe waved her hand. "Begone from my home, I have guests to attend to."

What a shrewd woman, Hermes thought. No wonder he liked her.

* * *

"You've been out a long while," Ares said, finding him on the walkways of Olympus. Without an inkling of armor on, the god of war appeared to be a god at rest — his injuries healed completely from the blessed weapons that speared him.

"Oh, have I?" Hermes asked. "I'm afraid time flies right by me. That little goddess, Circe, had many little pigs roaming about for me to look at."

Ares humphed. "Any man that bothers those women has it coming," he replied. "I hope she skewered them all."

Hermes' smile was small and pursed. *Preferably not,* he mused. "How fares the mighty Lord Ares this fine evening? Does the family not dine together at this hour or have you come from your tryst, perhaps?"

"I returned from a sacrifice in my honor," Ares replied, and fair to his word, he smelled like smoke from a great fire. A rarity for him. "Another general has returned to his people. The discord I have heard across the lands from lamenting wives and struggling queens… Glad to have them quiet now, though the feasts have been satisfactory. Finally the men can plan their future grievances. Days grow boring in idleness."

Hermes didn't walk with Ares often, but the two of them shared in overlapping prayers. Ares stood a few feet above him and was thrice as broad; Hermes hopped a yard up into the air to level himself to his face. "Then it'll be onto the next mortal fiasco, will it not, Brother?"

"Yes, the next one," Ares replied, with a knowing chuckle as they walked by Athena's palace, "unfortunately, not from *my* hand."

Chapter 5

From trips to Hades to delivering messages and hosting of games both on the earth and above in Olympus, Hermes crowned himself with a golden wreath of victory for his impressive speed and stamina. Olympian games were merely excuses for the gods to show off to each other and the other dwellers of the heavens. Apollo and Hermes nearly *always* hosted for the past three hundred years.

Did it give them an advantage? Perhaps.

Did they care to abide by all the rules they set? Not especially.

The games were held in a grand amphitheater with enough seats to hold all of the world's population. It swarmed with runners and spear-throwers, wrestling matches and feats of dexterity. Zeus lounged above them all in his throne, partaking in a large bowl of nectar and whichever little nymph sat upon his lap. Hard to say which brought him more delight as he laughed and presented gifts to the crowd. Hera, very obviously absent from her seat, moved amongst the games' participants as if she were inspecting them in a sport of her own.

Hephaestus showcased his newest builds: works of art for the gods, and prizes to be won by Mankind below. For a god to gift a mortal hero with divine armor and weaponry was to give them their blessing, but not immortality. Achilles, a very poignant example, now trudged depressing circles through the grain of Elysium.

Apollo held aloft a new batch of arrows with shafts made of bronze and the feathers of a turkey. He balanced one on his finger, apparently very pleased with the cut and weight.

"Hermes, what do you think?" he asked, presenting them along his bow. "Do they look mighty? Would you be struck with terror at the end of my draw?"

Hermes shifted a few swords around on their displays, swapping a bulky one for a thin blade on a pretty pedestal. A quick glance to the archer and he fluttered his wings. "I think I'd be struck with a sharp pain in my ass," he replied.

Apollo's excited smile fell crooked. "Shall we test it?" he said, jabbing the arrowhead at Hermes' rear, but the god flew above him. "Hephaestus cannot make everything for *you*, you know. Favorite, youthful god that you are."

"Who, me?" Hermes perched atop his brother's shoulders. "I'm not that youthful."

"Of us twelve — a child."

"How sad to be bested by a child, then," he laughed, letting his weight drop completely around Apollo's shining head. "Maybe next year I'll let you win without your chariot, Light-wrangler. Those beasts of yours impress even me with their speed."

A snorting sigh; Apollo rested his hands on Hermes' ankles, mindful of the sandals' wings. "So kind of you to offer *them* a compliment." The two walked like a conjoined giant down the stalls of Hephaestus' creations. "You know who I'm surprised is not competing among us? Athena. She's been quite distant as of late."

"Isn't she always?" Hermes said, patting a tune on Apollo's cheeks. There were a dozen wonderfully crafted shields beneath them. "I've seen her training when the night is high. She's been basking in solitude."

Basking wasn't really the right word for it. Under the stars, the goddess of war had been demolishing target after target with her spears. There were little tactical methods to her effort. Hermes would sooner be struck down with a javelin before he admitted hearing the frustrated cry coming from Athena's mouth. In feasts held in Zeus' halls, she sat stoic as ever, making only the smallest of talks with Hestia when the eldest goddess was present, or staring intently down her nose at Hermes so forcefully he needed to move seats.

If her eyes were not as wide as an owl's then it wouldn't be so unsettling. He wondered if Odysseus ever felt the uncomfortable gaze of his old mentor when he prayed for her guidance.

"Great Zeus!" Hermes shouted, throwing his head back.

Apollo staggered backward, choosing to let go of Hermes rather than risk being brought down with him. "What?"

"That conniving bitch!" Hermes replied, hovering above the ground.

"Which conniving bitch?" Apollo waved the spectators away. "Not Lady Athena, I pray? I've yet to prepare any eulogy for you if you speak like Ares."

Hermes pulled his tunic's pin tight. He had to grab his things right away. "I must go. All the excitement of the day made me forgetful of a prior engagement."

"Ah. Should I concoct some alternative reason for your absence at the gathering tonight?"

"I do a thousand and one errands, Father will understand."

"So you say…"

Annoying as it was to depart from the most anticipated event of the season, Hermes was more exacerbated by the ignorance of his *one request*. To play tricks on a trickster god? They ought at least be funny.

Taking up his caduceus and helmet, Hermes dove once more from Mount Olympus, passing the clouds to the land of men, and accelerating headlong towards the island of Aeaea.

* * *

It wasn't possible they were still feasting and laughing as they were *a year ago*. No way a man like Odysseus would loiter at one little sorceress' palace for the months of every season without complaint of home. Certainly, that palace was akin to a paradise after what the men had gone through, but what an embarrassment!

Their red and black ship remained beached, practically covered in sand across the deck.

71

Hermes coasted through the trees, spinning around large trunks and low hanging branches. If he burst right through the large windows, teeming with displeasure, he'd likely scare every man in the room. Not a goal, as tempting as it was.

His feet made purchase on the soil of Circe's wide-breathed flowerbeds. The chatter resounded from the halls, but a few crewmen walked with one another and a handmaiden or two outside in the gardens. Hermes put his hands on his hips and huffed.

Why did he do this to himself?

Inside, in that very chair from before, Odysseus sat in conversation with Circe as she worked her loom. They laughed and drank from deep goblets. No harm done, undoubtedly, but to enchant him with her hostess skill? A stupid, stupid man.

Hermes pushed his helm back and chose one of the men out for a walk. The young, tall one with the nice eyes. What was his name, his name, his name —

"Polites," Hermes said into the ether, and the man paused in his walking. *"Isn't it time for your king and crew to return to Ithaca? How long have you been loitering here?"*

The little nymph he accompanied stopped and questioned him, but Polites raised his finger. To his comrades, he spoke and broke them from their trance. How many months had wheeled by without their noticing? Autumn was returning again, that couldn't be! Rouse their captain to leave! It's been too long!

Polites, with a dozen concerned men behind him, waited to enter the hall until the witch goddess had excused herself to her rooms. They rushed to their king's side, pulling him up from the seat and to the corner of the room where no nymph could overhear them.

"Captain," Polites said, and Odysseus looked up to his eyes with a content smile.

"What is it?" he asked. "You're red in the face."

"My friend, this is madness — remaining here for so long. We've spoken long hours of home, and you yourself of your well-built house and native land. Have you no thoughts of it now?" His hands pressed down on Odysseus' shoulders.

"We've been recovering, Polites. With how much we've endured, do we not deserve a break from the perils of the sea?"

"Recovering has been wonderful, sir," he replied gently, but shook his head. "Though recovery for a month is one thing. How long do you think we have been within these halls?"

Odysseus mirrored Polites' head shake in disbelief. "Surely not so long as you imply?"

The men pressed him. Hermes made them urge harder, and Eurylochus spoke up plainly. "A *year* tomorrow, Captain. That is how long we have drunk from this witch's cups and feasted on her meals."

Odysseus' rapid mind and stubbornness brought that crevice back between his brow.

"I knew we shouldn't have stayed but you denied my suggestion again and now a year passes!"

"Eurylochus," Odysseus warned, teeth clenching.

"Every turn you have brought our crew to *destruction* from your heedlessness."

"Hold your tongue! I still have half a mind to divorce your head from your neck for speaking to me in such a manner," he declared and his crew held him back in their embrace, desperately pleading all the more until his temper quelled. "Circe has treated us well, we must admit that. But... I'll speak to her tonight. She'd promised to aid us and, even with no oath, I'm inclined to believe her."

Polites relaxed his hands. "Then we feast in luxury for one more night."

Hermes celebrated silently from the outside and flew around the palace to sit by Circe's window.

When at last night came, and the men fell asleep on soft mats to the gentle humming tunes of the river nymphs, Odysseus knocked upon Circe's door and entered without invitation. There, by the bed where Circe sat combing her long hair, he collapsed to the floor at her feet and pressed his cheek to her knees.

"Circe," he whispered in a sad supplication, laying out his pride before her. "Make good on the promise you once made me when I was weak and weary. It's time to help me home; my heart yearns for home, my friends' hearts ache for our land. Whenever you leave the hall, they wear me down and stir my sentiments. Please, lovely goddess, let us leave."

She hovered her hand above his head before combing her fingers through his hair, and he wept for a moment before she nodded. "Royal son of Laertes, you may depart my house if staying is against your will. I will no longer force you to remain."

Odysseus raised his face, his eyes dry at once.

"But," she continued, "it is no easy journey from here if you wish to avoid doom. Travel to see the great prophet of Thebes — the one who knows your past, your present, and of your future. The name is Tiresias; he has found favor with the Dread Queen Persephone. You see, Tiresias is dead, but his wisdom remains everlasting among the empty souls of Hades."

The king sat back on his heels. His skin grew white. "You mean… you mean to say I must travel to the Underworld to speak to *one* man?" His lip quivered. He ran his hands up his cheeks and through his hair, pulling at the roots until his breathing turned back to sobs. And he sobbed for a long while in the silence of Circe's room. The witch hadn't the heart to try and console a fated man.

Hermes nabbed a pebble from the polished floor of the courtyard and threw it inside where it soared fast and straight towards the pillow by Circe's arm. She looked up with a start to find Hermes glaring at her from the balcony. He gestured vaguely in the air — how dare she not call him sooner. Her full lips puckered and she offered the smallest of shrugs.

"Circe," Odysseus said and the woman kindly looked back at him. "Circe, *who* could pilot us on that cursed journey? There's no tale of any man who has sailed a ship to the House of Death."

"My dear king of Ithaca, let that not be a worry of yours. When you board your ship and let loose your white sails, sit back and the North Wind will speed you towards your destination. But should your concerns overwhelm you, an abundance of caution you wish to take, then burn a palm frond near the bow of your ship and your guide will be forever with you."

Sneaky, witch.

Hermes nodded. She could earn his forgiveness, he supposed.

He listened carefully to her direction as she dictated which path the mortals needed to take, mapping the way in his mind through the routes he was familiar with. To summon the prophet Tiresias was a process on its own, but Odysseus drank up every word, committing the rituals and sacrifices to memory. True to a follower of Athena, Odysseus was destined to remember it all faithfully.

"Do not allow the ghosts of the dead to come near the blood of the ram and ewe until you've questioned Tiresias yourself. He will tell you where to go, every stage of your dangerous voyage, and how you can cross Poseidon's sea to reach home at last," Circe said. She dressed the king in a fresh chiton and a sea-cloak and anointed his forehead with oil before gently kissing his cheek. "Take what supplies you need from my house, collect your men, and be gone, Royal son of Laertes."

Hermes climbed to the rooftop, overjoyed to hear the optimistic stirring of soldiers. The footsteps in the early hours of dawn ravaged the palace floors. A few ran to the stables to take a ram and a black ewe for the voyage, others heaved up pots of wine and honey and containers of oil. A jolly, little tune sprang up among each other. It made the young god's heart go aflutter… Until Odysseus broke the news of their destination and the joyful noise avalanched to broken hearts and anguished groans.

But there was nothing to be done about their complaints, the Underworld beckoned.

Like a pinprick, a sudden soul, lonely and ambling, clung onto Hermes' cloak. He pulled the tail to him, a tiny star in the sky of the woven fabric.

And *where did you come from, little one?*

"To the beach, brothers, we cast off at once!"

Oh dear, Hermes idled. Not the time to worry about a wavering soul; he'd deliver it to the Styx within the week it seemed. Charon was going to love this story.

Circe, donned in her robe and veil, called out from the courtyard before he took to the skies.

"Be gentle with them," she warned. "Whatever mischief you gods have, remember they are only human."

"I'm merely fulfilling my patronage, my dear!" That's all. Just a guide to show them along. "I cannot interfere in their fates. It's all predestined."

"So you say, so be it."

He ignored her tone and cast his attention to the sea. Pulling his helm up and over his eyes, Hermes flew high above the island, skin rosy in Dawn's first light. Despite a passion for speaking, he was an expert on letting his waking mind wander elsewhere as he danced with the breeze that rustled the tallest trees. To the beach, where the one black ship with the red bow and mended sail was heaved back into the water and boarded by forty-odd men. The crew scurried the running gear across the deck, keeping that sail as tight as they could. The wind was filling it fast, rolling the ship out of Circe's cove as easy as Hermes had guided them in it. No man needed to touch an oar; just the helmsman in the rear working with the wind.

Hermes arched down and took his flight to the water's edge, running through the foam and early morning mist. He heard Odysseus' steady steps as he paced the boat, his words of support to each friend that reached out to him, though there were few.

Gentle Polites' voice was endearing and full of respect. "Shall you burn it, sir?" he asked.

Eurylochus spoke up. "Who's to say what creature it will summon when a sorceress told you of it? Our course is true, we need no supernatural help."

Odysseus took his time to reply to the opposing opinion. "There wasn't any malice in Circe's advice. Her oath to never harm me remains forever, even away from her island. Polites, hand me the flint. What do we have to lose with some extra help?"

Before long, the leaf smoked and burned, its scent sending sparks through Hermes' core. Quite unnecessary now as he made himself at home in his mortal size along the ram of the boat, stretching out his legs, using the curving wood to rest his head up in his arms. He watched the sail above him remain impressively taut. If the helmsman maintained a straight line, they would indeed be heading towards one of the few entrances to Hades.

"Well, she lied to us," Eurylochus said, his voice growing closer as he rested his hands on the railing. He must've been the bow officer on his king's ship. "Better that than a… a…"

His faraway eyes met Hermes' and the young god gave him a little wave.

What a narrow-minded bastard, Hermes chuckled to himself as the mortal stumbled away from the railing with a stammering call for his captain. To his feet he rose, climbing nimbly up to the edge of the ship. His wings were far too excited to roll him onto the deck, but it was better to raise himself just as Odysseus' face appeared above.

That well-suited, likable face; definitely one from Hermes' loins.

"Hermes!" Odysseus said, his mouth stuck in awe. Hermes tapped it closed for him.

"You called for a guide?" Hermes replied.

Odysseus' eyes crinkled when he smiled. "Thank you, Lord Hermes. I've owed you that thank you for a long while now." He looked out at Hermes' cloak as it billowed like a flag in the whirlwind speed of the ship, and to his legs that jogged merrily in the air. "Would you join us on board? We would be honored."

The crew were wary to see an Olympian step on the same wooden boards they did. Wary, but *completely* captivated, to say the least. Hermes scanned through the men as he wore his pleasant smile. Usually he garnered immense satisfaction from feeling like the most important being in the room.

"Can I offer you anything?" Odysseus stood next to him and opened his hands.

"No," Hermes replied with a laugh. Not much mortals could offer to — "*Oh!* Oh, may I sit in the chair! The throne in the rear, set above."

Odysseus blinked, and the crew's attention shifted to the commanding officer's seat. "Of course you may, Lord Hermes —" He needn't finish his sentence before Hermes glided down the length of the ship and sat upon the furs with a kick and a giggle. The king scurried after him, unintentionally rousing more of the crew to follow.

"I've seen all you Greeks sitting on these in the years past, shouting at your men to *row faster!* As if the beaches would run away. How fun. Very authoritative, very high up, I can see why you enjoy this spot," Hermes exclaimed.

"Dear Hermes!" one crew member shouted, prostrating himself in front of the crew. Hermes glanced from Odysseus to the little mortals and several others followed.

"Oh no," Odysseus quietly tsked.

"Will you send us home at last, kind god of travelers?"

"We are hell-bound with little chance to escape!"

"Please, mighty Hermes, bring our ship to safety — tell us we need not be cursed to journey to Hades!"

Hermes leaned on his arm and looked back to Odysseus. "Should I have come as a human? This cannot be the whole of our ride," he said. Wincing as an older warrior moved towards the sheep with a hand on his blade, Hermes removed his caduceus from his harness and raised it like a king. "Can't have that."

The serpents sprang to life, hissing their song, and forty-five men immediately collapsed in a deep slumber like a downpour of heavy rain.

Great Zeus, what a welcome. He blew a raspberry, patting the officer chair's arms as he looked over them all. *Whoopsie*, he clicked his tongue.

"King of Ithaca," he said, and Odysseus woke at once, leaping to his feet with his fists raised. "Your ship's going off course."

The helmsman's seat was a few feet in front of Hermes and a step or two down. Odysseus leapt into the divot, gently removed his sleeping comrade, and shifted the oar back into its position.

"What have you done?" he asked. "My friends! Are they...?"

"It'll be like a dream for them, a faint memory of finding just a poor young man abandoned at sea. So generous of my lord to save me right before a great gust knocked us about." He smirked. "For now, though, we may speak in private. I know you've been full of questions since I dug out the Moly for you," Hermes said.

With a careful eye, Odysseus glanced over the men on the deck, down into the hold, and to his own lap. "Do you know who of my crew took the bag given to us by the Wind lord of Aeolia?"

"That's your first question?"

"It's been weighing on my mind. Every man pleads innocence and I haven't the heart now to punish them all."

"I'm afraid I've no answer for that," Hermes said plainly. "But I have a related question for you."

He worked his jaw, then looked up. "Ask it, I am ready to reply."

The god pointed at Eurylochus who laid halfway down the ship. "Your second-in-command? You're a clever man, full of ideas and schemes. He is… what's a *kind* way to go about it — he's arrogant."

Odysseus nearly let go of the oar to hide his wistful laugh. "He is my brother-in-law from Same. Paid my parents an incredible bride-price for my younger sister, Ctimene. We were friends back then, with our islands within hopping distance, though years of war has strained our patience for each other." He rolled his palms over the wood. "She looks nearly identical to my mother, it was no wonder he fell for her so quickly."

"Would she mind if your anger got the best of you and you beheaded him the next time he starts babbling nonsense?"

"Would she mind!" Odysseus exclaimed. "We are both of us: stubborn. I wouldn't really wish him harm, as much as he deserves it at times."

"Pity."

"And you, Hermes, herald of Zeus, what brings you to me?" he asked, and *damn did he get straight to the point*. "I accepted your appearance outside of Circe's house as a gesture of mercy, but now this feels unusual, to be beckoned by a palm frond over all the busy work you must do. You're here for a reason — you've told me yourself that coincidences *seldom* happen."

Hermes puffed out his cheeks, curling his legs up under him in an attempt to lounge in a small chair. Stroking his chin like he kept a wise beard there, he replied, "us gods only offer to do things that bring us entertainment or intrigue. Immortality can be terribly *boring* at times. The trouble you humans get yourselves into is what keeps our days flowing smoothly. Consider me here because your quest interests me."

"You must've been lending me some of the luck I'd run out of these years," Odysseus said, looking to the mid-morning sun. "Of all the gods to be interested in a cause like mine, just to get home, it's good fortune the very one is a psychopomp as we trek towards the Realm of the Dead."

"Don't sound too excited. Very few heroes had successful journeys into Lord Hades' domain. But… Yes, I'll assist you. Having my entertainment end so early on in its performance is disappointing at best. We must at least get you to Act Two."

The man's grin returned youth before Hermes' very eyes, but it didn't last, and the melancholy grew back like mold.

"War was Pallas Athena's act," Odysseus said.

"Yes," Hermes replied.

Zeus would know what the man was thinking about down to the fleeting side-thoughts. But Hermes could infer; to be abandoned by your closest god was akin to snuffing the fire of a soul.

"Did she ever appear to you like I am?" Hermes asked, throwing his legs over one side of the chair. No other god was on Earth as often as he was. Arguably.

"Not so substantial."

"Mm, she always preferred to be mysterious; part of her tactic to scare everyone at Zeus' table. She's lovely, by the way, to look at in this form. Measurably twice my usual height, lithe but looming. With eyes that see the whole room all at once." Like Odysseus' in color, he noted — that misty grey. "Was her voice far from you?"

"No," Odysseus replied. He lowered his head and took a long breath. "She spoke over my shoulder, right in my ear. Always when I prayed to her. In battle, in game, but not now. Not since."

Hermes picked at his nails. The clouds above them settled in white mounds of fluff; the ship was shielded by the storms by his very presence — Poseidon would only sense him aboard this vessel; and Hermes told no one who he was helping.

There was a reason he never chose individual mortals to bestow his immense favor on. He was among the youngest of the Olympians, and despite a few hundred years in his position, he still hadn't found any particular reason to invest his time and energy on one human at a time. Giving gifts of talents in thievery and knowledge left his hands free of guilt.

But gods weren't supposed to feel guilt over the lives of humans — that was what Zeus told him. And what Zeus said was law.

"Hermes?"

"You don't have to really hold the oar," Hermes said, rolling his head along his shoulders. "The ship will stay straight as long as I'm guiding it. I've made this trip millions of times before and I'll do so millions of times after."

Odysseus peeled his palms from the main gear and tucked his hands into the folds of his sea-cloak. The ocean air had yet to be warmed by the sun and his nose was as pink as the skin around his eyes.

"If I ask another question, would you be truthful?"

Hermes' brows dipped with his smirk. "Son of Laertes, you should know that's a silly thing to ask me. What's your question?"

"Of your journeys, have you been on Ithaca's shores? Seen her abundance of woods and a great lone mountain, the lovely walls of my palace at its peak? I built it myself, right around some of those trees my father gave me. The windows could swirl the wind around and make the upper halls sing. I still hear them… and my wife, she sang with the tune — a melody for our son when he was first born. His smile lit up the whole room. His laughter could bring any Ithacan to their knees in supplication. Since Agamemnon's war… have you been? Have you seen my family?"

It would be so simple to lie and say no, he hadn't been, but Odysseus knew that. Over eleven years, whether or not Zeus wanted him to deliver messages to that island, mortals still died.

"Yes, of course I've been to Ithaca," Hermes replied. "A rugged thing, but very pretty among the speckled islands that surround it. I never have a problem finding it as it misses the clouds that cover much of its neighbors. And your land faces the rising sun — quite good luck to begin the days with dawn."

On the draping furs by the chair, Odysseus climbed and sat, his chin upon the arm with a sparkle in his eye. "And Penelope? Telemachus? Are they well? Has Penelope changed in these years? Does my loyal dog, Argos, still play and hunt? My son — he'll be reaching the end of his boyhood now. Running fast with slimmer legs, I imagine. They were quite fat when he was an infant. Maybe he's skilled at climbing or honing his archery skills."

Hermes listened to the father go off on theories about his son with more rapture than he intended to. His visit to Ithaca was not for any good reasons.

"I didn't stay very long on your shores. The passing was about three years ago," Hermes exclaimed, sitting straight. "But, *ah*, my eyes did cross over your family's faces. The queen was vigilant in her duties. Prince Telemachus was clinging to his tutor's side, I believe. Hair like yours. Tall boy for his age."

"Tall like his mother," Odysseus chuckled. He ran the side of his hand across his jaw, watching the horizon. There must've been pictures of them in the clouds that Hermes couldn't see. "Penelope used to be quite troubled that she sat higher than I in our chairs when we hosted."

"Did she, now?" Hermes mused. This conversation was going to last the whole trip.

"She kept her chin bowed through my speeches — and I can speak for lengthy periods at a time —"

"No."

"But I've reminded her time and time again that no man will think less of me for standing shorter than my wife. They shall be too engaged in envy for how lucky a husband I am to have won her hand."

Hera would love him, Hermes thought, pressing his fingers to his lips to restrain his tongue. Odysseus simply kept going, recounting every memory he had of their engagement and marriage; how her very visage made his knees weak, her skin was like honey, her touch cool and calming…

With his serpents still singing, the crew could continue to rest for the remainder of the day, but that would be a bit too harsh, and their bellies would be empty, *and* the sell for just being knocked out by a rogue wave would be difficult if dawn suddenly turned to dusk. While Odysseus monologued, Hermes swept away his helmet and wings and dampened his loose curls. He replaced his dazzling, embroidered exomis and golden pins with one that was soaked and torn, held together with a fraying knot. His cloak with its one little soul vanished from view — leaving behind a tiny bottle with a speck of sand at his neck, secured with a leather cord. Gone was his gold jewelry and hidden away went his talaria. Without considering the caduceus staff in his hand, Hermes was simply a battered youth sitting in the captain's chair.

Pulling one fur around his shoulders, Hermes tapped Odysseus with his bare foot. The man was becoming so fatigued from surprises, clutching his heart.

"Maybe we wake up your comrades and prepare something warm for a midday meal?" he suggested, waving his staff over the ship. And before any of them could stir, the caduceus shifted into a dark, wooden cane. "I am just a lame, drowned boy; so humbled and thankful for your rescue, mighty king of Ithaca!"

* * *

The crew, at the insistence of an eccentric leader and the mind fog of specifically placed dreams, did eventually *accept* the possibility of a survivor hanging onto floating debris of a ship wrecked by Poseidon's storms; and they were lenient in believing the ship rattled them all when Odysseus showed them the matching bruise he had when he, too, collapsed against the deck.

Hermes got away with remaining in the comfortable seat where much of the crew gathered at the call for warmed wine and bites of bread. They sat and gawked at him, still shivering with sea water dripping from his bronze locks.

Eurylochus handed him a small ration of their meal. "Tell us your story, stranger," he said. "You clearly aren't someone summoned by burning palm nor desperate prayers of ours."

Odysseus rolled his eyes to the heavens.

"*Anastasios,*" Hermes replied lightly. "I hail from Taphos, where the wise king Mentes often sends out his sailors to combat those ruffian pirates before they steal away with incoming treasures."

"We know of them well, guest Anastasios," Odysseus said. "King Mentes is a good friend of my family."

"How did you end up in the Tyrrhenian Sea, adrift without becoming food for the sharks?" Eurylochus continued. A few of the men nodded in curiosity.

"A stroke of bad luck, maybe — punishment, perhaps, for leaving port without our great king's permission," Hermes said. "Our oars took on a life of their own, some broken and snapped. We were at the mercy of the West wind when a terrible monsoon maimed the masts and shattered our hull. With great effort we tried to make it to a nearby island, but it was far too late and we saw no light, not even the stars above us. I thought myself dead, wrapped up in the cold depths. But Oceanus must've had pity on me, and sent up wood dry enough to float on the waves. Two days I have been waiting and praying for deliverance. I am in your debt, kind warriors of

Ithaca."

"How is it that you are so young a sailor if you have a lame leg?" Polites asked. Hermes was trying his hardest to maintain his composure as Odysseus gawked at the manners of his friends, hissing to Polites with an exacerbated scold. "Forgive me! You do not have to answer my rude and intrusive question."

"Very unusual though," Eurylochus said. "You are too young to have seen battle for it to be from a fighting injury."

"Eurylochus," Odysseus sighed.

Hermes tucked his chin into the pelt and slowly stretched out his *oh so terrible* leg that would be an envy to Hephaestus. "I am no sailor," he admitted. "Just a bard made cupbearer. And this old thing, *bah*, an injury when I was a child racing my elder brothers. Fourth of five, I am. With two elder sisters to add insult to injury, though they tended to me with all the love of a mother."

They continued to ask and he continued to weave his mortal self's story — of his parentage and their backgrounds, what news came from isles near Taphos, if he had heard of any other generals of Greece returning home with their kin. Most did, he confirmed, though others were still off the beaten path. Very quickly, little Anastasios of Taphos became a crew favorite as he occupied their time sailing with pleasant talk and song. He was gifted a warmer cloak to clasp over his shoulder, and sandals to replace the ones he lost to the ocean.

While the sun traveled over their heads and began its descent to their portside, the men gathered around the front of the ship, where the horizon wrinkled and buzzed.

A distant hole of a cave, an entrance where the Acheron River took precedence. The River of Woes split off into the Styx, connecting the beaches where the souls wandered.

From the sea, the black ship swung onto Oceanus' river. Just a few more hours before that little cave loomed high overhead with jagged crags on either side jutting out of green, frothing water.

The grain of sand resting in the vial at Hermes' neck slid forward like gravity was calling it. He gripped the glass in his palm. *Almost there, be at ease.*

Odysseus paced behind him, speaking over and over again the ritual Circe told. His hands folded in prayer, his chin resting atop them. No other man aboard this ship was bearing the same weight on his shoulders as Odysseus; several deep lines mapped his face. Hermes rose, limping himself with his cane — as slow as he could physically allow himself — over to the stern.

"What if this prophet reveals to me that I'll never get home?" Odysseus murmured. "That after all this time of fighting, I'm doomed never to see my family again? I've tried to maintain my calm, to be merciful in hopes that it would please the gods enough to forgive what I have done, but it's brought me nothing."

"My dear son of Laertes, there's no doubt that you'll hear of things that vex and frighten you. The gods made it so from the start of your arduous Nostos and the Fates themselves have likely laid your *strand* out to Zeus for how your life goes. If you're doomed then you're doomed. What a waste to worry about it." Hermes patted the fibula brooch at Odysseus' shoulder; the face of an owl etched in the iron. "But if the prophet tells you otherwise… If he gives you the tiniest thread of hope that you'll live long enough to make love to your wife again, then isn't it worth it to hear those words? Regardless of the dangers that will very likely come with it — you have *pissed off* gods, so dangers will be ravishing you at every corner — won't you fight through it all again to see Lady Penelope?"

"I would do *anything*," he growled with a tight fist.

"Then face the prophet with some courage. I know you have it. And lucky you, you've a soul guide as your assistant."

"There would be little reason for Anastasios to leave the ship if he's lame and recovering, you realize."

"Yes, but Hermes always has reason to be in the Underworld! I have a full-time job, a slave to service! And what a *coincidence* it is that we're to run into each other *again!*"

He smiled wide and smacked Odysseus' arm until the crotchety man came to his senses and smiled back.

"Anastasios ought to bed down for the evening, then. We have a sack of grain skinny enough in the hold."

Chapter 6

Hermes glided over the Acheron in silence. The dark ship had brought up their sails, skimming the green waters a few feet behind him with all its crew craning their necks at this cave to the Realm of the Dead. They lined the ship's railings like an audience in an arena.

Acheron was a curious river. Souls that fell into its deepest waters were overwhelmed with their deepest miseries, drowning within their woes. It was unassuming along its banks where the souls roamed, who tested the water with their feet to decide if they wished to bathe further out. Sometimes they went in with purpose — those who haunted the beaches for eternity were apt to crawl in of their own accord.

Most mortals weren't used to the concept of a timeless forever. Their feeble minds couldn't fathom it.

From his cloak went the soul who had waited very patiently to fly into the cave where Hermes' staff pointed, the poor lonesome fellow.

"Listen up, men," said Odysseus, skin aglow from torchlight. "The land of Hades will try to incite you with visions and pleas, but you *must* hold your ground. When we beach the ship, bring the sheep to the sand and follow me. Don't touch anything or wander out of sight. Once the sacrifice is complete and I speak with the prophet, we'll leave at once."

"But sir," Eurylochus replied, wringing his hands. "This is just a cave — where are the spectres? What if this is just another trap?"

Hermes felt the tickle of anxiety on his back. He glanced over his shoulder and gestured to the shores nearest the crag. Odysseus commanded the helmsman to adjust.

"It isn't, Brother. Trust me."

Putting out his hand, Hermes pushed through the barrier that separated the realms with ease, and his vision flashed white as he spoke the words of the chthonic gods.

The illusion of a quiet river cavern erupted with the wails and echoes of screams. Dim moonlight rippled away to the hazy, green glow of the Underworld. Cold air rushed in and diminished two of the four lit torches as the mortals fell to their knees. The Acheron's gentle splashing reflected agonized weeping as the ship drifted by.

Hermes spun his finger in circles across it, disturbingly warm compared to the Styx.

"Dearest Charon," he whispered, "for that inconvenience I've warned you of, I beg you to allow the souls you've ferried to be called by this man. In exchange, I offer you blood and ichor to do with as you please."

The river rippled back at him. It was honest work.

Climbing up aboard the black ship's ram, Hermes rose to the bow. "Well, what do my eyes see here? Heroes performing some rites to win glory?" he asked, cocking his head. The crew, in a daze, gaped at him once more.

"Hermes! Clever Psychopompos, please come to our aid," Odysseus called. "We look for the beach where the Rivers of Hades branch off. Will you lead us?"

"What a fortuitous chance meeting, Royal son of Laertes. I can lead your ship. Command your men to steady themselves, the rivers grow restless before the shore." He winked, flew around to the back of the ship, and gave it a little push before drifting in the tepid air beside them. "Playing with the dead, are we?"

"We seek wisdom to go home," Odysseus replied. "Almost twelve years have gone by and our hearts ache for our island. We were told of a great prophet that Queen Persephone favors, and so allowed him to keep his mind's vision."

"I'm familiar with the one you speak of. If you're to summon him, be patient, for he has long ways to travel down here."

Down the river they flowed, around short rapids and the shouts of abandoned souls from either side. Some sailors held their hands over their ears, staring at the wood of the deck to not be tormented with the pain of the world around them. Odysseus stood firm at the bow, his fingers looped through the ropes of the ringing until the overhangs of the endless cave grew dark and misty. There they beached the ship and Odysseus ordered Eurylochus and his man, Perimedes, to bring the sheep down with them.

He dug a trench with his sword while the rest of the men relit their snuffed torches and set a cautious perimeter on the sand. Polites brought contributions for Odysseus' libations to be poured around the trench that was made like a sty for souls. He spoke aloud the offerings he would give to all the spirits, at rest and roaming, and to the prophet Tiresias alone once he made it to his home in Ithaca. At last he took the ewe and ram and, over the trench, cut their throats, filling the pit with dark blood.

Hermes stood above them all, watching and waiting.

When the blood pooled the foot's depth, the wretched ghosts of the dead clambered and clawed their way out of the river beneath his feet, tumbling over themselves like the bubbles of boiling water at the smell of fresh blood. Heavy shrieks and desperate cries lunged towards the shoreline in front of Odysseus. Faces of those who haunted his very dreams — the lost, unburied crew, half-dissolved in their corporeal forms, reached out to their captain. The men on the beach grasped each other, nails digging into their neighbors' arms, but poor Odysseus remained to guard the blood for Tiresias to drink first.

"Forgive me, brothers, please forgive me…" he whispered to their cries.

There was one soul, the fresh, little one, newly arrived, who approached the beach hesitantly, drawn to the blood, but intent on using the last of his energy to make a plea.

"Captain!" it called out.

Odysseus sank at the sight of him. "Elpenor…? How is it you traveled here faster on foot than I did on my ship?"

"By an angry god, perhaps, and Dionysus knows how much wine," Elpenor's spirit groaned. "I fell asleep atop the roof of Circe's palace and awoke with the hurry of our comrades, but I never thought to climb back down the very ladder I took to get up there. Right over the edge and headfirst I plunged."

Odysseus' shoulders fell with another tear.

"I beg you, Captain, for those you left behind so far away from here, your wife, your noble father, your son… I know when you leave this realm of death that you and our friends will put ashore on Circe's island. All I ask is you remember me! Do not sail off and desert me! Burn me in my armor, perform my rites, and leave the oar I swung with my brothers while I served you at my tomb so I may be at peace."

"I'll do all of it for you, my dear, unlucky friend," Odysseus replied with a gentle nod, his sword still by the trench of blood. "I won't forget a thing."

Hermes watched another phantom approach and his heart grew heavy. Veiled and slow, the spirit wandered close to the shore, its bony hand reaching not for the blood alone, but the man who guarded it.

Odysseus was abiding by his promise to Circe, waiting for that prophet, but the new sight brought any resolve to his knees with a fresh flow of tears.

"Mother?" he murmured towards the veiled ghost. His face had grown red, his nostrils flared, but his sword remained high up in defense. Dear Anticlea was forced to wait. "Oh Hermes, why did you not say — why did you not tell me?"

The god remained silent. He grasped his own wrist to squeeze. The funeral held for the old queen of Ithaca was reverent and in line with tradition, but grief kept her from Charon's boat, refusing to stand in the line without seeing her son. The coins remained in her closed fist. But now she couldn't look her son in the eye.

Hermes allowed himself a breath when the blind prophet's scepter pierced the veil of the living as he climbed to the surface. Tiresias addressed Odysseus directly, asking him to remove his sword so that he may drink the sheep's blood and tell the king all he knew. Odysseus sheathed his sword and stepped back, and Tiresias consumed a tithe of the sacrifice.

It was none of Hermes' business, but everything of his interest, to hear what the favored prophet of the lord and lady of the Underworld had to reveal. The words were like a whisper, unknown to the soldiers who remained pressed to each other several feet behind their leader.

"… A god will make your return formidable — I know — you will never escape the one who shakes the earth, quaking with unbridled rage for you still, a fury for blinding his son," Tiresias said. "But you and your crew still may reach your home, with suffering to endure, if you only have the power to restrain *their* desires and your own."

An island, he mentioned, one very known to Hermes, grazing with cattle. The crew was to leave them unharmed; if they did that, they may *all* reach Ithaca. Hermes narrowed his eyes toward the prophet as he presented the consequences of touching the beasts, the destruction and death, of Odysseus growing to be a broken man only to find pain wherever he went.

A ringing echoed through the cave, the call of the ferryman. They still had time, and the son of Anticlea still had blood left to let his dear mother speak after Tiresias departed.

"Tiresias," Odysseus was saying, "the gods have spun this fate out for me, I'm certain…"

Hermes walked along the water to the ghost of the aged woman and pressed his staff to the small of her back, presenting to her the blood at Odysseus' side. "Drink and speak, daughter of Autolycus, to your eldest son," he commanded when the blind prophet withdrew from the beach. She drank and saw her boy, alive among the dead, and pleaded to him. Hermes continued to patrol around the sand, intent on having no mortal lose themselves under his watch.

"Lord Hermes," Eurylochus said. "Do we not get to speak to our lost brothers too? Must this communication be had only by our captain?"

"Ignorant thought, to wish to be burdened with the sorrows of *dead* men," Hermes replied. "They'll not give you the closure you long for. These souls speak only truths when asked, nothing more. If it's their character you miss, then weep. That charm is left in the bodies meant to return to Gaia. The great campaigner, Odysseus, speaks with his dead mother to learn the politics of your land. Pray you'll return to it while he remains its king. No other man is worthy of that right."

Eurylochus shrunk into himself, examining the ground. "Forgive me, Psychopompos, you are right. I meant no insult by it, please do not curse me."

Hermes snapped, "I'm not offended by you. You are just a human."

Humans were handing over their own anxieties, siphoning into him like a lightning rod. He needed ambrosia, and lots of it.

"Mother — why won't you wait for me?" Odysseus cried, louder than he must've intended, as he waded knee deep into the Acheron. "How I long to hold you, take some joy in the tears that numb aching hearts." He tried to embrace Anticlea another time, her form wisping right through his fingers as he wept again.

"Captain!" Polites shouted. Eurylochus and the rest of the crew neared the shore, arms open wide for their king.

"Don't step into the river!" Hermes ordered, flying over to Odysseus as Anticlea hovered her hand over his cheek.

"My son, you are the unluckiest man alive! Your body must long for the daylight. Go quick and remember all I've told you, that one day you may speak of them to your wife," she exclaimed. The chime of the ferry grew louder, but Odysseus' grief rivaled it.

"Son of Laertes," Hermes said, putting his hand on his shoulder. "You are treading too deep into the River of Woes. Turn back to your brothers-in-arms and dry yourself. *Please.*"

Odysseus' somber eyes flitted across the ghost of his mother's face. "Hermes, why didn't you tell me," he whispered. "Filled me with hope just to trick me?"

What a mad accusation — you senseless man.

"Look back at our exchange and see that I didn't lie to you," Hermes replied, squeezing Odysseus' arm. "Remember what I am. What you are. My presence is not always welcomed; very rarely do I have the honor to be a bringer of joy. But you must get out of Acheron before you remain stuck here. *Your* presence will bring your mourning family joy. Turn back and dry your legs now. Let your mother be at peace."

Odysseus' left leg wobbled back, then his right. The ghosts moved through him in his retreat to where his comrades protected the trench of blood with their blades and number. Friends dried his face and wiped his shins free of the green residue that clung to the skin. They all spoke in tired, sighing words — hearing of their lost Elpenor's requests and the chance that they would complete the journey home together if they listened to Odysseus' commands.

Hermes flexed his fingers, sighing when Charon approached in his boat. The spirits of the dead lined up around the mortals, drinking and speaking their truths. It wasn't healthy for the living to remain in Hades for long — the air breathed their strength away from them.

"*Hermes,*" Charon grumbled across the placid water.

"Charon," Hermes replied. "Allow them more time."

"Your payment?"

"Mn. Yes, of course." Reaching into his bags, he pulled out a simple cup. Three strides to land, where a young woman spoke to the weary king, Hermes took Odysseus' arm and held it up. "With this, you have a few waking hours. Do *not* waste them."

He plunged his nail into a protruding vein like a serpent would its victim, and the warm blood of Odysseus streamed quickly into the cup. The son of Laertes gasped but didn't argue, holding his hand over the wound when Hermes released it. From his own side, he removed a dagger forged by the god of fire and held it to his vein.

He'd never done this before: offer such a commodity. He'd never asked if it was against his father's rules, but gods have fought and drawn ichor in war and games; a small, holy libation to another immortal couldn't be so bad.

The mortals watched in wonder as Hermes' ichor poured out into the cup, sizzling and hissing upon contact with human blood. Charon's boat hit the beach with a sturdy thump, and his hand lay open, waiting.

"Hermes?" Odysseus turned his head to follow.

Blood and ichor traded to the carrier of time. They're the warmest things Charon will have in eons.

The ferryman rolled the cup between his long fingers and brought the rim of it to his nose, as if he were a lord contemplating the essence of wine. To his lips, the cup tilted, and the concoction slipped into the haggard mouth.

Hermes discreetly pressed his own hand to the cut over his skin, which worked to mend itself together. Some salve from Apollo's conservatory would restore the arm to its pristine glory; Hermes didn't dwell on it.

"Dear Charon, my friend," he said, taking back the empty cup. "I pray this inconvenience isn't too burdensome for you. These mortals will be on their way once they're satisfied with the knowledge of their community; I'll see to it myself."

The ferryman pushed from Acheron's shores. *"Discretion,* Hermes," he grumbled. "The sky king is omnipotent."

Odysseus spoke with murdered kings, of warriors lost, and immortalized heroes in lamenting Achilles and Heracles.

The ghosts only continued to swamp the beach, desperate for the little blood that remained. Upon the final hour, the noise bordered on petrifying as spectres lunged for the flesh of the crew themselves. Falling backwards, Odysseus kicked sand into the trench as Polites raised him up and scrambled to his ship with Eurylochus leading the way.

Hermes pressed his shoulder to the ram and flew against it until the river hoisted its weight. They were to fight back upstream, but with a god's help in propelling the breeze, and the desperate strokes of the oarsmen, the venture wasn't nearly as futile as it could've been.

The blackness of the realm released in a *clap* to the stars and heavens above, with the nose-stinging smell of sea salt wafting right over the deck and the wind awaiting the sails to face their way.

A quarter hour of silence befell the ship.

"What a rest I've had!" Hermes, or rather, Anastasios, exclaimed. He rose, stretching from the pile of pelts at the rear of the ship. He scratched his nose while the crew dug themselves into their thwarts, and said, "Did something paramount happen that I've missed, my dear hosts? You look like you've seen a ghost!"

Odysseus, slumped in his chair, glanced back at him. In his hand he held a scrap piece of bandage, wrapping his forearm with care. It still bled, the blasted thing. Hermes scar in his mortal form looked like it was already healing for a few days' time.

Taking another pause, the captain turned back to address his crew. "We sail back to Aeaea, a straight path. Our friend deserves his proper burial. The wind remains kind, take whatever rest you need."

Begrudgingly, his cheek came down upon his hand, a weary man within a noble chair. Odysseus stared blankly ahead until Hermes rose to his feet.

"Your men will sleep and your ship will make it safely to Circe once more. If you have no fears for this next day's journey, I'll take my leave and return to Olympus," Hermes said.

"Has Anastasios grown tired of this realm, or just of me?"

"Neither," Hermes replied. A small smile tugged his lips. "But while I remain among you, there are risks to my giving future aid. And I need proper food and drink. Unfortunately wines and waters don't sustain me."

"What was that — on the beach? With the cup and our blood. You kept the ferryman from collecting me? Collecting all of us?"

Don't ask stupid questions, Odysseus.

"I'll return," Hermes said, taking up his wooden cane, "for your Act Two. Don't go ruining my fun while I'm away. I'd be terribly disappointed to come back and find you'd opted to stay another year with that witch, or crashed your ship into the crags."

He didn't wait to see if Odysseus thought of a reply or if he found the evasion of his question somewhat amusing. Hermes climbed up on the stern of the ship and disappeared from the realm.

* * *

Two hands smacked to the courtyard of Mount Olympus — a pretty pathetic climb on the last leg of the journey to the heavens. Hermes swung his foot up and over, thankful that night at home was apt to distract everyone in their parties. Dragging his hand up the back of his neck, he tore the helm from his head and shook out his hair and wings where the moisture of the

Underworld still clung.

Chattering echoes rolled through the roads. A few lesser gods and goddesses strode arm in arm together from one park of waterfalls to another park of roses. They spared him little glances, stepping in tandem like clockwork.

Sitting on the overhang of Olympus a few feet from Hermes, an eagle picked up its head. Its eyes shimmered gold and its scream rumbled the young god right back onto his ass as the bird shifted to none other than the Thunderer himself, clad in very scant garb for this time of night.

Hermes' wings whipped up to shield his face — not for any shame for seeing his father half-naked, he couldn't care less of that — but of the unlucky timing he subscribed himself too.

That son of Laertes was rubbing off on him.

"Hermes, my boy, there you are," Zeus said, his bare arms stretched out. He flicked a spare feather from his elbow. "Your absence at the games was noticed by many. You missed the dances, the wrestling — Poseidon took his fury out on several gods, it was quite the spectacle."

"You appear as if you were wrestling as well, Father," Hermes replied, and damn him for his smart mouth for Zeus' smile grew a little too broad. "Forgive my leave, I had business to handle under your Lord Brother Hades' domain. But I longed for our warm home and everflowing drink, so I cut my pursuit short. Shall I meet you in the hall, Father? I simply need to change —"

"Walk with me," Zeus said. He placed his large hand atop of Hermes' head and twisted him in the direction of a quieter path.

"Okay."

While in Olympus, Zeus could've taken any form of his choosing. Typically the older the immortal, the more forms they've constructed, but Zeus maintained a modest size: a few heads taller than Hermes, where his fatherly tugs crushed Hermes' cheek to his ribcage.

"You enjoy your conversations with that old ferryman, Charon, yes?" Zeus asked. His vision didn't venture into the realm of his elder brother, but he *was* still all-knowing.

"What he lacks in grandiose lexicon, he makes up for in his funny frivolities."

"Do you see Hades much as of late? I should send you with a personal message for him; get him to show his face up here for a few hours."

"I'm afraid he's almost as busy as I," he laughed. "I hardly even get to see Thanatos or his brother when they're at work."

"And who else accompanied you to the Underworld today?"

Hermes' mouth immediately grew dry. If there were sounds of water or laughter or distant clinking of glasses, he heard none of it now as he nearly stumbled in his walk — having kicked himself up into the air. Zeus gripped his shoulder firmly, not tight, but Hermes wasn't going anywhere; and his smile never waned.

"Nobody," Hermes answered just as quickly as the query was asked. "I was with nobody, Father. An immeasurable amount of dead mortals crawling about my feet, and the rancid smell of the rivers too, if we may count those. Do you smell it on me?"

The god king chuckled, deep and relaxed, and maybe Hermes wasn't going to simply be smote on the spot. "That's the smell of my brother you're talking about."

"Your lord brother keeps his halls perfumed with spring's lavender. You'd never know just outside of his walls are where the dead wander. He prepares diligently for the arrival of his queen."

Zeus hummed. "It's a struggle every year to quell the rage of Demeter to appease the loneliness of Hades. There is nothing I loathe more than when we fight amongst ourselves. And Poseidon thinks I allow things to happen for my own amusement, but *ah*, I merely abide by what the Fates have revealed to me. Dear Hermes," he said and the squeeze on Hermes' shoulder tightened. "We mustn't let mortal squabbles hinder the relationships between us gods, even for those humans we find favor in. It simply isn't worth it. Think of how Troy caused a divide between us! But your decision to sit among your brothers and sisters at my table, I saw, was a valiant move to begin healing our anger with one another. That was a good quality of leadership."

"I," Hermes replied, seeking some sort of response among the bushes they walked by on the stonework, "simply *try* to emulate your sense of Justice, Father. Though it's in my nature to try to make some fun out of it. Take Apollo — he's too easy to tease."

"I admired your relationship with your fair brother the moment he brought you to this realm. And your fun brings me great amusement. How four-hundred years flies. Your resourcefulness has made not only *our* lives brighter, but the gifts you bestowed to the humans before they even knew your name…"

"Father?"

"I'm sentimental tonight, forgive me," Zeus said.

"Nothing to forgive when you shower me with compliments." Teaching mankind how to write a more constructed language made it easier for everyone to communicate and organize proper worshiping rituals. It was a massive benefit to the gods as well and Hermes knew it too. But this promenade conversation had continued on a precariously odd path, and he was feeling the buzz under his skin. "I think I'm tired of standing upright, sir. With your permission, I'll retire to my halls."

"Yes, of course," Zeus said, removing his heavy hand. He studied Hermes' face — who had inherited most of his looks from his mother, Maia, with her rusty hair and appled cheeks — and tapped the lightning bolt pin on his son's tunic that coiled with snakes. "Rest, and remember that although you've the luxury to freely roam all three realms, you are always first at my beck and call."

Terribly hard to forget that.

"Thank you, Father. Have a —"

"Father." The voice was resolute, none other than Athena's. She stepped down the path's stone stairs in her long gown, looking more like a prophetess at this hour despite coming from the arena where many of the warrior gods were finishing up their late antics and sparring matches.

"My lovely daughter," Zeus replied. He took her hands and kissed them. "Your display of sagaciousness against Apate was astonishing! I haven't applauded so loudly in decades."

Athena inclined her head in thanks. "I am afraid I come with news overheard from your palace. Her Majesty has been shouting for you since she noticed your absence over the evening toast. I suggest, my king, that you have yourself bathed before presenting to your chambers. While it is lovely that the flower nymphs maintain a lustrous garden, their scent is like perfume that hugs the body."

What a kind, discreet way to tell their father he smells like sex. She was indeed the goddess of wisdom.

Zeus pushed his hair back over his shoulder and behind his crown. "So that was the shrieking I heard. Thought it was a crone, but alas, my wife. Blessed Athena, saving me from a worse scolding."

She inclined her head again, stepping aside to allow him the room to escape up the stairs where his palace glittered above. The eerie silence dissipated when the god king left them, and the sounds of the heavens flew about in faraway laughter and music. Athena weaved her fingers together at her waist and walked to the level where Hermes remained idle. She was far taller than him and very often grew in height in her most violent states — Hermes had to fly up to reach her face.

"Hermes," she greeted.

"Lady Athena," Hermes replied.

He was supposed to feel at least a sense of neutrality towards his sister. Most times he liked her company, sharing witty banter and clever schemes, but when she nary glanced at him, his feathers flared and his tongue grew sharp.

"Best to treat that cut before its scar remains," Athena said before he opened his mouth. "You are too young to be marked by blessed blades. Battleworn is not the image belonging to a messenger."

Hermes clapped his palm over the mark on his arm. "Messengers are the first and last on the fields of peace and war," he replied. "And through to the homes of those lost... or *missing*. But yes, I've every intention to visit Apollo before I rest. What of you, Athena? Finally broke free of the arena — unless we've only run out of spears to throw?"

Her footsteps were nearly as light as his. Her palace was closest to their father's. *She was taking the long way around.*

"Can you not sleep?" Hermes asked. Maybe she did feel something.

"Why would I not find sleep?" she quickly responded.

Right, of course she didn't listen to any of the pleading prayers sent up her way.

Hermes turned to the bushes. Going through them was a faster way to his palace. "I couldn't say," he eventually said. "But I didn't sleep much either these years. Thankfully, I worked to rectify that situation." He smiled. "Sound as a babe, now. I hope your night is as satisfactory as you *rightly* deserve it, dear Sister."

With a quick leap, he flew under the low-hanging trees, cutting through bush and hedge, holding fast to his cloak that he covered his big mouth with.

To Apollo's, a secret haven, but the god didn't need to know that; it would only fuel his brotherly hubris.

Apollo took one look at the golden line adorning Hermes' arm and told the universe he wouldn't ask, then immediately pressed his brother for answers. *It must have been during the games,* Hermes had said. So caught up and distracted by the day, maybe he was pricked by the arrow that Apollo was so keen on slugging around. The lord of medicine didn't like this lie — his face crestfallen as if he were truly the first one to leave a mark on an otherwise perfectly put together little brother.

Hermes didn't want to feel judged for helping the mortals more than he intended. He didn't have an answer that didn't stir up a lie to himself...

And he didn't have the reasoning for *why* he needed to lie to himself.

Chapter 7

A rhythmic buzz in his ear, the constant steady push and pull from side to side, it was reminiscent of the short time he spent in the cradle at his mother's home deep within the caves of Cyllene, where no god would dare bother them but Zeus. He was warm under his blankets, curled up under loose layers with his hair dancing above them. It felt like a day he could spend all the hours of from within his bed, ignoring the worlds, sipping nectar and listening to lyres and flutes play a new melody. If anyone needed him, they could come and supplicate, else deal with their problems themselves.

But these blankets covering his cheek were a little rougher than his silks. His bedding lacked the plethora of feathers it was stuffed with… and the buzz? The whooshing was no mountainous breeze, but the call of the ocean.

Hermes opened his eyes.

His body was heavy like stone, laying on the pelt of the ram that was once sacrificed to his father. Pulling some strands of wool from his mouth, a deep line formed between his brow.

Surely he went to sleep in his own palace, naked within his own sheets?

He sat up with a grunt. The salted wind caressed his curls while the sails of the black ship snapped taut and bellowed high above. It was late morning and the men were heaving back on their oars. Eurylochus paced from the bow to the middeck, speaking soundless orders. Above Hermes sat Odysseus, contemplating the mazes of his mind while twisting the skin of his lip.

Hermes spun his head to see where on Gaia they were headed. Too fast, somehow — his neck cracked painfully and he held it with a soft groan.

Odysseus broke from his thoughts, turning in his seat. "Hermes?" he said. "I thought you abandoned me when you didn't return at first light. I've had poor Anastasios ill with some ailment I've concocted for the reason why you slept so deathly still… Hermes?"

How was he here? Did someone cast a spell? Circe didn't have that sort of power to render his memory so muddled. And for him to be in his mortal form, *exactly* as he was before their journey into the Underworld, it —

"Hermes? Are you well?"

Quiet panic was socially acceptable.

Odysseus waved over Eurylochus and spoke to him while Hermes remained uncharacteristically stoic. The man scurried to the hold and returned with a small pot that he handed to the captain, and in a whisper, Odysseus said, "Circe mentioned you have an affinity to the trees that grow strawberries? She had them preserved and made into a jam for you to consume, perhaps. If you can?"

Eurylochus' brow was raised, maybe stuck that way, but he poured him a small cup of water. "At least he's awakened, Ody. None of us need *another* funeral pyre."

Hermes blinked and shook his head. His little, human hands took both the cup and jar. "No pyre," he replied. "Not anytime soon, I pray. And, *ah*, I do enjoy the taste. Thank you, my lord."

"Yes, you're… very welcome." Odysseus gave Eurylochus a nod and dismissed him back to his duties. His lips pursed. "But are you alright?"

He *was* all in one piece. Somehow. He feared that the leg he pretended to limp on would truly be that way, as he couldn't feel the hidden wings on his sandals, or the helm that often laid behind his head. The cane? He rested it in the crook of his elbow and, deep within, heard the quiet hiss of the serpents.

Thank heavens, he breathed, kissing the wood.

"Never better, my dear king," Hermes replied. Opening the jar, he stuck his nose inside to smell the sweet fruit. Eating for no nutritional benefit was still pleasurable at least; distracting. With a sudden urge to take the cup, he chugged its water down. It tasted like nothing. Curious how humans needed a liquid of nothing to survive. "What awaits you and your crew on these waters now? You're nearing some precarious islands of Italia."

"Circe warned us of the Sirens that rule over the archipelago."

"The *Sirens*." Hermes pressed his lips together and nodded. "Ugly creatures."

"Winged as they are?" Odysseus said. "One could believe you're related."

"Me? Related to *those* rancid daughters of Melpomene? You jest, son of Laertes."

"No, truly, with their affinity to song and guiding man — albeit to their doom — it's a fair comparison. You must see it."

He wrinkled his nose up at the man. Odysseus' eyes crinkled back.

"Teasing a god," Hermes said, eating more of the jam. "Very bold of you."

Odysseus worked his hands until his knuckles cracked dully. "I'm nothing if not bold. Bold as I am, I must ask about your arm again. In the past, I've witnessed Diomedes of Argos bring the blood of the gods to the surface of raging Ares' gut with a weapon crafted by the divine forge. Ares then pulled back from the Trojans, which immensely aided our cause. Gods cannot die from those injuries, can they? Your arm healed so quickly, I can't fathom a god or goddess ever falling to the hands of Man."

"To Man? Hades be, *no*," Hermes replied. "No, I've never heard of such a thing. We're gods for a reason. Age doesn't matter, and we're always regenerating. On Olympus we fight to hide our boredom — though in the most intense sparring, by some blades crafted by Hephaestus, or with the scepters of the three kings, ichor does spill. I visited my brother to remove what little scar remained." He held out his arm, to the smooth skin that freckled in the sun. "It's also important to me to inform you that it wasn't Ares' *gut* that was pierced through, but his cock. If you begin a curse by proclaiming: *Ares' cock!* whenever something goes awry, I promise you good favor from at least half of my family."

"'Ares' cock,'" Odysseus mouthed with a slight smirk. He pulled his fingers through his short beard. Likely not to be in his best interest to aggravate more than Poseidon.

And the jam was gone — damn.

He spun the empty jar like a top, feeling the ship's rocking more intensely than he ever did before. "Are you nervous to approach the Sirens? They're known to be callers of Death for a reason."

"No," Odysseus said. "As I said, I'm prepared to risk *anything* to get back home. Circe informed us about their song — the true secrets mixed with their lies that they lure sailors in with. She's gifted us beeswax to place in our ears. I only intend to give it to the crew."

"Ah, so you're just going to leap out and grab a siren as she flies by to chew your face off? Naturally resistant to her song: son of Laertes, mighty king above men, the *one* sailor to ignore their calls." Hermes patted his chest. "Even I knew I had to sing giant Argus to sleep before I carved his head from his body. Strength is not my forte. You and I — we're crafty men."

"I have no intention to fight them."

"Your perishing in such a manner would make me *very* upset, Odysseus."

"That's also not intended. Allow me to swear an oath to you." He leaned over the arm of his chair. "What time would be pleasing for me to die in your quest for entertainment? I'll swear to hold out through then, if not longer."

"You great fool," Hermes replied. His chin raised. "When you're in your tree-bound bed with your wife, having properly basked in her fruits, yielded her harvest, and swam in her sea — maybe then, I'll be ready to collect your soul. Until that hour, son of Laertes, you're stuck to suffer in this mortal plane."

"With you by my side?"

"With me by your — objectively *everybody* on this ship's — side. How selfish you are, trying to hog me all to yourself. No wonder your crew suspected that you hid treasures from them in that bag."

"Anastasios by my side, then, if Hermes isn't here for all the men to harangue," Odysseus exclaimed with a flick of his fingers.

"What *is* your intention for the Sirens?"

Odysseus coyly smiled and exclaimed, "I'm to be tied to the mast," as he turned to face the deck where Polites climbed the few steps to the stern with a fine, little syrinx in hand.

Hermes clicked his teeth together, mutely pulling the fabric he slept under over his chilled shoulders.

"We saw that Anastasios was feeling better," Polites said to Odysseus, his eyes so kind, and he turned to Hermes with an even softer expression that made the young god's chest tighten. "It made our friends worried that we may have lost you when you were unable to join us up in Lady Circe's palace. Though the captain readily prepared a warm bed and said you were content for the night, a few of us came down to the beach just to check on you. We, *ah*, also remembered your song from two days past and how much we enjoyed some sense of normalcy on the ocean. Circe allowed us to take a flute for you to play if you are willing — something better than those Sirens we cross shall sing."

He presented the syrinx to Hermes with a little bow, as if giving a gift to a foreign prince who sat beside his king. It was a modest flute for Circe's standards, wrapped by a careful hand with dark cording; the wood pipes, seven in total, were finely carved and covered with a beaded belt. Hardly unique enough to grace Apollo's collection, but Hermes was enchanted by the offering. He placed his lips to one pipe and whistled a quick tune. It trilled like an excitable bird.

These men only knew *Anastasios* for less than a week.

"Thank you," Hermes said, twisting in his seated position to lean comfortably against the commanding officer's chair. "I'll play as long as these lungs bear enough breath."

Zeus knows how much that would be.

His father seemed like the likely reason for why Hermes woke up on the ship like this in the first place. More reasonable than sleep-flying, though not impossible a scenario. The suspicion of casual, fatherly strolls from Zeus? Hermes was young, but not *that* naive.

"And sir," Polites said, wringing his hands. "Eurylochus was, *um*, expressing his disapproval for this plan against the Sirens. Wouldn't it be safer for you to also plug your ears? The Fates are taking unprecedented moves to end the lives of great Achaean kings. To lose *you* would make all our past victories worthless."

Hermes pointed at Polites and looked up at Odysseus. "I cannot believe I can say that your second's opinion has strong points. Cowardliness does breed survival."

"We're on our guard, and know they'll soon be drawing near. I may be able to learn something from their song; Circe told me, should I be determined to hear what those creatures have to say, Eurylochus and Perimedes must lash me to the mast," Odysseus said in earshot of the crew, standing from his chair. "Go fetch a rope, one tightly wrung, and leave it by the mast. When it's time, bind me as tight as you can until I can't move. Even if I plead to you all to set me free, lash me faster. Only when we leave that island far in our wake, you must free me *immediately*." He moved about the deck to procure the gifted wheel of beeswax that he began to warm in his hands. "Understand, Polites?"

"Yes, my king, I trust you."

Hermes wobbled to his feet. All the men at work had powdered sand by their seats to keep their palms dry and gripped firmly on their oar. They rowed with a steady pace since the breeze was kind, but none appeared too scared of the other struggles that lay ahead.

"Royal son of Laertes," Hermes said, limping over to where he worked the wax. "The crags that follow after these Sirens, that guard the Strait of Messina…"

"I didn't tell them," Odysseus muttered. "And neither will you."

He spared him a short glance before stepping down to the deck and walked to each and every man in his seat. A handful of wax was pressed deep into his comrades' ears with the last order to continue on their path. Around the ship he went, and to the center Hermes followed.

There was something incredibly stupid about Odysseus that made Hermes gravitate towards him, wondering what schemes the little human could concoct. *Reckless* was one epithet for him, but here he was: ensuring his comrades were as safe as he could get them despite his pride. Strange for Hermes to think about — this man had lost eleven ships' worth of men in a single day, and that swarm had tugged against Hermes' cloak like they were the wind and he was the bag.

How much did souls weigh on human shoulders?

Odysseus stood against the great pole. He leaned on it and flattened his hands against the wood, getting a feel for how he'd be bound.

Alright Odysseus, should you choose to be tied like an animal on an upright spit, so be it. Add to the epic tale you'll tell one day.

"This'll get in the way," Hermes said to himself. He pulled the sword at Odysseus' side out and stepped back from the captain to examine the blade. The bronzework of the grip was admirable, with braided detail welded around the sturdy metal guard. The bronze cast of the blade was immaculate, like it was hardly used. Odysseus had to have been primarily an archer, his whole physique was made for drawing a bow over a sword, throwing a spear over sparring with it.

The island of the Sirens appeared on the port side, shifting between misty clouds that settled above the waves. Eurylochus and Perimedes pulled the rope up, ignorant of their captain's uncomfortable grunting.

"Wait, Herm–Anastasios," Odysseus nudged his nose over to the wax, "do you need —?"

"Don't you worry about me, old man," Hermes replied over his shoulder, spinning the blade in swishing circles. It was a similar balance to his own on Olympus.

* * *

Sirens weren't beasts the gods thought about more than for a passing joke, or a titting sigh at the amount of humans consumed on their shores. There were no messages to pass along to that meadowing island whose grasses were fed blood, and the rocky coast grew larger with broken ships and algae-covered sails. Perhaps the only frequent visitors were an abundance of fish who enjoyed exploring new sunken victims, and the sharks who sought out fallen pieces of flesh when the Sirens swiped their quarry.

The men rowed and Hermes was plopped at the bow of the ship next to Eurylochus — who was entrusted to keep an eye out for bizarre lady-creatures, or at least any signs of them. Hermes sat with his face towards the center mast and the silly man whose hair was blowing to and fro into his mouth and around his eyes. No wonder he usually wore that stupid cap.

No, no, it wasn't a stupid *cap. It was a wonderfully stupid cap,* Hermes mused. Very practical for traveling and keeping warm.

"Are you comfortable, my lord?" he shouted over the wind, pulling his borrowed cloak up over his head. Eurylochus glanced down at him from his station, then looked back in silence to Odysseus, but Hermes kept his moving lips concealed.

"The ropes are quite warm, my friend," Odysseus replied, his nose red from whipping sea mist.

The ship mowed down a fleeting wave, then another, as the island drifted by within swimming distance, mile by mile when the hazy sun blurred in the clouds and the air grew balmy, a pain to breathe. What wind backed their sails ceased, the oars groaned with the extra weight, and the men hauled themselves forward and back to row the ship to safety.

Odysseus kept his eyes on the island, scanning skies for the beating of wings that accompanied the Sirens.

Like a roar filling a stadium, a high, rousing call floated over the mast, and the captain's determined search ceased. He remained still, staring frozen towards the shore.

"Come closer, famous king Odysseus — Achaea's pride and glory — and moor your ship on our coast so you can relax and hear our song!"

Hermes tapped Eurylochus' shins. Polites peered up from his central oar.

"Not in all our lives has any sailor in his black ship passed our shores until he has listened to the verse flowing from our lips."

"Oh, Odysseus —"

"Once you listen to your heart's content, you will sail on a wiser man!"

They sang in a voice descended from their mother, oh muse. Odysseus was straining his neck to continue to find where the voices echoed from, soft pleads from his lips.

What Hermes heard didn't sound like it was coming from the air.

He pulled himself up by Eurylochus' belt.

"We know all of the pains that your Achaeans and the Trojans endured on the wide plains before Troy's gates, the pains you've suffered when the gods willed it so — all that comes to pass on this fertile earth, we know all. Come listen and share our wisdom with your friends —"

"Your family!"

"Your wife!"

"Penelope," Odysseus whispered. His arms tensed against the rope and the island continued to run by. "Comrades, please, unbind me!"

Hermes hit the second-in-command again, and Eurylochus and Perimedes rushed down to tighten the ropes. Odysseus strained and cursed against his bindings. Hermes grimaced while the enchantment twisted into the psyche like fingers probing into the strings of a harp, pulling and strumming whatever note they pleased.

"I must know!" Odysseus cried out to the deafened ears of his crew. He wailed to the sky where the rising and falling notes stirred and spun. "Tell me more, I beg you. What wisdom hides within your song? Do not go from me — what of my wife? Tell me of my wife, my kingdom! What evils haunt my shores?"

The unheard song that spellbound Odysseus brought the man to tears, pupils blown wide.

Hermes trod down to the deck of the ship, cautiously allowing his gaze to wander, not to the sky, but to the railings. It was true: no man ever passed by the Sirens' shores without listening to their song. The creatures feasted on flesh and mind alike, placating their whims with the thought that every sailor was so pleased to be murdered by their hand. And no man who had heard them sing sailed out alive, for if they heard the song and journeyed away, the Sirens were cursed to die.

It was a punishment from Demeter — she liked issuing those out.

And if a creature was fated to die should a human sail out of reach, there would be no question that they'd venture to take that victim by force.

From up and over the black ship's rail, a screeching Siren soared. An avian body lavished in fine feathers of all colors, stained with blackened blood under her talons and claws; she bore the head of a woman down to her graceful neck, exposed beneath the down about her bosom.

The air whistled as she circled around the mast where Odysseus stood heaving in confusion. Such marvelous voices belonging to hideous beasts.

"Odysseus," the Siren sang.

The crew ducked into their low-stationed seats, yelping while they rowed, as another Siren swooped up from below with a wicked laugh.

Eurylochus drew his sword and Polites appeared around the other side of the deck with a bow drawn and helmet donned, ready to deafly defend Odysseus against these creatures.

"We know of your Penelope, King of Ithaca."

"Her lament can be heard across the sea for you, come listen with us."

Hermes' shoulders rose sharply. "Cease your lies, daughters of Melpomene," he said, drumming his cane to the wooden boards. "You've come to eat your fill and avoid your fate."

The two Sirens clawed at the mast to find purchase, dipping the vessel over starboard as their piercing green eyes bore down at the mortal-disguised god. Light, airy laughter churned from their faces, caws from women's fine lips.

"You hear our voice and do not wish to fling yourselves to our shore?" one asked.

The other slid down the wood beam, snapping at Eurylochus, who jumped back swinging, and held the wax firm to his ear. Large wings swept an arrow from Polites' war bow. The crew squeezed their eyes closed, rowing blindly in their bravery.

"You will still make a special addition to our meal. Just one man to hear us was a disappointment, he would have to be split up so small, but two *my sisters and I could manage,"* she said, drawing a talon over Odysseus' cheek.

Hermes felt the wind on the back of his neck and laughed. "So there *are* three of you," he replied. And pulling Odysseus' sword from his hip, the young god pivoted to avoid the pounce of the third Siren, her mouth open to bite into his flesh with shark-like teeth, catching the tiny pleats of his tunic.

Her lovely neck extended as she turned up, ready to take off into the sky again, but despite this form, Hermes was faster and, no stranger to the task, swiftly brought the blade down upon that womanly soft neck.

With a sopping thud, a pile of feathers tumbled to the ground with the rest of the body. The head caught between Hermes' fingers, and he swung it up to face the greedy Sirens.

"Take your own lives with honor or I will slay you all like the animals you are!" he cursed in the tongue unknown to Man. Hurling the head over the side of the ship, he raised the sword to the two that remained whose venomous eyes stretched wide and songs turned to cries.

They scrambled to avoid the fate of the blade, crawling back to the air. Feathers and blood, as their throats carved into themselves, peppered the deck; their song failing to bring any mortal to their urgent call. They would die over the sea or on the rocks of the island, but they would die nevertheless.

Hermes stepped away from the birdlike body at his feet. Its meat would be no good to the humans here and the guts would putrefy in minutes, leaving behind a wretched smell.

Falling back into his innocent limp, he turned to the men tearing the wax from their ears. Two could afford to leave their station, rapt at the bloody mess on board. Their attention was so locked on rowing away from the island that they didn't see who had slain the beast — clearly not the lame, young boy — but they helped in ridding the vessel of its corpse while Odysseus fell from his rope-prison into Eurylochus' hold.

All frowns, he wiped his eyes and face with scrap linen and examined his crew.

"Is everyone okay?" he asked, rubbing the burn lines from his wrists.

Eurylochus counted the crew, his brow never ceasing to twitch when he included Hermes among them. "Aye, Captain, we're all accounted for," he replied. "But what knowledge could have been worth the price of life? We were not warned the Sirens would come aboard!"

"Calm yourself, Eurylochus. They try to claim only those who hear them. Didn't you realize there was no danger for your or our friends with the wax in your ears? But," he said with a sigh, "I thank you for defending me when I couldn't do so myself."

Odysseus' rational eye shot straight to Hermes, who removed his cloak from atop his head, scraping at his ear like there was beeswax in there the whole time. Approaching close enough to touch elbows with Hermes, he held out his hand.

"You have my sword," he whispered, "thief."

Hermes slid the handle back into his rugged palm. "We're bound to the strait now. If you don't warn your crew, then prepare them at least to row like their lives depend on it. And you have a choice for which path to take them."

There was a decision already in Odysseus' mind, Hermes could see it on his face.

Before he turned to address his men, like a pendulum he swung back and took Hermes' by the shoulder. "I hate to ask when you've already done so much for us, but," he breathed, and there was a quake to his grip, "if there's any way you can save my brothers from this, I beg you to guide us."

The prayer was there, right in front of him, spoken to his face. But oddly enough, there was a barren hole where he usually felt those pleas.

Hermes' brows pulled taut.

He nodded, of course he nodded. He desired nothing more than to be sure Odysseus and those who treated Hermes with kindness — the flute hung around his neck under the small glass vial — were home before the season ended. And as he nodded, Odysseus smiled softly, but a pit was starting to form in the young god's stomach, a dread that he only felt in his own nightmares, a dread that felt incalculable and ungodly.

Fear that felt *human*.

Hermes flexed his hand, and the soft skin that had gripped the bronze of Odysseus' sword ached with developing blisters from just a mere swing.

Surely not, he thought, and brought his hands up through his hair.

No, his wings were still there under his guise, curled safely against his locks. He was still a god, just… *feeling*. He was just feeling, that's all. And what was a little blister anyway? Humans dealt with worse all the time. His caduceus was hidden in its poor cane casing, the gift from dear Apollo hardly ever left his side. All, but the items bestowed to him by Zeus.

Hermes would have to be a buffoon not to tie this trick to his father knowing of his escapades with the son of Laertes. A little punishment to humble him for lying — not that he did anything more than *omit* truths. He *had* been with Nobody for a fairly long time. Nobody was a decent strategist when he focused on tasks, just egotistical in the execution. *Who wasn't?*

Hermes pinched at the pin holding up his tunic, the discreet bolt that followed him everywhere, and looked up just as a cold gust of wind caught the sails with a thundering snap.

Mist rolled like tidal waves, washing up the sides of the ship. The Strait of Messina rose in the horizon, and just beyond it were Grecian seas — Ithaca not far beyond. Water moved the ship where it desired the craft to go, ripping oarblades from several men's hands and hurling them into the waking foam, but Odysseus urged the men to fight the current. He strode down each deck and clasped their shoulders.

"My friends, we're no strangers to danger, and this approaching danger is no worse than what we had faced in Troy or when that devilish Cyclops trapped us in his cave. Think back to that time: with my tactics and the courage we *all* roused, we made it out alive. Trust that I'll get us through this day too. I need everybody to work as one and follow my orders..." Odysseus relayed as the men on one side thrust their oars back into the storming current and the helmsman followed their lead to head for the crag and not the surging waters beyond the influx of sea-smoke.

Charybdis — the insatiable monster lurking just below the surface — would swallow up any vessel that dared to sail near. Her timing now was at its worst as she drank up massive gulps of the sea, and the oarsmen cried out against the force to fight the pull. Odysseus donned his armor and ran back down the deck with spears and helmets, passing them to his comrades who held on tightly to the ship's casting. Steering with all the strength they had, the black ship veered successfully towards the taller, narrow path, teetering on the precipice of falling back into Charybdis' current at any misstroke.

Odysseus said nothing of why he had armed himself and his crew. In a more innocent light, the image of him dressed as he'd been when he was general on the beaches of Troy may have stirred some heart in the men.

But the breastplate and helmet were for real protection, and his long spears were intent on drawing blood.

The cliff face rose like a great beast overhead. An eerie silence swallowed the darkness that the ship sailed into.

Through slight channels between the rocks, one could still see the gushing waves of the sea monster gargling and spitting up water, where one wrong move would pull them portside and send them crashing into jagged stone.

Hugging the starboard side, yes, that's where it felt safer. Eurylochus guarded the ship's bow diligently, Polites and a few others at the rear, Perimedes had four men roaming the decks with their spears held high. Maybe they expected some ambush, and they wouldn't be wrong. But it wasn't an ambush they were familiar with. Hermes stood by Odysseus' side at the center of the ship, a hand wavering by the bony tusks of Odysseus' helmet, as if he could manage to pull him aside in this condition.

"It's like a scene from my nightmares," Polites uttered, his gentle voice bouncing off the walls. He pressed his back against his friends' and squinted towards the angry water.

"Where is she?" Odysseus whispered. He scanned the rugged walls for the strait's other beast. One that would spell out certain doom if they weren't careful.

"Now I *know* Circe didn't tell you to fight Scylla," Hermes said harshly. "Odysseus, she's not a monster you want to battle." He continued to follow the crew members with his eyes, turning his face from the front to the back.

"But we have you with us," Odysseus replied. "Doesn't that change *everything*, when a god is truly on your side? Too many times I've taken the peaceful route, shown mercy and kindness, and have only had it thrown back into my face in the form of death and sorrow."

Hermes' tongue grew dry. He wanted to drop this pathetic, squishy form, grow to his true height, and simply rip the ship right out of the strait even if it destroyed the masts and smashed the rigging to pieces.

But nothing happened.

He still stood a few inches above five feet and he had no sandals to propel him forward at great speeds. A bead of sweat trickled down his cheek as the air grew humid.

Scylla had six heads to feed and vast crag walls to venture around. She could be hiding in any misty corner, watching the black ship like it was a little toy bringing her next meals.

With few sailors making it through the Sirens, Scylla's own belly must've been starving.

A warning bubbled up his throat, "Tell your men to spread out and —"

Hermes stumbled into Odysseus as the whole cavern roared with the empty waters of Charybdis, shaking the bedrock and tossing several stones across the decks. The rowing crew ducked their heads down beneath their oars, their helmets taking the brunt of the debris. Those standing grasped for the lines, and Hermes caught the first glimpse of the crag ghoul high above in the blackness, her eyes aglow whiter than the teeth she smiled at him with.

For the first time in his immortal life, he felt human terror.

Scylla's six heads, long tendrils like the bait of an angler fish, swung out to capture its prey — dumb, unsuspecting fish — and teared them upwards: so immediately went two men standing on the decks of the ship.

In a panic, Hermes dashed to the stern just as those men screamed out for their captain, lifted into the sky by horrible teeth crunching into their ribcage. The roar of tired warriors built up as they blindly fought back against the beast.

It wasn't a winnable fight, Circe made sure of that; she created this damned monster.

"By the gods," Polites said, thrusting his spear over Hermes' head, pushing him underneath his reach like he were Hermes' shield. "You ought to go below deck, Anastasios!"

What was Hermes doing? What was his plan, limping around the stern, unarmed and growing weaker by the second? Surely his father wouldn't let him suffer this way — being torn asunder and swallowed would be an awful punishment if he had to spend even a *day* within Scylla's belly before someone came to fetch him.

That is… he'd survive, yes? Just because he was stuck this way didn't make him human.

Polites hugged him from behind and pulled them far from the ledge as Scylla's shrilling third head plucked another man the moment he struck up a torch to see. The fire's orange light reflected against wet rock and the slimy, beetle-like skin of her body. Flesh shivered and flailed, whipping the sailor's body to and fro before swallowing him head-first down her gullet.

"Polites," Hermes said, pulling at his arms. "Don't be alone up here; go to your king."

"Someone has to protect the helmsman! If he goes, then we all fall into that whirlpool," he replied. The torchlight lit up the tired lines etched in his cheeks.

"But who will protect you?"

"We all protect each other the best we can. It's how Ody got us through Troy. It's how we will get you through this too, don't worry—"

Hermes wished he didn't see it: the black void, shining from the flames curling in from the side. He wished he closed his eyes and plugged his ears as several rows of teeth cracked into Polites' shoulder.

The Ithacan soldier still gripped his spear in the other hand and stabbed at the shell of Scylla's head. A pained cry was bubbling in his throat. Polites' pulse was racing under Hermes' tight grasp on his wrist. Behind them, Odysseus wailed back in agony, throwing his javelin at one head with swift, accurate anger while the remaining crew held fast their spears and shouted until their lungs grew sore.

But Polites kept quiet.

A gasping, little whine escaped while Scylla began to lift him from the deck. Hermes held on fast. Their grip was quickly growing slick with blood. Hermes dug his nails into his friend's skin and keened when Scylla shook them both like a dog with a bone. A terrible crack followed and Polites dropped his weapon.

"Great Zeus," Hermes exclaimed, grasping Polites with both hands. His plea was one of dozens screeching through the cave. The ship continued to move underneath them. Below was just water. A choking gargle from above brought Hermes' eyes back up. Blood dribbled onto his cheek. He was a dead man and they both knew it. "I'll get you through this," he said.

Polites nodded.

The warm light inhabiting such kind eyes that Hermes had the pleasure of knowing disappeared.

Scylla ripped a sixth man from the ship and made it known to all present with another violent flail of her tendrils. Hermes cried out, suddenly airborne, jettisoned forward until he was hitting ropes and knots on his rapid descent. From his hair, only the wings he was born with could stifle the impact of a flying god who was not prepared to face gravity.

There was the taste of blood in his mouth, even more getting into his eyes. Taking up his ears were the choking screams of those crew members, rising higher into the cavern, their arms flailing for help, calling for Odysseus, for the gods, for *anyone*. The awful heads flipped them like game and swallowed their bodies down whole.

Six small pieces of sand fell into Hermes' vial necklace.

The ship kept going, weaving around jutting stacks and columns towards the exit of the horrid path. The waters of the Ionian sea were within sight and Odysseus beat his fist against his armor to rouse whatever energy his comrades had left.

A cackling, wicked, inhuman laughter filled the abyss behind them, growing louder.

Hermes groaned, his skull dented into the boards. In front of him was the helmsman, muttering prayers, trying to hold the ship on course with all the might his quivering muscles allowed. Past him, the men in their thwarts, rowing until their fingernails were raw and peeling off.

And Odysseus, beyond tormented by his failed attempt to keep all the men safe, stood with another spear in hand, unrelenting.

He knew Scylla could eat her fill endlessly. Her glee at the amount of sustenance in her domain, the flesh that would keep her thriving in her immortal life, brought the six heads prodding back from the darkness. There were still thirty-nine souls on board.

"Hermes!" Odysseus shouted as the creature leered over them for a second

time.

Oh Zeus, he thought, wishing there would be a gust strong enough to push them just out of her reach. Gripping his cane, Hermes ran up to the helmsman and threw himself against the stern's powerful oar.

"I am still a *god,*" he said, raising the staff in the air.

Rippling free from its illusion, the winged, gold caduceus hissed loudly in the echoes of Scylla's lair. Heads to serpents, Hermes willed them all to sleep, the unfortunate man at the helm the first to fall limp to the boards while others thudded back in their thwarts. The weight of the water fought back against the change in power, but Hermes leaned into the blade.

His dear caduceus shook with the force of taming a creature the size of Scylla. One of her heads lurched itself like a battering ram towards him, but fell just short of the ship, teeth skimming the wood, and a thundering splash sent the vessel forward unmanned and without power.

Chapter 8

The two serpents hummed until even they couldn't any longer.

At last, the ship passed into the Ionian sea with calm waters and an open view that welcomed the colors of the evening sky; and maybe if Apollo was watching where the light was, he would see how his little brother ached with every fiber of his being.

Still a god.

Hermes' grip on the helm slipped away, the ship floating dead in the water. He stumbled to the deck with swollen ankles and puffy eyes, holding his staff as it shifted back to its cane appearance like it were the only reminder of who he was.

He was a god. He was just in a small mortal predicament at the moment.

The blood in his mouth couldn't have been his. It tasted of iron and had a texture he didn't agree with, like the gross bits in the squeezed juice of an orange. He spat and wept. It was that sweet Polites' blood. The mortal who now hung in a suspended time around his neck with five of his friends.

A sacrifice of six over the sacrifice of them all.

Palms slick with sweat, he gripped that vial. He couldn't bring them anywhere without his talaria.

You are a god, he told himself again.

Raising his head, he counted, with shaky vision, the unconscious bodies of the men on board. Odysseus laid facing the sky, weapon still in hand with the spattered blood of his friends staining the deck around him. Hermes dragged himself down the few steps to the lower deck, his bones feeling like clay wrapped up tightly underneath a bag of skin.

You are a god.

Not even the spell of his serpents, Kleistós and Anoize, could keep the exhausted mortals asleep long after their lullaby ceased. Bodies stirred and groaned, cracked and whimpered while Hermes crossed the boat to his great grandson.

A massive bowl of ambrosia sounded fantastic right about now.

Grooves of the wood pressed prints against his forehead. Twice he knocked his fist atop Odysseus' breastplate. "You unlucky man," he said into his arm. Humans were so warm. "Wake up."

Would he blame him for not saving his crew? For not preventing Scylla from ripping them from his very arms? When the captain moves to count his crew and see who's missing, how much will he hate Hermes for allowing his best friend to slip away?

Odysseus hissed between his teeth, seething before he even opened his eyes. The sky was bright orange and free of creatures, only the purple clouds that hung low on the horizon and silver ones speckled above.

"Oh Zeus," Odysseus said, and brought his hands up to push agony from his face. His shoulders rocked and he raised a foot just to slam it back on the ground; then did it again, and again.

"Ody, forgive me," Hermes whispered. There was shadow feeding at his vision — his father wouldn't let him die, would he? No, he was deathless. This was just a punishment. But he didn't feel deathless. He couldn't move much of the leg that Anastasios limped on, and his swarming thoughts couldn't find purchase anywhere. "Your friends, I…"

"I know," Odysseus replied from within his hands. "I chose this route; I knew its danger. An impossible choice as it was, it was me who chose it. The loss is mine to bear."

The crew slowly stood up from their thwarts, crying at the open sea around them, one finally lacking storms sent by angry gods and beasts determined to eat them. Some praised and others vomited, all weeping and grasping at their own palms full of splinters and calluses.

Eurylochus, bruised and disheveled, ambled up to the center mast and leaned on its beam. He sighed loud enough that the rest of the men let theirs go with it. The man's jaw was set. Hermes didn't need to be a god to insinuate what the mortal was thinking, as his dark eyes shifted down to where Odysseus just sat himself up.

Neither did Odysseus need to guess.

"If we went towards Charybdis, we'd have all perished," he said to his second. "We had a fighting chance against Scylla."

"None of us were cautioned about this Scylla, *Captain,*" Eurylochus shot back through tight lips. "We had no clue what we were looking out for — why didn't you tell us?"

"Don't you think, after everything we've gone through, if the men knew we were approaching a monster like that, they'd hide away in the bowels of the ship? And those heads would search like a hunter in its own territory just to *rip* us apart anyway. We needed men on the oars to get us through the strait," Odysseus stood up and pushed his nose into Eurylochus' space, "and I need *you* not to start rousing ideas of treachery. We're almost home."

"Then you will tell the families of the men we've lost that their husbands, sons, and fathers are *dead* because of you and your self-proclaimed guile," Eurylochus pushed back. "You can tell Polites' waiting bride that she waited thirteen years for no one."

Odysseus' fists curled. He tore off his helmet and threw it to the ground, like he was ready to pounce on his second for daring to speak to him, his king, in such a manner. "Tighten the front sail and have the men return to their oars. We're getting this ship under control."

Hermes bit down on his tongue just to shove his leg under him. A pain similar to when he was royally whooped from a grimy spar with his brothers. He'd have to apologize for laughing at Hephaestus for being so slow and grunty next time he saw him.

"Anastasios?" Odysseus said while the crew moved around them, trying to avoid the blood on the deck. He put out his hand and grasped Hermes' forearm. "Are you... okay?"

"I have no idea," he chuckled. Tears lined his lashes. "I've yet to leak mortal blood from my veins so I cannot be so bad, but I haven't the nerve to test any theories. My weapons are on Mount Olympus, half my consciousness may still be too, I can't tell."

"You can't tell." Odysseus cocked his head. "What does that mean?"

"I don't know. I had a walk with my father just the other night. He asked about you, or rather, he asked what I was doing with you — not in those words, but he knows I've been intervening on your nostos. He must've sent me down this morning," Hermes said, the cane wobbling to hold him upright.

There wasn't much to respond to when a god complained about his father, the god king himself, sending him out like a dog.

"I'm…" Odysseus picked at the latches of his armor before steadying Hermes again. "I know we wouldn't have made it out of that strait, nor passed the Sirens, in and out of the Underworld, and stood against Circe, without your help. I've never heard of a god choosing to stand among us for so long, but I'm grateful for it, and am sorry for what troubles I may have caused you. If you must return to Olympus to heal whatever damage wrought against the Thunderer—"

"I can't," Hermes interrupted. "My talaria, the gift from my father that allows me to go where I please, were seized. Without them, I've only my wits and a propensity to try and get myself out of trouble. Like how I was as a babe, but *pathetic*."

"So you're like me," Odysseus said, but Hermes shook his head and ran his fingers over the flute that dangled below the bottle of souls tinkling against the glass.

"No, you're like *me*. I've had the privilege of being well-liked while getting away with my tricks and lies, but it seems our luck ebbs and flows with the choices that others outside of our power make. I thought myself clever when I lied to Zeus that I was aiding *Nobody*. Now he's bound me to my mortal form to keep me where I was so determined to be."

Odysseus walked him to the officer's chair, step by step, an old man and his kin. Hermes thumped into the seat, sinking into the pelts as the oars found a quick pace with the wind, and all the hairs flew up to caress his cheek.

"I don't think you're determined to be here just for our entertainment value, Lord Hermes," Odysseus said, dropping the plate and gear in the chest beside them. From his things, he gently pulled out his stupid cap and tucked his unruly hair into it, and his sea-cloak to pin around his shoulders. Then he took another felt cap, a green one, and rolled it over Hermes' head until his bronze curls were neatly preserved. "Do you know me?"

What a silly question. He only asked silly questions when he had an answer already made up in his ever-ticking brain. Hermes had a plethora of just as ridiculous answers. *No, he was* not *here for entertainment, for everything was either traumatic or awfully boring and there was very little in-between.* But he could not exactly bring himself to make the humans dance for him at a time like this.

Playing a note or two on the flute, Hermes pressed his nose to the wood pipes. "I know you," he replied with all the truth capable of this tiny form. "I knew your mother, and your mother's father far too well. More than anyone else on this ship or anyone alive in your kingdom, I know you."

There wasn't any need for a god to explain any further than that. He continued a little tune, something that all of the crew could hear. A melody long and soft that carried calm on the wind that filled the sails. His cheek grew damp though he didn't see any rain from the sky, and the mist spat up from the oars hardly could fly high enough to strike him. He played for an hour without stopping, slipping to ones his brother had written for the lyre, but sounded rather fine on a human-built flute. If his muscles were going to ache and his vision was going blurry, at least acting the bard used the ceaseless breath he had.

* * *

Odysseus washed his hands and, in his silence, studied the island in the encroaching shadows of night. He was warned of this place with its lush pastures and calm coves — the island that radiated joy and peace. Wearily, he commanded the helmsman to continue on past it, to venture home and avoid any disastrous fate that awaited everyone there. Eurylochus jettisoned himself to the captain's deck and took Odysseus by the arm.

125

"You are an unyielding man, Ody, clearly with a fighting vigor ten times the strength of ours. Look at your brothers — they are half-dead in their thwarts, starved for sleep after constant labor through the jaws of death. Now you *forbid* us to set foot on the first *kind* land we have seen? Forbidden to rest and have a decent meal in peace again?"

His fist squeezed Odysseus' wrist.

"The crew is drained, the night is among us, but why not desert this haven within our reach; let hidden winds of the night ambush upon our blundering, and with their gales, tear our ship apart and cast us out to sea. The gods must have that preference for the lot of us, it seems," Eurylochus spoke loudly for all to hear. The circles under his eyes grew purple; his nostrils flared. "Damn the night. Allow us to set our supper here by the tranquility of these waters. We will sit tight by our ship and at daybreak, board again and make for Ithaca."

Through his speech, the crew shouted their enthusiastic support for the second-in-command. Eurylochus' posture straightened; bold-breasted and eager to be on the winning side of a doomed objective while simultaneously speaking out against the warning of their *king*.

Brother-in-law or not, Hermes thought, Ody would be right in punching him.

But Odysseus let his gaze waver over his crew, his shoulders falling limp. Ithaca was right on the other side of the Ionian sea. It was the original distance between Troy and home, a straight shot there. Poseidon hadn't taken notice of them since they arrived on Circe's island, but the risk would surely be worth it. His fingers curled into his hair, and he dared threaten to pull them all out by the roots, but let his tension slip through a sigh.

"My brother," he said, and Hermes heard the grief burrow into his heart, "I am but one man against all others, the advantage is yours."

Eurylochus smiled.

"Swear to me, all of you," Odysseus continued, and his voice rose to a plea. "Should we come upon herds of cattle or flocks of sheep, none among us in his recklessness will slaughter ox nor ram. Just eat what we have from Aeaea — it's plenty and given to us freely. Do as I say and we'll keep peace."

Tired, worn hands excitedly drummed against the boards of the ship. The crew swore an oath at once not to interfere with any of the herding animals that roamed the island. They thought only of safe land and soft, dry sand to sleep upon.

Like a usurper lord, Eurylochus cheered among them, rousing their spirits and shaking their shoulders to push the rest of the way into a sheltered harbor to moor their vessel. Odysseus' knuckles grew white while he gripped the edge of his chair Hermes occupied, pinching his nose with the other.

The island of Thrinacia was one Hermes only passed over on his trips. In a way, it made him smile to see it, always aglow in the dead of night, like it was where Helios stored his shining light when he didn't carry it. It was home to fresh springs that sprouted lovely nymphs that tended to his cows. Helios wasn't keen on inviting Hermes when he was younger, give or take four hundred years ago — something about knowing how cattle reacted around him and the situation with Lord Apollo's favorite cows. Hermes couldn't place it.

He'd never done anything wrong ever.

That he didn't set right soon after.

Throwing buckets of stone into the shallow water, a quaint echo of tired giggles intermingled with sobs as the day's events had a moment to settle on the mind.

Shrouded with their cloaks and holding aloft meals to prepare from their storage, the crew peeled themselves off the ship and splashed to shore to lay their spread. Hermes rose to follow, leaping to take off like he had always been able to do, but his leg, like the story he told, did not allow it, and he crumpled to the floor.

Odysseus grabbed his waist and picked him up like he weighed nothing to sling over his shoulder as they disembarked. A different feeling than flying, slightly more humiliating, but it took the ache from his body away and that was fine enough.

Leaping from the ship though — *great Zeus* — his ribcage rolled against Odysseus' back, and the man was as hard as a rock.

"Don't kill the boy," Perimedes said, preparing a fire on the rise of the beach. "Perhaps he can sing our libations tonight. To see, of all of us and those we've lost, that he survived this far -- the gods must favor him."

His captain sighed. "Don't put our one guest under duress. Shouldn't we allow him the same peaceful night we long for?"

Hermes wiggled his feet until sand flooded his sandals and Odysseus adjusted the cloak around his shoulders and the pileus cap on his head. He was certainly looking like a dirty, bloody peasant in the company of dirty, bloody sailors. His attention flew to the ground where the sand fit between his toes. Raising his good leg, there on the surface of the ground was a footprint — plain as day.

"There should be a small stream," Hermes said to Odysseus, "that we can wash in just beyond the large rock garden. I cannot look at you all knowing we're covered in the ichor of human flesh. Command those that prepare the food to clean themselves first; then I would like to bathe... *Please.*"

The son of Laertes was more than willing to do what was asked, throwing out his hands to the men and gesturing to the wall of stone, sending with them new barrels to fill with fresh water.

How did mortals do it? All the anxieties and pain inside yet they had so much to handle without acknowledging any of it.

Hermes once mocked a sculptor for creating ugly renditions of Demeter and her daughter to be sold for idol worship. He lied and declared any person that purchased such things would find their crops dead by the next season and would return to light his shop on fire. The old merchant replied that he'd already promised the statues to a patron, and in his stance of defense accidentally destroyed the idols. He merely gawked at the broken pieces with no words remaining on his tongue. Pain in his eyes was there, but there came no tears. Hermes had expected tears.

Not from himself, not now. The wetness on his cheeks returned under their dry canopy of ivy and stone. He carefully flitted a finger under his lashes, the globular drop traced onto his nail. It didn't feel absolutely horrid to cry; his chest hurt more, but the water adorning his fingertip was happy to be free of him, and he of it.

The problem was that more merely continued to come and he only had ten fingers.

Didn't he already have bad feelings on the ship? Wasn't that just supposed to be it? The emotions come *back?*

"Ody, would you help your lame ancestor to the waters? This human form is malfunctioning," he whispered, limping to grab hold of the man's shoulder.

"I'm still working to understand," Odysseus replied, taking him up under the arm.

"It isn't like you don't personally know other children of gods. Several fought with you, some have died by you."

The rise of the beach was modest, but the smooth sand was dastardly to climb up when gravity wanted the sandals to go down. Hermes puffed out his cheeks.

Human skin was so fragile even eye-water burned it.

"But you," Odysseus stammered, searching the trees that scattered around the stream, "to have you physically next to me. To have been by my side for so long already."

"For the time, I… I'm failing in my one duty as a guide." *Damn the tears, he felt like Aphrodite was near to force her rampant emotions upon him.* "What I'd give to get you to Ithaca and your family now, on my honor. And that's a phrase I seldom use honestly."

"You're not failing, Hermes. You're clever enough to know that I'd be long dead without you." Odysseus shook his head and let his frame relax at the tranquility of the little clearing, where the men could be heard just over the stones, and no haunting dangers lurked beyond the trees. "For my family — I see them everywhere: in my dreams, my waking thoughts, thinking of how they are, what they look like now. I fear I've concocted some pretend voice of Penelope; she's the siren I'd succumb to without hesitation."

They settled on the tiny stone bank where the water lapped lazily down the hill to meet with the ocean around a few bends. Simple, the way Helios liked it. Hermes pulled off his shoes and immediately grabbed for where the wings of his talaria would be. Their wispy feathers were so much lighter than his own ones, but his fingers only combed through air and the auburn hairs that curled up his legs. Fingernails dug into his shins the longer he tried to feel for them.

"I'm acutely aware of how you can expound on great lengths over your wife. I'm afraid the only other person I know who could manage such a thing is my uncle, Hades." He wet his hand and rubbed the dried blood flakes from his face, and unclipped his cloak and tunic. "Truly the happiest union within my family. It must feel lovely," he said, as Odysseus scrubbed his own cheeks clean, "to know love so intimately."

"Surely love is not a human invention when there is Aphrodite," Odysseus replied. His surprised hum of approval to the stream's warmth made Hermes chuckle. They waded further in to submerge themselves and Hermes sat on the silt beneath the running water.

"It's a different kind." Hermes shrugged. "To explain how gods love to mortals is like asking *dogs* to serve you wine."

Odysseus wrung his hair, looking like he needed oil that didn't exist nearby. "It can be done. Mine could if I trained him."

He brought up his legs. "It's a hierarchy of respect. Love for one is put aside for love of another more important. My father likely doesn't *enjoy* that I'm being so disobedient at Lord Poseidon's requisition. Not that my uncle knows, exactly, and I assume Father won't mention this infraction. He was just preaching to me about respecting our family instead of dawdling in mortal problems." The wings hidden beneath this form's hair rustled from their bath. He tucked his chin between his knees. "Even if *we* are the ones to have caused so much of your grievances."

"We've caused much of our own, too."

"I was there at Paris' trial of the apple. I played the Gamemaster at Zeus' request and watched my family trick that fool into choosing one goddess over the others. As if it meant anything other than stirring discord. And a whole war started up over it."

Odysseus seemed unconvinced. "Human nature's full of contradictions: jealousy and devotion, rage and mercy. We make *choices*. The young prince of Troy didn't have to take away Lady Helen. I'm not so blind as to believe she was taken against her will, but Paris had the *choice* to be a respectable man and leave a king's wife be. But he didn't, and so that was his consequence. Gods involved or not."

Hermes picked at the water as if it would follow his fingers. "But there are some choices only the gods give you, and neither of them are fair. Meant to just close our eyes or watch it occur; and we're not to care too deeply. For your lives are short and ours are eternal."

A watery wave of mood-ruining betrayal came splashing straight into his face, pushing him backward until his nose dunked under, and with the gurgling of the stream against tightly fitted stones and grass, it was like the whole water was laughing about it. There was no chance to protest, Odysseus moved his large hand and sent another.

As if the man were not also melancholic, listening to his crew on the beach sit and cry about their fallen comrades; as if he didn't lose his best friend in the most painful manner mere hours before. But how many times can heartache make a man bleed? The scars of war dotted Odysseus' arms and thighs like a tactical map — cuts and harsh lines of quick spears and arrows that were sent off their course and spared him. There was an uglier gash in his side beneath his ribcage where the skin was still red and patchy, stitched together and only healed for over a year or two.

Hermes remembered when the king was surrounded by Trojans on their beach, alone with his weapon while he stalled for time. When, afterwards, those beaches were full of corpses, massacred and crushed by the hundreds, and Hermes remained to collect every soul.

The vial of sand still remained fixed around his neck — one thing he could not remove even if he wanted to. It was not five or six hundred as it could have been when his cloak was filled with starlight: the men Odysseus had already grieved. It was just six. Six that still brought about weeping.

"I don't like your Human frailty," he said, wiping his face. "It doesn't suit me."

"No, it doesn't," Odysseus replied, rising from the water. "But your empathy does, I think. And if you're my great grandsire, then," he shrugged into his tunic, "we can learn more from one another while you deliver me home. And I can tell my son of how he comes from one of the greatest gods I've ever known."

"You're just fanning my ego, and I tell you, sir, gods invented hubris."

"Come dry before you catch an unsuitable human cold and have to bear it for the rest of our voyage. Sickness and the rocking of a ship are a ghastly duo."

He redressed in clean linen that Odysseus helped drape for the night; the rest of their clothing laid next to the stream's bank to dry. The noise from the crew would be too loud for any water nymph to try and steal them away in their amusement. Hermes' scent was all over the place, they would know not to touch them. Beyond the ship, where the harbor let out to the great sea, the sky was dark and full of constellations without a cloud in sight. Some stars drifted so close, he could simply reach out and touch them.

Laid out before the few dozen men, a few fowl smoked over two fires, with boiling pots of lentils set near them; a great aroma wafted around the beach, a lure to Hermes' nose. The youngest of the crew was sent around with the bread and cheese, and Hermes was handed the collection of spring water to pour each man his cup despite Odysseus' protest. But the cups were brought over to pour instead of making him limp around — no offense to xenia taken.

They spoke of fond, personal memories of the men they loved most that no longer sat among them, shedding tears until sleep came to all without any help from the messenger god's staff. Their snores blew up sand and several found comfort using each other's limbs as pillows. Hermes pulled his himation over both shoulders and laid on the sand by Odysseus.

That man still slept like Penelope was within his arms.

Soon she will be, Hermes hummed, pushing the silt into a small mound between Odysseus' hold, like he was building the shape of a woman the way Prometheus created mankind out of mud.

Chapter 9

"Hurry up, throw the lines!"

"Heave, men, til her ram won't budge!"

"Perimedes, climb aboard and move the helm's oar to its starboard side!" Odysseus shouted over the pelting rain and gruesome wind that whipped outside the sheltered beach they awoke on.

When a sudden storm blew in from the south, pushing the moored ship on its side before the men took notice, there was a panicked rush to pull the thing aground before it could be ripped apart. Storms around the island of Thrinacia were rare, opting to fly into Sicily instead. The island itself remained blissful, basking in a hole of light between the clouds so its lord's sun could warm the golden meadows and comfort the cattle.

But its beaches were growing violent and the sand spun in frightening twisters that Hermes would avoid entirely if he were flying by.

While the crew beached their black ship, Hermes was tasked with dragging their supplies further inland. A slave to Zeus, a slave to these men, very little difference, but Hermes was diligent in whatever he was assigned. He brought the pots and the chests to the far reaches of the stream bank as it swelled with water and sped to the sea. The ripples coursed with energy, called to the ocean by the master of the tides.

Poseidon had found them.

If Hermes was any less human and any more audacious, he'd stand naked on the beach and kick the foam for good measure.

Instead he set up a modest camp — the way Ares described them in the raiding parties he'd sneak within, just with a little Hermes flair — tying thicker fabric along the trees from limb to limb, tight enough to hold his weight. He laid atop it for a moment until the lack of ground beneath his back eased some of the cramping, and approved the design for two more *Hermocks*. Extra rope was worked free of their knots and he left them in tidy bundles by the men's things.

Their spears couldn't draw ichor he discovered when one sliced into his finger; which was such a huge relief, despite the muted pain, that he succumbed to crying again.

He sharpened their tips for spearing fish when the craving overcame them. The stream, just a few minutes walk up, expanded outward and was saturated with tuna and anchovies. They were fat fish; Helios bragged about his twin daughters who lived on the island and their kindness towards all its animals. Probably another reason Hermes was never a visitor; his reputation with Helios' daughters was ambiguous at best.

If Helios knew he was here, then he knew of Hermes' current predicament. *How embarrassing.* Though the lord of the sun was not apt to gossip.

"— at least until the storm passes by," someone shouted.

But they should've known better by now: if Poseidon knew they were on this island, they weren't leaving anytime soon.

A firm nudge to the small of his back sent Hermes over a log he just rolled for the men to sit on. Up and around his feet went, somersaulting as gracefully as a lame leg could allow.

"Ody, enough with your teasing," he grumbled, shaking out his hair.

But it wasn't Odysseus sneaking up on him.

Eurylochus stood still half-armored from yesterday. Much of his hair was looped behind his ears and kept from his eyes with a deep yellow, leather fillet. The palms of his hands were raw and red, as were the highlights of his face where the wet winds had angrily beaten them.

"I assume the ship is safely on shore?" Hermes asked, taking up his cane.

"Yes, no thanks to you." He couldn't decide whether to cross his arms or not. "But when did *you* start calling the King of Ithaca, son of Laertes, the Lord Odysseus, *'Ody'*? A guest — one we've pulled into our company by sheer happenstance of the gods if you will," Eurylochus said, gesturing to the sky, "should not be referring to his host by familial names. We have known you for less than a week."

"I beg your pardon. I have heard you say it, and in my naivety thought it was a name he was fond of," Hermes quickly replied. "And oh mighty *king* he is, that Odysseus. Yet second Lord Eurylochus, you appear to be dressing the part of that role today."

A brow twitched with the vein that rocketed along his forehead. "Are you mad, boy?"

Hermes was tongue-in-cheek. "It's possible. I did spend an exuberant amount of time in the ocean. Perhaps the salted waves shook up my mind. It seems to have kept your king and captain amused for the days I've been present."

Eurylochus stalked to where Hermes had dragged his things, a trunk of fine wood and bronze, and opened it. "In those days we have lost seven men. I care little if Odysseus believes you are some eromenos to him, but I saw you when we were avoiding those Sirens. You who had no beeswax in your ears to protect you from their song — a lame boy who slew a beast without looking back."

"You'd be surprised at the upper arm strength of those who are lame. Have you not seen Lord Hephaestus? There is no better illustration of that power than he." Hermes yanked himself to his feet. The tall grass along the bank was damp from the little rain that made it through the tree cover, and his sandals sank an inch into the soil.

From Eurylochus' chest came the sharp *schling* of a dagger whose grip disappeared under his fist as he turned around, his brow arched at an absurd angle. The distant roaring wind through the harbor sounded like screams of women in agony.

"What *are* you?" he growled. "Did that witch, Circe, summon you to trap us here? That damned woman always tried to keep Ody longer than he must, *trapped* us for eons when we could have been home by now. But no… and now we are here with a storm circling yet *another* foreign island. And you appeared to us when we first left her halls."

Ah, this man was delusional.

The blade would not truly hurt him, though the image of being impaled over and over again, as there was no doubt this foolish man would stop after one stroke, was rather… displeasing.

Hermes wobbled back, and hopped nearer the water where their voices may carry towards the beach.

"Sir, I am no one but who I said I was. This goddess, this Circe you speak of — I have no past with her, I have never met her!"

"I do not believe you." Eurylochus' heavy steps forward were coated in adrenaline as his arms shook with anxious rage. The warrior caught up to him in seconds, like chasing a child, and gripped the elbow that kept the cane steady. Hermes' damned knee buckled, splashing into the water that had since grown terribly cold. "I will not have another beast take my friends; dooming us to remain lost to our families. What about *my* wife? What about *me?*"

Hermes fumbled for Eurylochus' hand and pressed his thumbnail into the soft skin of the veiny wrist with all the force he had. "It's not me who will doom you! You've heard your lord — it's the animals on this land you mustn't touch. Keep true to your oath and you will see home and Ctimene again."

Eurylochus' whole body seized for a tiny moment and a rim of tears lined his glare, but the grip did not waver.

If this form bruised, Hermes' wrist would don new black tattoos. He'd look like Poseidon.

Eurylochus pulled him up like a hare ready for skinning.

"You think you can manipulate me? Speaking all the lies that witch sowed into Odysseus' mind and pretending to know my wife; as if discarding you just to be safe and to preserve our supplies wouldn't be worth it even if you *were* just an unlucky, stupid boy." He rotated the dagger and pushed it against the soft tissue between Hermes' ribs. It was cold; a soulless blade.

"Eurylochus!"

Odysseus' fist came down hard upon his brother's cheek. The crack echoed like thunder as he stumbled to the side, pulling Hermes along with him until both plunged into deeper water. A fair gush of it rushed right up

Hermes' nostrils worse than the times he would collide with dolphins and fall into the waves of the sea. He'd prefer that, really, right now.

"Release Anastasios at once, Eurylochus. You shame yourself!" Odysseus trudged through the stream and pressed for the dagger. "You were as ruthless in Ismaros when I demanded benevolence towards the—"

"Oh, don't start that with me! They were allied with the Trojans," Eurylochus spat. "What difference was slaughtering them in broad daylight to sneaking within your horse in the dead of night, killing men while they slept? What difference is there between killing this boy to prevent catastrophe and you *throwing* that *infant* from the heights of the palace? Why are *my* actions any different from yours, Odysseus? Why must you insist *I* always be in the wrong?"

Hermes thought his arm may pop right out of its socket with the way the younger continued to yank him away from his captain's warning hands. A rough palm held onto his face, thumb probing into his cheek while a brick of an arm squeezed his windpipe. Eurylochus maneuvered to snap his neck now that Odysseus commandeered the weapon and was staring at him like a wolf would an ibex.

Just stick me on a spit after this. Make my offering to Apollo if you must choose one, Hermes contemplated. Though if he didn't bleed from human blades, he didn't think his bones could break at mortal's hands, even in this form; and he certainly didn't have to worry about being smothered. Still, the pressure was beginning to hurt.

"Eurylochus, gods forbid you violate xenia," Odysseus said, and he was fuming under his composure. "You dishonor Zeus himself by doing this. Release the boy; he's done no wrong. *Polites* enjoyed his song — would you wish to never be reminded of our dear friend over a theory made in trepidation?"

"Ody, if anything goes wrong, they'll blame you," Eurylochus replied, shaking his head.

Odysseus worked his jaw and slowly set the dagger into the belt around his waist. "I know, Brother, but I'm not wrong about this, I swear to you. Let the boy go. Have the men bring up the rest of the food and wine we have in our hold and *you* may divide it among us as you see fit, but be wary — we must make it last."

A tight click of teeth. "You should have followed Diomedes," Eurylochus said, dropping Hermes to the ground, and Odysseus released a long breath through tight lips.

"I know."

Maybe his offering shouldn't be towards Apollo. His brother would either laugh at Hermes' punishment or shoot down every man who wished to feast on his innards. Dionysus, then... No, that would be worse.

Despite spitting out the water that rushed up his nose, Hermes didn't desire Eurylochus to be slain outright. At least not by anything Hermes had to do with. Turned into a rock, perhaps, or a mouse.

His conscience did flitter with some guilt.

He could admit that much.

Every hour he felt smaller than the hour before. *A tiny human,* as Odysseus lifted him from the stream and delivered him to his floating bed invention. Large hands twisted his wrists and inspected his neck. He mouthed words that were so kind and flourished with fatherly worry, but so useless and demeaning and not at all comforting to Hermes' centuries old heart.

"Enough!" Hermes shouted, smacking Odysseus away. "I am a *god.* I do not worry about *death.* Death is my comrade, and I fly by his side when Man calls out his name with their final breath. It's *I* who saves, not who needs saving!"

Odysseus fell to his knees as the young god prickled with static and the language of the ancient gods slipped in and off of his tongue with ire and chagrin. "Hermes, my lord sire, forgive me," he said, lowering his gaze. "You are correct, always. I feared what would befall my fool of a brother if I didn't intervene; my comrades are distressed and I've put them in this situation."

Right away it felt wrong. Not this man, the rage that was simmering over the pot was not for this man. Hermes was not a god who lost his temper.

Often.

Across the top of his thumbnail was a sliver of Eurylochus' blood, bright and gleaming.

"I am a god," he said again, aloud to his kin.

"Yes," Odysseus murmured. "The most favorable one I pray will still allow me to call him a friend."

"I *will* bring you home. When I'm again myself, I promise you, Odysseus of Ithaca, we will fly hard against the winds to bring you to your beloved shores." Hermes grasped Odysseus' face and kissed the top of his head, where his hair was twisted and swept back with a braided tania that encircled his forehead and disappeared beneath the strands. It was much more dignified of a true king. "Don't move. I'm moody and while I fix something up for you, I fear I may accidentally shift you into some creature."

And so the mortal stood as still as a statue while Hermes snapped himself free of the fog that swam around his brain. There was a minuscule pouch tied to his belt, one that could only hold a few coins and terribly awkward to compare to the usual satchel of endless depths that he carried. From this pouch he pulled his inventory and made modest work with nimble fingers, twisting fishing wire around the shafts of three feathers until it was sturdy enough to curve to the shape of Odysseus' ear, where he tucked the earpiece and moved the hair around it.

"You have a competitor who's biding to be the leader amongst you," Hermes explained, fluffing up the barbs of the multi-colored vanes. "If this doesn't remind them of their true king, be it then a symbol of my progeny. Or in your crew's senseless minds, a reminder that the reckless son of Laertes listened to the song of the Sirens and lived to tell the tale. These are the only pieces left of those beasts. If you discard them, I'd take personal offense."

Odysseus followed each of the feathers with his hand, breaking the first smile since being startled awake that morning. The earpiece went too perfectly with his attire and complimented his silvered roots that remained hidden by the dark brunet pieces pulled over them; but those signs of stress and age were apparent in the whiskers along his face.

"What happens now?" Odysseus asked, rising as the first of his crew climbed up and around the boulders keeping the terrifying wind of the sea at bay. Hermes tucked his legs comfortably in the hanging bed and wrapped a dry cloak back over his shoulders.

"Waiting, I imagine," Hermes replied, rolling back like the small, little *eromenos* he was called to be. "Could be some time."

What an insinuation Eurylochus had. In some circumstances it could be comical, but coming out of the multi-transgressor, it lost some of its irony. To be an eromenos was to be submissive and feminine, often holding a lower status to his lover. If Hermes were his full size, he could crush Eurylochus' head with one hand.

He idly watched the men cup their cheeks in their palms and blow heavy, warm breaths to get the painful red out of their faces. Some collapsed into the tall grass where the sand crunched into the soil underneath. Others found where their things were placed and sifted through their supply to grab cloth and hats to roll themselves into.

"Hold on, friends," Odysseus said. "We'll make a fire before anyone's body gives out on them for the morning, aye? Timon, fetch some smaller kindling in these woods behind us, go no further than twenty paces. Perimedes, clear the center and be sure it reminds dry. Anastasios?" He turned to Hermes. "Where did you place the flints?"

"They're kept with your second's, my lord," Hermes replied, gesturing to the opened chest where the fool had grabbed his dagger before.

Odysseus' brow lowered, but his thoughts were his own. With a short breath, he nodded at the chest. "Poli… *ah*, Phidus, do you mind," he said.

He spent five more minutes dictating orders, of who was in charge of what — though he kept his promise to leave the distribution of rations to Eurylochus — and who was to keep on collecting water by the stream.

The men obeyed with tired frowns, but the tasks were completed, and before noon, the whole of the crew crowded again around a fire, drained from false hope of leaving for home. But the island was quiet inland and they were safe where they were. An island sacred to the sun god would bear no ill-will towards its visitors if they remained peaceful.

"Anastasios, are you still awake?"

Hermes hummed his assent, opening an eye. "How may I assist you, sir?" he asked, his bed swinging lackadaisical over a man's napping form. Did it come across as rude to not rise to a seated position when addressed by a mortal king? No one seemed to care.

"What songs do you know? Perhaps something to calm our anxious hearts." Odysseus was two men away, sitting cross-legged on a cushion that certainly had been through the war.

"'*What songs do you know?*' My lord, please," Hermes laughed and tooted a line of notes as he thought. A hymn would be too on the nose; and the heavens knew these men didn't feel as if the gods were being of any help. A paean, then, of sorts. "I know the best that would appease both man and god." He brought the flute back up to his lips and started something deep and low.

The men relaxed on the ground where they lay. The fire cracked with the moisture of the wood, saved from the cave before it could succumb to the sideways rain.

Hermes was humble enough to admit that he was not his brother when it came to composing, but he was an excellent student and a brilliant inventor; together he could trick the sound of a chorus if he split his breath into multiple pipes.

This was the men's time for prayer and meditation, though if they prayed to him he couldn't hear them. Who knew how many prayers were sitting in wait or lost to the ether. Prayers unheard were for Kronos in Tartarus to eat up, and no one wanted that. Zeus would have to allow Hermes his rights sooner than later.

He made the Achaean language easy to rhyme, it was melodic by nature.

"Oh feathers gleam down the mountains pass

O'er the fine trees and long dewed grass,

Cross to where my lovely house do fare,

And rests amongst my humble wife and heir."

The syrinx hummed its low notes, taking afternoon sleep with it over most of the men as they tucked their faces into their arms or sipped at their warmed wine with dreary thoughts of home in mind.

"Tell me dear feathers does light still shine

On my home, my hearth, and that family o' mine?

Oh send me the kind wind that carried you far,
Take up my whole soul to be where they are."

Apollo had described Hermes' singing voice as unfairly tenor and hypnotically smooth. A human's trusting tone with an echo of the gods. But Apollo's voice was both gentle and warm at the same time it was vicious and scathing. He was so used to hearing it everyday; despite being away from Olympus for long periods of time, he always came home and saw his brother.

Was this pathetic? To feel homesick after two days when Odysseus and his men haven't seen home in twelve years? Hermes closed his eyes and furrowed his brow. He could just play for them at least. Even for wretched Eurylochus, he played.

For the third day, he played while they continued to rest.

The sixth day, he was still playing. The men ventured to their ship to sweep off the sand that was blown by the incessant storm onto the decks and filled up the thwarts.

On the twelfth day, Eurylochus told Odysseus that it would be best to start fishing in the stream to make up for their food preservation. The captain agreed. Three men speared sixteen fish. Hermes continued to play.

The fourteenth day startled the crew, as the first sign of the cattle that roamed the island appeared. Its large nose sniffed Hermes as he lay on his tarp, tickling the young god's face with its whiskers. Odysseus stood with his arm out to calm his men — they were not to touch the cow at any rate, just in case. Hermes cupped his hands around the beast's broad head. Its brown fur was fine and soft, gently brushed in straight lines down its neck and back. After a few minutes of tasting Hermes' cheeks, the cow excused itself and wandered away into the woods with a wide-swaying jaunt.

The crew didn't bring up the bizarre action until the sixteenth day trapped on the island, when they were awoken by *two* cows now at Hermes' bedside, and they watched the poor Anastasios get rolled off his high bed by their heavy skulls, and *thunk* to the ground with a stifled grunt. Two sets of whiskers inhaled his scent with breaths strong enough that Hermes' hair and clothing fluttered up against gravity, like the cows themselves were mere vacuums.

Hermes wanted to laugh. He wanted to cackle at the irony of the cows of another sun god willingly coming to see him. It would have been so easy to lead these sweet creatures away to some cave like he did Apollo's. Though he didn't know this island as well as the lands he was born on. Much from the air to be seen were just coast, streams, meadows, and in some places, desert.

But laughing outside of being simply tickled by the hairs on the cushioned, wet noses would strike up as very odd as the men pulled him free of the bombardment. Being dragged a few feet wasn't enough — the cows just continued to amble forward, sniffing at his feet and ankles.

Odysseus ordered the crew to disperse at once. "Let's get them back to pasture, gods be willing," he said. "Lay no hand on them. Take a stick and attach with rope a bowl of grain; just a little. We'll walk them back the way they came."

Excited to get out of the little sanctuary they were trapped in for two weeks, the men quickly dressed and prepared the bait as their captain had instructed.

The woods weren't dense, but tall trees with heavy foliage atop kept the ground cool. Not much grew in terms of berry bushes and flowering plants along the dirt path they followed.

They weaved through the trunks in a staggered line, with Odysseus placing himself in the center, watching the trek with cautious eyes. He never returned Eurylochus' dagger, it remained tucked into his belt, wrapped in leather strips.

Hermes hopped himself to his side. Days of doing very little did some wonders to the lame leg; the hopping was more of a jack rabbit than a dying dog.

"Anastasios," Odysseus greeted. He cleared his throat and awkwardly pointed to the cattle who turned to look at the bronze-haired boy with a sparkle in their big, brown eyes. "Could you do me the greatest favor and go up front so the cows continue to walk? I don't believe we'll be making any progress if you're behind them."

"We can put the boy on the stick, sir. They may follow faster," Perimedes chimed in and roused a chuckle from the crew. Two humorously chuffed Hermes on the shoulder as he went around the cows, who gleefully followed him next to the bowl of delicious grain.

Delightful creatures. Rare, immortal ones.

Hermes recalled Helios' choosing only the strongest of the bunch, though they couldn't breed, and therefore the herds that roamed this island couldn't grow in number, but the sun god cherished and knew them all by name. They knew all the winding paths; meandering with the mortals for a good hour inland until gentle calls of friends, a resounding echo of *moos*, rose from a great opening in the trees. The dirt led way to fields of golden grass, flush with hay and clovers.

Every man gaped at the herds in front of them, scattered as far as the eye could see — hundreds of them in pristine condition, their winter coats shone with oil in the sun overhead. Yet Odysseus' shock was towards the sky around them. Where the sun overhead warmed the island, the white, puffy clouds curled and darkened heavily at the borders. They swirled and twisted angrily on the verge of calling lightning if the godly brothers so willed it. And beyond the scope of the island were clear skies and calm seas.

A circle of storms surrounded them alone.

The escorted cows graciously munched on the wheat they followed now that it dropped to the ground. Hermes found another, an oxen, also intrigued by the strange human who smelled very similar to their owner. Quietly he held his tongue as the ox nearly threw him with the force of his nose.

"There must be enough to feed every man, woman, and child in Ithaca," a man, Timon, said, stroking his hand across the fur of the one who had continued to visit them.

Odysseus hissed, "do not touch them — what have I said before? Do you want to be the cause of our demise?"

"Well, Anastasios has done so already, so if we are doomed, blame him!" Timon replied. He pointed at the boy. "He is riding one as we speak!"

Near three dozen faces turned to stare at Hermes as he steadied himself on the back of the ox. To be fair, it wasn't his fault that he happened to fall forward onto the thing instead of backward onto the ground. Odysseus' face struck horror.

"It ran its head between my legs, my lord," he explained. "If I didn't wish to be impaled, I had to roll over its back!"

"Well keep *rolling*, Anastasios!" Odysseus yelled.

"If I were to fall from this beast, I'd become lame in my other leg!" Hermes yelled back. The oxen was starting to walk away. He leaned down and looped his fingers around the wide neck; it had been a few hundred years since he rode on cattle. "You'd all mourn the curve of that leg, how masculine it is becoming."

"My friend," Odysseus said, with an immense sigh in his chest. He jogged along the beast and held out his hands. "Please, let us not tempt my mutinous crew with disobedience any more than they already have been."

Hermes fell into his arms. "Do not put the blame on me," he replied. "I'm simply a magnet for stupid creatures who wish to be stolen. Had I not already promised to never steal from my family, and if I were back to my glorious self, these would be ripe for the taking." Placing his cane firmly to the grass, he stood as straight as he could manage, looking Odysseus in the eye. "But I think it'd be too easy, and there's no fun in that."

Odysseus shook his head and quickly monitored the whereabouts of his men — they basked in the sun, sitting comfortably on the dry grass, enjoying the peace of the meadow. Then he looked out to the horizon.

"What do you make of that?" he asked.

"That's a very petty attempt to keep things under his control," Hermes answered without hesitation. "If my uncle relents, then he'll appear weak; and as a king *and* a middle child, well, appearing weak is his greatest concern."

"Then how can this end?" Odysseus tugged on his hair. "When will the suffering be put to rest?"

Hermes stared at the storm in its silence from atop the hilly, perpetual eye. Realistically, the mortals could not hope to survive on this island forever; they didn't have the time. Poseidon had all the time in the world. To wait a few weeks for them to starve was a blink of an eye from Mount Olympus, especially from a god who had lived for millennia.

But it wasn't Poseidon that Hermes thought would be the deciding factor.

"Ody," he said, "I think the only one who can truly set you free is the one who started this in the first place. Where did the anger stem from? What specifically did you do?"

"Well… I've told you, haven't I? I blinded his son —"

"No, not Lord Poseidon," Hermes turned to him. "I'm speaking of your former divine patron, Lady Athena."

The confusion that crossed Odysseus' face preceded a rush of blood to his cheeks. "What do you mean by that?"

"You allowed Ajax the Locrian to live after he committed blasphemy in raping that prophetess who pleaded to Athena for protection."

"I—"

"He was allowed to then board a ship and sail off, was he not?" Hermes cocked his head. He felt the ruffle of his own hair despite there being no breeze.

"I fought against that ruling. *Me* alone — I wanted to condemn him to death. I had the stone already in hand and I swore I'd be the first to throw. He… he hid from us in another temple, pleading innocence. Believe me, I was prepared to drag him out by his hair, but Agamemnon declared that my doing so would anger yet another god, and I was forced to withdraw," Odysseus exclaimed with growing dread. "I know Pallas Athena didn't like Ajax even before we raided Troy. She helped me win against him in Patroclus' funeral games — embarrassed him in front of the whole army. But it was Poseidon's storm who struck the son of Oileus down and sent our ships off course. Some of my men said they saw the trident rise from the waters themselves."

Hermes frowned. "My friend, it was Lady Athena who had asked that of him. She was the one to send our father's thunderbolt down upon your fleet and those of your allies. Yes, the king of the seas continued the fight, but it's the goddess of war you need to be seeking forgiveness from. *Whatever* you have done, whether it be simply that Locrian man's fate or if something else occurred between you two — appeal to her, and there may be an end to your suffering sooner than later."

Athena was never a goddess to speak much of her quarrels with humans, especially those who she once favored. But Odysseus was an all-around fine man; a clever, but tired human with a tendency for deceit and display of hubris. Yet he was attentive, and showed admission when he was in the wrong, which not many others could bring themselves to do. Certainly a quality even gods would dare not hone.

"I say all this," Hermes said, as Odysseus stood in his silence, watching the abyss between reality and the mind, "but I think you already knew it."

He shook his head again. "I did not."

"I think you did."

His grey eyes were too similar to Athena's — the calculating stare that could hide sorrow and shine with joy in the same quick look. Sure, Odysseus was Hermes' descendant three generations down, but he was Athena's protégé. And they probably quarreled like a parent and a child. That's why Odysseus has not heard from her since the war, and why Athena had no qualms against throwing lightning mere leagues from the mortals she fought besides, and immediately crushing others she disliked.

Hermes raised his hand at Odysseus' guilt-mongered composure. "I'm not asking for you to tell me what it is you did," he said. "But you must plead for Athena's mercy. At the very least, *speak* to her, even if she does not answer your prayers. She has great sway over the god king — far more than I do, she's his favorite."

She probably never had to be stuck in mortal form for so long either. Hermes' stomach was longing for ambrosia; he was dreaming about it. Immortals couldn't die of starvation, but damn did it feel like he could.

Clearing his throat, he let his hand fall on Odysseus' arm. "That is what I make of *that*," he answered, pointing back at Poseidon's siege of the island.

Chapter 10

On the twenty-first day on the island, the supplies from the ship ran dry.

Hermes curled up on his *hermock*, hugging his staff to his chest as he hid under his cloak. There was a faint weakness planted in his core. It could've been the longing for home, to drink and bathe in nectar, to bask in Olympus' golden glow. He didn't think immortals could get sick.

The crew frantically set traps around the woods, snatching small birds and waited by the water for any sign of fish. They must have been smart fish, knowing if they swam downstream they'd be speared. If a man could boil water angrily, Perimedes could get it done — trying to make some sort of tea out of the grasses he plucked from around the camp. It smelled awful, probably was going to taste like dirt.

A wide circle of trees had to be cut down to feed the three-week fire, though Hermes vigorously defended the ones he kept his inventions on. Only once did one floating bed fall from its supports, but the men were too fatigued to care about falling on top of each other; they'd fight about it in the morning until Odysseus peeled them away and sent both to do fruitless tasks.

Eurylochus sat on the rocks amid the men that often took up their oars near the front half of the ship where he laid charge. They sharpened their harpoons and curved more wire to fashion into hooks, and they did so with glowering faces.

With the arrival of the twenty-ninth day, Hermes awoke to shouting and bone hitting bone. A fight over a large river fish, caught between two spears. Hunger was ravaging their minds. Odysseus' voice, the only one of reason, berated them individually, like children. *Every meat caught was to be meat shared, even if the portions divided were minuscule.*

He was so bored.

A worse punishment than being stuck without his wings, without his palace, without his brothers and sisters to bother.

Human days were longer than he remembered.

Father, please, Hermes begged, pulling his knees up to his chin as his insides melted in flames. The bed curled around him. *Let this island prison be done with.*

An extra warmth piled atop his frame. The least he could do was peel an eye open.

"Ody," he said, the bright feathers behind the man's ear came into focus before his face did.

"We aren't losing you, are we?" Odysseus asked, pulling the tarp tighter around one tree trunk.

Hermes laughed dryly. "No," he said.

"Very persuasive."

"Immortals can't die like this."

"Is Anastasios immortal?"

"Of course he is," Hermes mumbled. "But he's unable to properly consume human food, as tasty as some can be so I've learned. So his stomach is noncompliant; and his muscles long to run and fly and-and-and not be sedentary. He's not made for that."

"I'm going to go inland to pray," Odysseus said. "That's all that's left for me to do now. We've reached the threshold of our sanity, I fear, and I don't wish for my comrades to resort to cannibalism. They'll probably try to eat you first."

"I would taste delicious," Hermes said with a tired hum. "Alas, they'd be disappointed to find my flesh poisonous. Perhaps the revelation will startle them back to their senses — that they've been teasing and prodding and..."

Odysseus picked the curl of hair from Hermes' eyes. "This effect on you isn't something you have prior knowledge on, is it?"

"I'm afraid I am the first for many things. Arguably this is better than being trapped in a bottle, or chained to a mountain as an eagle comes every day to eat of your guts, but," Hermes shrugged one shoulder.

The hand holding his hair up gently came back down to pat his head.

"I will return in a few hours. I'll pray for you, too."

"Very kind."

The warmth combed out of his hair, leaving the tarp swaying in the remnants of the southern wind pushing through the land. The grass around the camp was so dead from being stomped on and laid across that it cracked like sticks under Odysseus' feet.

Whispered between the trees, Hermes caught Eurylochus' gravelly voice.

"Captain, we need to speak of an incident that happened earlier in our trials," he said. He sounded nervous, the way he used to sound before little Anastasios joined the posse.

"I'll be back before the day's end, Eurylochus," Odysseus replied. There was a pause and further snapping of dry grass. "Keep the men in line. I'm going to make an appeal to all the gods on Olympus that one will show us mercy."

"Show you mercy, you mean."

"Eurylochus, just — just do as I say."

And with that there was silence. Silence that lasted for as long as Hermes could maintain a listening ear. An ear that heard the gurgling of water as it rushed past stone and hidden traps; the leaves above fluttering in the neverending storm, hanging onto their branches with all they had; the crackle of a low fire, tired of burning, wanting to rest; the absence of the birds' song, the lack of fishes' leaps, no cicada beckoning or even of mortals' keen laughter.

The shores of the Styx had more life than the little inhabited riverbed on the island of Helios.

Three hours later and the one noise that came up over all the ears in the clearing was the deep, wind-journeying *mooing* of the hundreds of cattle that grazed in various fields, a mere hike from where they all sat starving.

Someone stirred from their seat.

That wasn't good.

"Listen to me, friends, my tormented brothers," Eurylochus spoke and all fatigue washed away from Hermes as if he heard the sound of the bugle. "Every way to die is dreadful, there is no denying that." He walked between the men, who raised their chins him with every ounce of energy they had remaining.

Hermes lifted his head from his resting place. Several knuckles cracked as he gripped the cane kept under his blankets.

"But to die by inches — to starve *slowly* to death — that is the worst of all. I can see it in all of you and you can see it in me, how we are withering away. So rise with me now, let us select our choice from the herds, a few of the several hundred here. We will slaughter them and give half to the gods who rule over us. If we ever make it home to Ithaca's shores, we shall erect a marvelous temple to the lord of the Sun and line its walls with glorious gifts!" Eurylochus raised up his arms, his chest heaving in its exalting. "But should he be furious with us for doing what we *must* to survive, destroying our ship before we reach our home, well… I would rather die at sea, swallowed by Poseidon's waves, than perish on a sickening island here by hunger."

To Hermes' horror, the crew cheered at their second-in-command's speech.

Every single one of them rose with anticipation for the great feast they were to have in the matter of hours. They collected rope and blades, some went to the beach to prepare a separate site for sacrifices. Hermes rolled himself off the bed, stumbling on the dirt that intermingled with the fecal smell of three dozen men over the course of a month.

There wasn't anything he could do — but Odysseus had to be warned. This was the one condition that the prophet gave them.

A tight-fisted, rough hand clawed itself into Hermes' hair and pulled him up by the roots like he were moly in the ground.

"And I think we've found the easiest way to rouse those oxen to follow us!" the man said, tugging Hermes back.

The instinct he had to turn this mongrel into furniture came out of his human mouth as a pained snarl, and he swung his cane down upon the man's shin. Gold did not feel like wood, and a heavy caduceus didn't leave the flat bruise a solid stick would. The man yowled, throwing Hermes away from him into another's grasp — a terrible game where he was the ball.

"You'd benefit from a real meal, you know," Perimedes said. "The captain's taken a fair liking to you; wouldn't want you starving either."

"Your captain told you not to touch the cattle, nor the sheep. You swore an oath! You all swore an oath, you fools!" Hermes shouted back. If they killed the cattle, they were doomed — if they *killed* the cattle, they were *doomed* — if they were *doomed* then he couldn't *guide* them home.

He could see the lines being drawn from the Fates to these men, even as they gagged him with a strip of leather to stop him from calling out to their king; those strings were fishing lines coated in blood, dozens of them skyrocketing to the heavens.

It was always meant to be this way.

How the knowledge crumbled his heart, that Zeus knew the men could not resist trying for everything to not die a miserable death against a heinous enemy such as Hunger.

Hermes' hands were bound, bait on a stick to coax unsuspecting cows from their pasture. He glared at Eurylochus, who carried more rope over his shoulder, the two of them at the front of the line that encircled one field.

They rounded up a few of the best ones they could find, ones with lovely horns and innocent eyes. The oxen nuzzled up to Hermes, moths to his unwilling flame, pitter-pattering across the dirt to the sand where the remaining crew waited with bated breath with their knives and spits.

Hermes' skin was buzzing, being tied to a post of the beached ship like a horse that would run away at a moment's notice. He ground his teeth into the leather bit and seethed with every pull of his bindings. A groan came from the black ship as it dug deeper into the wet sand. The ocean licked his ankles.

Poseidon surely would know he was on the island now.

"Stop!" he ordered between the gag, his feet kicking up several inches from the ground as the lightness under the curls of his hair returned.

But the men paid no mind. They prayed to gods that wouldn't hear them instead of heeding the one in their midst. They brought the blades to the cows fleshy throats and carved deep into them, one by one, filling the sand with their blood as the immortal beasts cried out one last time.

Oh, to see immortal creatures be slaughtered at the hands of humans, Hermes lamented. And the humans sliced them up and skinned them like they did at any feast. They used water as a libation as there was no more wine, their voices like tiny, useless whispers in the back of Hermes' head. The smell of the meat wafted inside a great smoke — the cloud blackened as it curled into the heavens.

And the sun that always pleasantly drove across the blue sky suddenly went dark.

And day became night as if the chariot simply dropped from the clouds.

Poor Odysseus staggered onto the beach, his eyes already wet with tears as he screamed out at his men. The words were probably in agony, spoken in distressed horror. Hermes couldn't hear anything but the buzzing in his head that grew louder and softer with the waves that washed onto shore. Why was he gone for so long? *Dear Ody, what kept you? Was it my Father? He does as the Fates recommend so many times.*

To each man, Odysseus grabbed a fistful of their tunics, their armor, their hair, and pulled them to his face. His ire rolled out in groans and pleas — what mutiny, what utter betrayal his own men committed while he begged for their release. What a hypocrite they made of him to the gods themselves!

Hermes couldn't keep his head straight, trying to pay attention to the scene unfolding in front of him while his mind sent tiny shocks through his body.

And then—

Olympus.

Zeus' palace, shadowed for the first time in Hermes' life, the halls filling with bellowing anger. There was that holy chariot, the one that rivaled Apollo's in the sky.

Helios stood in his blinding golden armor at Zeus' throne, his face too emblazoned to look at, but his words were known: retribution or consequence. The sun would shine for Hades if something was not done.

And Hermes then felt his whole body shudder as Zeus opened his mouth and replied, "Sun, you'll continue to shine over Mount Olympus and for the mortal men across the green of the earth. As for the guilty ones," he chuckled, "soon enough they'll take to the sea and I'll strike their racing ship down and tear it to splinters. They'll feel no more of your warmth. Is that satisfactory for the loss of your herds?"

Zeus leaned forward on his throne with a patient smile as Helios thought up his response. His golden eyes flickered beyond the sun god to where Hermes observed his own presence waiting, and the young god felt his chest grow tight.

"Are you satisfied?" Zeus asked again.

Hermes did not need to breathe, but he gasped, snapping back into his own senses. His eyes rolled back to see the beach and the bitterly weeping men shove and point fingers at one another. The sweat running down his arms from his palms soaked the rope at his wrists, and the flax abraded his skin until what was once soft turned blistered and red.

The image of a decimated ship flashed in his periphery, and he did his utmost best to ignore it as Odysseus took his turn yelling at Eurylochus, the man's clothing gripped like iron in Odysseus' hands. A betrayal of a brother of all things. A brother led them all to their ruin.

Pulling harder on the binding while the tide rose to tug at his knees, Hermes ripped one hand free with a crack and a groan. The wrist popped itself back into place, falling to his side as the rope noosed itself around his other. *If he gnawed his own hand off, it would grow back — eventually.*

Quick splashing of legs to the foaming, cold water and Odysseus was there, knife in hand to cut him free. His poor face was stained wine pink, the tears rolling with the rain that spat down on them from the clouds overtaking the rest of the darkened island. He said very little while he cut his pitiful great grandsire free and carried him to the drier sands, his own knees crumbling beneath him as he shook. But he quickly dug into his bag and pulled out that silly, green hat to fold over Hermes head.

"Your wings," Odysseus breathed pathetically, astonished through his woe. Hermes put his hand to the side of the hat, where the gentle feathers between his hair curled up warmly. "Hermes, can you get us out of here? Please, I beg you."

The young god looked at his palms. They were still human despite slowly healing from superficial wounds. Everything else was still human; and he had no talaria to carry more than himself a few yards at a time. "I'll still get *you* home, Ody, I promised that," he said. "I don't break my oaths."

He took the large hands that grasped onto the sides of his face and held them tightly. There was a painful growl from Odysseus' stomach, the smell from the roasts was awfully enticing. And the men, despite their scolding, continued to feast on the meat and taste the inner organs.

Having Odysseus so near the water felt improper; Lord Poseidon could rise from the next wave and pull the poor soul beneath the tide. Hermes tucked his arms under Odysseus' frame and lifted, the pain in his leg that kept him lame had disappeared like an old bruise. A few paces from the mutineers, but on the upper half of the beach, the two laid restless in the sand.

If it didn't kill Odysseus, Hermes would let the man eat him. It was the least he could do for being such a failure. The temporary pain would be some sort of atonement for the embarrassment he was feeling.

He kept touching his head. Those speckled feathers were so dear to him, as if two limbs were amputated for weeks, and took so long to grow back. The feather cuff around Odysseus' ear stuck out from his own hat, which flattened his long hair over his eyes.

But what was there to see? The same drudgery as always. Odysseus pressed his fingers into his sockets and took another shuddering breath, the names of his family still at the forefront of his tongue.

The morning after the slaughter — *or was it?*

Who could tell without the sun coming over the island? It skirted around the beach, a red haze in the distance covered by the clouds. Helios and his grudges were seen by all; and what a shame it was to insult the lord who provided the light and warmth to the land.

Hermes climbed to the tops of the tall trees further inland, where he plucked the few figs that grew where Man didn't think to reach, hovering for as long as he could until his arms were full. He brought the fruit to Odysseus and didn't speak a word of it to the others as they only continued to roast and flick the bones into the flames.

By the evening, there came a horrendous moaning from the fire as the meat rotated over the embers. The moaning curled like the lowing of the oxen, not only from the flames but from the raw flesh that sat in covered bowls. It filled the cave — a nightmare come to life.

Even Hermes' lip curled at the display, witnessing the skinned hides crawl along the sand like sea slugs dragging their way to nowhere. It was obscene, an idea that Hera would concoct to torment unruly mortals, and executed by Dionysus in his youthful madness.

The men watched as they ate, and Eurylochus dared to approach the thing and suppress the movement with a stone before retreating back to the other side of the fire. Those dark eyes of his flicked back to Hermes and Odysseus, but his expression was unreadable: contempt? Rage? Forbearance? His arms lay limp by his sides, his chest sunken.

Eurylochus went about throwing the covered raw meat into a bag to tie off instead of letting them moan and cry from wooden bowls. No grip mightier than the one he kept on the string of the sack, as if he let it go, all the noise would forever escape to torment them.

It was him, all that time ago.

Hermes slid his knuckle between his teeth and bit down on the bone.

The sand crunched as Odysseus sat up, cracking his knuckles against his knees. It didn't take long for him to notice the golden-brown eyes boring a hole in the side of his face. An unspoken communication: Hermes' look. Odysseus worked his jaw, breathed through gritted teeth, and shook his head.

If he were to believe it, what good would it do now?

"Tell me what you're thinking?"

Odysseus shook his head again.

"Ody, tell me."

"I could've had my wife and son in my arms by now," he replied through tight lips. "Gods damn me — I could've had a second child at this time, wrapped in fur, drinking from Penelope's breast. I'd be teaching my boy everything he should know to be a man while experiencing what it's like to be… to be a *father*. What will Telemachus think of me? Will he think I abandoned him? Would my wife remarry and be stolen away from my — from *his* court?"

"I'm," Hermes said quietly, "not always the most *attentive* father." He peeled another pear for Odysseus. "But when I can, I like to see what mischief my offspring are up to, for that tends to be an inherited trait." He wiggled his nose. "Not every god does that, but we know when our children need us, when they call to us. *Obviously* that hasn't put you in a good spot when Poseidon's son pleaded for him to avenge his loss, but… if you're longing for your boy, doesn't that make you a good father?"

Odysseus folded his arms across his knees and tucked his chin inside, seemingly unconvinced.

"Telemachus may not realize how much you're fighting to get to him, but when you see him, he'll know. And all the time spent in worry and doubt on both of your parts will be thrown aside the moment he's in your arms. You are *humans*; it's in your nature to feel all these things. *Hope* will keep him watching the horizon for your ship, and hope will drive your queen to remain steadfast until your return."

"You sound very confident with that," Odysseus sighed.

"I was there to deliver the box that held all your realms troubles," Hermes exclaimed. It was one of his first tasks at his father's behest. "Despair is still locked away. You, my dear friend, are to hope just as strongly that your family will caress you once more. Maybe the honorable Penelope of Sparta will be waiting with a bath, fresh oil, and a damn comb for your hair. Shameful, Odysseus, that you've allowed the treachery and agonizing tribulations to distract you from upkeeping your usually immaculate grooming."

A tired smile forced an even more exhausted chuckle from him. "I'll keep that image in my dreams to persevere."

"I shall keep the image of you with your crown and silks, seated on your proper throne in mine," Hermes replied. "It'll please me very much if I was the first libation you pour at the celebratory feast you host."

"For you, son of Zeus, anything."

* * *

The terror on the beach went on for six entire days until all the meat was gone and the men began their arguing again. No one paid any attention as the tide pulled back, dropping beautiful shells and abandoning crabs to scurry back to the water. The waves had settled to silence; the silence rumbled in their ears, contending for the spotlight great Helios provided, sun shining through the parting clouds beyond the island as if there were no malice done.

Hermes fluttered to his feet, analyzing the speed at which the storm dissipated.

That wasn't right.

It was Eurylochus who was the first to recognize that the ocean was calm enough to leave. His unscrupulous energy roused the crew and a great cheer rose, stirring their captain who laid hungry on the sand.

No command was given. A few of the men climbed aboard the boat, discarded the debris that covered the deck and pulled up their reliable oars from the hold. Many cared little for the chests left up at the river camp, the call of Ithaca was more enticing than the few things they had on them. Odysseus stared at the water; it was too odd, and Hermes agreed — the gods were up to something.

If Hermes were on the ship, nothing of great disaster could happen; if he were standing among the Ithacans on the deck, with their captain and king in the rear... Not as if he had a choice.

The black ship was being hauled back into the harbor within the hour.

Odysseus had climbed aboard, one hand firmly wrapped around Hermes' slight wrist, as if he were to let go, Hermes would bail on him now after all they had been through. If anything, he would forget that he was capable of some flight again and begin to float off like a kite. The breeze was pleasant and finally came from the correct direction: a straight path towards Greece's Ionian islands.

It was almost too perfect.

The static in the young god's head rose in pitch and ventured off to cling to his bones. Hermes puckered his lips and forced out a breath as the sails were unfurled at Odysseus' hesitant order.

He didn't hold onto his cane for support, it was tucked under his arm like he usually held his caduceus when not using it. Nausea bubbled up his throat, and maybe he should've placed it down. But he dug his nails into the top of the captain's chair and blew out another breath.

Thrinacia shrank behind them, brightening with golden sun the further the ship sailed. A pinprick of light on their backs and the empty void of the ocean in their sight, Hermes felt like he was on a ship in a bottle. His hand flung to the vial around his neck and the six specks of sand that waited patiently to be delivered.

His head filled with static again.

Odysseus lifted his cheek from his weary knuckles. "What do you mean?" he asked.

Hermes blinked. "Mean about what? I... I haven't spoken."

"You asked if I was done," Odysseus said, pulling his brows taut. "And I suppose, yes, I certainly feel like I am. With what I cannot be sure, but you know what *I* mean."

"I do," Hermes nodded, but the nodding turned to denying, "but I did not speak."

The static shoved itself under his tongue.

"I believe this has gone on long enough," the voice came from Hermes, but the message was not his own.

The young god fell back, clapping his hands over his mouth while Odysseus ripped himself from his chair, the grey of his eyes so bright and full he looked like the moon.

"Hermes?"

"Forgive me," Hermes muttered, looking to the sky as the clouds returned. An immense squall hurled itself against the sails, cracking the mast and tearing out every stitch that the sailors had mended. *Pop, pop, pop.*

Around them, the waters churned black like ink from a great monster or the hair of Poseidon himself, but the panic Hermes felt was not for any arrival of Poseidon — it was the crackling of thunder rolling strongly overhead.

Chapter 11

A murderous blast deafened the men as the forestays keeping the mast steady shattered into pieces. The great pole careened backward towards the stern. Hermes flew to tackle Odysseus from his horror-stricken daze, the two of them rolling to the deck alongside the men. The mast barrelled down into the helmsman, his skull crushed open like an egg and left his body flopping lifelessly down next to them. Blood splattered out to mix with the seawater. Hermes continued to pull Odysseus further away from the stern as the dead man's soul chased after them to hide within Hermes' vial.

"Stop!" Hermes shouted, his call among dozens as the crew screamed and clung to each other. This wasn't fair. They were stupid, but this wasn't fair.

Odysseus was without words, gawking at the sky as arms of lightning peeled open the clouds and the very essence of the lord of the skies, king of the gods, the mighty Zeus, loomed over the ocean.

He was massive, a storm in his entirety to the mortals far below — a step away from his primordial form that would've melted the eyes of any that looked upon him. To Hermes, he saw the drawn face between the clouds and lightning. Zeus' lips opened, and from it, the static in Hermes' mouth made him speak his father's words, hot ichor trickling from his tongue, *"Say goodbye. You've had your fun, but now it is time to go."*

"Hermes!" Odysseus cried, he clung to the young god's arm as the dull skin glowed from underneath. "Don't leave me, please."

"I— I don't want to leave you," Hermes replied, snapping back. He wiped the ichor from his lips, and through the storm, as it shrieked and the ship lurched, called to the sky, "Father, have mercy, they're just human!"

The very air rumbled around them.

"They've aggrieved Helios and I have made the deal to carry out their punishment so that their kind may bask another day in light. Now take yourself to Olympus —"

The tattered clothes he wore shifted and pulled back to his fine silks and delicate threads, but Hermes would not move even as the lightning smashed next to the ship. Zeus hadn't sent down his thunderbolt, there was still time.

"No! Father," he pleaded through a pinched throat. "I witnessed the atrocity wrought upon the sun lord's fine cattle, but it was only done in desperation. Badly done, yes, but I've come to understand mortal's th—"

There was a horrible hiss that drowned out Odysseus' panicked shout. As the hairs on Hermes' arm stood straight, the world turned into a blinding white light.

A blink — more pain than he had ever felt before in his whole existence. His golden skin burned until ichor poured out of the smallest holes that the lightning tore across his body.

So this was fear of *death*, as he crumbled to his knees. A bloodied god, revealed to the men just as he vomited out the ichor that coursed through him onto their ship. If it were Zeus' thunderbolt, he'd be dead; in an instant, Hermes would've burned up like the pile of feathers and parchment he was.

Even in his anger, Zeus was merciful.

Guess he was supposed to feel grateful.

Odysseus clamoured to reach him, and he looked so much smaller now with his crew as Hermes held up his god sized hand to stop him.

"Do not touch me," he commanded. The last thing he wanted was for his friend to be poisoned by his lifeblood. His heart sent pang after pang through his body; each beat more agonizing than the last.

"Hermes," Odysseus breathed before Hermes was plucked up by Zeus' immense fingers, grasped like a bird, and thrusted into the clouds, leaving the poor mortals to their fate.

He tumbled into the scattered visage, eaten even, caught surrounded by the lightning that made up the god king's form. The space where he fell was tiny, and he was shoved into it like mail in a bag. Ichor continued to pour out from his burned skin to scathe the rest of him. In the quiet of this jail, he looked onto the continued destruction of the ship. A body was thrown into the sea and pale arms raised up for help.

He whimpered out another plea.

"Father, my king, I beg you. The son of Laertes didn't partake in the slaughter of Helios' cattle; he never touched them. He's not guilty, he doesn't deserve this punishment."

"No, but you *do, don't you?"*

"Let my punishment be my own, and I'll serve it without complaint –– but please, Father, this man is my kin; you don't need to kill him! You have a *choice*, great Father, for Helios can't find this man at fault. Odysseus is a good man. He longs for his home. He deserves a chance, he's lost so much already."

Despite the silent response that pierced his ears, the prison cage that kept him immobile moved slowly, and the bitter, blue lighting shifted gold and calming. The shape crushed Hermes' knees uncomfortably against his cheek.

Zeus was changing appearance and he was stuck inside of him.

A good man.

The bemused thought from his father ripped through Hermes' head. He fluttered his wings to get some air to lungs he didn't really need to fill.

Nearly human sized: that's what Zeus shifted to, and from his eyes, the ship that hung onto its beams with single nails, and the few men that were left scattered on its deck, were cast in the king's holy glow.

"Odysseus," a gentle voice cooed out — and it wasn't Zeus' although it came from his throat. It was the voice of a woman, a woman who the mortal king knew intimately.

Hermes wept. This was a cruel trick.

"Penelope," Odysseus whispered. He pulled himself to his feet, his shins blistered and bleeding.

"Would you give me up to save your brothers?" Penelope asked, her arms held out to receive a forlorn husband. "If you were to choose now, my love, to live forever at sea with the men who fought with you… or just a few more years by my side…"

Hermes kicked at the prison walls, shoving Zeus' stomach with the pointed end of his staff. "You twist my words!"

And poor Odysseus, weary and worn, wobbled slowly to his wife's warmth. She was the oasis in the desert he was lost in. "Penelope, I've lived only to see you again," he replied, and Zeus held him to his breast.

"Won't you kiss me, then? If that is your choice?"

Hermes heard the distant and desperate cries of the crew. Eurylochus and his terrified rage, clawing at the ship to keep himself and his brothers-in-arms afloat. There were their prayers, flooding into his mind —

Hermes, guide us home.

Hermes, tell my wife I love her.

Hermes, send this mirage away.

Hermes, please.

Hermes, help.

Hermes!

The golden Penelope took Odysseus' face between her hands, gently wiping the tears from his lashes, and tucked her nose to his, waiting. It was his choice to make, his move to play.

And he did.

He kissed the image of his wife, to be with her for even just a moment over living eternally with his comrades whose dying curses to him went spiraling to sea. The ship cracked and splintered, left in utter darkness as Zeus' Penelope slipped from Odysseus' fingers.

A good man, Zeus laughed.

The wooden planks ripped from the keel as the deadly thunderbolt came crashing down upon the center of the ship. In the shadows of Hermes' prison, his cloak sputtered with new stars, one after another, a dozen… two dozen… Every man he once knew, rejoining each other in the vacuum of Hermes' split-tailed cloak. He wept harder, watching heart-broken Odysseus scramble around the ship, grasping onto ropes and calling out his name over the whipping winds.

"Hermes, are you still with me? Hermes!"

"Odysseus," Hermes said aloud, hoping he could hear him in the fathomless depths of Zeus, but the image of the sea was fading, shrinking until the destroyed ship looked like a tiny toy in waters that swallowed it up piece by piece. And he heard no more prayers, no more thunder or roaring waves.

Just him and his twinkling souls and the endless tight blackness around him.

He blew out a breath and pulled up his cloak, bringing the iridescent fabric to his eyes, and counted every star; the bold ones, the dim ones, the ones that flickered with impatience or worry, the six that had already been waiting for so long…

I've got you, he thought. *Odysseus, I have them.*

As treacherous as they had been, they were just human.

* * *

Ephemeral, or rather, it *could've* been an eternity, but from where the sun was in the sky when Hermes was dumped onto his palace courtyard, it *must've* only been minutes.

The marble flooring froze his burnt skin to the tiles, glowing ichor scattering all over. A hiss slipped through as he peeled his cheek from it, struggling to put a knee between, to rise and face his father.

The draping blue fabric drifted by, still sparking with bits of lightning between the weaves. Zeus paced and he didn't pace often.

"You've made me a liar," Hermes gasped. The puddle of ichor that dripped from his face reflected the seared skin above it.

"It'll not bother you long, a liar is what you are," Zeus replied, scratching at his beard.

The scampering of the palace nymphs halted as they caught sight of the two gods; the halls had been empty for far too long without its winged master fluttering among them.

Zeus knelt down by Hermes' side and twisted off some of the chiton's melted fabric from his son's skin. "Fetch Apollo," he said to the nymphs.

"Tell him to cease his mourning and bring his supplies. His brother is home."

Hermes wanted to stop the tears from bubbling up and pouring over his lashes. They stung his cheeks and made him weak in his anger. "Father, have I not always done as you've asked of me? Could I not have this one thing?"

"Because I favor you is why you're at home and not strung up in a bird cage somewhere over the mountains of Egypt," Zeus said. He gently laid his hand on one of Hermes' bare ankles, his voice tender. "But you lied to *me*, of all people. And you're more clever than that! You know how I'm trying to calm the quarrel with Poseidon, and yet you go to aid the mortal he seeks to punish."

"He is of my lineage," Hermes hiccuped, too wounded to move, so he continued to cry toward the ground. *He was my friend.*

"Oh, my dear boy. I too have mourned mortal sons and grandsons of mine whose fates were out of my hands. I've witnessed you carry them to Hades and could do nothing about it."

"But I *could* do something. I *was* doing something!" To shout only brought up more ichor that stained the floor gold. It shifted to an ugly shade of black the longer it was left to congeal.

Zeus patted Hermes' back, as if that would offer any help.

"If I'd allowed you to bring that man to Ithaca now, Poseidon would never forgive me. I've told you, Hermes, that our love for one another must *always* come before our liking for mankind. We are forever, our relationships must persevere. Mortals live because of us, and so we must continue to maintain our strength and reputations."

His hand shook as he wiped his mouth, unable to grasp at what nonsense his father was speaking. "I thought that mortals were created so we had reason to exist at all. Without them, without their worship to the pantheon, what good are us gods?"

Zeus' passive expression twitched. His sigh was deep, shaking the walls as he got to his feet and released Hermes' leg. "Perhaps it's because you are still to reach your first millennia, you don't yet understand, so I won't hold it against you. But let me make this perfectly clear: We existed before humans and we will exist after them."

At that time, the palace gate opened and Apollo rushed in with the nymphs right on his heel. Clothed in cream and lavender, his golden hair left unkempt and sprigged with hyacinth bulbs — his mourning clothes, as he assigned it centuries ago. He staggered to a stop at the sight of them. His lips parted, but he bowed his head without a word.

Dismissing himself from his fatherly affections, Zeus paused at Apollo's side and gestured back to his groveling son. "Hermes was caught in one of my storms. Take care of him and put him to bed," he exclaimed.

Apollo's skin went white as he vigorously nodded, and sent his nymphs to collect more linens.

When Zeus left the palace, Apollo's cracking voice escaped from his throat.

"Great heavens, Hermes, what have you gotten yourself into?" he cried, running over to fall on his knees. Very delicate hands probed at his brother's face, picking up his cheek and jaw to look him over. Apollo had readable expressions, a welcome change even though he winced and scowled and titted as he wept at the state of Hermes' body. "I haven't seen you in... in..." he blubbered, lowering himself even more to embrace him.

"You'll ruin your clothes," Hermes muttered.

"Let them be stained," Apollo replied. "I hold the ones I love." He glanced to the steps, of the length they would have to travel to get Hermes back to his bed chambers. The palace handmaidens returned en masse to the courtyard. "You two, go prepare a lukewarm bath; you, take the aloe from my things and start preparing it, leave the gel in a cold pan. Hermes, can you w — oh."

Hermes struggled just enough to grasp his brother's shoulder in a vain attempt to kneel upright. "What?"

Apollo let his hand glide down the singed calf where Zeus had gripped. Tightly embracing the ankle bone was a golden cuff, and attached to this cuff was a chain. The chain linked on for a few feet before fading into the ether.

"I believe you have been grounded," Apollo said, grimacing as he tried to lift one chainlink.

Hermes cried to look back at his foot, his skin throbbed like a thousand hearts. He heaved until he felt sick, but there was nothing in his stomach, so he convulsed and groaned out more tears.

Apollo shook his hands. "No, no, little god, it is alright, all will be well, I… I will help carry it if you can help me carry you. How's that? Your feathers are still present and I know you hover so nimbly."

"It hurts." Hermes shook his head, but he worked to rise anyway. Apollo cupped one arm under his and with his other, heaved up on the chain. Its strange rattling sounded distant and deep.

"I know."

With assistance from several nymphs, they managed to get Hermes up into his chambers, where everything had been prepared multiple times through the weeks in case he came home. No steam rose from the bath, but the water was already soapy, and Hermes watched the bubbles float around as Apollo and their nymphs worked on carefully peeling his clothes from his chest and back. One returned from the courtyard with his caduceus in hand, another carefully hung up his cloak by his bed, gentle with the starry lining.

He'd never bring souls up to Olympus; it was an incomplete job.

The bathwater shifted yellow when he was lowered in, cuffed foot propped on the edge, and Apollo washed his skin. A goblet of nectar was brought, the scent alone was hypnotic to him, and he choked it down to fill his insides. It aided in the pain, but the wounds from Zeus weren't going anywhere anytime soon, even with the god of medicine applying salve to every burn.

After forty minutes, it was as if Hermes had physically never gone down to the mortal realm; his hair was cleaned and combed, his body ached, but was fed. Although his skin was wrapped in bandages, it was free from the salt of the ocean and dirt of the ground, and of the ichor that fell from his burns. A loose robe was draped over his shoulders and Hermes laid in his bed.

Feathered mattress, silk sheets — all things he missed. A heavy tear tumbled down one cheek while he lay silent. His room was cleared and cleaned, ready for similar treatments for the days ahead. Apollo rinsed his hands and applied oil to his wrists, quietly ordering the maidens about for music and ambrosia. He looked very fine in his purples, Hermes thought. The first time he recalled seeing the color on his brother, he was hardly into his second century and Apollo was into his fourth.

"Consider yourself lucky that you will be fed by the most handsome of the gods," Apollo said, climbing up onto Hermes' bed to lay at his side. The strum of a lyre sounded from beyond the chamber door.

Hermes peeled his lips apart, the words coming to him before he could think about their strength. "You love humans, don't you, Brother?" he asked. His voice sounded better once the nectar healed his throat, but it was a pathetic whisper.

Apollo spun his finger around a bronze curl. "I do. Some more than others, you know this. Many of us love humans."

"But yours was something more — something different. Like that Hyacinthus. The pretty man who chose you over all others, who died in your arms."

"I… yes, he… that was my fault. I could not help him."

"You pleaded to Father to make you mortal," Hermes said. "You loved him so dearly, you wanted to die with him too." Apollo's blooms within his hair were the very flower formed from his lover's blood.

The god frowned, raised his face from the pillow and sighed out, "Maybe I should leave you to rest; this is quite the unpleasant conversation." But a shaking hand weakly gripped his fingers.

"Please, Apollo, I want to know why I care so much." Hermes blinked through his tears. "Not even for those I find pleasing — for all of them; their vanities and humility, their adoration and hate… My heart feels so heavy, but Father, he —"

"Hermes," Apollo said. He laid back down, combing his nails through the curls. "We have lived for fractions of what the first gods lived, of course we would view the mortal realm differently. Think of their domains, those of the ocean, of seasons, the sky and fire… All these things exist without humanity, yes?"

Hermes looked up at his brother through singed lashes. The light that radiated from him was serenity.

"Even our elder siblings of war, violent or tactical, I care little of the specifics; their domains involve us squabbling amongst ourselves. But you, my dear, shrewd little brother," Apollo continued, "what lies in your domain?"

"I'm a trickster," Hermes replied, but Apollo hushed him.

"I am monologuing, it was rhetorical."

"Sorry… Continue."

He placed out his hand and counted in front of Hermes' face. "You are an inventor: of instruments I love so that they all love in tandem, of human language from their written to their conversation and song; you protect the shepherds and their lifegivings, as well as the roads they take in travel; you give mortals both rest and boundless energy; you carry their very essence to and from their world. Do you not understand what you are, Hermes?"

His chest protested against expanding while tears just continued to flow over his bandages.

"My clever, stupid boy, are you not a *god of Man? * Is not *everything you are* tied so intricately to humanity? Dare I say, the only one of us who is on the earth more than you is our little brother; and he goes to revel in many mortals' rituals and customs that you began. Probably bathes in wine on the daily. Artemis and I dabble with mortals, for certain, they have much to offer. But you, Hermes, care because that is who you are. Make one man rich beyond belief, greatly humble another — you walk among them like you belong there because, in part, you do. Why do you think our father gifted you those winged sandals?"

"They're far lighter than this," Hermes said, unable to lift the chain around his ankle.

Apollo hummed. "This punishment will not last forever. Father's ego has been bruised and he stresses over our family's state. We are still recovering from the war's transgressions. And you must recover from…"

"My run in with a storm?"

"Yes, that. I'll be with you every day until it heals."

"How long does it take to heal from *lightning*, anyway?" His throat was beginning to hurt again. With a sniffle, he tucked his cheek to Apollo's chest, nearly lulled by his massaging hands. There weren't many comparable cases of gods being struck by Zeus' lightning. His thunderbolt, yes, and those beings then ceased to exist.

"With an abundance of ambrosia and all of my *love*, we will have you on your feet in no time," Apollo said, nuzzling his nose into the feathers that unfurled with Hermes' tired laughter. "And there will be no sign of burns on that handsome face of yours."

The lyre continued to play for the daytime hours, the sky outside growing rosy and dim. Hermes drifted in and out of a restless sleep.

A god of Man, he thought, yes that made sense. But that meant he was failing that too.

His cloak glowed in the candlelight, the horrible reminder; its colors cast right through his eyelids. Thirty-eight stars drifted like fish in a sea of limbo. He knew the souls could feel the calm around them, but their inner thoughts would be so full of turmoil. It took the Underworld to begin to relieve them of their strife.

"Are you brooding?" Apollo asked.

"Of course not," Hermes lied.

"Well, stop it."

The sun rose and fell and rose again, Helios on his regular timetable.

Inside the palace of the Messenger, nymphs from its walls and Apollo's worked on transforming it into an oasis for the infirmed. Having stairs and high levels that a flying god couldn't traverse while grounded was terribly inconvenient. Linens were cleaned and brought through the neighboring gates with more herbs and cooling ointments. It garnered plenty of attention from the lesser gods who tried to peek in windows to see the Olympian who broke the rules.

In his rage, Apollo sent blinding light from the halls, scaring away all who attempted.

Only other Olympians were allowed to enter, and few made that journey in the forthcoming weeks.

Artemis arrived first in her hunting attire, slipping away from her duties to make a call. With her she brought her dames who carried pots of mountain spring water, cold enough that the young women wore gloves to protect their hands. It was a discreet gift that Zeus would scold about rushing the healing process, but the Leto twins were not going to let anyone stop them from fulfilling their kindness to the young god who spared their mother.

It was Ares who came a few days later with Aphrodite wrapped around his arm, thus completing the old Trojan faction of the war in being the first to visit. Ares provided plenty of compliments for Hermes standing his ground, fool-hearted as it was. He eyed the heavy cuff around Hermes' ankle and ran his palm against the grain of his sheared hair before Aphrodite took it, and provided Hermes with a gentle kiss while she cast calm over the little palace.

Dionysus, the youngest of them, with his crown of ivy and grape vines twisting down his berry-colored hair, a single himation thrown over his shoulder, was the last to visit within the month. He brought with him the fleece of a ram from the earth, left draped over a chair for Hermes to run his hand through from his bath. The color was too familiar to Odysseus'. He hated it; he loved it.

While the bandages on Hermes' arms were replaced, Dionysus rambled on about what the mortals were doing, how some returning home from the war were going a *little* crazy, while others settled perfectly content with their families. In either sense, festivals and feasts and funeral games were raging and Dionysus found no boredom to be had.

Hermes grunted as Apollo flipped him onto his stomach to address the fern-shaped scar that proved to be quite difficult to heal. "Dio," he said, taking the generous serving of nectar from his brother, "how far have you traveled these weeks? Have you seen the son of Laertes among any of the peoples?"

Dionysus cocked his head, rolling his drink between two fingers, and tapped the rim to his lips thoughtfully. "A son of Laertes," he hummed. "I cannot say I have. That is your Odysseus, yes? The short one with thick hair and skin luscious enough to bite into?"

Hermes blinked. "Yes, that one."

"Mm. No, haven't seen him. *Although!* There have been some mild celebrations in that kingdom of his. I believe the prince was gifted with many things for his anniversary of birth. There are also a handful of youths on that island without fathers, I've noted. Little jackasses, several of them."

Apollo poured the cold water over Hermes' skin and followed it with the aloe. Hermes held the goblet out in front of him, face pressed into the pillows while every muscle in his body flinched at the touch.

"It's a generation of young men who will be very ill-disciplined," Apollo said, shaking his head. "Until we must intervene to put them in their places."

Adolescents playing fools were a dime a dozen. Unless they were absolutely blasphemous, the gods typically could wait for them to venture a step into adulthood before turning them into whatever flea-bitten animal suited their nature.

Hermes turned his cheek. "But you've seen the prince? He's well? Have you stayed as a guest in the halls or were you just passing through like you always seem to do?"

"My goodness," Dionysus laughed. "I didn't expect to be interviewed, I would have brought more drink. There *was* an air of melancholia, but the health of the mortals were unblemished. You really do worry about that family. My good brother, why don't you call for Hypnos? Have him turn off your anxious thoughts."

Oh if only he could in good conscience do that; the idea that he could go back to laughing and causing inconsequential mischief, running the fields and hosting a new round of games like the master of ceremonies he loved to be.

But the damned Odysseus could not leave his head. His very blood was mixed within Hermes' ichor. Charon tied their wild journeys as one when Hermes paid him the fee for his aid.

Biting his tongue, he feigned sleep while Apollo pulled the bandages around his back. If he tuned into listening to the music around the room, he'd be able to work on crafting a new song or the like.

Like the song he made for Odysseus.

Damn it.

* * *

When Persephone's beautiful flowers returned to Olympus, weaving up walls and taking over the walkways, Hermes found enough willpower to walk on his own. Pleating a fine green and gold himation, his handmaiden draped it neatly over his arm and added back a glittering band of gold across his forehead.

"Lyricaun," he said, and the pink nymph paused in her nitpicking. "A few things."

"Yes, my lord?"

"If I sent you and a few of your girls down the mountain to retrieve some of the herbs that Lord Apollo used for my sake, I'd like to replenish his supplies. And, *ah*, of course the talaria are not currently in residence, but if you could keep their case clean; my staff and helm as well."

"It would be our pleasure, sir," Lyricaun replied with a small smile. "We've just been very happy to have you back home. Spoiled, even, for all your company. Are you sure you don't want any help making it to Zeus' palace? There are so many stairs."

He shook his head. "I'll be fine. Taking my time may be just what I need."

The skin around the shining cuff was pale from the weight that kept him tied to the ground. Hermes pulled up on the chain, twisting it like dozens of snakes around his arms until the pressure on his leg eased enough to walk, though he moreso *ambled,* from his courtyard. To go right would lead him directly on the route to the grand Olympus palace, so naturally he turned left.

Clatter of metal as the chainlinks clinked together ruined any stealthy attempts to keep himself free from prying eyes. The lesser gods on their daily merrymaking finally had their chance to gawk and commit to memory the image of the messenger carrying a pile of chains instead of his usual bag of letters. He wished he could say the weight was similar. There were days where the messages were neverending and his arms were dead by the end

175

of his shift.

He stopped halfway around the bend of bushes in the direction of the arena. It was too early for any great games to be afoot, but it was certainly occupied. The whistle of spears and the deadly thuds of them hitting their mark was scarcely unrecognizable.

What to say, ye crafter of words, Hermes mulled.

He pressed an open palm against his back where the bandages still held him together. Not as noticeable thanks to Apollo's attentive care, but Athena would know — despite not visiting his halls, she likely knew what occurred the moment it happened. Or she *would* if she ever cared to look back at her disciple.

An unfair transaction — was it a duped client from an inadequate patron, or insubordinate follower to a divine mentor? Odysseus was far from a perfect man, daresay he was perfectly *flawed* in everything he had done; but Athena, who strived for perfection, must have known that *before* she chose to bestow her favor on him.

To dream about bringing a sword down against that goddess was foolish. Though Hermes fantasized about the possibility of succeeding in a duel, he wasn't dumb enough to be like Ares and have his ass served to him on Athena's great shield in front of the entire pantheon.

Maybe as, like, a joke or something one day. Far from now.

Far, far from now.

Trudging by the arena's wide gates, the inner field had been cleared. Even Athena needed to make her way to Zeus' table if she were to avoid the king's questioning. No one would dare train while the goddess of war was about, probably throwing spears with all the fury in her heart, and the lesser gods finally appeared in the crevices of the arena like deer approaching a clearing.

"Tell me, Argeiphontes, why we have book-ended our meetings on this path?" Athena asked from behind.

Hermes pressed his shoulders back, eyeing her reflection in the shine of the arena pillars. She was still dressed in her armor, braided hair pinned back out of her birdlike face, and unwrapped the leather from her hands.

"And you are twice injured. I have told you before that it does not suit you."

"Nor does capriciousness suit you," Hermes replied, carefully pivoting around. His sister's brows lowered. He toed a dangerous line, so he might as well put his entire foot in. "I find myself twice injured because of an obligation to fulfill the oaths I make to mortals. Tell *me*, Pallas Athena, why have you rejected yours?"

"I beg your pardon?"

"Odysseus, the royal son of Laertes, general of the warriors from Ithaca, I'm sure I needn't go on with his numerous epithets. You know who I've been aiding these past two years; who I've spent all hours with before his comrades wrought Helios' wrath. Now he's lost to me! And it all started because *you* couldn't let this one man's ship flee to his home." He threw his chains about, neither in anger nor in humor — some odd mix of the two where he couldn't help but laugh a little at the insanity of it all. "So *seclusive*, Athena, since that day. Have you slept since then? Content with knowing that your student who adored you is suffering in this very moment, if he has not already swallowed all of the sea's water —"

The hand set to strike his cheek stopped a mere inch from his face. Athena's form nearly broke from her Olympian stature, hunched like a lanky, long-necked barn owl whose firm grey eyes shifted a void-like black before reverting at once to how she was.

Hermes blew a sigh out of his nose.

"Do you care about him or not?" he asked.

Athena shook her head. "No more than any others who pledged to me," she said, turning quickly around on the path that led to the great palace. Hermes pulled his leg along to keep up with her.

"You cannot lie to the inventor of deceit."

"Hermes," Athena snapped, "you are the most emotionally intellectual brother of mine, but do not make me speak of my disappointments. I have no regrets for issuing my punishment. The misfortunes the son of Laertes is going through are... they are of his own wrongdoing."

There was a compliment slipped in there, Hermes noted. Not expected, but he was going to mentally file that away for later. His sister was making an escape.

Dragging his chain up stone steps was a mistake, but he bit his cheek. "I spoke to him about Ajax. He told me he urged for the man's death after what he committed in your temple. He was the *only* general to do so, and was simply outvoted and overruled by his commander. It couldn't have been that which angered you."

Athena pressed her fingers along her forehead and continued her pace. They walked up two more flights before the glittering palaces could be seen between the large buildings of Olympus' markets. Hermes legs shook as the ground plateaued, and heaved the chains over his shoulder.

"For crying out loud, Athena, if you don't wish to speak it, let me *see* it. Show me what he has done that's caused you to sever him from your guidance. Take my hand and let's be done with it. I'll not bother you over that mortal again if it truly is so dishonorable," Hermes said, holding out his palm once given the chance to step into her way. His ability to share information with other deathless gods made conversations go so much quicker.

There were hundreds of years of life that separated Athena and Hermes; if he probed deep enough, he could see all of her story, hold in all that information, but he only cared for the specific time during the war. What was it poor Odysseus did that insulted the goddess of wisdom?

He pressed his palm closer to his sister's chest.

Take it and show me, he repeated.

Fine.

She grasped his hand with long, slender fingers, cold to the touch, and Hermes' vision lapped backward.

Falling down to Troy in the dead of night, wind snapped through his hair. The immense wooden horse, wheeled into the city by its own workers, cracked open with a downpour of Grecian soldiers who silently assassinated the dwellers in their sleep. Odysseus was among them in his armor, the shine to his helmet carried an ethereal glow. Several men raced to the gates to push them open, allowing their comrades in from the outside, and then the city took flame.

From Athena's vision, the landscape stretched miles. She witnessed men storming into homes of the laborers while keeping an eye on her two protégés: young Diomedes in his golden cuirass, so full of faith and valour, ran several Trojans through without hesitation; and Odysseus, crouched low to the ground, snuck around the city towards the high-towering palace.

Hermes watched the king dodge arrows and throw accurate spears, clearing his way down the halls, bound to his mission.

Kill the son.

That is what struck through the man's mind and it bounced around Hermes' skull. Through the panic and calling of handmaidens in the palace halls while the city burned around them, Odysseus kicked in the final door that stood in his way.

And oh…

It was that flattened, little baby that Hermes had delivered to Charon not too long ago, small Prince Astyanax. He remembered Eurylochus' harsh words about this encounter; Odysseus' silence.

Odysseus peered around the room, like this was a mistake to only have the cradle of a swaddled infant with a slain nursemaid at its side; an arrow struck perfectly through her neck, a stray shot from a neighboring tower. The warrior king lowered his blade and glanced at the child who cooed and waved his chubby hands at his presence.

"This cannot be the son you meant," Odysseus said, turning around the room until his eyes settled on the invisible form of Athena for a moment before gesturing back to the child.

Like the breeze, Athena answered, *"It is. Born of Prince Hector, he is fated to avenge his father and bring Troy to its zenith."*

"He's helpless," Odysseus whispered. The man carefully took Astyanax within his arms, and he cradled the babe like a father would. *"Can I not just take him with me? Or send him off with another far from here? His spite would be with Achilles, not I. There's no honor in this."*

Hermes felt Athena's frustration grow. The breeze in the room pushed right over Odysseus' shoulder and blew the drapes of the balcony open.

"You must kill him if you wish to save Achaea's future. He will grow to only burn Ithaca to the ground. The task is simple, Odysseus, the most simple of the ones you have faced these years. Now be quick with it and return to the courtyard. We have more important matters to tend to."

He ambled the few steps to the balcony, where the screams and rallying cries deafened even the stars above them. Astyanax grasped Odysseus' pinkie, and with a babbling coo and a bold proclamation of *'papa,'* made the king stifle a sob, wiggling his finger over the baby's face until he could gently break free.

Hermes shook his head.

Oh, Athena, asking him to kill a child — like his own son he left behind at the beginning of this unrelenting war, the one who possesses all his thoughts in his waking hours. You must've known it was a folly command, Hermes pressed, stuck helpless in this memory.

What came across to the goddess as incompetence and weakness to do what was necessary, only came across to Hermes as sympathetic mercy. But the child did die, no doubt, peeled from the ground by his people who remained.

Yet Odysseus didn't move from the balcony, holding the heir of Troy with growing trepidation while Athena's black shadow sharpened and expanded across the nursery. She put her lips to the mortal's ear.

"Odysseus, you must."

"Athena," he pleaded. *"I... can't. Not like this. I'll find another way. There is always another way."*

In an instant, shattering the tension like glass, came a heavy clatter in the hall before three weeping women crumbled into the room, shoved by a young man with blazing red hair. The son of Achilles, with fire in his eyes, gripped the princess of Troy by her roots while he scanned the bedchamber.

"Odysseus!" he shouted. *"You are needed by the old man. Quit your dawdling and get on it so we can all go home. Troy is ours. Are you bewitched? Come on!"*

Stalking to the balcony, a crying Andromache in his hold, the aptly called Pyrrhus took one look at the infant smuggled in Odysseus' arms, grabbed the thing by its leg, and heaved it over the edge of the palace.

Odysseus stumbled back. Under his helmet, his face contorted with ugly lines before immediately detaching itself from any emotion at all as the infant's mother wailed in agony. If Hermes had hands in this memory, he'd cover his own gaping mouth.

He pulled away from Athena's hand.

"Are you mad?" he cursed, startling a few passing goddesses into running off. "This is the tide-turning moment that persuaded you he's a man not worthy of your protection?"

Athena's frown deepened, but her voice remained as monotonous as she could maintain it. "I warned him of the consequences if that child did not die. He wished to see his family again, and if the boy prince remained alive, then that was impossible. Astyanax's death was for the good of the cause and Odysseus should have known that."

"Good, but not right! How ridiculous," Hermes complained, running his hands through his hair. His feathers stuck in all directions while he paced in his limited capacity. "Damn us all, Athena, you *know* what he saw in that babe. He'd probably have *done* it too if you gave him more time. Treating him unlike your Diomedes. If you're to be crass to one of your mortals, might as well be so to all of them."

"Odysseus had also revealed his name to Polyphemus in an act of hubris which exacerbated his troubles. I had taught him better than that," Athena said, crossing her arms.

And yes, true, that bit was inane and idiotic of him, and perhaps a trait he inherited through skipping a few generations.

The chain pulled at his ankle sharp enough to force an annoyed hiss. He crouched to his foot and tried to dig his finger around the cuff. Athena looked on, and a hand slipped from its resting spot to rub away invisible debris from her arm.

"But you said you were with him," she said, no, whispered, "when Father destroyed his ship? How did he react?"

"React?" Hermes scowled. "To seeing his friends drown? Or being left alone in the pitch blackness of the ocean, knowing fully well that our uncle waits to kill him? Oh, he was acting *so* brave, Athena. Not at all like the terrified mortal trying to survive in the world we use as our playground." He threw hand as if to push her away. "Like you said, all he wanted was to go home. He was so scared about his son, my dear sister. You've no idea what your abandonment has done to him."

Gathering the chain back up into his arms, as impossibly unlimited as the length was, Hermes stood back up and suffered to take a few more steps closer to Zeus' palace.

"Maybe you'd sleep better at night if what you speared was the guilt you seem so possessed to deny. But what do I know — I'm just a messenger."

Chapter 12

Another month dragged by like the extra weight Hermes was getting used to, fluttering up a step or three at a time every venture to Zeus' palace. It wasn't a place he wanted to go, but every day spent in his bedchamber was another day listening to the frightened calls from his cloak. He heard Polites in his sleep at times — the sweet man and his gentle forgiveness, trying to overcome the constant screaming of Eurylochus. Even if Hermes had his cloak moved across the room and placed in his chest, it didn't stop the voices shooting straight into his mind.

He sat at the grand table between the twins, across from Athena and Poseidon. The former nary regarded him, and the latter had already snuffed Hermes twice for being in places he had no right being. Zeus had calmed his brother the month prior before the floors could shake, which was great because Hermes did *not* like being lifted from the ground when it wasn't of his own accord.

Although the potential image of Apollo throwing himself across the table to bite their uncle in the arm for being handsy with his finally-healed-patient did strike Hermes to be a little funny.

Demeter placated that side of the feast with her soliloquy about all she and her daughter had accomplished in the blossoming spring. The more she spoke, the more she glowed, and the ambrosia filled itself in the large bowls scattered around the buffet. It was the fullest Hermes had felt in months, but he was prone to slipping under the table with the damned chain phasing through the marble when he was idle for too long. Artemis had silently pinned his hand against the arm of his chair so she and her brother could eat and drink without worry of losing him.

"The longer we go on with secrets, the longer I cannot fulfill my son's one request," Poseidon said, his fist cracking a plate. His tone was directed towards Zeus, but the chilled glare never left Hermes' sulking frame. "It's insulting how long it has taken to kill that mortal; as if you all think I do not hear the dissident whispers around Olympus and my own domain, mocking me for being *incompetent.*"

"Brother," Zeus replied, "if what you desired was to have the son of Laertes suffer, then that request is already in action. Killing now would be unnecessary work, after all. Your son only asked for him to never reach his native shores." He waved his hand and added, "if you hear whispers through these halls, you've all the power to bring them to me, and to punish those in your own realm."

"Some whispers come right from this very table," Poseidon muttered. He was as dark as the sea was when the ship crumbled away. "Did you swear on the Styx, Hodios Hermes, to be such a nuisance? To think your crafty scheme in aiding that human would not be found out?"

Zeus leaned forward on his throne. "My son is paying for his trespasses, Poseidon, I've ensured that."

Hermes stuck his tongue forward against his teeth. Zeus made sure to sew his lips closed to prevent any sly remark from slipping out. No, no swearing on the Styx, but by everything he had, he would. He'd swear on that oath-binding water in an instant.

Athena quietly set her goblet down. "Good Father," she said, "you say the son of Laertes is not yet dead?"

"Of course not," Zeus replied. Athena glanced towards Hermes. "But he's paying for his insults. Let us leave it at that. I'm tired of quarrels in this house —"

A long rumbling rolled over the palace that brought all eyes to the Earth-Shaker, but Poseidon shook his head. Nothing to be worried about, every god quietly shifted to face the entryway. Green fog rolled along the halls with a tepid, cold gust. Demeter sighed, sitting back in her throne with her arms tightly crossed. Zeus turned in his chair with a practiced smile, for if there was one thing he hated, it was being interrupted.

But if there was one thing he found mildly pleasing, it was surprise visits from his eldest brother — the king of the Underworld, lord of the dead, Hades himself.

Hades marched barefooted through the marble corridor, bedecked in silver and deep greys as dark as ash. He typically kept his beard short through the cold months while his wife remained with him; she liked weaving her fingers between the fuzz while pulling him along the Underworld palace. But it had a month's worth of growth returned to it; so did the shadows under his eyes as he scanned the festive table before settling a charcoal gaze on Hermes.

Hermes waved.

Hades clicked his bident to the floor and turned his head to Zeus.

"My, Hades! What an unexpected surprise for you to join us!" Zeus exclaimed, leaping up from his seat. "I cannot think you're here to barter with Demeter for your beloved again. What brings you to my halls from a land as busy as yours?"

"Funny you ask," Hades replied, raising his head taller than his youngest sibling. His dark hair fell straight to his lower back, undecorated save for the sparkle of diamond. "You see, it typically *is* unabashedly busy in my realm with how much bloodshed you and your kin like to spill on the earth."

Zeus laughed coolly, tucking his chin into his hand.

"It is partially my fault," Hades admitted, "for not noticing sooner. When Lady Persephone was home with me, I thought it was a wonderful coincidence that the influx of souls had suddenly diminished. You cannot blame a man for being enamored by his wife."

Hera rolled her eyes as Zeus nodded along.

"But then it came time for her to leave us; and I sat down to toil only to find that my paperwork was practically nonexistent."

"That's a good thing for you, no?" Zeus asked, picking up his nectar. "You can finally relax for once!"

"The Underworld is missing hundreds of souls, Zeus. My numbers have been off for *months!* And here you are," Hades shouted, thrusting his hand towards the table where Hermes was forced to stand at the under-king's bidding, "keeping *my* psychopomp on Olympus!"

Poseidon rose from his chair. "He is Zeus' son and he is serving his sentence for his lies and disloyalty against me."

"Oh, get over it, Brother," Hades said, sauntering to the young god's seat. "This one was agreed upon to serve under *my* jurisdiction between his duties to Zeus. By keeping him here, the souls of mortals are stuck on the earth." His cold hand settled on Hermes' head, though it was rather comforting.

"Well, we cannot risk him breaking loose to search for the mortal who offended me." Poseidon tossed his himation over his shoulder as he rose up. All others looked on as the three kings stood at a crossroads. Hermes almost blushed at the attention.

"Well, I cannot have the foundation of death's cycle begin crumbling because you all waste your time crying over whatever mortals do to offend you. By holding Hermes hostage, you require me to take him by force. He will have no time to fly anywhere other than where the souls await him. Zeus, you know this is in our contract — the psychopomps have very little choice in the matter when they are bound by duty." Hades pulled Hermes back from the table, clinking the golden chain along with him with ease. "Release him to me."

"Zeus, no," Poseidon argued. "Lend him another in this snake's stead. We do not skimp on our punishments because of the disorganization of the Underworld."

Hera smacked her hand on the table and gave her younger brother a warning glare as heat began to radiate from Zeus' shoulders.

Hermes clicked his teeth — *and so the family will quarrel because that's what we do best.*

Running his hand through his mane of hair, Zeus closed his eyes and chuckled. When he lifted his head to the table of gods, his contempt settled on Hermes as if it was solely his fault for starting it all. "How about a compromise, eh? Get both of you out of each other's business," *and out of my ass,* his face read, "but maintain some equity. Hermes will be allowed to serve in his capacity as psychopomp — I did agree to that, Hades. But he must be escorted to every site, released to collect and dispense, then to return to his bindings."

Poseidon worked his jaw; Zeus continued.

"Apollo," he said, and the god shifted uncomfortably. "Summon your chariot. You're to bring Hermes to where he is called. If he escapes you, then you'll don his chains upon your own wrists, and will be incapable of drawing any bow or working any instrument."

Oh, Father, cruel. To set brothers against each other simply to save face with your own.

"Are my instructions clear, boys?" Zeus descended to his seat.

Apollo glanced at Hermes before nodding. "Yes, Father. I will see it done and Hermes returned home at once."

Hermes found his tongue at last. "If that's your will," he replied, the weight of Hades' hand leaving his skull.

"Take care of it now. Hephaestus, relinquish the talaria to him."

Hermes sat on the back of Apollo's chariot, donning his helmet as the four white horses with flaming manes busied themselves in trampling off the edge of the mountain. It was astonishing to see the golden chain lengthen all the way down to the earth as he dangled his feet from the chariot cockpit. But to feel the wind rush over him, to pull at his star-studded cloak and ruffle his wings, Hermes could pretend it was he who was flying again.

To escape and search for Odysseus was his first thought if he was given free reign to fly out; it was natural that Zeus would know that, but to pin any new punishment on Apollo was unfair after all he'd done to alleviate Hermes' pain. If it were any other time, perhaps, then he wouldn't feel as bad to let Apollo split his comeuppance. It would be in good fun.

"Don't think about sliding off," Apollo said, holding tight to the reins. His red and gold cape nearly blocked Hermes from seeing his face, but he knew it was stern.

"And miss out on this view? Brother, we must get you a shorter chiton so the others can know what they miss out on," Hermes replied, turning back to the lands beneath them. He counted every town they passed over, knowing each by name.

Apollo huffed. "Just tell me where I must go."

Like a beacon, the caduceus naturally pulled towards wayward souls. When they flew close enough for Hermes to see the spirits panicked or lost in their home or in the wilderness, as most deaths outside of war were more peaceful or accidental, he scooped them up, adding to the weight of his cloak. After one town, they flew to another, and another island after that well through the day until Nyx spread her hands over the sky and they disguised themselves as a shooting star along the horizon.

Hermes whistled out a terribly long breath. He carried almost four hundred souls on him; most of them being infantile or elderly made the cloak calm at least, but standing behind Apollo? The speed nearly choked him.

"And that's just *one* day's work," Apollo said, slumping along his chariot's railing when they stopped above the entrance to the Underworld. "Making up for a nearly fifty day holiday, though, I suppose that isn't too bad?"

"Suppose away," Hermes replied. "It's a blur after a while." He pointed at the cuff until Apollo hesitantly summoned the borrowed power to release it, and quickly jerked to the edge of the cockpit. Apollo flinched to grab him. "Aw, Brother, you think I'd just fly off and leave you like that?"

"I don't know what I think of you right now; you're unpredictable." Apollo drew back with a wary eye. "How long will you take in Hades? I'm tired and want to go home."

Hermes shrugged, balancing his toes on the ledge, his ankles lighter than ever. He felt like the next breeze could simply blow him away. "I'll not stay long. I give direction and I make peace with them. Under an hour if I don't speak to Charon as well."

"If."

"You know me," Hermes laughed.

He let his head tilt back and his body follow suit, falling from Apollo's glowing chariot and into the swallowing cave of the Underworld. The air shifted in an instant, a nostalgic feeling, as Hermes gracefully weaved through the tunnels.

Hades was right, it *was* quiet. Even the souls that had been lumbering on the beaches for years had the chance to be brought to the judges to find out their fate; very few remained, silently standing in the sands, staring off into the endless abyss of the river.

His favorite rock to perch on remained unbothered on the corner of Acheron and Styx's banks; he was a little worried it would up and move away out of spite. Wiping his face dry of any errant tears, for the souls didn't need to know how pitiful he became now, he held out the golden rod and called them forth.

They shot out like volcanic sparks from his cloak. Pale blue faces falling to the white sands with wide eyes and nervous hands reaching out to Hermes like he was their mother. From a small group to a large crowd to a massive horde, he resisted the urge to hover above them all, and allowed them to grasp his legs and the floating corners of his clothes.

With gentle words he instructed the elderly to take their coins and go to the ferryman, that they would be taken to judgment and find rest for the remainder of eternity; for the deceased newborns, he plucked a downy feather to follow and play with, having the older children carry them about. Organizing hundreds of spectres was not what he believed would take up much of his time — but it was the forty-odd number of them that brought him to the ground of the beach.

The six were horrid to look at: mangled and missing limbs, faces crushed and bodies full of rowed tooth divots. Three were not recognizable at all, though dear Polites still was. Armless, a mangled chest of teeth, his face was still serene. Upon seeing Hermes, he fell to his knees, not knowing he fell to his old Anastasios. The psyche of spirits were frozen in time, but many of the men knew, for they saw him before their ship was crushed, and fear stuck to their charred and bloated faces.

"My gracious hosts," Hermes said to them, trying to keep the sorrow from his voice. "You are where the Fates have called you to be, along the River Styx. This is the entrance to your new home, where if the judges are willing, you'll rest without any more pain or worry. On these shores you may find a few comrades you have known in life; others have crossed over through waiting in time, which," he paused, finding Eurylochus' callous stare over the crew, "many of you will have to endure. To be buried at sea is not a burial at all, I'm afraid. You'd have bettered your chances to die ashore so your rites could be performed."

Not for him to judge, he sighed.

"Take this path here, down to the water's edge. Await the ferryman and plead your case with modest words," he continued. "After all this waiting, he may be generous enough to take some of you across without coin."

With that bit of knowledge, nearly half the men, especially those who had followed Eurylochus' mutinous orders, stumbled away without another word. The rest were cautious, taking in the warm glow Hermes' body emitted, as if he were the last bit of warmth they would ever see. Dear, kind Polites carefully picked up his head when Hermes knelt down in front of him.

"Polites, friend of Odysseus, you have done me a great service," Hermes said.

"Have I, Psychopompos?" Polites asked and looked at him like he did the day he was ripped away.

"Indeed you have," Hermes chuckled. "I'd like to repay you for your kindness." He reached into his satchel and pulled out the gift. Pressing the syrinx to Polites' remaining hand, he covered the flute with his palm. A pile of coins, plentiful enough to pay for several crossings, rested in the ghost's hand. "Save two for yourself and choose the best of your friends who deserve a quick, safe passage. Your king would want this for you as I do."

Polites stared at the shimmering coins. *"Thank you,"* was all the energy his spirit had to say. Hermes smiled. It was something pleasant to sense that this man would not know anymore suffering, would not know his best friend's pain, and could not know Hermes' guilt.

He couldn't mope around with Odysseus' crew any more than he already did, giving them the exclusive guiding experience down to the shore. Charon stood on his boat in the middle of the river, taking with him the first batch of the newly arrived who had their payment at the ready.

"Did you miss me?" Hermes asked, flying over the waters. "Waiting all by your lonesome for me to bring in some entertainment."

Charon dug his oar deep into the river. "Knew you'd be awhile," he replied.

"I suppose you would. Still relishing in my great grandson's blood as well as my own." Hermes crossed his arms, letting the still air carry him alongside the ferry. "My uncle asked if I swore on the Styx to aid the son of Laertes, but lest does he know I've gone and tied my whole fate to him, eh? I cannot doubt that Zeus knows of this; he tries to walk the middle path to avoid more conflict after Troy. My brother waits for me just outside the realm to reattach the shackle I've been carrying for several weeks…"

"Mn."

"You must've seen Hades leave to argue my case for me. Tell him I'll return his gesture in kind one day, would you?"

"Mmn."

"Thank you, Charon," Hermes said, rotating to his stomach. "I missed you as well, but alas, I must get going. I'll see you in a day's time again to continue our lovely conversations."

Charon offered a tiny peek of his face from beneath his hood, which for the man, was a great deal, and Hermes was pleased to have earned it.

Dusting his sandals over the waters, Hermes skimmed the surface back to the white beaches of familiar faces. Over several hundred of Odysseus' men: all of whom had followed him into Troy, survived the war, and perished on a nostos that would have taken less than a month if not for the gods.

Hermes closed his eyes and didn't look back at them.

Rising up the cavern, until the suffocating air of Hades bloomed with the sea breeze, he nearly overshot the chariot that lay waiting for him. The four horses tapped at the ocean mist and huffed in the cooling night, their flaming tails lighting up the entrance to the Underworld like blazing whips ready to attack Cerberus if the mighty guard dog saw them as a threat.

"You're still here," Hermes said, a little disappointed that his brother couldn't have just allowed him to fly home.

"You did say under an hour," Apollo replied, tuning his lyre. "I thought you'd be longer. I pictured you holding everyone's hazy hands and walking them to Tartarus or the like."

"Do you have any idea how the Underworld works?" Hermes settled onto the chariot and pushed off his helmet. He lifted his carved calf up a few inches towards his brother.

Apollo knelt and reattached the cuff. "Why would I have to? Didn't you tell me I was banned?"

Fair enough, the god of medicine had tried a handful of times to resurrect mortals; it made Hades a decent bit aggravated.

Hermes chuckled and scooted back to lean against Apollo's legs as he stood to take the reins again.

But the smile didn't last, staring out at the endless waters where his kin was lost among the thousands of islands. It wouldn't take an awfully long time to search them all; he needed a few hours — just a few hours. He could fly faster than he ever had before, searching until his ichor boiled inside, and he'd know that son of Laertes was near.

And he tried it. When given more slack, Hermes would abuse it, flying off immediately to Ithaca. The cuff returned for another six months. And when he was released on good behavior to continue with his job, he flew across Crete and along the shores of Circe and the giants. Again, the cuff would return for twelve; freedom to bondage, rewards and punishments.

On and on and on and on, tirelessly, for seven whole years.

* * *

On Olympus, he sat on the edge of the mountain, watching the ethereal chain swing between white snowy clouds. Misbehaving had cost him most of his outings, and fulfilling his duty to Hades was kept to two very overworked days of the week at the insistence of Poseidon — who was so infuriated, part of his palace wall cracked under his blown fuse.

It wasn't that big a deal. The wall was easily mended by Hephaestus and his crew.

Hermes felt zero guilt towards his uncle. There were times he wished he could wrap the sea king up in the heavy chain, strung by the neck, and cast him out over the mountain's cliffside. But Hermes was small and Poseidon was not, and to be struck by his trident would a terrible and ugly injury.

Dawn had only begun to stretch her fingers across the horizon. Hermes hadn't slept that night, dressed only in a himation and wrapped with the ram fleece gifted by Dionysus. He heard Helios' chariot take off, and the Titan god's bellowing call that began the day. There was the Sun — blinding and warm. There weren't many times he would be awake at this hour to see it, but his boredom presented itself in either insomnia or manic episodes that the Leto twins were obliged to sit through as Hermes theorized every possible strategy to get out of his bindings. Perhaps one led to the other.

An armored calf stepped up to the ledge next to him, the flow of the Aegean blue cape followed right after. His heart nearly leapt from his chest.

"We must go to Father today," Athena said, standing like a statue overlooking the sky.

"We're speaking again?" Hermes asked up over his shoulder, where his sister and her grey eyes glanced back. "You've been very skilled at evading me for the past decade, I'm surprised I still have the ability to see you."

Athena, in all of Hermes' shock, sat down next to him. The click of her armor was an alien sound. When she timidly tucked her hair behind her ears, Hermes was partly convinced that this couldn't have been the goddess at all.

"I do not like to be wrong," she said bluntly, "but it would be unbecoming of me to not admit that you were correct to be displeased about my inaction with… Our lost sheep."

"Okay."

"I have contemplated what could be done given the circumstances." Athena kept a wary eye out for listeners. "You told me once that I did not care for his weakness towards his child. I am apt to prove you wrong, Hermes. I shall travel to Ithaca this day and see to his son."

His feathers perked up like a dog's ears. "Athena!" She covered his mouth, so he mumbled through her fingers. "It cannot be good there; those ingrate children have grown to be audacious adults without the king present, or so

I've heard in their libations, at least. The prince Telemachus will need your aid."

"I will convince him to go out and search for his father," Athena said, patting Hermes' face away. "In his learning about the king's exploits, perhaps he will be better prepared to receive our lost sheep when *you* bring him home."

All of the excitement that had avoided Hermes like the plague year after year suddenly overcame him in a fit of cackling madness. To have the goddess of wisdom on his side, on Odysseus' side again — *Hermes could keep his oath* — the thought almost brought him to tears.

"Can I kiss you, Sister?"

"Absolutely not."

"I'm going to anyway," he said, pressing his lips to her porcelain cheek. "But what'll you say to Father? One more fault against Poseidon and I believe I'll be spending the next decade pinned to the ocean floor to feed his seahorses with my ichor."

Athena stood elegantly, wiping the early morning dew from her hands. "Poseidon shall not be a problem today, I have made sure of it."

"By the Styx, you've killed him."

"Hermes."

He leapt up, his chained leg painfully resisting the flight his wings wanted to achieve. "I can see no other reason why he'd not be at a gathering," he exclaimed, following her as fast as he could.

"Just wait. Go change into your *usual* attire. I will see you at the palace."

"When you go to Ithaca, will you tell me about them? Some knowledge I can bestow him to ease his very fragile heart? Athena?"

There was a painfully slow five hours before the gods and goddesses were expected to be seated around Zeus' table. Hermes bathed himself in oil and had the best of his silks and linens brought to him — gold woven in patches all over a green chiton, pinned together with the serpent-wound lighting bolt. The nymphs of his palace giggled with the time they had to individually curl his hair and tend to his wings now that their lord was back in his light-hearted moods.

He walked with Apollo like he did every time, playing out how he imagined Athena got rid of Poseidon — the palace was empty and his chariot was gone, but his nymphs remained so he couldn't have gone down to his underwater palace. Unless he was having strange one-on-one time with Amphitrite, which was *unlikely* — Poseidon had more mistresses than Zeus since his wife cared little for his company. He must've been somewhere in the mortal realm.

A twinge of anxiety crept up Hermes' spine.

If he were anywhere near where Odysseus was kept, Athena ought to hold Hermes back, he was about to get reckless.

The empty sea king's throne at the table was an odd change when the others arrived — first Artemis, then Apollo and Hermes, Hephaestus appearing in his braces rather early, Ares and Aphrodite danced in after a very obvious night of intense sex, followed by Demeter, Athena, and eventually, their majesties in their usual splendor. Dionysus was somewhere on Gaia, basking in his own preferred drink. There was a heartier mixing of seats here, many biases and complaints from the war were starting to heal; Artemis didn't mind lounging closer to the queen so that Hephaestus could sit closer to and pester his actual wife.

While plenty of usual side conversations took place, Zeus stared at his brother's empty seat like there was a joke he was missing out on, but levied his concern with a heaping amount of ambrosia. For once there was no need to keep Hermes' mouth shut for conversation, though a strange follow up occurred when the young god said nothing at all, looking expectantly at his sister across the table. How *pleasant* the table was without the Earth-shaker this morning. The god king's posture straightened.

"Certainly, I must've been deceived by someone, for we lack a member at my feast," Zeus said, looking around his company.

Athena gently laid her napkin in front of her and creased the fold. "Father," she said, immediately listened to by all. "There have been a great number of victories with the Æthiopians at the edge of the world. In their celebrations, they wished to bestow many gifts to Lord Poseidon for his contributions. I believe there are several days worth of festivities and sacrifices that your great brother had desired to revel in."

She glanced at Hermes. *Victories won in the far reaches of the world where they cherished Poseidon the most of all Olympians.*

"I see," Zeus said, spinning his drink. "Poseidon does enjoy his gifts. Good for him."

Athena smiled, a horrifying expression for her.

Hermes shook with impatience, holding his tongue was becoming increasingly difficult. If he made it through without uttering a word, he should be given some sort of prize.

"There is something that weighs on my mind, good Father," Athena said after another minute. "It is about a mortal who I first wished to make an example of, but I fear our punishments have been intertwined, and he received far worse a fate than I wanted for him."

Zeus listened and tapped his fingers to the arms of his throne like a tiny rainfall. "Ah, you speak of Laertes' son, that Odysseus."

"I do, my king."

He grunted as he sat back in his seat. "Where he is, I'm humble enough to admit I did not intend for him to remain there forever."

Hermes leaned forward against the table. *Keep pushing, Athena.*

"I have spoken," Athena continued, "with several members at this —"

"Conspiring behind my back, my dearest daughter?" He almost sounded offended.

"To save your time from mortal frivolities. We think the son of Laertes has undergone enough. Twenty years away from his homeland, for Man, that is a quarter of their lifetime. He has called out to me, and I have heard his plea." Athena gestured around the pantheon. "If I forgave him, Father, could you? Let him be free from the place you have sent him."

Zeus hummed and strung his beard with his fist. "He was yours at the start," he thought aloud, "though he did commit acts of pride that my brother cannot forgive… but he is *away* at the moment."

Hera tapped her nails to the smooth plates in front of her. "I could send my heraldess, Iris, to the distant coast to keep an eye out for the end of their frivolities," she said casually, as if she didn't take great interest in the mortal.

Zeus' held-in laughter rumbled the room. "Very well," he said. "Hermes."

He tried so very hard not to pounce right out of his seat, thankful for once that the chain kept him grounded. "Yes, Father?"

"It is not Odysseus' destiny to remain in the hands of the Titan child, Calypso. Go to Ogygia and command her to release him. He's to make his journey to Ithaca." Zeus snapped his fingers. The cuff shattered to pieces and Hermes left the floor on instinct.

Tread lightly, the god king said for only Hermes to hear. *I cannot intervene should my brother find you out.*

Hermes nodded, he didn't care for something that far ahead. If Ogygia was where the mortal was at, then Hermes would be there faster than the wind could hope to carry him. He spared only a second to acknowledge Athena, the goddess and her grand strategy. *What a deadly combo they could turn out to be.*

Out the palace, through the courtyards, lesser gods gasped at the sight of the divine messenger on his duty once more. No feet even kicked off the edge of Mount Olympus for a flashy takeoff — he dove right through the cloud cover like a falcon pursuing its quarry.

Chapter 13

To think he was so close to this island during a dozen rounds of soul collecting — an isolated land, hidden to the world by Zeus. It was a punishment for Calypso, the powerful nymph who dwelled there alone. During the war of the Titans, well before Hermes' time, she assisted her father, Atlas, in fighting against the Olympians. She was just a child then, even by deathless standards. Hermes believed she was still within a mortal's lifespan when she was banished to Ogygia.

The weather that surrounded the clouded island rolled with grey clouds above, and deep, dark waters below. It was nothing any sailor would wish to journey into; there were paths of calm streams that went around the island and a divine feeling to avoid the shores at all cost.

Pulling his helmet further over his eyes, Hermes whistled over the rocky waters, zipping in and out of rogue waves like Athena's spear on the battlefield. Thousands of years alone on an island to an immortal was a long time, and no doubt Hermes would drive himself insane if he were in Calypso's shoes. But several years for a human who was already past his prime was asking for torture.

Hermes ran head first through the barrier that surrounded Ogygia, and the rumbling sky ceased at once in lieu of the glow of an afternoon in which divine weather settled and foamy, blue waters washed against the cliffs. The young god skipped on the foam as he skidded to a stop. Behind him looked like an eternal calm ocean. A misty rainbow burst from the corner of the earth and flew over them, vibrant in its colors.

It was a little, perfect paradise. He was ready for the gloom.

That was unexpected.

Flying over the island lush with green woods and tall caves that spit out blossoming ivy and soft moss over its stony faces, Hermes carefully settled on the ground. Nothing felt solid, even the grass underfoot was as if he were walking on pillows. Spinning his golden staff, he strode along the path to the greatest of the caves, where Calypso kept her palace.

He heard her voice first, lovely in its song; it danced on the warm air in a hypnotic tune. A large hearth greeted him in the entrance of the cave, burning sweet-scented wood that pierced right through Hermes' nose. He shook his head. If the music and the smell made *him* woozy, any mortal would be useless against her.

Above him sat birds by the dozens, some perched in impossibly tall trees: ravens, hawks, and owls alike, all resting in the perfect, gilded birdcage. The feathers by Hermes' ears unfurled in protest to the idea of being a mere decoration.

Akin to Dionysus' utopias, a never-ending, winding vine of clustered, ripe grapes hung from the doorway. It brought him along a path where a handful of happily bubbling creeks branched off down the cave's many cloistered tunnels, leading to opulent flowered meadows of violet and herbal greenery. Dragonflies littered the air.

Hermes stopped in his tracks.

Maybe for some goddesses like Demeter or even Hestia, this would be quite fair to call an abode. A lavish vacation spot to rest one's legs, but only for a week or two.

Kleistós and Anoize, the serpents enshrined around his caduceus, hissed Hermes *out* of the spellbinding trance, all but biting the hand that held them aloft. He hushed them, letting the staff rest on the crook of his arm, and continued pressing deeper to where the singing was the loudest.

And there she sat working her loom, throwing the shuttle back and forth with a gentle hand, weaving a marvelous piece of herself and an older man. Her hair was loosely tied back in a thousand braids, decorated with seashells and flowers, woven with ivy the same way her island was. There was little need for her to dress modestly, so often alone on her island which she kept as warm as Mount Olympus in a perpetual pleasant summer. Her breast lay bare, and neither she nor Hermes batted an eye toward the nudity.

It was quaint: her presenting as mortal when she could easily encapsulate the entirety of this room. The metal click of his staff's point hitting stone silenced the singing.

Calypso stared at him for a long while, slowing the shuttle until it rested in her hold. Hermes glanced around the cavern; Odysseus was nowhere in sight.

"God of travel and stories, why have you come here?" she asked, her timbre light and airy. "You are a beloved friend and I've longed for your visits, but they have become far too rare these centuries. I see you have yet to grow a beard." Her pleasant giggle was sincere.

Hermes smiled and let his mind sift through ideas of how to avoid angering her; if she had any hold on Odysseus, he didn't wish to see him injured in her rage.

Calypso slid from her stool and sauntered to a small, wooden table for which she brought out and set between them. "Tell me what is on your mind. I am eager to be of assistance, to do whatever I can do *if* it can be done at all. Take a seat, here."

And so he reclined, and she carried in plates of ambrosia and freshly mixed, red nectar akin to wine he had seen poured out at many feasts. She watched him eat and drink, her eyes as dark as the grapevine above them, her cheek resting patiently on the soft palm of her hand. She even handed him a napkin before he could request one.

"From one god to another," he replied, "you ask why I'm here. Now, my darling Calypso, I will share with you the whole story and spare you no indelicate words as you've commanded." Hermes kicked back in his seat and folded his hands in his lap, nodding to the stool the goddess was sitting in before. "It was Zeus who ordered me to come. No choice of mine, I admit — who would *willingly* make this awful trek across brackish wastes of the sea for so long? Your island near borders Tartarus, miles from home. There are no mortals in sight, not a soul around to offer sacrifices and burn the fattest picks. A *nightmare* for anyone to journey this far."

"You have come before," Calypso responded, dragging her fingers lightly over her braids, "to keep me company."

Hermes wiggled on the cushion. He sure did.

"Zeus has sent me now and I have no way to thwart his will," he said. "He claims that you keep prisoner the most unlucky man in Greece."

"Prisoner?" Calypso startled up out of her seat. Hermes continued his message.

"He fought against King Priam's Troy for nine years and with his cunning, had it sacked on the tenth; when he set sail for his home, he was complicit in angering Lady Athena and lost his way. His crew has since perished and I was told the winds and currents forced him here. Zeus now commands you to release him immediately."

"Hearts of stone, you gods have!" Calypso retorted.

Hermes peered up at her from his seat, keeping within him all the composure he had learned from sitting in silence at Olympus' table. "It's not his fate to die here. Destiny ordains that he'll see his loved ones and reach his native land where they await him."

The island nymph roamed her cave with her fists balled, shaking her head like a pendulum. Hermes quietly fluttered to his feet.

"Lords of Envy, you creatures feel belittled when a goddess takes a mortal lover when *you* all venture off, free to stick your shafts where you please!" Calypso clawed the empty bowls from the table, sending them clattering to the plush floor. "Murdering lovers of even the most powerful goddesses — Dawn witnessing the archer goddess shoot Orion down; or Lady Demeter and her lover, Iason, whom Zeus dispatched with his lightning — you all now turn to *me* with your spite? Who am I to any of the Olympians?"

The flowers blooming in the cave began to spout a rancid smell. Hermes moved around the table, but didn't follow too closely to Calypso's tangent. They had similar spats a dozen times before.

"I saved this mortal man!" she cried. "From the winds and the currents, he arrived on my beaches half-drowned. I tended to his wounds, his needs, and all his wants; I cherished him greatly in my welcome. He *loves* me, Hermes — we bask in joy here together, as we have been for so many years. I promised him immortality, but you come at Zeus' decree to take him from me."

She stopped by the entrance and hid her face in her hands.

"Calypso," Hermes said. "The man doesn't want immortality; he's even rejected that from Zeus in favor of returning home to his wife, his child. How can he be happy here?"

"How could he *not!* See how beautiful I have made it for him! We lie together every night — I feel his desire. He pleasures to be with me, I hear him call my name."

Hermes worked his jaw as pity rose for Odysseus. She had no choice but to release him, whether or not she wished to argue about it. But the sooner he won their tift, the sooner he could be underway.

"Calypso, sweet goddess, when you bring him to lie with you," he asked, nuzzling his nose to the back of her neck. He whispered, "does he hold you like this?" Gliding his hands over the nymph's sides, he traced her body with her own fingers. "Does he kiss you tenderly, like so? Hold you closer to his chest, weave his hands through your lovely braids...?"

Guiding her through the times in the distant past when they, too, laid together — Hermes was a tender partner when he slowed down to be. Did it compare to how this mortal man that she'd declared her own spouse lay?

"When... when I told him to, he would do all a good husband would," Calypso hiccuped. "We love each other."

"You entrap him against his will, little flower and you know it," Hermes said, waving his finger. He stepped away from her, sighing with a rousing pulse of disappointment.

Calypso's eyes flashed. "If he goes out there and wishes to be destroyed on that barren sea, as our *Almighty* commands, then so be it!" Her skin was thoroughly flushed as she stormed away from the daylight, wrapping herself in her own long hair. "But I have no escort to give him, no ships in reach to call to my bidding or extra hands to man his oars."

She worked hard to avoid Hermes' gaze. She picked at her loom and bent down to collect the tossed cups and bowls. He remained in the center, his patience wearing thin. Wiping her face, she shook her head, then a quiet addition came along.

"But I have the trees and tools he may use. He may have all he needs, but I cannot help him beyond that. Is that adequate, *Argeiphontes?* To avoid the rage of your father?"

Hermes acquiesced. "Release him at once, do as you have said, and you'll not force Zeus' hand in making your life a living hell."

"It already is," she spat. "Be gone from me, away from my island. It shall be years before I think to forgive you awful gods."

Not to be told twice, the messenger sped from her cave.

The calm, colorful vibrancy of the sky before had darkened to a mellow slate, as if the sun drifted too far from the sky. Clouds crept along the highest points of the island, and the waters licking the cliff splashed violently back into the sea.

Now where o' where was his kindred?

As if Hermes would simply go home now that he had no chains to hold him back.

He circled the island, zipping past the beaches and over the woods, barren of life. The breeze blew towards the ocean, like a heavy push, and he allowed himself to follow it to the white-washed bluffs. And there, standing weakly by the ledge, was a man.

From afar, he was dressed very finely, wrapped in rich, bright linens. His hair and beard had grown longer, aged with silver that matched the glimmering bracelets at his wrists and shins. A prisoner in paradise.

Hermes dipped under the tall cliff and lifted his chin skyward.

This poor man was precariously close to tumbling right off the cliffs. His shoulders quaked and his chest heaved deep echoes of lamenting. If the island followed its goddesses emotions, then it paled in comparison to the mortal standing above. He muttered to himself and shook his head. A shaking hand reached out to the void of the sea; several pebbles fell free of their hold.

Hermes scrambled up the crag just as Odysseus veered too far, catching him under his arms in a desperate embrace, one that shoved the man's feet right back onto solid ground. A bare cheek pressed to the bearded other.

"Hello, old friend," he whispered, holding onto Odysseus as the panicked, grief-stricken sobs came out in shocked gasps.

"H-hermes," Odysseus said. His voice was hoarse, half-faded from his cries or from its under-use.

His hair had grown to his lower back, verily oiled and cared for, though tangled by the wind. But his beard was too long to be reasonable for a handsome face. Unacceptable, really.

"What is this," Hermes muttered, leaning back to take Odysseus' face in his hands. His fingers tugged into the curly, unkempt whiskers. The creature on his chin was gone as soon as Hermes willed it, back to a reasonable length of a man of good wisdom. It had cut twenty years from his age — and Odysseus *was* only a man in his fifties. "Much better, that was painful to look at this close."

"Hermes," Odysseus wept, crumbling to his knees.

Hermes threw back his helmet so his friend could take in his face too, the apples of his cheeks wet with fresh tears that slipped as he laughed.

"I thought," Odysseus gasped, "I thought you had died. I thought I got you *killed*. My friend, my only friend. I was so lost." The rock beneath them bit at his calves. "Hermes, I cannot go on like this. I've tried everything — to be merciful is weak, to be malevolent is lonesome. I've walked on glass and have bled with every step. This life is… it's unwinnable, my friend, oh my dear friend."

He folded smaller beneath Hermes' grasp, trying with his leftover strength to all but climb into Hermes' skin. Gathered like a babe, the young god slipped him away from the bluffs and to the cushioned grass of the nearest meadow.

"It's true," Hermes said, "that this life of yours is a game never to be won. Us gods are rather cruel in our games, even to each other if we can be. Be selfish or be selfless, but do whatever you must to stay alive."

"Take me from here, I beg."

"You needn't beg. It's been *commanded*. I've been released from a prison of my own making to finally bring you from yours."

Odysseus raised his haggard eyes from the ground. "What?"

Breaking the fine jewelry from his worn skin, Hermes chucked the cuffs to oblivion. "Zeus has declared it's not your fate to remain trapped. You'll step foot upon your shores again," he said, ruffling his hands into Odysseus' hair. "Great grandson of the god of wanderers, you'll see your wife as I promised."

"Hermes," his name laughed through disbelieving tears, "to see you today is like seeing my boy. You still look to be the age he would be now — so grown."

They could spend an eternity laughing and crying, bonking foreheads until some of Hermes' divinity washed off on him. Prince Telemachus, as far as Hermes knew, wasn't taking after his father in the amount of hair possible to grow. *Boy* remained very much the correct term to use. The correct term for Odysseus would be a *ram*.

"You must make your way to the beach," Hermes said. "As I'm not allowed to intervene in getting you *out* of this bottled island, Calypso will provide you with the supplies you need to build a boat to depart."

The mention of her name deflated Odysseus' joy, the lines on his face growing deep and shadowed. "Please don't make me face her again. One word and I find my body moving without my consent, dragged to her bed. Please, I cannot go another night."

"Ody, under my watch, she wouldn't dare. Nothing but another god will make her comply. Zeus has declared his will and if she opposes it, there'll be a price to pay. Just allow her to give you the tools; you needn't even look at her." Following his gaze, Hermes continued to place himself at his center. "Focus on crafting your vessel, focus on your dearest Penelope, focus on trying to guess where I'm hiding."

"Why... why would *you* be hiding?"

"Calypso doesn't know I know you. As far as she's concerned, I showed up only to be an ass, which I did incredibly well, just so you know. If she suspects we are friends, *hm*, I imagine she'll second guess if what I told her were truly Zeus' orders."

They hesitantly rose to their feet. Hermes kept his ready hands under Odysseus' elbows. It all must have felt like waking up from a wicked dream, one impossible to claw out of when all you knew was that the world around you was wrong.

"I also *really* want to see if you can guess," he added, smoothing back Odysseus' hair and straightening his chiton. "I've been out of practice. But put on a brave face, venture to the beach, and with the speed you find, you'll soon be *free* of this torture."

He loathed to leave the man alone.

Odysseus slipped down the path of decaying grass, rubbing his arms like they were flint and steel, keeping watch over his shoulder for the goddess who dared to call herself his lover, his immortal wife. Nonsensical whispers sent from his tongue, fumbling quickly to the sand. There were footsteps along the beach, deep ones, *trenches* would be a better word. Dug near the water, the high tide rose only to its edge, unable to fill the lengthy hole.

How many times did this man pace on the shore? Would Calypso allow him near the waters after pulling him from their foam? She tolerated him to sit along the cliffs and Hermes was afraid to admit that if he didn't interfere, he'd be collecting his descendant in a far different manner.

Nudging his cloak back over his shoulder, Hermes disappeared from prying eyes, flying several feet back from his charge. Should he turn into a crab? Would a rooster here be too obvious? The irony would be hilarious — trying to be sneaky and yet appearing as the most unusual bird on the island.

Maybe not hilarious to Odysseus, not yet.

On a simple branch he perched, eyeing the lilac path where Calypso stepped down with her own brewing anxiety.

"Ody?" she called. Hermes threw up in his mouth a little.

Odysseus' shoulders raised to his ears, facing the ocean, stuck, alone between two immortal captors.

In a fit of fidelity, Hermes plucked a feather from his hair, laid it on his palm, and blew it towards the shore; it dutifully brushed past the king's nose, caught before it could be lost to the sea. Odysseus held it near as Calypso paused a few feet behind, his face stained from the onslaught of tears.

"I've come with news," she said, "so you do not need to grieve so ardently at the life you are wasting by my side. You can take my tools, cut the length of timbers from whatever tree you like and make them into a durable raft — one that will sweep you far and away from me — who you *loathe* so deeply." Pulling a robe about her shoulders, the rest of her hair fell free from their light ties.

Odysseus kept his lips pressed so tightly they turned white, watching her from the corner of his eye. The feather twisted and twirled between his thumb and forefinger.

After a moment she continued, "I will stock your raft with food and water, with the wine you like, so you do not hunger on your journey. Whatever clothes you desire are yours, and I release you from your binds to this island."

Rushing up at once, the high tide pushed past the invisible barrier and nipped at Odysseus' feet, filling the trenches he had created. A gasp puffed from his nose as he stumbled away from the summer sea.

Calypso reached out to comfort him, but even then he curtailed from her soft hands like she had the touch of death. "I release you, but it must be those gods on high who are willing to guide you home. They balk and laugh at our lives, whatever pleases their monotonous existence."

"How do I know you don't look to trick me?" Odysseus muttered. "So many times before you've filled my heart with hope only to force me abed and forget the days that have flown by. Now you send me off to the endless seas?"

Hermes settled on his stomach, his face held up in his hands as he kicked his feet. *Get her, my boy. Throw out all your frustration, she cannot harm you.*

If Ody wished to get off of Ogygia soon though, he really was supposed to be getting started.

He guessed he could do Odysseus a favor, sending a few trees within the wood falling to the ground. Their echoes interrupted the building retort that Calypso was ready to unleash.

No aggravating the already sad man, tsk tsk.

Hermes mosied the beach as a vibrant green tortoise, watching Odysseus collect himself once left alone and immediately get to work. He dragged the fallen trees to the shore, pulled over his broad shoulders, and laid them next to each other in parallel lines. On his knees, he peeled and cut them to size, winding heavy rope around each beam until they moved as one, the size of a grand bed. The sun ticked to early evening and the king of Ithaca smoothed out a strong beam for the mast. With no help, he hoisted the great piece skyward and moved the makeshift deck around the keel, hammering the iron nails until his shaking hands struck themselves and Odysseus cursed loud enough to fill the wind.

"Ares' cock!"

No tortoise had ever laughed before, not before now. Hermes curled himself into his shell, an untamable swell of pride rocking him over onto his back. There was no aiding him, flailing like an idiot on the sand. His progeny unknowingly, in his own frustration, caught the god of mischief so off guard that now a lone tortoise — clearly just minding his own turtle business — was upside down, wheezing from his shell.

How he missed this mortal, a good man.

One gentle lift from rough hands flipped Hermes around again. A laughing, flying tortoise, being brought to sit by the becoming-vessel's side. He peeked out of his shell. Odysseus worked on the sail despite his swollen fingers. Looking up at the man's profile, Hermes' heart swelled.

He had added the feather from Hermes' wing to the small ear cuff beneath his greying hair. It stuck out gracefully against the worn feathers of the old sirens, whose colors had diluted over the years.

A hand lightly patted the winding curves of the shell.

So Hermes' hiding technique needed some work. That was fine. This was good.

Odysseus worked silently into the night and through til the next day. Calypso brought crates of food and wine and watched him from behind, but her beckoning and empty apologies fell on deaf ears. He hardly ate, locked onto his building until his cracked hands bled. By the fourth day, the raft grew twice in size, a vessel any fisherman would envy, and the sail, once secured with rigging, filled with the muted wind that stirred from inland.

Once the supplies were stored under the small half-deck, Odysseus stood on the raft and looked it over.

"It looks nice," Hermes said from atop the mast. His cloak billowed like a mighty flag of travelers. "Ready to launch her?"

"Must I bid farewell to the goddess?" he asked, pulling a sea-cloak over himself and securing it with a silver pin.

"Would you like to?"

"No."

Hermes chuckled and raised the modest ship from the sand, gliding it over invisible waves until it coasted along the foam. He whistled his mortal on. Odysseus splashed through the swash and leapt up to his vessel, a tired laugh of relief when the sails pushed out.

Seven years since he had been on the ocean, yet when he grabbed the lines and pulled against the tarp, the ship rocketed from the island in the hands of an expert. Hermes flew above him, keeping watch on the divine wall that kept Ogygia isolated from the rest of the islands of the expansive sea. He tucked his nose under his helm and brought out his staff, flying inches in front of the craft to break it through.

The ocean swelled under the tied beams. No longer was it a bright blue surrounding a paradise, but the inky, salt of the distant world's stream. This very same water eventually ran into the Underworld, and therefore shared its haunting hue.

"Easy there, Oceanus," Hermes quipped, circling down to rest his feet on the rising bow of the boat. It lowered back down, and the strongest winds then died off, tossing Odysseus to grasp the mast. Hermes twirled in his excitement. "And just like that, Ody, you're free!"

That fact took a few minutes to digest. Odysseus just continued to sink down the mast's beam. Which, very well, Hermes could do that too. The young god removed his helmet and sat.

Wasn't he supposed to feel overjoyed? He was allowed to go home. His family was within reach.

"My friend?" Hermes asked. "You're safe now. There's nothing around us only because you've been cast to the edge of your world, but fear not! The stars are the same that shine over your beloved Ithaca. You can see them still, just you wait, I'll show you myself!"

"Twenty years," Odysseus whispered, and Hermes lowered his hand from the sky. "I'm not the same man I once was. What if she doesn't recognize me? What if Telemachus loathes to have this... this *creature* as a father?"

"Yes, and *what if* the queen has grown a lizard's tail? What if that treasured prince has one arm, or what if your hilly island burst from a volcano after centuries of being dormant? What if the sun never shines or the ocean burns to ash or we gods get cast away by our successors? Oh my, what if humanity loses the ability to speak, to read what wonders I have taught them to scribe!" Hermes threw both his arms up and rolled back. "I can do this too, you know: worry about utter nonsense. It won't change anything. Your ladyship — she'll know you. Don't insult her by thinking she couldn't. And your son knows not of any creature for a father — he's in good hands. A guide is with him now, too, teaching him to come to know you."

There was all the time in the world to let Odysseus sit in his thoughts. The sun was dragged swiftly to the west as the day left them behind. Not much headway without any strong winds or oars, Hermes hummed. Blowing a little gust to keep them going wouldn't attract too much attention from his family. Little things were natural; helping seafarers was definitely in his domain when Poseidon was away.

They were going to have to be careful about using the sea lord's name. Like a summoning spell destined to bring Hermes' passenger right to his doom.

No thank you, Uncle, you can stay right where you are with the Æthiopians. I pray they are dancing and smoking all the victims by your temple so you grow drunk on merriment.

A quaint nudge to the sail and the small vessel continued its way east. The path was long by sea, longer in a one-man craft.

"Here," Hermes said, holding out his caduceus.

Odysseus looked up from his brooding. "What?"

"You have no oar, you hairy oaf," Hermes replied. "Take it and start rowing."

Watching him test the touch was entertaining, tapping the golden rod thinking it would electrocute him or turn him to stone. It looked funny in his hand — the jewel affixed at the top, fluttering its ethereal wings; the serpents felt the change in ownership, breaking free of their frozen state to hiss in protest. Odysseus immediately held the staff back.

Hermes giggled, pushing the two snakes' heads until the staff shifted into a long, sturdy oar. "Don't fear those two. If they didn't like you, they'd bite right away. Kleistós would knock you right out, but Anoize is the dangerous one. She's how I was able to make your comrades forget they saw me…"

He bit his tongue. *Very smart, Hermes, very smart. Pat yourself on the back and then eat a rock, you imbecile.*

Pushing the oar through the heavy water, Odysseus let his thoughts sit on the ocean's surface and Hermes tried not to fidget through his contemplative silence.

"I've taken so much life," whispered the man. "By my orders or with my own hands, even my inaction, I've sent men to their early graves."

"Ody, my dear friend, you'll give *me* silver hairs if I allow you to sulk in your self-pity. You row, I'll talk, and when it's your turn to speak, you may talk about your memories of your lovely courtship and happier thoughts, yes?" Hermes leaned on the little deck and propped his feet up on the mast's beam. "If it brings you any comfort, I walked them to the ferryman myself. Those that are ready to cross have the means, I took care of it all."

"Are you allowed to do that?"

"My job as a psychopomp is very unregulated," he chuckled, though the humor didn't quite reach. "The guardian of the rivers already knows me too well; he relishes in our bound journeys, the kinky fiend."

Another strong stroke, Odysseus' melancholy turned to confusion. Not every day one hears a god gossiping about his deathless colleagues — and Hermes had so much gossip to share.

"You once asked about why I offered your blood with my ichor," he said. "I've tied my time with yours. For as long as your heart beats, I voluntarily committed myself to finishing what I've started. Makes it a little complicated to keep me from interfering in your difficult nostos. You have *no* idea how boring it is to be chained to the earth — I actually think it went all the way down to Tartarus! Imagine me! Having to drag a chain like that around Mount Olympus, and in front of all the lesser gods too!"

"All that for me," Odysseus shook his head. "That wasn't a good choice with all we've gone through; the pressures and pains of being human are nothing a god wants to have."

"Not a good choice, no, but it was the right choice. And I'd do it again despite angering my father. You're the baby *I* refuse to throw from the palace."

The oar shuddered, caught by a swell and slipped from Odysseus' hands with a sharp stifle, but Hermes calmly summoned it back and dipped it into the water himself until the rocking eased up enough to hand it over.

Dear Odysseus scrutinized him from the front corner of the deck. Fallen open like a big, old book, the son of Laertes allowed every conflict from that night pass his face. Hermes observed the Troy scene play out again from the mortal's point of view, pleading to a voice who never even showed herself to him. *Kill the son, kill the son, do what is good for your people or there will be consequences.*

"I cannot see where Prince Telemachus will find any monster in a man who didn't want to murder a helpless infant," Hermes said so casually without accusation, like it wasn't about the old general whose grey eyes had formed red rashes around.

Odysseus rowed until the sun disappeared and Nyx began her starlight chase across the sky. There was a brief spat about rest and taking watch; preferably the queen of Ithaca would like an *alive* husband when he arrived on their shores, and Odysseus wasn't going to make it if he passed out at an inopportune time. It was lucky enough to be within the summer months, for the breeze in the dark wasn't biting nor struck up any bumps on the skin.

Cloaks were more than enough to bring some comfort to sailors, and Odysseus, as he crawled to the center of the raft, cocooned himself in his.

The clothes Calypso gave were rather extravagant, maybe too nice, to be laboring at sea with. Yet with some folds and spreading about all that extra cloth, they provided a makeshift pillow and a thin blanket to tuck around his legs.

Hermes, in hand with the magic oar, shifted it back to the sleep-charming caduceus. Not that he needed to use it, his poor man was toeing the line of unconsciousness before his cheek hit the beams. Ahead of them drifted the Great Bear, her constellation stalking over the horizon, and the cherished Pleiades — above the hunter drawing straight his bow — to the left where Ithaca waited far across the seas. If they kept the Pleiades to their portside, they were on the right course.

"I can keep going," Odysseus argued, staring at the white stars. Hermes didn't doubt it, he'd seen him awake for days on end.

The young god replied, "Why should you? I'm here to keep your craft at ease and straight on its route. Half your troubles are mine to bear, so take half a rest. When Dawn returns, I'll wake you."

"Hermes?"

"Yes, my friend?"

"Thank you," Odysseus said, "for not forgetting me."

Oh, the damn mortal was going to make him blush.

"Ody," he laughed, a mere whisper, though his wings fluttered happily, "you're rather impossible to forget."

A heavy hand pinched at the draping cloth of Hermes' cloak. It was empty of souls, of course, and Odysseus shouldn't have any inclination that the fabric once held all several hundred of his companions. But the pinch became a grip, and he pulled the long cloak to his face, his shoulders silently rocking like a faraway earthquake. Hermes propped his knees up to his chin. There was a dim light shining from his staff, a torch in the blackness.

And he thought. It was his duty to think now, plan ahead for what could be obstructing the nostos. To anger the god of travelers was a difficult and ridiculous thing to do, but he was toeing the line when talking to Calypso. Such a naive goddess, needing to lie to herself to feel happiness.

Hermes sighed.

Prayers from around the world filtered into his head. They were much less violent when he was in their realm: little breaths from their last libations for the night — the offerings filling him with vigor.

"Bring us safely to Pylos, divine Hodios Hermes, to beach on her sandy shores without harm and without delay."

The voiced prayer cracked through all the rest. A voice of a young man, restless and eager.

Hermes unclipped his cloak and let it remain at rest with Odysseus as he flew up as high as he dared to go, staring beyond the stars of his beloved mother and her sisters, down to where the kingdom of old Nestor sat on the coast of the Mycenaean state, a hundred miles from Ithaca. Cupping his hands around his eyes, he scanned the ocean. An opulent ship sailed in the night, lit with torches. At the high end of its stern, atop the half-deck, sat that very young man wrapped in fleece, his chin tucked to his chest.

A man stood beside him, back straight and elegant, a single hand resting on the top of the throne. The man's face turned towards Hermes, over four hundred miles away — not even a speck in the sky — and inclined his head.

The young god laughed, practically rolling in the air.

"Your path be swift and your ship be strong," Hermes replied. He watched his great-great grandson leap from his fine chair, excitedly grasping his new friend's arms for *great Mentor, I have heard the god's response!* was loud and clear over the curve of the earth. Hermes folded his hands across his chest, swooping back to the tiny raft that held onto the old, lost king.

Perhaps a little faster wouldn't be so detrimental, he thought, summoning his staff to become an oar once more.

Chapter 14

On the seventh day came a large crag that brought heavy groans to both man and god. The sun, which provided most of the day's travel pleasantries, disappeared under the roiling fog that spat out of the abysmal cave. The two travelers knew this was coming, continued rowing knowing it was coming, yet were so surprised to see that the damned strait still remained in the spot it always had been at.

The audacity!

"Nothing says expertise like going through this a third time," Odysseus said, securing everything he could beneath the shallow deck. He'd been shunted through by Zeus' storm, taking on Charybdis alone by clinging onto low hanging branches and allowing the pitiful planks of tied wood he had been drifting on be swallowed up. He had timed his fall into the monster's mouth to the gurgling water spitting back up, sending him and his craft tumbling out into the Tyrrhenian Sea. It left him exhausted, unable to control where he sailed to.

Hermes ran his hand through his curls. The looming entrance bore a deeper sense of dread than the opening to Hades did.

"I *do* owe you for last time," he said, puffing his cheeks. The more divine intervention used, the more noticeable it was, but there remained no message sent about the *Lord of the Sea* finishing his bountiful celebrations.

Odysseus pointed to the hanging sword that sat in its sheath on Hermes' belt. "That would kill Scylla, would it not? No more heads grow from her tendrils, do they? Tell me now, Hermes, or I'll start my venture around the crag by swimming."

"She's not a hydra," Hermes complained. "And we cannot both be stupid — of our two lovely, beastly ladies, you know you'd be better off with Charybdis."

The ship swirled in one of the monster's many pools. Odysseus tightened his grip on the ropes while Hermes nonchalantly floated above the beams.

"I may, perhaps," he said. "But my raft is not guaranteed; and there's such a long way left to go — I can't have it be destroyed. Not until I reach Ithaca."

"No, no, your raft can go through Scylla's cave. She wouldn't bother with an empty boat. There were plenty of men in the past who succumbed to the Sirens where their ghost ship would sail through that cave unmolested."

Hermes' idea was stirring a wicked grin upon his face.

Odysseus locked up from stowing the sail and paused, letting it unfurl again. "I'm getting in the water," he said, turning to the edge to avoid Hermes' cackling.

"You can't tell me you haven't thought about it. That the idea of it doesn't bring up your morbid curiosity."

"I cannot *fly.*"

"I'd carry you."

"No!"

Hermes plopped his helmet atop Odysseus' head. Without the plume of the average war helm, or the flourish of Hermes' wings that curved around the metal, Odysseus looked very silly. It was lovely. Hermes secured the strap beneath the bearded chin before he could fight back.

"In case I drop you," Hermes said.

Odysseus curled his rough hands around Hermes' throat. "I've killed for less."

"And I've done more foolish things," Hermes replied, tickling Odysseus' elbows.

Odysseus didn't move despite the ship sailing faster towards the swallowing whirlpool. With a sly step, Hermes was off of the boat, hovering with it as it twirled and rocked and took on the rapid waters.

"It's going to Scylla, I'm hoping you come with me!" he shouted, striking the side of the vessel with his staff.

It veered violently to the left tunnel of the cave where the waters moved deceptively gentler. The son of Laertes bounded across the beams and vaulted to Hermes' waiting arms, smacking the young god back a good three feet while he clung to the lithe body.

"If you can take *any* form, why don't you give yourself more muscle to grab onto," Odysseus grumbled, trying to find a secure way to remain above the water. They opted for the back, for Hermes to carry him like baggage; else he may be tempted to drop the mortal for insulting him, or turn him into the ram he basically was to carry over the shoulders.

He didn't fly with passengers... ever, really. The talaria and his own wings supported him and they were fully capable of withstanding a mortal's weight, even one as dense as Odysseus; but if he went as fast as he normally did, the sun-worn skin of his progeny may burn right off.

Oh well, in they went!

It was as terrible as they both remembered, even above the violent action underfoot.

The ugly gurgling made the smoggy water feel like spit when it soared around and whipped them in the cheeks. Tucking his nose into Hermes' back, Odysseus let the helmet take most of the strikes; but *oh*, poor god, lifting his cloak to cover the lower half of his face — what a sacrifice he took. It would've been simpler for Hermes to fly up and over the crags, but fly too low with Odysseus and Scylla would climb her rocks to grab him, and fly too high? The man's breath would be spent.

Roaring reverberated up the walls. It was astonishing the caves along the strait had held up so long.

Through the immense columns far off on the other side of the cavern, the little boat floated on, unbothered, like a forgotten toy in a bath rocking gently along the pull of the river.

Hermes jumped over a rushing rock that Charybdis ripped from its walls. It hit the stalagmite behind them, shattering into a dozen pieces. *A little faster, there*, he urged himself, kicking up mist as his talaria thundered against the waves.

"Hold on," he warned. Odysseus pulled in closer.

With a parting salute to the sea-creature, Hermes launched them through the cave faster than three dozen oarsmen could row. The shout from his backpack was lost to the air well behind them.

But then he was skidding, skipping along the surface of the Ionian Sea like a stone along a still lake when the cave's ceiling disappeared above them. *Stopping, stopping,* he whistled. Better to change the weight — and up Odysseus went, two stories skyward while Hermes adjusted his chiton. The one he layered on top always liked to slide around his shoulder when he specifically pinned it to his underlayer.

"HERMES!" Odysseus plummeted passed him.

"You're fine," he replied, snatching his hand. The man swung around like a pendulum, up and over, until he dropped into Hermes' arms.

Shaken, but no more worse for wear, Odysseus lifted the helmet from his eyes. Hermes bonked it with his forehead.

"We're out! Not too bad. We've beaten your boat, but I can float around with you until it comes out. Shouldn't be longer than another two minutes — that water was *moving.*"

"My insides are still moving," Odysseus said and Hermes held him thoroughly away from his body.

"If you're going to be sick, be sick that way."

Odysseus shook his head and lowered his hand from his mouth. "I'm fine, just... get me to the boat before I change my mind."

* * *

On the twelfth day, a steady stream took control of the raft. The two of them sat cross-legged from each other while Odysseus carved shafts for the arrowheads he shaped. Hermes once watched Apollo make his arrows, casted heads in bronze to keep the edge sharp. These were cut and barbed from flint and stone, whatever Calypso had included in her gifts, attached tightly to every shaft he finished.

There were no feathers inside her supplies to use as fletching, not even fowl to pluck as the meat would rot before they found any safe land to beach and cook it. From the splinters overtaking his mortal's hands to the four feathers placed behind his ear, Hermes sighed and dug his own fingers into the down of his head, pinching one close to its molting stage anyway, and plucked it.

Then he plucked another…

"Cut and shape them as you see fit. They'll be sure your intent flies true to its quarry," he said, holding out what made up most of his left wing.

Odysseus, breaking from his tired stupor, stared at the fletchings in abject horror.

His voice cracked. "What have you done?"

"They'll grow back. I'm a god, remember?"

"Yes, but," Odysseus cautiously took them, shielding each from the wind, "these are… You look like a strummed fowl."

Hermes clapped his hands to his head. "Then don't look at me until they grow back! Mighty Zeus, I was trying to be kind!"

"And I'm grateful, but —"

"No, no, it's too late. Make your arrows and shoot me to put aside my unseemly appearance now."

"I have yet to make a bow."

"Stab me, then, Ody. Must I spell it out for you? Good grief —" His other wing perked up, an antenna to an incoming prayer.

"Dearest Hodios Hermes, bless us again as we continue on to Sparta! I am to meet the famous King Menelaus, the man who brought my father and all his allies to war to rescue his wife. My visit to King Nestor went splendidly! He gifted me his youngest son, Peisistratus — well, not gifted, of course, but…"

Hermes snorted.

"I could use your skill for eloquence and persuasion, Lord Hermes. Mentor declares it would do me some good. I need to find my father. Could you lead me to him? Are these too many demands? I should stop, right?"

"Are you alright?" Odysseus asked. He had scooted closer in the time it took to hear all of the Ithacan prince's pleas. The divot in his brow matched the day Hermes was overtaken by Zeus' speech, now with a few more wrinkles.

The one-winged god took a long look at Odysseus.

Yes, he supposed many parts of him passed down to the prince: the gentleness of his grin, the dark hair that curled in smooth waves...

Mentor, oh Athena, you are plain in your disguises, he mused. *Still too shy to show your face to this family?*

"I was receiving a prayer from your son," he answered truthfully. "He too is on a ship, sailing down the coast of the empire."

"What?" Odysseus exclaimed, throwing his hands atop Hermes' knees. "My son? You've heard my boy? What does he ask for? How does he sound? Why is he at sea?"

"A prayer, yes, also yes, and," Hermes nudged the man's face back, "he begs when he finds his father, that the old man has bathed before they embrace one another. He sounds sweet, though a bit flustered. Some children are, usually, when they pray for something real."

A bittersweet smile settled on Odysseus. "He looks for me?" he asked.

"It appears he was persuaded to speak to your old allies. Arriving in Sparta tomorrow, come daybreak if I'm willing."

"Be willing!" He pushed back against Hermes' knees, prostrating with all the room he had. "Oh, Hermes, please be willing."

"You're embarrassing yourself, my friend. As amusing as this is, there's no need. The son of Odysseus will make it to every harbor he pleases with no delay on my part. It'd be rude to deny the queen her own prayers of his safe nostos."

"We must hurry, then, to greet him when he returns home: my son—!" Rolling to his feet, he took Hermes' staff and thrust it into the waves, the gold having little time to turn to its wooden oar. The vessel lurched forward with the extra strength. "Fill the sails, dear sire, I care little for the things that hold you back!"

Hermes tucked the arrows and knives into the hold. *Another foolish request, but who was this god to decline a faster voyage?*

Hopping unbalanced into the air, he inhaled as much as his great lungs could take and blew the canvas taut with a confident snap.

* * *

On the seventeenth day… or maybe it was the eighteenth — time moved so slowly in the mortal realm — a line of land was spotted far off in the distance; the rise of a sandy mountain, covered with green speckled trees and stone houses. The sky was still pink with Dawn's sweet fingertips, the shadows taking a gentle blue hue.

Odysseus sat on his makeshift bed, mindlessly sifting his fingers through Hermes' wings now that they had grown out. The god laid in his lap with a small finger harp, snapping a lullaby tune the two of them had made up in the past week.

"That's Same," Odysseus whispered, as if speaking louder may break a beautiful illusion. "There was a boar I hunted there like the one I struck down with my grandfather all those years ago. To avoid my spear it ran through the caves, but I knew a route from a small cenote in the center of the island. Caught it unawares. Athena was always so proud of me back then."

"She apparently liked to mark you too," Hermes said, tapping the old scar that took up a large portion of Odysseus' leg where the hair didn't grow. "Does that all the time to Ares." He strummed a few more notes.

Odysseus admired the island, and contemplated the challenge that awaited behind it. "My mother told me," he said, and his voice grew angry, "of the young suitors harassing my wife for her hand. How long it's been since she passed, and this treachery in my palace has only been growing in my absence. For *years* they've been breaking the law of xenia and I've not been there to issue their punishment."

"Perhaps that's why Zeus allowed you your freedom — to do so on his behalf," Hermes yawned. Almost three weeks with little sleep was calling it close for the divine. Odysseus' lap was rather comfortable though. Good for Lady Penelope. He imagined her hair would also be played with while her husband was lost in his thoughts.

Not many husbands were so gentle; Hermes would write a thorough review.

The raft rocked as a quick ripple moved inland. It was so minuscule, if they were standing it would've been practically unnoticeable.

Hera's heraldess, Iris, pierced through his head. *"He has left Æthiopia!"*

Oh.

Oh no.

Hermes sat up at once. Odysseus watched the vein form on his forehead and climbed to his feet, holding tight to the rigging.

"Athena," Hermes called.

The sea continued to ripple as the seafloor itself shook with every step the furious god took. Odysseus stared longingly at his beloved islands.

Hermes flew about the deck. If there was any time to lighten the load, it was now. He tossed half-empty crates of food overboard, emptied the casks of wine and water, hurtling the things like discuses. The wind built up, pulling the boat against the resistant waters. Gathering a rope around his arm, he'd pull the ship on his own strength, but what did discretion matter now? If he carried Odysseus in his arms once more, they could glide right to the Ionian isles.

Skimming the waves, he skipped in a quelled worry to Odysseus' side. The man grasped the mast with both hands as the raft wobbled.

"Time to go," Hermes said, dropping his caduceus in its belt loop. The wind whipped his cloak's long tails back out to sea while the raft lurched sideways. Still, he walked along the waves, waiting for Odysseus to take hold of his shoulders, his neck, anything.

But Odysseus' attention was behind him, eyes wide enough to see the pupils constrict, full of panic and despair.

Hermes' flared gold. "Come, Ody—" he shouted, almost a command, an unfinished command.

Heavier than a boulder, the hooves of Poseidon's immense cavalry collided with his side, tearing the young god away from his friend and sending the raft spinning back.

His ribs flexed cracked, trampled flat on the waves. In trying to keep himself above the water, he tucked his knee and slipped between the rest of the stallions' massive legs.

The sky grew black.

Zeus was going to deny ever knowing about this betrayal.

A flush of rapid foam pulled further out to sea beneath Hermes' sandals, building up on itself as high as a tidal wave: a mountain of inky, furious water. From the depths struck three heavy prongs, piercing the air with horrible screams, ripping through the ocean as it rose to the clouds overhead. As large as Zeus could grow in his lightning cloud, Poseidon grew in his sea.

No definition from Man could exist except the unequivocal Sea Monster.

Son of Zeus.

Shit.

Hermes dodged another stampede of the endless horses who rose and fell in the growing storm, twisting a relentless typhoon around them. Wisps of thick mist slapped his cheeks and drenched his hair. Wind with the strength of the Titans sent him tumbling back right past Odysseus' raft like a loose kite.

He heard his poor friend call out as he clung to the mast.

Tricking the gods to change their minds the moment I turn my back? Poseidon's eyes opened in this form, a cold glow under the blackness, full of ire. *You'll regret making a mockery of me.*

The moment his talaria dipped an inch under the surface of the water, Hermes knew he was caught. A dozen, clawing hands gripped his leg, and again, Hermes was violently ripped upwards. This was a different fear than Zeus. His father in his wrath was not resentful of Hermes, but his uncle had no qualms about serving a harsher punishment. Zeus' justice was quickly served with a slow recovery; Poseidon's, like his temper, lasted as long as he pleased.

Poseidon's hand swallowed Hermes whole. Dense and cold, the water that formed the god wanted in all its might to force itself down his throat, to get into his body by any means to force some petty submission. But Hermes had a great propensity for breath, and legs that wouldn't stop kicking until he was fighting against the surface like a spear thrust in battle.

What use is there protecting this mortal when he has caused me so much trouble? Poseidon rumbled. *If I am no longer fated to kill him, Hermes Dolios, because of* your *amorality to your family in favor of Man, then perhaps through you I will get my fill of vengeance.*

The words were clear and tired and bitter as Hermes breached the outside and sucked in all the air he could. So high up against the dreadful wind, frost formed on his curls. "Poseidon, you're clearly mistaken! Let me explain and we can come to an amiable resolution. I don't abandon Olympus in favor of Mankind. To love one is to aid the other. Don't you underst—"

He was doing very well in finding his speech before Poseidon reared back his immense arm and pitched Hermes through the black clouds rumbling above their heads with the willpower of a hurricane.

A shooting star, Hermes tumbled over and over and over towards the edge of the world, the skin of his body singed by the sheer speed as he fought to slow down.

Space thundered around him. Not from Zeus, but the strength of the Earth-Shaker and his trident, churning the waves and whipping heavy gales from the domain of Aeolus.

No storm had existed as immense as this in his lifetime, and all just to torture *one* man?

To disrupt the blessed nostos, one protected by the patron god's own presence. Diplomacy's chance had come and gone. Poseidon succeeded at one thing, and it was just to piss him off.

Hermes' wings flared out. There was no patience left in him for the elder god.

You think, dear Uncle, I won't be the eternal nail in your side for this?

Burning his feet on the sky, Hermes dug his hands into the air, nails clawing into the ether. There wasn't a wind in this world that could hold him back, and his uncle was a fool to think he wasn't still the fastest god in this realm of humans or immortals otherwise.

He was a god of words, of prayers and pleas, of trade and wit and everything in between — and facing Poseidon and his storm, grasping steadfast to the corners of that wooden vessel, Odysseus only needed to raise his voice to the heavens.

"Hermes!"

And Hermes was there.

His form raced to catch up with himself, molding together like feathers and paper and the words that they held until he finally ran flush with ichor. He grabbed Odysseus' arms and heaved him up out of the waves onto his craft. Odysseus' muscles shook under the frigid air as the sea god spun the cold currents to the surface. The tears he shed intermingled with the salted, spitting swells, continuing to fall even after Hermes wiped them away.

"If I had just died alongside my brothers on the field of Troy," Odysseus cried, "I would have had a hero's funeral, and my glory would be spoken across the lands by my comrades. Not this — this wretched death."

"You will not die," Hermes replied over the gales. "I refuse to allow y—"

He heard it before he felt it.

A hissing burn of scalding water shot up behind him as a near-mortal sized hand grasped his neck.

"Y—you," Hermes stuttered out. His sight flickered like a candle flame. He was becoming sick of the interruptions, now this was just rude.

Poseidon's trident protruded from his gut, diagonally set, just below his heart. The material gold rippled from underneath its watery image. Each prong was barbed, hooked on Hermes' glimmering chiton.

An odd feeling: the stinging pain pulsed through every nerve in his body as ichor rushed to try and heal the skin around it.

Holy blades — *great Gaia*, Hermes winced, the hold on Odysseus slipping away. Poseidon's large hand came around to grip at his face like a ready assassin prepared to snap his thin neck.

"Do you know what happens to papyrus when wet? To voices when the lungs are full of water? To little gods who swim too deep?" Poseidon said with a sneer.

Hermes bit sharply on his tongue and coiled his hands around the outer prongs of the trident as they teetered just feet away from the unstable boat. Kicking his feet did nothing but bubble forth more ichor. His head fell against his uncle's grip.

This couldn't be it, this was a terrible end to the story. Hermes didn't care for terrible stories.

"Poseidon!" Through the wind and the rain, a wrathful voice cut his thoughts short. "Your grievance is with me," Odysseus shouted. From his side he pulled the golden sword of Hermes from his belt.

The conniving thief must have taken it when Hermes wasn't paying attention.

He laughed through the pain as Odysseus heaved the blade with expert precision, the shining metal plunging through Poseidon's exposed face. Ichor exploded from the god's eye in a disgusting display of curses and crazed cries, pouring hot over Hermes shoulder.

Poseidon reared back, retreating into the sky with Hermes flailing like a speared fish.

"That's my boy!" Hermes hooted, spitting up his own innards. He continued to pull his weight over the trident.

"Now," Poseidon said through gritted teeth, "that mortal will die." With an insane grunt, he tore the sword from his face. The blade plummeted to the sea.

A terrible wave came thundering down atop Odysseus' head, smashing the headmast to smithereens and hurled the sail far into the winds. The ship toppled violently across the sea, its captain thrown from the deck. And the old general disappeared under the inky void.

Hermes swallowed the ichor that built up in his throat and screamed out to Odysseus until his tongue grew heavy.

As long as the ichor was inside, he would be fine. Definitely what his brother taught him.

He scanned the waves for any sign of Odysseus breaking the surface, but the little man was nowhere to be seen. Poseidon only laughed, a humorless, apathetic cackle, holding his trident out while his other hand covered his wound.

The rumbling sky echoed from afar.

"Even I must answer *my* children's prayers; hear *their* pleas," he muttered to Hermes. "Isn't that what you've preached these past years? I promised redemption for my son. You wish to make a liar out of me?"

There was nothing left in him to feel pity towards his uncle's argument, towards his wounded pride.

Through labored breaths, Hermes took one last hold of the barbed edges of the trident. The light hair along his arms stood up, a buzz overtaking his body. "Not a liar, no. We can't answer every prayer," he said, crying as he pulled himself free with a sickening slurp, "but Odysseus' fate is in *my* hands."

He fell a mere three feet before the blinding light surrounded Poseidon, and a deafening *CRACK* sent both tumbling in separate directions. The lightning bolt sizzled away, thrown by an austere warrior; the mighty chariot of Athena pounded overhead.

Go, Hermes. Find him, she exclaimed, drawing her spear to face Poseidon, her helm pulled over her cheeks.

Straightening himself, he dove into the ocean, a bird swooping to catch his food. The deep waters were warm within the storm, but the spinning light distortion sent the surface in every direction. If fish wouldn't be able to tell which way was up, how could a man? Distant booms muffled by the eerie silence of the sea brought a violent image of war back to Hermes' mind.

Athena was powerful; they could prevail.

Crashing waves above had enough wayward force to push Hermes sideways as he propelled himself deeper. From his stomach drifted his lifeblood, a golden luminescence swarming in clusters in the undertow. He glowed like an angler fish, willing Odysseus' body to create at least a shadow in his light.

The clothes gifted by Calypso were rapidly weighing the man down. Somehow, even her spiteful kindness caused him only strife. They floated half-torn off in his attempt to fight to the surface; Odysseus kicked against an unwinnable gravity. With quick work, he discarded the beautiful water-logged garments and moved his arms.

Down he continued, down, down, down until his shadows reflected across the sea floor.

But he wasn't going to drown, Hermes wouldn't let him. Taking Odysseus' face, he filled his lungs with breath.

With the talaria stirring the mess beneath, he kicked for them both to the surface. Poseidon's rage in his fight against Athena sent crushing waves one after another, barreling into Hermes' head as he shielded Odysseus from the worst of it. Brine poured from Odysseus' nose while he coughed and gasped between each swell.

Truly stuck within a bottle, where the king of the ocean shook the contents with all his might.

High above, blazing beams of light forced gaps in the black clouds: a burst of sun as a second chariot raced out of the heavens.

Hermes lacked the strength to fly out from the sea, but whooped until his lungs hurt when the glorious twins of Leto drew their bows taut. Artemis, on the back of Apollo's golden chariot, released a barrage of arrows into Poseidon's reformed oceanic body.

Odysseus began to slip from his grasp as they tread the black water. No matter how much Poseidon withdrew his attention from the storm, it still pummeled them with all his trident's power. Stampeding hits of horses' hooves ground them back under the waves.

They needed to get to land.

Hermes spun in place — they had gone off course, pushed north of Ithaca. The closest island shifted like a mirage through the clouds.

He hadn't been to that island in decades; very few mortals died there.

Without need for communication, Athena grabbed a hold of the winds and ceased their circling anger, lashing the storm's worst flat on the path ahead. Poseidon's cavalry scattered like mice.

"Swim, Odysseus," Hermes commanded, throwing his shoulder under the man to keep his nose above the surface. His weary legs eventually kicked, and four arms and four wings beat against the swells.

In mortal time they swam, stroke by stroke.

Odysseus raised his sharp eyes from the water, seeing the distant shore as they crested a wave. In what little energy he had left, he built up his pace. Hermes felt the warmth radiate from him, though it was fading fast, eaten by the sea.

Hours or days, it didn't matter, Hermes didn't allow Odysseus to slip through his fingers. The jagged reefs below his feet led only to deadly, jagged cliffs with a powerful surf that sought to crush mortal bones against cutting rocks.

Up with another swell and down onto those rocks, Odysseus gripped to the surface with all his power, blood pooling from his hands. A single cry to Oceanus for mercy slipped free with the remaining divine air in his lungs before Hermes bore the brunt of his progeny's weight.

And Oceanus knew the young god and his kin well and, in his kindness, calmed the next surge, peeling the waves back enough for Hermes to hoist them to the calmer shore of the river's mouth. His ichor streamed down his legs from the three gored holes in his gut and dyed the sand a murky black as it grew old and dry.

That isn't good, he thought, dropping to the ground in what felt like his greatest marathon run ever.

Odysseus lifelessly thumped in the sand beside him. Coated in cuts and seaweed, his swollen body was tinged blue. Hermes scrambled to his side, taking Odysseus' head in his sand-covered hands.

He wasn't meant to die, not this man. It was his destiny to make it back home. Hermes had promised him; and he had made an oath in return to not die until he was basking in his wife's glory, and only then if Death was ready for him.

"I am not willing to take your soul," Hermes muttered, pressing the damned spirit back into Odysseus' chest. "You keep that thing in this stupid, fragile body until I say so!"

He didn't intend to drip any ichor onto Odysseus' bare skin. In his panic to move away from the body, he only managed to smear the gold fluid across more of the lacerations. There was a hiss, like lava meeting water, and himself be damned there was nothing clean on him to wipe it away.

He really was a failure. Some god of Man, unable to keep his one traveler, someone of his own lineage, alive on his journey. His heart wanted to fold in and disappear, pressing against his ribcage. It had never pounded so hard before.

So this is what despair feels like — when everything is all for naught.

Hermes curled his wings over his face and wept, angrily pounding the spectre of Odysseus back again.

And Odysseus coughed.

Wheezed, really.

Rolling slowly to his stomach, brine gushed out of his mouth with tremendous force until his nose bled. He held his stomach as he cried through every nauseous pulse. They laid there, two idiots, practically nude, covered in their own fluids and sand. Hermes gaped at Odysseus, stupid, while the ichor tended to the nicks along the human skin before trailing off with the rest of the water that dripped from his tangled hair.

When Odysseus rallied some energy to look up from his lethargic stare with the sandy ground, he was met with Hermes' crimson-stained smile as the god's hands were coated with mortal blood. Hermes tried to understand why the ichor did not immediately dispatch Odysseus for the Underworld — how he was able to deny the soul its departure. It went against everything he was taught, every other encounter he was witness to. Touching ichor equals death on contact. And yet...

"Aren't we the luckiest bastards in the realm," he said. A weak laugh sent him collapsing into the sand.

He lowered his shaking hands to his tattered chiton, opting to simply rip the lovely fabric away to reveal the messy tear of godly flesh rather than let it fester. It was no different than getting cut from Ares' sword, or impaled by Apollo's arrows. The hole was just completely through his body and there were three of them. Sand was inching its way inside.

It would be *fine*.

Odysseus struggled to drag himself over, nose still dribbling with wine-dark blood. His lips quivered, the morning wind coming in from the sea was cold and froze his wet skin. "Hermes," he whispered, for his voice was nonexistent. "Where are we now to say we're lucky? This isn't my sunny Ithaca."

"This is Phaeacia," Hermes replied with a grunt. He pressed his palms against the wounds, quelling a hiss. "The people are favored by Poseidon, but don't fret, it only means they make headwinds in the ocean. Their nautical prowess is known on Olympus. We're just at the top of your beloved Ionian islands."

Being prompted to sit up, Odysseus ripped the cream silk that sparkled with speckled gold into strips, kicking away sand to get closer to wrap it around Hermes' abdomen. His whole body was vibrating from the cold. They needed to head inland before he froze to death. Dense woods laid ahead of them just beyond the banks where the wind wouldn't pierce.

"W-what if wild beasts drag me off as their meal?" Odysseus breathed in his anxiety.

They picked their way out of the bank, leaving one set of footprints behind, and fell into the grassy reeds with anticipatory sighs.

"I'll be sure they eat me first," Hermes said, holding back a yawn. He couldn't be the first one to admit his exhaustion.

But Odysseus didn't care to disguise his fatigue; he stumbled blindly into the wood, clinging to trees and his friend as he went, until they came across a soft-floored grove. He crawled towards two, single-rooted olive trees on instinct — their bushy leaves tangled up in each other cast a dark, impenetrable shadow underneath. No rain could slip through; the ground lacked any life except the soil that grew it and a mass of dead leaves from a forgotten winter.

Like clockwork, Odysseus took the task of clearing out a space for bedding down. Leaves clung to every part of him in bits and pieces before he used them to cover himself, a shield to the world of the living. He finally looked up through half-lidded eyes to Hermes carefully crouching by the small opening.

"There's room," he said.

Hermes chuckled. This was definitely not his bed of choice, but he was no longer averse to trying things the human way. He crawled inside and unclipped his cloak, folding it under their heads. As he laid back with a quiet groan, Odysseus immediately pulled him near, his arm around the god like the many times he had done to empty air when sleeping.

Warm and pleasant enough, Hermes mused, holding fast the makeshift bandage around his abdomen.

"Forgive me for losing your sword," Odysseus mumbled, sleep overwhelming his mind.

Hermes found the embrace very comforting. "It was worth it," he replied, letting his eyelids close, "just to witness the surprise on his face when you blinded him. The king had it coming."

"I don't like when my family is hurt. I can't control myself."

The arm relaxed and labored breath calmed, merciful sleep took Odysseus as the sun rose beyond the blessed olive trees. Hermes turned his cheek to the man. In him he saw the same way his brow creased, the parting of his lips, and curve of the cheek… some things that two generations before could not breed out.

"Yes," Hermes whispered. "Me neither."

Chapter 15

The young god felt Athena's presence the moment they came to the olive trees, but only as the day continued on to evening did her sneaking around wake him from his rest.

Sister, what continues to bring you away from the prince you've sworn to be guide and guardian to? he questioned, squinting up at the layered branches. *You've played our savior and condemned Poseidon back to Olympus. Shouldn't you return to your new warrior?*

Her voice replied in haste. She wasn't often one to rush along. *I shall set the dominoes up to fall in the son of Laertes' favor. Come tomorrow at daybreak, be not yourself. These people know us gods too well and to look as if we interfere would frighten the wise king.*

And where, then, are you going?

I will go home, she answered. *To be the voice of reason when the kings collide.*

Ah, certainly not a job Hermes wanted to bear. He hummed, content with the short interview. To think they could've done this seven… ten years ago. But where was the story in that? Not that it was all around flattering to show how long it took for the god of travelers to get this royal man home.

Odysseus slept like the dead, not a snore nor a sigh to be heard. Hermes pressed his ear against the warm chest in search of gentle drumming. *Yep. Still there.* The cuts along his large, roughed hands had sealed shut, tiny remnants of ichor holding them together.

Oddly peculiar. He wasn't a demigod unless Anticlea got real frisky with another deity. Or if Autolycus, when naming his grandson, imbued his own demigod blessing upon him. Though what thoughtful grandfather would name an infant after his own angry, sardonic mood? *Oh, Ody, you could have been named something sweet like your nurse offered up; I could be calling you Polyaretos.*

But remembering his solemn expression holding true the godly blade, Odysseus was a fine name for him.

Hermes closed his eyes again. It wasn't often he had an excuse to rest for a whole day and night. He dragged his finger over his bandaged belly. His back was numb. Like his friend, he too was slowly healing, though without proper care he risked it scarring. He enjoyed baring his chest too much to have it marked up.

No matter — Apollo would be on it the moment Hermes was in sight.

The next daybreak, as instructed, Hermes was no longer himself. The disappearance of the split-tailed cloak left Odysseus' head to thump against dirt. There was noise from that man now — the growl of hunger, and the uncomfortable mumbling that came with it. Odysseus pawed out in the bed of soil, searching for the traveling companion that accompanied him for so long.

His hand met a smaller creature, something soft. In a panic that some wild beast crawled its way into his sanctuary, he tightened his grip before he opened his eyes.

Hermes crowed loudly in his face, puffing up his luxurious saddle feathers.

Odysseus' firm grasp did not waver. "I will eat you," he said, his voice returning.

"I do taste delicious," Hermes blipped like a fleeting thought in Odysseus' mind. He stamped his feet along the crunchy leaves, crushing them to fertilizer. *"You cannot stay in here forever. Come."*

"Why are you a cock?" Odysseus asked, slowly crawling from his olive tree hideaway. The gentle sun lit up the grove and revealed just how awful the man looked in his present state. It was so horrid, Hermes immediately prayed to Athena himself that this plan of hers was foolproof.

"The Phaeacians do not get visitors often, but they're familiar with my lovely face and the usual mortal forms I take."

Odysseus cracked his neck and stretched out his arms. "Why not take on a different mortal form? Be an older man, then. Or a woman if you feel so inclined."

"This one allows me to be completely unquestioned."

"Yes, but then I look the fool for talking to a bird."

Hermes wandered around the grove, nearing the trees opposite the ones that hid the sound of the open sea. There were washing pools not too far from here, and high upwards from there lay the winding, pristine town. Phaeacia climbed modestly in height, though at her peak was not its palace, but temples to honor the gods. The palace lay on the slope next to them, wide and airy, with colorful draping silks that could be seen from all corners of the island.

Athena's scent permeated the breeze — her plans stretching all over this utopian community.

Odysseus lumbered behind him, stalking through the tall grass like a mountain lion looking for its next meal. A cryptic beast, even, naked and disheveled, unlike any man that claimed to be a king. He scanned for rabbit, for deer or boar, willing and hungry enough now to catch them with his bare hands.

Hermes flitted in small circles. Unwilling to watch his human weak with hunger, he searched along the tree branches.

"Some berries, Odysseus," he said, flying up to a low hanging stem to poke at a red one, rich with juice. Seven of them, nothing large, but it was food in an otherwise empty stomach.

The heavy splash of a ball and the resounding echo of shouting sent Odysseus against a tree, his fists closed ready to fight.

"What are they here?" Odysseus asked. "Are they violent murderers? Every land of Poseidon's bears only misery…" The shouts turned to laughter, the call of youthful women, which to most would have eased their worry, but the poor man couldn't relax. "Say these aren't nymphs who haunt the springs and wood, say it before I dare see for myself."

Hermes wandered along, for where there was splashing and giggling there were very often pretty, nude girls dancing like young goddesses. He wasn't going to lead Odysseus to anything less than peaceful — he was tired of infighting. His rooster form was missing some down feathers along his breast, no need for more plucking and skewing.

There was no prodding necessary, Odysseus wasn't willing to wait around and waste an opportunity for aid, no matter how small. From the olive trees, he stripped off a dense, leafy branch and shielded his groin for some modesty amongst his brine and sand-caked skin, and hair that desperately needed some attention to detangle and oil it strand by strand.

In the afternoon sun, the crustiness was all the more horrid.

He frightened the young women.

Of course he did. They scattered like lovely doves the moment he made himself known along the clear, washing streams.

But one stood her ground. The most courageous of the pretty girls, draped in the finest garb and shining diadem. No more than twenty, with hair as red as the walking beach crabs, she held her chin high as she perched upon a smooth, flat rock, regarding Odysseus' approach with the gentle eye blessed only by Athena herself.

Odysseus held his branch steadfast, falling to his knee and inclined his head like a suave suitor. "Here I am, Princess, at your mercy — are you a goddess, or a mortal like I? If you're one of the gods, you must be Artemis in the flesh — in your build and bearing, your grace..."

He flourished her with all the compliments a well-spoken, desperate man could bestow. Within the praise to her beauty and poise, he revealed some of his story: his army, a long campaign that doomed him to live misery after misery, from Ogygia and facing Poseidon, to being here now, *oh what torments will the gods give him next?*

"Grant some compassion, Princess, *please*. You are the first I have come to after all that I've suffered. I don't know this land, or the people in its city, nor anyone else on this shore. If I may beg you, my lady, to show me the path to town; allow me a rag to cover myself or any cloth you could spare… May the good gods give you everything your heart desires: a good husband and home, an everlasting harmony — for there's no better gift than that. When a man and wife possess their house, their two minds and two hearts work as one!"

The girl brought a thoughtful hand up the gentle curve of her arm and grasped her elbow. "Stranger," she said, "friend, you are hardly a villainous man and certainly are no fool. You know it is the gods, mighty Zeus, who hands our fortunes and misfortunes out. He has given you pain out there, it appears, and I am sorry that you must endure it." With a small smile, she inclined her head. "But you have landed on our shores, reached our city, and so will never want of clothing nor food nor gift. I'll show you to the town. We are Phaeanians, and I am the daughter of the generous King Alcinous. *We are beloved* by the deathless gods. They have hidden our precious island from other mortals so that no conqueror would ever lay waste."

She called to her handmaidens, who hid behind stones with their braids and twists hanging loose around their shoulders. They threw their veils up and over themselves before Hermes could weave between their long legs. Pretty like their lady, though not clever enough to show any attention to the luxurious rooster ready to kiss their feet.

"Tend to our wanderer well," she ordered. "Every stranger and beggar comes from Zeus. Take him to our picnic, bathe him, and keep him warm from the cold snap that offends our waters."

Hermes scurried along as the maidens brought Odysseus down to a sheltered spot of the river where the wind could not disturb them. They presented a fine shirt and a cloak to wear, laying them neatly on a slab, and handed over a shining golden flask of oil. He took it with shaking hands.

Odysseus lowered his chin and asked of the maidens, "if you'd stand a good way off, so I may bathe — I dare not do so in front of lovely, young girls. I'd be embarrassed to stand naked in your presence."

With light giggles they left him to the river. He lowered himself in the waters, the sand caked to his skin taken by its gentle current. Like an infant sitting in a tub, he took a long minute to come to, splashing his face with large cups of it, sending the brine downstream. Hermes waded in briefly, then found a pleasant spot on a nearby rock heated by the sun.

Present him as I would, Athena's request sounded in Hermes' mind.

Hermes raised his head to Odysseus. *"You're already looking much better,"* he said.

"I feel somewhat better," Odysseus replied, combing his fingers through his scalp. "It's been ages since oil has touched my skin, I've forgotten how nice it is." When he left the water, he took the flask and coated himself in the olive oil.

As he applied it to the ends of his hair, the curls appeared thicker, darker once more — akin to Dionysus' luscious waves. Gone was the silver hair born from years of stress, Odysseus had been returned to the polished black ram he was. Across his arms, his muscles shined; to his legs, he seemed to grow in height, like a warrior trained in the fine arts of Athena. From her good wishes, Hermes lent his power to pour splendor from Odysseus' shoulders. Even his old friend, Diomedes, would find this sly son of Laertes thoroughly in his prime.

Hermes added a little sparkle to the cloth that Odysseus dressed himself in.

For the pizzazz — humans love pizzazz.

Running after him as he returned to the princess and her entourage, Odysseus and Hermes took in the sight of her glorious painted wagon and fine mules while the women took in the sight of the transformed man. From a beggar to an anointed warrior of the gods, his bronze skin gleamed in the light.

And there was a cock that silently whisked by his side.

The princess tucked her lips behind an elegant hand, whispering to her maiden, "if I marry, let it be to a man like this. The gods cannot *all* be against him, he appears to be one among them." Clearing her throat discreetly, she gestured to their picnic they brought to the shores. "Come girls, give him wine and bread, our leftover dates and tagenites, and do so quickly."

A pink rosé was poured, light and sweet. Odysseus scarfed the plates of food down like he hadn't eaten a full meal in decades.

One young handmaid lifted Hermes from the ground with gentle hands. "How wonderfully blessed this morning has been! Dear stranger, you have a rare guardian to ward off ill luck. And what a handsome rooster he is, too," she said, bringing his wings to her cheek. "Oh dear, he appears to have been in a fight, poor, pretty thing."

Odysseus wiped the dates' juice from his lip. "He enjoys the compliments from a girl as fine as you," he said. "Must've known of your presence, his call alerted me to investigate. I'm fortunate to have listened."

Hermes let the girl smooth his feathers down while Odysseus finished his breakfast. It surely felt nice to be treated with civility after everything he'd gone through; to know this food wasn't forcibly given nor laced with potions and spells.

He still planted his stories with cautious lies, woven so intricately it was impossible to know. If Hermes were not himself he wouldn't have noticed, but mortal lies resonated like flaming effigies in speech.

The princess — who introduced herself by the name of Nausicaa — requested he follow her wagon alongside her girls, that they may escort him near the town through the harbors which hugged the island, where workers busied themselves crafting immense, beautiful ships in Poseidon's *royal precinct.* It took no guesses to see that this was where the people's pride was: their slipways full of carvers and rope-makers, mounds of perfectly polished oars. A smooth, but tapered wall clung to the rising hill above them on which the town was built. Five towers, strong and tall enough to kiss the skies, ringed the wall.

There were too many eyes who knew princess Nausicaa; and seeing her with a handsome and strange man when strangers *never* come up to the shores of Phaeacia would place her in a precarious situation. Gossip be that she'd either taken a shipwrecked man to be her husband, or he: a god newly arrived, to take her as *his* lover.

Too much scandal within the possibilities. She would leave Odysseus at the entrance of the town for him to work his way to her father's palace. If he could make a fair impression to the king, then that was his quickest route home.

It was an offer more generous than many — and better than being thrown to the gutter like an unwelcome beggar.

She directed him to a grove, blossoming like spring although the summer rippled on around them. Poplar trees were planted as an offering to Pallas Athena around a glistening fountain and meadows stretched beyond the island's possibilities. Within it was her father's estate, she claimed, where Odysseus could wait a few hours before making his way up to the palace on the hill.

"When you arrive, go straight to my mother," Nausicaa warned. "Grasp her knees and win her heart. Only then will my father be willing to offer you a ship."

"A wise king," Odysseus replied. He bowed his head and picked up the primping rooster from his throne of a pretty girl's arms. "Thank you, dear princess."

Nausicaa smiled from atop her wagon and inclined her head. Moving her whip forward, the mules continued on until the man was left alone in the grass, his feet still without sandals. His shoulders gradually rose. He ambled to the trees with Hermes in his embrace, like one would hold a child, and looked along every flowering poplar tree. Their heights were as great as Athena, Hermes would know it. He saw these trees often near the Underworld — the queen loved to tend to them along her own groves, which brought Hades much joy.

He was placed on the ground when Odysseus fell to his knees along the row of greenery. The sun had moved between their branches, casting fluttering shadows across the meadow.

"Hear me, daughter of Zeus, whose shield is everlasting and whose eyes see all," Odysseus whispered to the breeze. Hermes settled beside him. "Athena, hear my prayer at last — for you've never heard me when I was in pieces, a wretched man, a woeful champion left behind to suffer at the hands of the acclaimed god of earthquakes. I've called to you on the high cliffs of Ogygia; you must have been merciful enough to allow the good god of travelers to find me."

Hermes hummed.

"Grant me that same mercy here among the Phaeacian people. I haven't known human love and kindness for so long; I have forgotten what it feels like, what it sounds like, how it looks."

Hermes.

Hermes rested his head upon Odysseus' thigh and wished away the tears that threatened to fall from the man's eyes. *"She heard you,"* he said.

Olympus must have been stirring in chaos with Poseidon among them. Not a fiber of his being wanted to check in on anything up there. If Athena was in the ranks, then at least the palaces still stood.

If he were not a god, Odysseus' pets of stress would have crushed his rooster bones.

"If you say," Odysseus replied. The island's noises were so foreign to him, but the breeze was all the same. It commanded the grass to sway and the trees to dance like they were sitting among a symposium. "The princess says you gods bless them?"

"Blessed, cursed, there is little difference, isn't there," Hermes exclaimed. *"To be hidden away from Man, so far that coming here is like traveling to the far reaches of this realm, means they do not know culture far much beyond their own. If that's not something a man cares about, then this is a utopia. But to be trapped in a single place is hellish to me."*

"If I were to be chained up to Ithaca, I don't think I would mind. I miss the way the sun shines through my bedchamber windows; seeing the fishermen out in the harbor while the shepherds tended my flocks. I can retrace every hall and stair within my palace, committed it to memory before I left for Troy. That's my utopia: where my son and wife wander in wait."

"It's a lovely palace."

"Has my son sent you any more prayers? Have you heard him?"

"Last I saw, he was en route to your brother of Sparta, to be hosted by King Menelaus and the infamous Helen. She's resigned herself to be a happy wife. I've never seen a couple who started a scale of war as great as Troy return to

domesticity so quickly. Ah, but you don't care about that. Prince Telemachus travels with his most loyal men. He is tall, though lean. His voice is still young, like yours in timbre but the pitch of a boy's. Queen Penelope must love to hear him speak. And he speaks fast, sometimes his prayers are in a single breath."

"Penelope does that when she's nervous," Odysseus laughed, rubbing his face. "He must've learned that from her."

"And you just cry."

He wiped his eyes, shaking his head. "Well, I cannot lie to you of all people. You have come to know me better than most."

Another half-hour was enough time for Odysseus to consider that the princess reached King Alcinous' house. And Hermes smelled Athena's presence on their journey to the gates before the little girl carrying a jug of water *oh so coincidentally* crossed their path. The jug was large and filled to the brim, but the child never wavered in holding it. That was one of Athena's faults with humanity — overestimating how much mortals could handle.

Odysseus humbly placed his hand over his chest. "Dear girl, would you show a stranger some kindness in guiding him to the palace of he called Alcinous, the king who rules the people of these faraway lands? I know no one here in this city nor the farms that surround it and am weighed down with strife."

The girl with grey eyes smirked. "Yes, sir, I know the palace that you ask of; the generous king lives beside my noble father."

Athena, you spinner of tall tales, Hermes said.

She spared a glance to the rooster. "Best to hold onto that one as we must quickly make our way; the men here are not so keen on strangers, they are cautious of everything not from their lands. Only of their flying ships — gifts from Poseidon that dart through the waves like birds."

Hermes fluttered up to rest on Odysseus' broad shoulders.

Do not be getting lost, Athena replied. *We must make his time here move hastefully.*

They sped through the city streets, clouded in godly mist to hide them from prying eyes and provocations. Across the overlook of the harbors,

Odysseus gawked at their immense size and industrialization. Luxurious grounds where the nobles met always appeared above them, as if another man needed a higher perch to look out at the vast glittering ocean which remained calm around their shores. Of these perches, one led through covered marble halls to the palace that Odysseus had asked for.

The little girl stretched out her arm. "Good, old stranger," she said, "we have come while the king's sons are feasting. Go in with courage, for every gamble is given to the man who is bold. You will find the queen first — called Arete, for she is an answerer of prayers."

The royal queen of Phaeacia was a descendant of Poseidon: he sired her grandfather, and Apollo slew the girl's father. The king took her to wife and she became the most revered woman in the land.

Arguably.

Odysseus may have him beat by the way he speaks of his Spartan princess.

"Queen Arete lacks nothing of good sense and sound judgment. She is gazed upon as a god by her people, and of sorts by her husband," disguised Athena continued.

"Then I must win her sympathy," Odysseus said.

If only Hermes kept count of how fast Athena got herself out of there, running off with the speed of a mortal with legs twice as long, only to dissipate into the ether in her retreat to the mainland.

Very smooth, Hermes said.

I am attending to the prince, she responded.

As if you're not shy simply talking to him now; pretending to be a hundred other people.

Does he suspect?

You know more than I do that he wouldn't have been your champion if he was stupid. I'm sure he's suspicious, but he's tired and longs for home. Genuine help is a rare commodity. Dear sister, let's keep this line of communication between us open — tell me, did Father speak with Poseidon?

Odysseus silently approached the bronze palace doors.

He has, though the Earth-shaker rages on, Athena said. *He is not pleased with the children of Leto interfering, nor with either of us. Your wound, Hermes, has it sealed?*

Like three lovely stabbings. *As much as it will for now, yes.*

His ride stopped, hesitant in the entryway. A rush of emotion poured from Odysseus' heart.

The Phaeacian walls were as radiant as a god's temple, with brilliant friezes full of color that followed the long, glowing hallway. If they were underwater, it would be similar to Poseidon's palace, where the golden inner doors reflected warm light, and statues guarded each new room. They had the perfection of Hephaestus' handiwork. Thrones by the dozens sat against walls of the innermost chamber, covered with brocade sewn by the crafty women of the kingdom. Phaeacian lords equally would sit to dine and drink on unending feasts well into the night, accompanied by neverending servants.

The further Odysseus crept into the abode, the more luxury was simply draped at his feet. Pure wealth, yet trade was nonexistent, simply gifts from gods when they came to relish in King Alcinous' hospitality.

Odysseus stared in awe of it all the same way Hermes did of Calypso's nature utopia.

From the windows, orchards as far as the eye could see were lined with trees bearing ripe fruit year round: pears, apples, grapes, figs… if they bore strawberries, perhaps Hermes would come around more often.

Gawking spellbound at marvels must've been a family trait.

Odysseus snapped out of it, finally moving with swift feet where those lords were pouring out their last libations to Hestia and the giant-killer and guide — Hermes felt a swell of energy in his chest with their offerings. If it was a restful sleep they wanted, he would grant it as soon as they allowed his man a word.

Shrouded in Athena's mist, Odysseus went straight down the hall towards the larger chairs: those bearing the king and queen. His heart beat loudly, the vein in his temple pulsed against Hermes' side before the young god leapt off of him. and Odysseus flung his arms around Queen Arete's knees — the divine mist whisking away from his form.

And the room fell silent like death on the battlefield.

"Great queen, daughter of the gods," Odysseus beseeched. "After everything I have suffered through, I beg for mercy: yours, your generous husband's, the noblemen who dine with you. I pray the gods will flourish them with fortune and happiness all their lives, to pass to their sons and their sons' sons. For me, all I ask is a convoy home to my native land. How far away and for so long I've been from my loved ones where every day is a trial of suffering!"

Queen Arete, her auburn braids wrapped up around the crown of her head, bedecked in hanging beads of gold, pressed her hand to her heart as she watched Odysseus crumble from her knees to the ashes of the hearth in front of her, his head dipped so low he nearly prostrated himself.

Hermes lurked along the walls as the lords were frozen still. Soundlessly he rounded the chamber, and found amongst them the eldest lord to nip at the heels.

Broken from his silence, the nobleman rose from his seat.

"Alcinous, this is not right!" he cried out. "Are we not blessed by the coming of a stranger? Look how he sits on the ground like a slave at your holy wife's feet. Your people are awaiting your word, my lord. Raise up this man and seat him among us. We are not immune from Zeus' great law!"

Signaling to the servants to mix up more wine, King Alcinous, clothed in gold and embroidered waves along his himation, extended his hand to Odysseus and pulled him rightly from the hearth. To his other side he ousted his first-born, the most beloved son, from his throne, offering it to the worldly king. A maid brought him a pitcher of water to rinse his hands, and a table of bread and delights from the island was set up by his side.

With a stomach like an empty pit, Odysseus ate. Another round of libations, unusual after Hermes, were poured out to Zeus who guarded suppliants. Not at all an insult to Hermes' usual position in feasts — he felt rather relieved at the welcome.

The king stood after all the extra wine was poured and enjoyed. "Lend me your ears, my friends — lords and captains of our great island — as I speak from my heart now. Tonight you will return home to sleep, but at dawn, I call the elders to assemble. We will sacrifice to the gods and turn our minds to our guest's passage home. A new friend we have gained, and he will be one to witness our hospitality aboard our ships, bear no more strife or pain, and see his homeland soon enough, even if it sits on the very edge of the seas.'

He gestured kindly to Odysseus.

"He will be a guest of my palace, as many of the gods have sat beside us before and shared in our feasts."

Odysseus sat up warily. "King Alcinous, *please!* Don't compare me to the deathless gods, not in speech nor in your mind. I'm just a mortal man. If you know someone burdened with the worst of sorrows, I'm nearer to him than the divine." He pulled a piece of bread from its loaf and pressed it to his lips. "Hunger is a beast, my lord, and I'm honored to be given such a wondrous dinner to suppress the monster that growls within my belly. And if you at daybreak keep to your word, hurry, I beg, to set this unlucky guest on the beaches of his home. If I could just see the sun rise above it, my men, the house I've built with my own hands... I could die peacefully thereafter, and merciful Hermes may guide my tired soul."

The men applauded him before they took to their own homes, but Hermes stood in the center of the shimmering chamber, the night breeze casting his invisible cloak aside. He wasn't thinking often of the time he would have to carry that one star on him to Hades. Not soon; he wasn't willing to. He'd block Thanatos from arriving for as long as he was capable.

But mortals still died, eventually, ultimately; the curse of living.

To Odysseus, the rooster that roamed the empty room now came up to settle at his feet while the king and queen sat in the quiet of servants clearing the dishes and goblets. It was Arete who pulled herself forward in her chair and took a long look at the clothing the man wore, her voice sharp and direct.

"Stranger, I must be the first to question you as you came to me likewise. Who are you? Where is it you come from? Who gave you the clothes that you wear now?"

"She reminds me of Hera," Hermes said.

Odysseus ran his fingers over the chiton the princess gave him. "What a story it is, my queen, to recount to you from the beginning. I will be truthful in my retelling the recent journey for how I have come to be here, spare you nothing as you wish," he lied. "But to recount the last twenty years will take more than this night."

So he spun a tale, so very close to the reality of it. Of his time on Ogygia and how the goddess had a stroke of mercy to release him; his almost three-weeks at sea… All perfectly recounted with one main ingredient retracted.

Not once was Hermes mentioned to be at his side.

He would laugh if his laughter as a rooster was not just as obnoxious as his godly form, maybe more. Why would a god invest so much of his time into aiding one mortal? It would make Odysseus' earlier claims of being just a man, free from divine influence, false.

And his white lies now were so delicious.

At the mention of the princess Nausicaa and her tactful offers, Arete's stern eyes shifted to her husband. Alcinous rubbed his thumb against the gloss of his throne in the same way he pressed his mind around Odysseus' story.

"My daughter never escorted you here, my friend," he said, "but she was the *first* to offer hospitality?"

"Don't try to find fault with your flawless daughter now." Odysseus backtracked with a noble raise of his hand. "She insisted, but I dare not follow. The embarrassment *I* would find if you took offense at seeing me with her in my state. Are we men not already so suspicious, dear Alcinous?"

Anger didn't even dust Alcinous' brow. "I would never, friend. Why, after seeing what kind of man you are, I would welcome you to even wed my daughter, become my son-in-law if you so please. I would give you a house and great wealth if only you stayed."

Odysseus feigned a smile. "I'm a married man of many years, good king," he replied. "Though your daughter deserves someone greater than I for her deeds. My life is owed to her. But I only desire to return home."

"Indeed." Alcinous nodded. "I've chosen tomorrow evening for your departure. On that voyage home you will sleep so soundly while my people sail you through calm and gentle currents. They fly as if on the wings of the giant-killer's golden sandals — can cross the world in a single day."

* * *

They sang praise to Zeus and relished in each other's gentle company while Arete had a bed made up in the covered porch of the palace, where a mild breeze shifted through the columns and jostled the flaming ornate torches. Blankets layered over heavy purple throws, woolen robes and another covering — a perfect nest for a human. And how Odysseus grew overjoyed at the sight of some place soft and warm.

The royal couple left him to the colonnade. Echoes of a gentle drizzle patted along the rooftop, just enough wetting to water the meadows and ripen the fields. Odysseus laid surrounded by feathered cushions, staring up at the bronze ceiling.

Hermes stretched out next to him until his knees popped. *This was nice, similar to home.*

"So the wondrous god of guides lacked to aid you in your endeavors, I heard," he said with a snort.

"I figured you wouldn't want the expectation to spread across the seas that you'd be holding the hand of every single wayward, groveling man for years at a time."

Too true. He was far too busy for that. And many groveling men were annoying.

"Are you going to sleep in *all* of my beds?" Odysseus grumbled, holding tight to a pillow with a strong arm. "Must I fight you to defend my wife in our own bed?"

Hermes wiggled his way to lie sideways. "I'll not be sleeping tonight, I don't think," he replied. "I'm behind on my duties. But while you rest here safe and sound, when you awake, I shall be back, assuredly. And you *are* safe here, Ody — I swear on the Styx."

Tired grey eyes blinked at him. "Day tomorrow will be long," he whispered.

"But the convoy home will be swift. The fastest they have ever sailed while I'm aboard."

Odysseus could not stay awake to contemplate any further, slipping soundly into sleep like a man succumbing to drowning. Just one more day that they would both make it through.

Hermes summoned his staff and flew to the large windows. Beyond the island, the weather could be much worse. He pulled his helmet down over his nose and took to the sky.

Apollo, dearest, he sent out, holding tight to his bindings. Flying was a strain.

His brother took no time at all to reply. *Mighty Zeus, Hermes, at last you speak! Lord Poseidon seeks to rip your home from its foundation. We have been lit in conflict on the Mount, I do not think I will even find my bed tonight.*

Excellent, I need you to meet me at the gates of Hades. Bring your balms and your gentlest words. I look skewered worse than when your sister snipes a fowl.

The silence was all he required to picture Apollo's face while he zipped from society to society, collecting all the lost souls needing to be judged.

I fear one day you will kill me, brother, Apollo sighed. *I shall be there.*

And thank you for coming — with Artemis, even. I was as surprised as Poseidon that you stayed true to your word. I expect Father will want words when my task is completed. I'm ready for them.

A melodic hum. *Just stop being struck by the kings' weapons. You are aging me, Hermes. I think I felt stubble growing before it burned off.*

I love you, Hermes said, holding his hand out to an old gentleman spectre to welcome him to his twinkling cloak.

Yes, yes, you're more sappy for now, I understand. Just get to the gates, I am nearly there.

Chapter 16

When Dawn came, King Alcinous rose with Odysseus by his side to show off the harbor where the great ships were built and cared for, and Hermes arrived to see Athena back at it again in another disguise.

The king's *herald*: rousing the lords and captains to be quick in their arrival to tend to their curiosity. He debated if he should just sit back and bring over a cup of nectar to sip and watch her show — the goddess who claimed she wanted very little to do with bringing her former champion home.

He settled atop an empty post among others that supported carved boys presenting cups of fire to the sky. He could do so too, easily. Probably was the most handsome of the bunch. All eyes were too enraptured by the dazzling stranger; and if not on him, then on Athena who roared at sailors to be faster in preparing the black ship. She must've been enjoying herself; she always tried to sway every scenario to her will. If this one didn't align with what Hermes wanted, he'd be doing his utmost to contest her. What luck he had this time.

"My Lord Hermes," the prayer of Prince Telemachus was not unwelcomed in the slightest. *"We raise the sails and set our eyes back on Ithaca —"*

"Sail straight and true, Son of Odysseus," Hermes replied. *"You'll reach your homeland."*

It was the prayed laugh that got to him, almost breaking his fixed composure.

Athena, what sort of new champion were you molding out of this one?

Telemachus didn't sound like the sort of warrior that would want to throw an infant off a balcony either. Hermes wanted to wrap *him* up like a babe instead.

Maybe Odysseus was planting these seeds in his head.

A parade of princes and lords, and sailors once their tasks of preparing the boat was finished, overflowed the grant hall of the royal palace halls for morning feasting and entertainment. A dozen sheep, eight boars, and two ox were all slaughtered in sacrifice to feed the masses — Hermes was drunk on the smoke, stumbling into his rooster form to slip into the covered room.

And poor Ody, subjected to a blind bard's enrapturing song on the lyre — a tale of Troy and the bitter clash of words between Odysseus and the great warrior Achilles that occurred before blood was drawn on the battlefield. The audience listened in wonder while Odysseus hid his face in his cloak and wept.

A long day indeed.

The king noticed the tears, and without insulting his guest, prompted his people to go out into the fields to entertain with games and contests so that their new friend could tell the outside world how talented they were. There was a vacancy in Odysseus' eyes, the one that could only be filled by his family. The time couldn't go by any faster.

But Hermes was a lover of sport, and games were within his domain. If he wasn't going to be discovered immediately, he'd join the fun just to beat all the young boasting princes.

The work Apollo did on the wounds that mirrored each other on his back and belly was rather impressive. A suture made of the same strings Apollo crafted his lyres with closed the three holes up completely. Hermes' skin only revealed the lightest of marks, like lavender blooms down his sternum and the straight of his spine. It was rather painless now, like a dull ache. He could decimate the competition if he wanted to.

He really *really* wanted to.

But he was picked up from within the crowd; not by any curious bystander or another pretty maiden, but Athena in a male form. She eyed the competition during their foot races and wrestling matches, their field and discus — when a proud prince approached Odysseus to ask a challenge of he whose thighs and arms, the build alone, must have been skilled at sport.

Did we make it too much? Hermes asked, stretching a wing out in Athena's strong arm.

He has always been muscular. All my champions have been.

Yes, but he was slighter than Diomedes. I think you've projected a little, Sister.

No, Athena argued, *his stature merely made him appear so. I fixed him.*

Hermes rolled his eyes. The poor men chosen by Athena had little room to just live. Nevertheless, Odysseus did look incredibly handsome, but Hermes was going to find it annoying if he had to look *up* at the man from now on.

Another prince had joined his brother in what was turning out to be a goading ceremony toward the King of Ithaca. No longer was he an athlete, no, he must've been a profiteer here to collect their gold to take home, for his cargo was obviously pitiful.

Odysseus leaned forward on his leg, leering down at the bold prince. "You speak reckless words without thought. I can see that the gods don't hand out their gifts at once: no build and brains, nor Hermes' flowing speech. Apollo may bless an ugly man with fine looks and grace, charming all who see him. Another man," he said, giving the prince a once-over, "may appear godlike, but is inept in his words — just like you, my fine, handsome friend, where that mind inside is worthless. Your slander is ignorant: I'm no stranger to sports. In my youth, I was crowned among the best."

He stepped down the podium where the lords watched and briskly moved along the field.

"Despite my struggles and suffering these years, you've fanned my anger and roused my fighting blood." Seizing a heavy discus from the pile unused by the princes, he whirled around and let it fly, zipping long over the audience in the distance. Athena ducked her head with everyone else as the people gasped.

Hermes felt Athena's spirit soar as she stood back up and proclaimed to Odysseus, "Even a blind man could find your mark. So far from the crowd, it has almost cleared the field. Nothing to fear in this competition, sir, no one can beat your distance!"

So she said and so Odysseus laughed.

Hermes rotated his neck as far as a rooster was capable. *Athena.*

Her smile fell. *Do not speak to anyone about that.*

I don't think they'd even believe me if I did! He fluffed his feathers. *Why do you not just speak to him as yourself? After everything you two have accomplished together during Troy, before it, even, as he was young when you selected him, I'd think you wished to make amends.*

Athena could not run from him now that she held him up from being kicked by strangers. *Laertes' son calls to me because he is acutely aware I had started his suffering in the first place — you solidified that understanding when you told him to ask for my forgiveness before knowing what it was we disagreed on. If I started his suffering, then I must be capable of ending it. I held the threads to his life and have done so since he agreed to serve me in his boyhood. I cannot appear to Odysseus now, little brother, and remind him of what once was. The best thing... The* right *thing to do is to let him live free of being my champion. I released him from his expectations.* She paused, looking back to the ocean. *Besides, I have work to do with his son. He would hate to know Telemachus has agreed to me, but it is a necessary choice given the circumstances within their palace walls.*

I haven't told Ody of how bad it has become yet, Hermes replied.

For the best. He need not sit here in worry. He requires all his strength; and his mind works quick, he will figure his plan out moments before it happens.

She loved him. And unsurprisingly from the goddess of wisdom, the decision for a god to release a mortal from their oath was an act of mercy. No champion truly lived a full and happy life. Not even Hermes' — whose "champions," if he could call them that, were usually great thieves — saw the world as a wondrous place. His talented Autolycus, who could make the things he stole invisible and relished in his schemes, was not a cheerful man in the end. And Odysseus' name, "he who causes pain," was a direct consequence.

I'll not speak of your taking Prince Telemachus' fate into your hands, Hermes told her after the sports concluded and the Phaeacians offered to show their guest their prowess in dancing.

The bard's new song struck up tales from Olympus, and Hermes caught his name within the story of Hephaestus capturing Aphrodite and Ares in their act, and summoning his brothers to come mock the duo. Poseidon was among them, though the king didn't laugh, not even a smile at the scenario. He had begged the god of the forge to release them, that Ares would pay the price of his insolence, whatever Hephaestus and the other gods found fair.

Would he be so willing again — when the acts were against *him* by the others, would he be willing to listen and agree to what the pantheon agreed to as a fair punishment?

When the audience began to part, Athena set Hermes on the grass, running her long fingers over the feathers of his back.

Go to him. I will see you again in Ithaca.

She was too apt at disappearing into crowds. He could argue that she toed the line of his trickery domain more often than not, though she'd deny it.

Odysseus was receiving gifts when Hermes glided over to his lovely chair. The prince who offended him earlier presented a silver-studded sword and good wishes towards his wife: two things that Odysseus welcomed kindly. The sun was beginning its descent in the sky, the time drawing near but not fast enough, as the party returned to the grand palace where even more gifts were showered upon him.

The man cried upon being shown a true bath — the tub decorated with colorful stonework. Treated like an honest king, he was washed by maids, scrubbed with oil, and dressed in a warm fleece and shirt. Brought to the feasting halls, he ate and drank, and praised the bards who provided such blessed music, weeping again to his own request to hear the story of the Achaean victory over Troy.

And from his weeping, Alcinous asked him to recount his nostos, all the trials he bore, the challenges he won, and the losses he faced. Odysseus, predestined to be a storyteller, wiped grief and fatigue from his eyes as he spotted Hermes by his chair.

"Just a few hours more, then Ithaca awaits."

Through more tears and precise words, Odysseus told of it all, sparing the audience no lack of emotion until his voice grew hoarse and his arms tired. The lords and servants alike were spellbound by his tale, the king taken by his humility amid his suffering. Hermes sat agog over even *more* gifts that the men supplied Odysseus, to be sent with his chest to the ship that would carry him home, so that even if his native land was robbed blind, he would want for nothing.

Another offering to Zeus — for, truly, it was Zeus everyone had to appeal to — and as the sun dipped low enough to paint the sky in hues of pink and orange, Odysseus was ready to depart.

He turned to Alcinous and raised his hands joyfully. "Majesty, shining like a beacon among your people, make your libations and send me safely along. I bid you and your family, your good people, farewell. All is good, my heart swells from your generosity. May the gods of Olympus bless your gifts and your mighty sailors for me; and rain down all kinds of fortune upon your lives forever."

"I pray for you to see your wife unchanged and your loved ones unharmed and healthy," Alcinous replied. He called for his herald to bring about the wine to mix and pass around to send Odysseus on his way. The King of Ithaca offered his great cup to the queen as he rose from his seat, prepared to be escorted down to the harbors for his nighttime departure.

Odysseus stepped aboard a ship manned by fifty-two oarsmen. Smaller than what he was accustomed to for great ships that traveled so far, but his knees were buckling at the mere idea that he was hours from home. The Phaeacians were truly excellent crafters — the ship like a chariot on the sea.

He settled into a quiet corner of the deck, wrapped warmly in his cloak. A rooster happily settled onto his lap for his large hands to take hold off, running tired fingers through the down.

"There you are," he said, though there was hardly any energy left in him to speak.

"Here you are!" Hermes replied, heating his mortal's lap. *"The next time you open your eyes, my dear Ody, you'll be home. You'll see your son, grown, arriving not soon after you; and your good wife who has been waiting to take you into her*

arms."

The sound of a weighty rope being tossed back to its post was the lightning before the thunder of delicate mist that washed over the deck, like a spell of sleep to overcome him. And the ship careened down the southern tip of her home island as if drawn by Poseidon's mighty horses. Over the wakes, she surged, the oars overpowering even the fastest flying birds. No troubles befell the vessel, nor the inhabitants on it. Hermes poured his energy into calling to his mother, her star shining bright to guide the ship along to the Ionian islands where Ithaca awaited, her harbor shielded from wicked gales by jutting headlands.

* * *

In the early morning, before the sky even shifted blue, the Phaeacian ship drifted silently through Ithaca's gentle bay. Spotting a welcoming cave, whose olive trees waved their branches, and whose northern opening was the only one allowed by mortals, for the other was kept to the gods, the sailors drove their vessel so fiercely that half the length of it was beached.

Hermes disappeared from the craft, flying high above them as the men came to lift Odysseus from his resting place and carry him to the dusty sands. Not even the roar of a fire could wake him. They surrounded him in this cave with the plethora of treasures and hoards: gold, bronze, silks and linens, all hidden from passersby's eyes. It surpassed all he once had from his wartime raids, those lost to the deepest depths of the ocean.

Without dawdling, the ship left, and cast off back to their shielded island. Because its sailors were so kind and its homeland generous, Hermes was pleased to bless their voyage, but his divinity was abruptly overcast by one higher than him.

The poor ship was doomed to the seafloor.

Hermes sighed and dropped his arm. It was the price to pay and he shook the feeling of the souls perishing from his mind as Odysseus, at last, broke free of his deathlike slumber.

He awoke with a start, leaping up from the rug he was laid upon and scanned the land around him. With the keening from his lips, he didn't seem so pleased, and Hermes flew down to stand by his side.

A stranger, Odysseus looked, changed again by Athena's crafty magic. Hermes was going to laugh if it wasn't so ridiculous at this point. The mist she harbored clouded Odysseus' eyes, his home did not look like home to him, but Hermes appeared the same — in his green and gold with his split-tailed cloak.

"Am I a man so clothed in misery that I'm lied to by all?" he yelled at Hermes. "Being sworn to be brought to my Ithaca and yet left to rot in some no-man's land? I know Zeus'll have them for this; he punishes all who transgress him!" Stalking over to his gifts, he counted them all in his anger, as if a stolen item would be the final straw.

Hermes let his head roll to one shoulder. "Yes, the ship that brought you here has certainly been punished," he replied with a frown.

"And you!" Odysseus said, thrusting his finger at Hermes, his face red. "You've told me nothing but sweetened lies, haven't you? Do you derive so much pleasure from thrusting me from coast to coast while I beg and cry like a dog? This is the entertaining play you've longed for — my tragic tale?"

Hermes raised his brow. If he did not know the circumstances, he'd find that accusation to be immensely insulting. A dry smile drew across his features before falling into a grimace.

"Be silent and turn about. There's a young man across the beach," Hermes griped. "Dry your pathetic face and speak with him, *then* tell me I'm as cruel a god as you say."

Turning down the beach, white sand blinding in the morning sun, Odysseus approached the man who held a spear for hunting and threw himself at his feet, begging to know where he was, who it belonged to, if it was an island or just the shore of the green mainland.

He was so accustomed to begging for mercy at this point, the flowery language poured from his lips.

The man, no native at all to Hermes' knowing eyes, crossed his arms. "You must be some fool, stranger," he said, "to not know this land! Its name is known around the world. An island that lacks spaces for running horses, but holds good country for goats and cattle. Timber never runs low and the waters flow through their streambeds year round. A small island, but not poor at all in its grain nor its grapevines. Even those as far as Troy have heard the name of Ithaca."

Odysseus staggered to his feet, taking in the homeland he'd waited twenty long years to step foot on.

"Ithaca," he said, his mind turning. "Yes, I... I seem to *have* heard of such a place. I hail from Crete's broad land far across the sea..."

He launched into another brilliant story full of lies that delighted the listeners about who he was, how he had come to be washed up here with all his fine gifts...

"Best you bury those deep within the cave for now, new friend," the man said with a coy smile. "The palace is strung up with many selfish men who seek power and wealth. If you make your way up there, you will find little room to be welcomed as a guest. They have nearly run the missing king's supplies to the ground." With his spear he pointed to the rolling hills. The mist over Odysseus' vision pulled away as he saw his high-roofed house above them all.

"Bless you, friend," Odysseus replied with a new sheen in his eye. "I shall do so according to your word."

The arrival of another ship not far out from Ithaca's shores pinged in Hermes' brain. When the definitely-not-*another*-disguised man left Odysseus to the beach, Hermes landed himself in front of his kin, who collapsed to kiss the ground of home.

"Forgive me," Odysseus said to the god's feet, "for doubting you, Hermes. I had no reason to do so. You said you'd bring me to my native shores and you have fulfilled that much. If this is where you part from me, then I thank you now. I must plan for how I'll deal with these suitors who lord over my home and seek to touch my wife."

Hermes crossed his ankles and tapped his chin in as thoughtful a way as he could pose when insulted and pleased. "Very well," he huffed. "Good luck with that."

And he was gone.

Sort of.

Hermes wasn't so mean, though Odysseus deserved it for speaking rudely. Lying to Athena was all he needed to find forgiveness, however. It must've also been a welcome change for her from the way Odysseus acted in giving his name to the Cyclops.

Forgiveness on both ends by speaking falsehoods.

He still let the mortal king push his own gifts deeper into the cavern alone — the work of a dozen men done within the hour.

A strange sort of rage stirred and contorted Odysseus' figure as the scent of Olympus wafted over the island. His shadows along the cavern walls revealed not his shape, but the memories of his self past, clad in regal armor, wieldy sword in hand. He sat with his head in his hands, frozen in time, contemplating in muttered whispers what scheme would fare best against men he wished dead.

A new Trojan Horse to get inside his own palace.

If Athena spoke to him, it was out of Hermes' earshot, though her presence remained by the distant, young prince's side.

Up the hills he eventually climbed in choking silence while Hermes witnessed the transformation with each step: his lovely clothes to rags too obscene for even the poorest of peasants, the gloss to his skin shriveled and his divine dark curls fell away.

Hermes cupped his hands over his lip-curled mouth to keep from gagging at the ugliness Athena bedecked him with. So cruelly necessary, it was like pulling feathers.

About halfway to the summit of the rocky hillside, where the blue ocean could be seen for miles, a boisterous little rooster stomped his way after the old beggar of a man, who turned his head at the rare bird's display. His grey eyes were dull now, lacking sparkle, but they crinkled softly at the fowl.

"As if I wouldn't see you to your wife's bed," Hermes said, flopping his saddle feathers. *"It was implied in my promises, I'm surprised a man as shrewd as you didn't catch on."*

They weaved through straight trees, ones that would cut great for ships, and made their way to Odysseus' old swineherd. The presence of the pigs safe within their pens was oddly nostalgic; the lodging was surrounded with a sizable wall of stone and a fence of pear trees, but sitting on its foundations, maintained a lofty view of the land. There were twelve sties kept for fifty pigs each, their snores echoing like a rumbling cloud. Boars slept in the outer fields, not as many in number now due to the immense gluttony of the men who invaded the lord's palace.

Hermes heard the guard dogs before the four of them rounded the corner. Subjected to Odysseus' quick thinking, with sturdy hands, he was thrust high into the air as Odysseus crouched down to confront the barking hounds. But the beggar had not the face of the infamous king that commanded respect; and Hermes inevitably waited to be trampled upon and chewed.

The swineherd dashed from his post, lobbing rocks at the dogs to disperse them before they had the chance to gnaw off Odysseus' old-man nose.

"The luck you have to be alive, stranger!" the swineherd said, catching his breath. He was known to all as Eumaeus — purchased as a boy by Odysseus' father, Laertes, when he arrived on Ithaca's shores a prisoner. "I would have finally been shamed by the gods if I allowed my pack to tear you apart. No, I am already a heart-broken man, disgraced with every one of my master's hogs that are sent for other men to eat at his table."

Eumaeus helped Odysseus to his feet, hesitant to pat the bird in his arms.

"Come, my friend, come into my place at least. Eat your fill of bread and have some wine. Then tell me how it is you came here." He tiredly gestured to the modest farmstead with high walls. Inside, he covered a seat made of twigs and brush with a shaggy goat pelt, something pulled from the man's own bedding, and nodded towards it.

Odysseus' cheeks warmed. "Thank you, my dear host," he replied, taking the seat, Hermes still in hand. "May Zeus and the gods on Olympus give you your heart's desire for the royal welcome you've received me with."

Eumaeus waved his hand in rejection of the overly kind thanks. "We treat every stranger and beggar with the best we can do. Unfortunately we servants have been cowed by the young lords who have planted themselves here for the past several years. If my old master were present," he choked to say, "he would treat us well — give us a good house and repay us for the work we have done. You would be sitting in a true chair by a finely carved table, but alas: he is long dead…"

Presented with a loaf and a small bowl of mixed wine, Odysseus waited in silence as Eumaeus left the room to slaughter a pig for an afternoon meal.

His old friend considered him dead. Of course, why else would he not be amongst them, knowing it was prime in his heart to be home with his family? It was the only reasonable thought for rational men.

Odysseus sighed. "I hate this," he whispered, squeezing Hermes' sides. "Waiting to tell the people I love that I am here. The deceit is vital, but I loathe every minute of it."

"To know of their devotion to you is needed. You'll get it and then they'll know," Hermes replied.

The swineherd returned with the quaint meal, sat across from them, and shared his own sorrows of how these suitors had squandered Odysseus' land, ate up his immense riches as if there was no care in the world. And truly, the son of Laertes was a wealthy man to be capable of supplying so much to so many year after year.

Emotion swelled Eumaeus' voice while Odysseus scarfed down his meat with the veins of his temples throbbing with every complaint.

A pause in his torment, Eumaeus sipped gingerly at his wine and cast a glance down to the bird in his guest's lap.

"What is this fowl — have you brought him to offer as a sacrifice to ask for leniency in your pains?" he asked.

"No, he is my friend."

"Ah."

Odysseus licked his lips. "Tell me, friend, who was this master of riches you speak of? If he fought and died in the honor of Agamemnon, perhaps I know him and can give you news of his true whereabouts."

"You would not be the first to offer information to please his wife and win his son over. We welcomed liar after liar, but the queen is wise and their stories only drive knives through her heart. Through many different ways we have heard how King Odysseus perished. Even I cannot stand to hear more of it — he was a brother to me," Eumaeus said through gritted teeth, discreetly wiping a tear from his cheek.

His weeping roused Odysseus' heart. "You seem to insist that he's never coming back based on lies. But I will not just declare it, I swear as the gods do on the Styx that Odysseus is on his way," he proclaimed. His boldness dared to continue, "I don't ask for reward for my deliverance of news — I hate a man who does such things. Your king, master and brother, *will* return and will come with a vengeance to take on any man who has offended his wife and son!"

Eumaeus was too driven by grief to believe his own disguised master's words. He shock his head and whispered the prince's name. "That godlike son of his. Those deathless ones whisked him away to search for his vanquished father and now these horrid suitors lie in wait like sharks for his return, ready to destroy the royal line from Ithaca. If that boy is killed, I… I will never recover."

Hermes wiggled from Odysseus' lap and fluttered to the doorway. The prince's ship was still a day out at sea, following the coastline of the mainland northbound.

Behind him, when prompted, Odysseus went on with his very long, dishonest backstory with more vivid detail than any other mortal could possibly conjure up. A drama to make a bard holler in envy. Some truths were weaved into the tall tale, which only made it more believable, but Eumaeus was a great skeptic of this stranger — tired of the many claims to know his old friend. They squabbled back and forth like old men indeed, a crafter of words against a builder of walls, the wind against the mountain.

"Ody," Hermes exclaimed. *"Give sacrifice to the god of tricks, for your friend should know the gods are indeed at play here; and we may prove to him that your words ring with some truth."*

Odysseus glanced at the rooster, then rested his hands on the soft of his seat. "Good host, you must find me odd after I called that bird my friend," he said. "In truth, he is, rather, my friend who once walked with me as a young man — you're correct that a god led me here to you. My companion was naive and insulted the crafty and cunning giant-killer for allowing our travels to be so miserable; he's been turned into this cock as punishment. An offering to the god may appease him and change my friend back to the man he was."

That was unexpected for the aged swineherd. A story so preposterous, it would be insane to believe it, but all the worse to not take it as truth when the gods were involved. He raked his hand over his beard and looked at the bird in his doorway. "It is a rare thing to see," he replied, his voice wary. "When my herdsmen return for supper, we may make the first offering to the son of god and nymph."

When the servants returned and washed themselves, they greeted their strange guest, and prepared the hearth for their evening meal. They prayed for their king's return home, slaughtered the fattest hog for themselves in spite of the palace dwellers, and Eumaeus, to his word, offered the first slice of meat to Maia's son, Hermes.

And oh, how Hermes missed frightening mortals with harmless pranks.

The colorful rooster crowed and cried, stumbling back and forth as its wings flapped in such a panic even Odysseus pulled away in alarm. Out the raised door Hermes fell. The sound of barking hounds echoed towards the hut, and in horror that this rare bird would be eaten alive, two of the herdsmen leapt up from their seats to rip aside the draping cloth.

One man cursed. The other fell to his knees and quickly pulled the cloth of the doorway right off of its nails, scrambling over to cover the naked, young man who lay damp in the dirt and stuck with feathers.

No limp this time, he had control. Merely shivering from the *frightening* ordeal of transforming back into a *definitely mortal* body.

Eumaeus and his men gaped, rubbing their eyes when the boy was brought inside, the dogs licking at his heels.

"Anastasios!" Odysseus gasped, ever the actor, holding his arms open, and Hermes stumbled right into them. "Oh, you stupid boy."

"Forgive me, my friend!" Hermes wept, then lowered his voice. "You're absolutely disgusting in this form, I hate it so much." His face was pressed further into the disheveled, dirty fabric as Odysseus thanked his host a thousand times over.

"Boy, you," one servant said, shakily sipping his water, "were turned into a bird? For how long?"

"Felt like *eons*,' Hermes replied, curling the ragged cloth around his waist. "Be careful of the things you say, my friends, for the gods are always listening. We arrived alive on this kingdom's shore — I should've been grateful and not *insulted* the god who very well saved us time and time again from certain death…" He spoke to the men, but he turned his eye on Odysseus who chomped down on his choice meat given to him, knowing he'd have extra from the food that Hermes would only pretend to consume.

When everyone had their fill of bread and pork, the men bedded down where they sat. A wind stirred up outside, another night of rain sent by Zeus for every day passing where Hermes didn't go home. The servants slept on their covered straw, wrapped in the very cloth they wore to work, but Eumaeus stood to leave, apt to sleep among his swine to protect them. While Hermes lay curled up amongst himself, he listened to Odysseus try once more to win his old friend's heart. A tired loss — the man simply laid his fleeces and furs by the fire and gave his disguised master the cloak off his back before stepping out into the rain.

A quiet beat passed, where only the hearth cracked, before Odysseus opened up the wool cloak and Hermes slid inside for warmth.

"He cares so much for my goods and doesn't believe me to be alive," Odysseus whispered. "I don't need to test him further, I trust him. Too much danger awaits my son for me to continue stalling."

"Sleep without worry. I wouldn't let my great-great grandson fall into a trap devised by stupid Man." Hermes dug himself deep into the bedding. "Great heavens, I pray to myself that this ends quickly so we can get you out of these dreadful rags — what was she thinking?"

Odysseus said nothing more, though Hermes would have to be the most grand idiot to not feel the way his chest heaved. His human was a cry-baby, and that was okay.

Chapter 17

Telemachus was so alike to his paternal grandmother that the similarities to Hermes' own features made it impossible not to stare. Through his father's genes, he inherited the curved nose and strong cheekbones that carved neatly into his face, lit up by the sun as he ran up to the swineherd's house early in the morning. Dark hair waved over his eyes, kept back with a silver braided cord that laid across his forehead — but his eyes were most certainly of his mother's: striking and bold, like the bioluminescence of algae.

He skipped the step and clung to Eumaeus' doorframe, his jewelry and heavy spear clinking against the wood as his cloak rushed to keep up, falling over the happily chirping guard dogs nuzzling his legs. Twenty years of age, still beardless. Though from the shadow along his chin, it was trying to come through; like the Fates were waiting for the right time to turn this boy into a man.

Eumaeus dropped everything he was doing to rush over and hold the prince close, kissing his cheeks until they were pink like a father would his son.

Hermes fiddled with his honeyed wine, watching Odysseus instead as his brows pulled in close at the sight of the boy and his breath drew in through clenched teeth.

The true strength of holding oneself back when all that's desired is right in front of you... Odysseus, you are better than I.

Hermes stood up in the corner of the lodging and bowed his head, waiting for the swineherd to cease his sobbing at Telemachus' safe return.

"Oh, hush, old man," Telemachus chuckled, leaning his face away at last. "I've come to see you to ask of my mother's health, not to plainly show you mine. Does she still hold strong in my absence, or has some scoundrel beaten her coy game?"

"She still waits for you in her halls, unyielding as ever, but not without tears — the poor woman." He took the spear from the prince's hand and, at last, Odysseus rose from his seat and offered it to his son.

Telemachus' shining eyes looked upon Odysseus and gently raised his hand to stop him. "Please, remain seated, stranger, I am sure we will find a spot for me," he said. Glancing at Hermes, he offered a polite nod of his head.

A well-bred son — what a *welcome* change, no wonder Athena became fond of him.

Was it offensive to Ody if he admitted that, or would the man be happy that his son wasn't an ass like the boastful suitors in his house?

The king worked his fingers, never letting his gaze falter from the royal boy's cherub-cheeked face while another pelt was laid over sprigs for him to sit on. The clothing he wore flaunted the wealth of Odysseus' family. Like the gods, the embroidery was sublime: tight and intricate even along the tunic's neckline under his sea-faring cloak. Dyes were bold and evenly spread, an indigo blue that couldn't rival the color of his iris. Gifts, no doubt from Odysseus' old friends, Menelaus and Nestor, mingled with his Ithacan garb, sparkled in the low light of the hearth.

It was funny when polite mortals asked their friends to explain who it was their guests were instead of asking directly. Perhaps they learned it from the times the gods didn't care to know what strangers had to say — *who is this strange man in my temple* — or the like. But Eumaeus introduced Odysseus and Anastasios to Telemachus with his typical air of skepticism while putting away the little meal they dined on.

Telemachus listened attentively, his brow slowly furrowing.

"You wish to stay in my house?" he asked, not in anger, but concern. "I'm afraid it cannot be done — I have little power and my mother is too burdened to protect you, my friends, from the men that exacerbate every problem in my halls. They would take you as someone to abuse with their reckless nature and that would break my heart to know I allowed you to suffer their biting words. But clothing and rations to fill your bellies, that I can promise."

Odysseus grew solemn. "My young lord, my own heart breaks hearing of your struggles with these suitors, here against the will of your royal family. To know they harass your wise mother and plot your demise..." he said. The rage in his chest simmered over a growing fire. "Tell me truthfully, do you let these suitors treat you with disrespect? Have you no allies among your own brothers? If it were *my* house — if I were the son of Odysseus or even the great king himself — and they treated me and my family so, I'd rather strike them down where they stand, or at least go out fighting, than witness them bask in my goods."

Telemachus slowly cocked his head, as if he had heard this move to household war somewhere before. Picking at a ring on his finger, he shook away the curiosity and sighed, "I have no brothers coming from a line of only sons. Nor are there any men I trust within my own house — dear Eumaeus, of course — but even my mother's maidens I worry are conspiring against her as they sleep with those intruders. A plague of deceit and betrayal racks the foundations of Ithaca. I pray to Pallas Athena as often as I can... her will has been, *ah*, very much like yours, dear stranger."

Called it.

"The gods are always pressing their resolve on our lives, but Athena's a powerful ally; when you have the wise goddess of tactics on your side, then the god king looks kindly upon you," Odysseus replied.

Hermes rolled the edges of his extremely skimpy exomis. "Other gods outside of the war domains are also quite advantageous," he exclaimed.

He liked some praise, dammit.

Telemachus turned his smile at once. "Oh, I have heard from the wayfarer Hermes! He's answered all my prayers thus far — it gave me some reassurance on my travels, but forgive me, you must hear of princes *all* the time assuming their importance to the gods. You, my friend," he said to Hermes, "sound so familiar. Have you visited Ithaca before? I dare say you look as if you could be a cousin in distant relation."

Hermes laughed. "No, I hail from Taphos. Never set foot on these shores, I fear. Though it is a beautiful country you have, my lord."

"Taphos," he said. "A family friend I was told, Mentes, rules over that land. He had visited before I left on my excursion. Persuaded me, in fact, to investigate my father's legacy."

"Of course he did," Hermes whispered into his hand. "That is all well, I'm in no rush to return home. But as for your troubles, allow us to unburden you and the assiduous queen."

"I cannot see how, and I certainly cannot ask that of you," Telemachus said, looking at Odysseus' haggard form. To Eumaeus he commanded, "My friend, go quickly to my mother and tell her I'm home from Pylos and that I'm safe in your house. Tell this *only* to her. I cannot afford more plots against my life — I will wrinkle before I grow a beard."

"Shall I not tell the good news to King Laertes? He has been wasting away since your departure," Eumaeus said, and Odysseus' grief only grew, squeezing at his lungs.

Begrudgingly, Telemachus shook his head. "Should any of the suitors have an inclination of my arrival, I fear my fate will be that of my father's. If my mother wishes to tell him, she'll send her most trustworthy maid. Come back when you are done."

When Eumaeus left them, Hermes prodded Odysseus with his foot, and at the same time, Telemachus turned his ear to the distant hoot of an owl not far from the little house.

"No time than the present," Hermes said only to him. *"Your scheming needs more players and none are better than the royal son of Odysseus, blessed by Athena, I swear."*

It must've felt humbling, to be presented to his son in the tired, ugly form he was disguised in. Having to rouse more courage than a general in war to find words to speak to the boy who was an infant when he last saw him. All the horrid echoing memories of screams and death were put asunder by Telemachus' mere presence.

Now that was a power on its own.

Hermes melded into the shadow of the corner, not minding his own business, but far enough to be forgotten.

"You look at me like you know me, stranger," Telemachus said, and his voice dropped to a whisper. Twisting the same ring, he scanned the grey eyes of his father the way an artist examines his sculpture. With a tentative breath, he asked, "Do I know you?"

Odysseus centered himself across from the prince, sitting forward and straight. His skin may have looked shriveled and his muscles weak under his cloak, but he sat with all the regality of a king and warrior. Hermes heard his lungs expand with a great nervous inhale before the man replied, "I do know you."

Telemachus leaned toward him.

"I was there when you were seconds old," he confessed. "Swaddled in the robe your mother wore when she paced in labor, you were given to me. I cried as you cried and laughed when you did. You loved your queenly mother's breast almost as much as I. I know you favored your left side no matter how many times your nurse flipped you over. You could fit into my helmet with how small you were those first weeks. I don't know what it was your mother was feeding you, for your legs grew so plump before my very eyes," Odysseus said with a pitiful laugh.

Telemachus' face was frozen in its confusion.

"I don't understand," he murmured. "Are you some god? Is this another test for me?"

"I'm your father," Odysseus said. "The very Odysseus you've suffered and searched for every one of your twenty arduous years, who was so unwilling to go to war that they used my love for you to take advantage of me — to take me from home."

Unable to help himself any longer, he wept in front of his son.

"What is this magic?" Telemachus said, not knowing if he should feel manipulated or relieved. His shoulders raised to his ears. "You cannot be Odysseus — he has been lost to us for so long, but he would *not* be a man of your age unless another curse has befallen him. I've seen every etching, every sculpt of his face, my mother described him to me in avid detail. I know him by *heart*, do not deceive me just to wound my soul!"

"Telemachus, you must look at me harder then and see it to be true."

In Hermes' mercy as Telemachus blinked tears from his lashes, the flickering image of Odysseus' true form revealed itself. Like an picture through mist: the dark hair, the laugh lines, the sparkle in his eye…

Telemachus nary needed to reach out and touch the face before Odysseus enveloped his strong arms around him, and the young prince's shaken cries bubbled up and out, held in for far too long. And Hermes confirmed that wailing like birds must run in the family. They watered their cheeks endlessly, Odysseus unwilling to release his boy from his grasp.

"How? What? When?" Telemachus rattled out all of his questions in between his gasping.

Hermes didn't need to sit through another retelling of the whole story as Odysseus would, no doubt, tell it all from beginning to end. He ghosted outside of the lodgings, finding the air with the boars to be less of the sappy mess happening inside. Wiggling the little, sharp sting away from his nose, several quaint snorts echoed his own sniffles.

They were ugly things in a cutesy way — the pigs. Not as strange to look at as the old crew. Hermes pet the tallest one on the head and wiped his hand on his tunic.

"Well, what's next in your plan, Sister?" he asked, letting his head loll to his shoulder. Athena stood by the window in her armor, listening in on the royals' heart-to-heart. "I brought Ody home, as I promised myself and him. Good on my part, didn't doubt myself for a second. This is your war front now, isn't it?"

"It is high time the suitors died," she replied, smirking at the Ithacan family. She lowered the flimsy fabric covering the opening. "Father would expect it to be done."

"Yes, I understood that much. You'll be working behind the scenes, I imagine. Leading the prince to where he must be, who he must attack and the like. I get to cheer on the old sack of bones from a distance." Hermes dug his sandal into the dirt, picking out a flat stone with a toe. He gave it a slight kick.

Athena lowered her gaze to him. "You wish to be more involved."

"Yes! I mean," Hermes flopped his wrist and stood on his toes, "I'll be here *anyway*. Would be a waste not to utilize my many skills."

"Do not worry," Athena said with the smallest of chuckles. She weaved her long fingers through Hermes' hair before pushing him back towards the hut. "The son of Laertes is already scheming a role for you. I think you will like it."

* * *

Hermes did like it. He liked it very much.

Walking along the wide-stoned path to the palace with its double doors, high walls, and brilliant columns, he admired the grandness in its simplicity. Not to mean it was *boring* from the outside, the architecture alone made it tower over the rest of the island. Half of it was built into the hill. A large olive tree, forty feet tall, burst from the roof of the main residence, the walls having been constructed around it to accommodate the massive growth.

Hermes stood in Prince Telemachus' clothing: a chiton and cloak gifted from Sparta, and new leather sandals from Pylos. On his belt, he summoned a sword, and tucked it neatly into its serpent-etched scabbard.

Another suitor in the flesh, the most young and the most handsome if he said so himself.

Infiltrating the masses couldn't be done by just anyone, Odysseus had argued, but thank the *gods* that Anastasios was very persuasive. A hundred and eight suitors to deceive — men from all over Odysseus' kingdom: Dulichium, Same, Zacynthus to the south, and a dozen from the mother island — and their servants too. Some loitered in the palace's front gardens, lounging in the late morning with drink and music. Woven mats were placed over the muddy puddles that formed from the many night's rainfall; the sun now was too enticing to not enjoy it.

Hermes rounded a corner, brushing through unnoticed, as the few guards were busy idling with the older men who had tents put up by the dozen.

The pull of death tickled his cheek.

Hermes paused to inspect the inner courtyard with its woven banisters draped along the walls. No man nor maiden lay dying yet, every human was moving about. His eye lowered to the ground, to a dirty mat half-covered with shit, shoved in the corner by the entry door. On it rested a haggard, old dog — some skinny, matted thing full of ticks and fleas — whose paws were worn and muscles weak.

The beast was far beyond its years.

"Hello," Hermes whispered, crouching by the hound. "Poor thing. I'm sorry that animals, no matter how dear, have no afterlife to be brought to..." Gliding his hand over the dog's head, the hound whimpered and leaned into the touch with as much strength as it could muster. His face was whiter than the clouds above. "You must be Argos. What a good dog you are. Stay strong just a little longer, your master is coming."

There was the smallest twitch of Argos' tail, what was left of it, that is.

Hermes hummed, scratching gently under the ears. "Such a good boy, indeed. I'll see what I can do."

Odysseus was going to hate to see the puppy he trained still alive only to be neglected, a skeleton with skin. But Hermes couldn't stay. No suitor cared for the old king's useless property.

He continued onward through the courtyard and up into the central hall. As the largest room of the palace, with three thrones at its zenith, most of the suitors loitered around the hearth, feasting on leftovers of their morning meal. Along the ceiling were brilliant and colorful frescoes from Odysseus' paternal line, their first king to the current, some unkempt and fading.

Athena's influence was vomited all over the place.

Ody must add some new things when he reinstates himself on his throne. Missing a couple of rams, maybe a handsome god with wings and a staff...

"Another? Stranger, you are several years late to the party — there is little hope for you to even speak to the queen. She is a stubborn bitch who delays all her decisions," one man said, spinning Hermes around by his shoulder to give him a look over. "Young and rich as you may be, she doesn't accept most of our gifts. Best you run along and not waste your time. There are others among us who have a better chance for the crown."

Hermes stared at the clammy hand that gripped his shoulder. He could turn this man into a worm without blinking. The suitor was gangly, if Hermes had to pick a word — the way the scarlet chiton hung off his shoulders made it seem like he hid a protruding ribcage and a stomach that took in more wine than bread.

"My friend," Hermes purred dryly. "You consumed too much honeyed drink this morning. You know your dear ally, Anastasios! We shared a whole barrel just last evening as the lyre was plucked and the songs flowed well into the night." He pinched a finger of the suitor and lifted it from his person. "I believe this was the very hand that grasped that young girl's thick upper thigh when she served us, was it not?"

The eyelids of the suitor fluttered, and he retracted his hand to rest at his hip. "Why you're right," he said with a stupid chuckle. "I nearly forgot. Girl probably hadn't felt a man's touch in her life with how rigid Penelope's orders are to them. What Ithacan queen follows Spartan laws?"

Hermes took a piece of unused linen from the table and wiped the foreign sweat from his skin. "You should go somewhere else now," he said with a smile, holding the top of his sheath.

The suitor pivoted on his foot, clueless, and sauntered like a lame ostrich to a table full of his companions as they emptied platters of their bread and olives.

Every man varied in build, complexion, age, and attractiveness — most displayed their wealth on them, with colorful beading sewn into their tunics that matched unopened chests left by one of the vacant thrones at the top of the hall. Bating Queen Penelope with new clothes, jewels, art, and throwing up other useless items to a woman who didn't want to be courted was really a *trying* tactic — a siege against the foundations of the fair lady's psyche. Swords and daggers hanged low on their belts. They ate her supplies and roamed her halls, slept in the chambers that surrounded her private quarters where the tree stood high and mighty, like mites trying to nibble away at the bark and infest the roots, taking Ithacan maidens into their beds.

Hermes breezed through the many hallways of Odysseus' palace, keeping note of who was where, which men favored each other, and who stayed with themselves. The virgin maids shuffled quickly through smaller corridors, avoiding the courts and tall rooms, with their chins tucked into the laundry or food they carried.

Where they went, so did Hermes, discreetly finding his way to the grand stairs that led to Penelope's chambers. An open walkway over the steps cut from what must've been Telemachus' room to the private bath.

He had no intentions of disturbing the queen, though she was grateful enough for Telemachus' safe return that he felt the *one* prayer to him that she had uttered in the past three years. Ever since the suitors took control, her words were rare to the god of guides.

He stopped in the hall.

There was the god he could imagine her prayers went to.

"I didn't think you'd actually join us," Hermes said, pausing by a large woman that stood in the center of the wise queen's stairwell.

"Mother did not argue against it when I discussed the circumstances with her. Reuniting a husband to his wife was very much a winning case," Ares replied, folding his hands in front of him before glaring down every suitor whose nose poked within view.

"Very unusual for you to take a female form. Couldn't resist standing out?"

"The queen does not trust men; few of her ladies as well. If I can provide a sense of some aegis, then it is worth the lesser form."

Hermes nibbled on his lip. It was honorable in its humor. "Well, if Athena can do it on a regular basis, my brother, you are just as noble to reach her height. I'm happy you're here. I won't stay by you long — pathetic suitor that I am, ready to bestow gifts onto the queen in exchange for her hand. *But!*" he said, summoning said gift, "I believe she'll find these offerings adequate enough to accept now. Will you give them to her?"

He presented a handful of arrows. The smooth and straight carve done with an expert hand with the arrowheads of stone chipped neatly into a point. Each feather was divine, both in appearance and source, attached perfectly to the shaft.

"Her husband was stupid and left them on his craft before Uncle sent the thing all the way past Crete. I went bald for a whole day for those," Hermes explained. "She may recognize his work; she may not. Fun either way."

Ares took the arrows and inspected them as a war god would. "I would say you surprise me, Argeiphontes, but somehow this secret warfare seems right for you."

"I haven't the slightest idea what you mean," Hermes said, strolling backwards down the hall, an excited skip slipping in. "The son of Laertes is drawing near, Ares. I believe I have the smell of hot iron in my nose." He wafted the hallway. "Could be his soiled clothing though. Athena has made him hideous. Not for long — not on *my* watch!"

* * *

As Telemachus predicted, the suitors were not keen on inviting a beggar into the house that wasn't even theirs.

When the prince suddenly arrived at court, fresh from his voyage, his hair wind-swept from the strait he passed through on his mighty ship, several of the men fled the room — their plan for some allies to kill the boy at the beach was still underway; they'd be attacking a ship with no prince aboard.

Telemachus glowed among them, avoiding cold stares and offering a polite toast to the day as a servant handed him a cup and a welcoming kiss. The suitors stalked Telemachus with their bitter glares.

A dark energy inflamed Hermes' heart.

But Athena was watching her young charge with her all-seeing eyes, their plan brewing within the prince's mind. Hermes had his own to wait for.

Four hours after Telemachus' arrival, Eumaeus came and sat near the prince where the cooked meat rested and waited to be carved; their new stranger followed inside the palace.

Complaints began at once. The second Odysseus hobbled into the court with a crude walking stick, dressed in rags unfit for a dead man, playing the aged, old peasant with intense dedication, the suitors' resounding whines were fit for a nursery. Hermes was well settled on a cushion by the columns, basking in the absent queen's hospitality, huffing and puffing at Telemachus' mere presence. He could play his role just as well.

"And what is this?" the Ithacan suitor known as Antinous, son of Eupeithes, crowed. His voice was loud enough to convince others of his authority and respect, but he was no more than a brat with a beard. Perhaps his ego was already bruised from the verbal lashing he took from the queen just yesterday — who, in her exhausted rage, screamed at him and the men around him for the better part of five minutes. "The gods really do mock us now by sending in pigsty filth as we eat our meals! Is it not enough that we must feed hundreds, that we also invite the fleas to nibble on our crusts?"

Telemachus stood up from his chair. "Antinous, you clearly care more about *my* house and *my* goods than I do; how fatherly of you," he said and clicked his tongue. "By Zeus' great word, give the stranger something — I don't forbid it, but the gods know you never care for what I, nor my mother, say as long as you can gorge on my chattels yourself."

Antinous possessed the darkest heart of the men that surrounded him; black as dried ichor. He smiled, a sharp canine cut through his lips. "My dear prince, who here is more generous than I? Most of the gifts that line these halls are mine if not Eurymachus'. I present the queen with the sweetest conversations, no one can deny that." He looked at the beggar with venomous green eyes. "Here, sir, why don't you have a seat?"

A footstool squeaked violently against the floor, pulled from beneath Antinous' chair before he kicked it up and hurled it overhead. The solid wood splintered into pieces against Odysseus' shoulder, but the man was resilient, having taken blades and arrowheads through his body — a stool was nothing to move him. Nevertheless, it stirred a few passive suitors over, offering the beggar some of their scrap pieces of bread and picks of meat they didn't care for.

They filled a single plate. How a hundred men managed that, Hermes would never know. With a brilliant flair, he dropped a handful of figs atop Odysseus' rations. He wanted to brush the grime off of the king's clothes, reveal him now to the men, and let he and his son slaughter the lot of them. Hermes was rarely this patient; he'd already done his fair share of waiting these past mortal years.

Odysseus staggered by the table with the scraps, the gears spinning in his mind as he stopped in front of Antinous. "Sir, you couldn't possibly be the poorest man here with your fine looks and drapery. Perhaps I intimidate you? For I was once a man of wealth. I gave all I could to any beggar that appeared in my house and yet the gods still saw to my ill-fate and made me into a tramp after all the hardships I've survived. Perhaps you wonder: *will that be me next?*"

"Get out of my face," Antinous replied, his lip curling. He thumped into his chair and ripped his wine cup from the table. "You have been given abundance by the masses already, leave the hall before I give you another hardship you won't survive."

They quarreled another round. Hermes settled beside Telemachus. The poor boy had his bread crushed between his tight fist at the abolishment of his father. Hermes laid a discreet hand on his arm and gave it a quick squeeze.

"Trust me that he's gone through worse. This gloating buffoon and his hubris will get his comeuppance. The gods aren't pleased for this to continue for much longer, young prince," Hermes whispered.

"I have waited years to find the courage to take a stand," Telemachus said, hiding his anger in a cup. "To see them abuse my father now — Athena will have to hold me back from beating him senseless before it's time... metaphorically of course."

"From the way Antinous speaks, he deserves it. There he goes, threatening his own king with a flaying. He must've been dropped as a child; just needed to be from a higher wall," Hermes exclaimed, sitting back once more.

He scanned the windows that overlooked the surrounding ocean. Athena's shadow stretched longer across the floor the deeper the orange sun set, like teeth devouring the room.

Odysseus retreated to the back of the hall, sitting on the ground to eat what meal he had collected. It would be the last ill-befitting meal he would have, as there would be a king returned come the morning. Not a word came out of him. Just chewing with a soulless look in his eye, the two men of the house brooding for all it was worth.

Hermes glanced at the table, then back to Telemachus.

"You ever thought about growing strawberry trees?"

"Strawberry trees?"

"Yes, they are Lord Hermes' favorites. They say he truly eats among mortals when they are present; and wouldn't it be fun to host a god as kind as he?"

Telemachus' eyes flashed as he grinned. "Of course, Anastasios," he said. "Tomorrow then, I'll order for some strawberry trees to be planted in the orchard — a thank you to the guide for bringing my father to me."

"I think he'd like that," Hermes nodded. "Best not to make the gods upset."

"No, certainly not."

The way Telemachus regarded him was a mirror of Athena's knowing stare, but it was swiftly taken from Hermes with the approach of the queen's servants, carrying a long weapons' rack over their shoulders. At the center of the procession was Ares in his guise that Hermes couldn't stop himself from chuckling at. Struck on this rack was a long line of axes, each placement perfectly parallel to the next.

This was not in Athena's plan, nor Odysseus and Telemachus'.

Hermes raised a brow at Ares.

The god of war walked slowly around the hearth as the suitors gawked at the strange display put forward in the middle of the court. At one end, the end that looked toward the thrones, Ares placed down an empty quiver.

And not a second later did the curtains of the hall split apart, and the lady of the palace strode in. She was tall, aged just into her late forties, with hair dark like ink that prominently displayed the silver strands in her braids. Her veil dipped below her knees, floating on like a cloud; above it: a diadem of bronze and turquoise. Penelope's face was set in a stalwart frown — the suitors nary even rose to honor her entrance, though they ogled her body and lovely features hidden beneath a well-draped peplos. The energy of Aphrodite radiated from her, one that Ares knew intricately enough to replicate.

Gripped in her hands was a wood and horn-enforced palintonos bow. Unstrung, the curve of it so pronounced it could be mistaken for a lyre. A cold glare cast over the invaders of her home as she stepped up to her throne. Telemachus rose from his seat, overjoyed to see his mother, and her gaze softened towards him, but a discreet two fingers lifted from the bow — *wait.*

A challenge?

Hermes folded his hands and rested his chin upon them.

How exciting.

Chapter 18

No one loved a game more than Hermes, once again stuck as a bystander, uselessly admiring the facial journey of every suitor while the woman they had spent *years* trying to woo laid out her demands.

"This," she said, her tired voice firm like iron, "is my husband's bow. It was given to him as a wedding gift nearly thirty years ago by a dear friend. With it he had hunted boars and deer from across quarries, pierced creatures as small as quail and large as lions. He had left this bow to me when he was taken to war." Her jaw shifted. "You men have all been *very* patient with me as I mourned his absence. In truth," she lied, "it has taken me so long to reveal myself to you all because of a promise I have made to my good husband. Before he left for war, knowing well of its dangers, he said to me to wait for him, wait as long as our son remained a boy. But should he grow into a man, take another husband and leave this land."

Telemachus absently rubbed at his bare cheek. The color was beginning to change to the cool-toned hue of hair ready to prod from their hiding spots, but the boy still had weeks before one would grow out.

"And there are just so many of you," Penelope said with a shake of her head. "I couldn't possibly decide between men courting me so *differently* from my native country — the charitable Eurymachus, bold Antinous, kind Amphinomus… So I will let the gods decide instead. The first man to string this bow and shoot an arrow through twelve axes without disturbing them shall be my husband and sit with me here on the throne, to rule over Ithaca and all her lands until my son is wed."

She took the arrows Hermes presented Ares, held them aloft, and dropped them into the quiver before leaving the unstrung bow on a peg. Odysseus gaped at the feathers, still in pristine condition, as Penelope stepped back to her throne to oversee who would dare try the challenge first between the rabid bickering.

Peculiar, the line of axes was aligned perfectly to her chair. She could peer down every one of the twelve holes within the weapons, waiting.

Telemachus took the opportunity to finally greet her. With gentle arms they embraced, and with a stern, quiet voice she scolded him for continuing to hang around such insufferable men. It was a fun conversation to eavesdrop on. Hermes rested his elbows on the table, keeping his eye to the suitors and ear to the royals. Odysseus in his rags studied the queen; his haggardly beard hid the smirk at the game she was playing.

The entire family were liars! Hermes blessed their tongues. The amount of spite that poured from Penelope's character brought him a wondrous pleasure he hadn't enjoyed in some time. No wonder Ares was her first god to call for.

Five suitors humiliated themselves by being the firsts to try the bow, so enraptured by Penelope's beauty and the idea of simple kinghood.

This was a far better plan — this added entertainment. He laughed and continued to pour drinks to his neighbors, forcing their staggering and clogging their throats. Little need to watch over Odysseus, the wolf hiding in the sheep's pin; they had forever a connection of the mind. So while the king brooded and plotted, spoke to passing maids and suitors' servants, Hermes oversaw the intoxication of a good five dozen men in the next hour, glowing as if he were young Dionysus.

Telemachus slid from his throne and walked around the twentieth man to try the bow — the *monstrous thing,* they cried — and slipped into the crowd. As if a famous pick-pocket ran in his family line, he swiped swords and daggers from the tables, their owners up chiding at one another for his go, or lost in a drunken ramble, mocking the tramp that stood by the sconces.

Carelessly, the suitors fed Odysseus more bitterness with their taunts, and planted deep displeasure within the three gods who hid among them.

When the sun disappeared from the sky and Nyx began her chase, Penelope stood as the forty-fifth suitor failed to string Odysseus' bow, and swiftly exited the great hall. Choruses of jeers and offers of more gifts tried to coax her to stay, but the queen was done for the night — being around them was strenuous enough for any woman.

If Athena has not said so, let us start something now and begin this party's end, Ares said, disappearing from view.

"While we take bets on who is the strongest among us," Hermes announced, hopping up onto his chair, "why don't I entreat us all to a song? If you've forgotten, I earned much of my wealth and fame through my bardic talent — the most blessed of Apollo's mortal muses, I dare say!"

"You dare say!" one suitor called.

"I do!" Hermes boasted. "Pass me some lyre and I'll prove it. Perhaps a powerful chord while Antinous tries his hand at stringing that bow. My dear sir, you have not gone first. I am surprised by you, acting like you are beneath the old king."

"I am not so foolish as to waste my chance in going first," Antinous said with a dismissive wave of his hand. "It is a resilient weapon. To be the first demands all the strength to even begin to bend it! Let the string be stretched with everything you men have; I will have my go when the time is right."

One man's servant handed Hermes a finely tuned lyre. Strumming a quick note, he murmured out a little ditty, a melody he and his brother once crafted, before singing out a classic and known tale. It brought a sense of normalcy to the room as they ate and drank and whined under the strain of the wicked bow that already defeated over half of the suitors.

Odysseus stared off to the halls that led up to the chambers of the queen. "I grow impatient," he only breathed, but Hermes heard it well.

"Leaving me to guess if you mean to bed down your wife or to slaughter these ghastly pimps," Hermes replied only to him, altogether laughing along to a horrendous dance three men began between them. *"Though I can say one will precede the other."*

"Telemachus has done his part and hides within his quarters for now. My loyal Eumaeus is at his beck and call…" He paused as a bone was hurled in his direction. Pulling his torn cloak up, he blocked it from hitting his face, and it thudded against the stone wall behind him. "The good servants here are tired of never ending feasts and abhorrent treatment."

Hermes was quite talented at multitasking: playing the lyre, singing tale after tale, listening to Odysseus whisper his unbridled rage, and to top it off, a quiet prayer came through once more from the woman upstairs.

"If the sun rises come morning and these men are still loitering about my halls, if the bow remains unstrung, for only my husband could ever string the weapon, please bring me to where the royal Odysseus rests in Hades. I cannot take another day, I cannot take another man."

She was more resolute than Odysseus had made her out to be from his memory of her. How they both have changed. Would they know one another if they spoke face to face? If only they laid out their hearts now and compared them to their hearts of twenty years ago.

Hermes added an extra verse to his song, one for all to hear.

"Mighty Zeus on great, old mountain high,

Be this a night of revelry

To fly on and on for hours with friends,

No drink runs dry but our true fate descends," he said to laughing toasts, and he knew his father heard it, for Nyx's talons dug deep into the corners of the world, and Helios' chariot was held off from departing come dawn.

Day would not come until the deed was done.

Antinous scowled as another suitor took the bow from the hearth's edge to warm it and rub it with grease, perhaps to force it to bend, but to no avail. They had worked their way around the room, humiliating themselves one by one for being weaker than the great Odysseus. He flexed his fingers on the table, dragging his wine cup with his thumb while his time to test the stamina he boasted about rapidly approached.

* * *

Hermes sat atop the table, surrounded by the torn apart meat of supper.

The suitors ate like savages.

Given, they couldn't help themselves — Hermes' song filled their heads with delusion. Their laughter was painfully loud, bickering about things they never conversed about before. Hermes tied their hands as if they were little puppets to play with the longer they sat in Odysseus' chairs.

Hours had flown by, it was well past two in the morning.

"This is a waste of time," shouted Antinous as the man next to him failed to string the bow so spectacularly that it curved back to smack him in the jaw. He slammed the palm of his hand against the table and shot to his feet, his chair tumbling back. "Have we no sense? This is just a ploy by the queen to mock our pride, a challenge set only to stall the inevitable. No one here can string this trash! Are we just going to let it continue to kill our chances one by one?"

Stalking around the line of axes, he rattled every one of them as he passed. They resounded a metallic hiss. Hermes gently calmed his lyre's own hissing strings.

Odysseus shifted in silence at the back of the court, keeping Antinous in his line of sight through a forest of people.

"We had everything prepared! If that cocky boy didn't sneak by us, if we all had gone down to the shore and caught him unawares — we wouldn't be sitting here begging a *woman* to choose one of us. There would be no choice, she would have to take a husband, damn it — we would take her! No woman can go long without a man leading her way," Antinous said with broad strokes, pointing up towards Penelope's chamber. "Without Telemachus, the best of us would already be sitting down on the throne that's grown cobwebs since we arrived here! How is that helpful towards the *citizens* of this land?"

He roused a handful of banging fists on the table, agitation growing like the tide.

Hermes tuned the lowest note of the lyre, listening to Odysseus' heavy beating heart, matching the tune to the deep thumping.

He was ready. Hermes was glad to oblige.

"When morning comes," Antinous proclaimed like a commanding general, "we seize the palace, take what is ours by force. We have the numbers, we have the money. Three years has been a generous enough wait, hasn't it? How many more gifts can this woman glean from us? Her selfishness will be her demise —"

"Selfishness," Hermes spoke so softly it deafened the room. Three little chords echoed the word: self-ish-ness. "My friends, I've a song for just this instance: the ire we feel churning in our hearts. How unfair this all is! What a waste these years have been for those who are *most* important as they gave and gave and received no respect back. Why don't you have a seat there, Antinous, the true leader among us. If you cannot be the king come morning, enjoy the throne for this final song. The queen needn't know and the prince is not with us to call you off."

Standing on the pedestal, at the head of the court where the three thrones sat parallel, Antinous ran his fingers along their arms and laughed. The queen's chair was overlaid with soft furs, and he agreed to bask in their luxury. "Maybe Penelope *should* know," he said, lounging back with his wine, his legs spread wide. "Perhaps she will find this seat more of a comfort."

Hermes' teeth caught on his lip as he smiled. "I'm sure she will very soon," he replied. He hopped to his feet, lightly dancing over the mess of the feast of the table that laid to the left of the thrones. He may have grown an inch, hard for the men to tell from the way their eyes wearily blinked in the tired, drunken daze.

"Oh feathers gleam down the mountains pass
O'er the fine trees and long dewed grass,
Cross to where my lovely house do fare,
And rests amongst my humble wife and heir.
Tell me dear feathers does light still shine
On my home, my hearth, and that family o' mine?
Oh send me the kind wind that carried you far,
Take up my whole soul to be where they are."

As he sang, the clothes he wore from Telemachus shifted in the torch's illumination. The bright wool to tattered black silk, so subtle, a trick of the light, no doubt.

"The gods heard this prayer, and one happened to know

That the lovely house was full with strangers to show
The wife their gifts, their wealth, and their pride,
All to be rejected, adjourned, and denied."

The suitors drummed their fists on the table, stupid to his intent. Hermes kicked one goblet with lukewarm wine into the lap of one from Same.

"And the god flew down, for his feathers were sent
As signs of fair luck and good intent —
He came to me and opened his arms
Revealed knowledge with wit and distracted with charms.
Said these strangers in my house scorned my begotten,
Harassed my wife and must have forgotten
The deathless gods demand hospitality —
These suitors grow bold and need reminding of mortality."

Hermes' words grew bitter. His next kick revealed the gold in his sandals. Platters of half-eaten food clattered to the ground, splattering juices and gravies on their legs and feet. Several pushed away from the table, mumbling curses and raising complaints to their throned ringleader.

Antinous would find he could not move from the throne whether he wanted to or not. He threw out his chin and cussed out to the overstepping bard. "Anastasios… this isn't a name I recognize after all! Who are you? What business do you have to stir our anger? Stranger, you will get yourself killed for this!"

Only now did the suitors cling to their belts, finding no blades at their sides nor weapons by their food. The young prince had deceptively swiped them all from under their noses, for very little attention was given to his presence in the first place: the one who was deserving of all their respect.

Of course it was expected: when many rob one, one may rob many in retribution.

Hermes leapt to the smaller table that curved towards the back of the chamber, so that most of its seated could look upon the royalty without straining their necks. The table was cut in half with the rows of axes in between, the quiver empty, the bow gone.

"Who took our swords?" cried one.

"We've been fleeced!" hollered another.

A shadow ran down Hermes' face. His eyes, unblinking, dripped with ink-like sap, melting away his clothes strand by strand, as his boyish features split into an inhuman grin. Sharp needles pushed out from his forearms while his playing darkened.

"Who are you — one asks, who sits on the throne

After gloating and feasting, preaching nonsense, unbeknownst

That the one who stands are the feathers intact

Who heard the king's prayer and came to enact

Justice, godsent, on those who've done wrong."

Out ruptured his wings, censoring his cold stare as he shed his mortal form like one ripping open a papyrus envelope: a sickening tear of skin, feathers and ink bursting through seams unknown, spattering on the table beneath his feet, pouring into black puddles that pooled quickly across the floor. His arms extended with long-fingered wings, his feet curled into talons.

Two dozen suitors fell back, clambering on the floor, their eyes frozen on this monster whose body nearly torn in half — a floating golden heart between ribs of paper and ink. Some clasped their hands together, others pleaded in shaking voices.

Antinous sat still as a statue, his cocky smile stuck on his face.

"Fear not," Hermes sang, as the lyre melted in his fist, *"for I'm a god of Man, a guardian of souls. I'm not here to kill you. No, not I — the one with that pleasure tonight is your host."*

The string of the bow hummed a loud, beating chord as it was strung. Odysseus pulled the arrow notch back to his chin as he aligned the point through the twelve axes. His eyes were cold, unyielding, locked onto the beast of a man sitting on his wife's chair.

"Die," he said, opening his fingers.

The arrow shot straight. Across the room it went: one, four, seven, twelve — no time to spare for Antinous' eyes to widen as the stone tip grew larger before him.

It embedded itself in the soft muscle of his throat.

The suitor choked, gasped, and the hundred and seven remaining among them screamed in horror.

Odysseus tore off his rags and pulled another arrow from his side, nocking it on the bow, and shot the next man without a second's delay. Here the suitors saw that the haggard beggar, one they mocked and assaulted, standing like a haunted creature, was their king who was gone for twenty years.

Chaos in the great hall, Hermes cackled — a terrible, scratching sound to mortal ears. Taking flight in this primordial form, his body traveled through the wails and shrieking of startled men. The outer doors to the palace locked, dozens of torches blew out, and the shadow of Athena flew adeptly over to the prince's chambers.

Five men were dead before Hermes even flitted into the hallway, tumbling with a hidden wind. The air rushed between the gaps in his body, splattering ink across the stone.

Men scattered everywhere, splitting into groups large and small as they scrambled to escape the throne room where Odysseus laid them out by the dozen. Ugly crunches and squirts echoed far as he tore arrows from backs and faces.

It was *music* to the gods' ears.

"You dogs think I wouldn't return from Troy?" Odysseus growled, loosing another arrow. "You waste away *my* property, you lie with *my* servants, plot the death of *my* son, harass *my* wife! You deserve no clemency, not even Asphodel."

A silver spear whistled in the dark — the highlighted armor of the prince glimmered with Athena's influence while he joined his father's mission in tearing down suitor after suitor. Two men fell to the boy's weapon as he swung it close and tore the point from a bloody shoulder-blade.

"If you are truly the King of Ithaca," one man said, Eurymachus, hidden behind a column. His voice shook as he spoke. "Then your fury is justified! We have abused your family's kindness, that is true, but Antinous was the head of the snake. It was he who truly wanted the young prince dead! He pied for your throne, your power! We are weak in spirit, we let him speak such ill things, but we were against the ploy." In a pull of cowardly courage, Eurymachus revealed his face to Odysseus. "We will pay you for the burdens we have caused, and speak no ill of you — take twenty oxen from us each, and as much gold and bronze as we have in our homes to soothe your heart, my king!"

Soothe his heart? What payment would be enough other than their blood?

No mercy would be given, the king was far beyond reasoning with the damned.

And Hermes didn't blame him. Mercy was hard to come by in this realm and the one above.

The sound of Eurymachus' body, with an arrow through his breast, toppling over the table and spreading half the meal across the floor, stirred another round of panic. He gasped and kicked like a fish, slamming a weak foot into the chairs until he fell still and silent.

The suitors needed to find their weapons — it was fight or flee, and there was no fleeing from this palace. Hermes closed and opened doors like a cursed labyrinth, sending men running into the prince's spear and others back around to fall at Odysseus' feet. In his dark, wispy visage, their souls chased after him — desperate to find purchase within the psychopomp, like fireflies in his open chest, not wanting to be left alone in the halls of their demise.

It turned into a child's game: hide and seek, the hunters and the hunted. Suitors skulked in every dark corner, running blindly through the halls trying to find a way out. They flocked in greater numbers if they were brave enough to fight back, others remained silent and lonesome in their despair.

The joyous shock a dozen endured when they found the armory open, their stolen weapons from the court hidden inside. If they had just taken a minute to look around at what was missing, which pieces were absent from the chests and racks... they could've predicted that Odysseus would appear behind them, bronze helm over his face, a heavy shield at his back, and two long spears in either hand.

Like rats in a maze they cornered themselves. Angry howls or hopeless pleas had little effect on the king's ear.

Hermes gathered himself in his corporeal body back in the corners of the throne room. It never happened that he remained in his primordial state for longer than a moment. He patted his face and brushed the muck from his legs, glowing brighter than the dying hearth's embers as fifty-six souls clung to his cloak, still shaking from fright.

No desire to greet them; he hoped they suffered in oblivion.

A quivering, cold hand struggled to grip his talaria. Hermes looked down his nose at the man who wore an arrow as a pendant. "My l-lord," he croaked out, "save me."

"Save you?" Hermes asked, his brows high. He laughed coolly and gestured to the field of corpses. "I'd sooner let you all *rot* outside of the Underworld, doomed to relive your final hours over and over again, just to have a *taste* of what your king has suffered these past twenty years while you feasted on his supply. My love for mankind stops where their disrespect begins. Now remove your hand from my foot before I remove it for you, lest you wish your ghost to be amputated for eternity."

The suitor said nothing more. He pulled his hand back to his chest and died.

Ares loomed into the room in his Olympian stature as well, ducking under the doorway. His wide gait was stiff and his dragon helm's tail was aflame with the surrounding sounds of clamour and bloodshed. He was three times the size of the human thrones, but he didn't storm off to join the fighting. In his unseen presence, his little champion for the night burst into the court.

Her hair was braided back and her once lovely peplos was torn at the knee, revealing leather greaves at her shins tied tightly to her sandals. Penelope ran to the axes, leaping in the dark over several bloody bodies that flooded the room with toxic stank. Not even the windows could be opened over concern that the suitors would throw themselves out of it — for taking their own life would be more merciful than this.

The queen yanked two axes from their stand. Her muscles flexed with the weight while she quickly worked to secure one to her back as she held fast to the other. But it wasn't enough. Hopping around the room, she ripped bronze bands from the dead suitors' wrists, sliding them up her arms as if they were a mobile shield.

Hermes stood there, mouth agape as Penelope then stalked out like an Amazon warrior, while Ares joined his side.

"Brother," Hermes said, as no mortal would hear them speak.

Ares shrugged. "She is a woman and this is her house. How could she sleep after hearing the wails of the men who have done her wrong? Let her partake in the bloodshed, slaughter all she sees, she has earned it."

"Look at us all teaming up for the first time in decades! Athena's off with her young boy, likely throwing him down the hall to impale another, mine is — *ah* — somewhere in here acting like Retribution incarnate. What a lovely sibling outing!" Hermes chuckled. Another soul with a speared hole through the thigh zipped to his cloak. He didn't even need to approach it, they were finding him. "I find Athena's a rule-breaker, don't you?"

"By rule-breaker, you mean she cheats? Always," Ares replied. The red holes in the blackness of his helmet grew brighter than the moon as he inhaled with glee. "This won't go on much longer now that the queen has already severed both head and limb of four men."

"So fast?"

"She is Spartan. Ask Apollo."

Hermes set his hands on his hips. Mapping out the palace, Odysseus mowed down every man in his way coming from the armory, and Telemachus — rapidly wearing himself out — silently cut through shallow halls, catching suitors off guard. Telemachus wasn't the masculine figure Diomedes was despite that man also being Achaea's youngest general and Athena's other champion; the youth was strong-willed but terribly sheltered, his heart raced as his breath came out in quick bursts of adrenaline.

Athena, the boy's going to pass out if you don't let him rest.

Athena's shadows splintered like glass around the palace walls, through every corridor and around each room. *He has more fight in him*, she replied.

Hermes took to the air, zipping over the carnage and down the hall where painful grunts of thrusting spears and cracking of bones rang. There the boy was, being pushed back against the stone by two men grasping his weapon with everything they had. Several others took notice from the hall and started on their way over, resentful grins on their faces.

Cursing under his breath, Telemachus kicked out their shins and used his smaller size to slip under the spear and tumble between them. But his face was stark red, and even in the dark with Athena's influence, the arrow he ripped from another man's ribs to shove into the back of a suitor's knee drew blisters in his palm, and it took a terrible three minutes to wrestle the other to the ground.

Telemachus' helmet went rolling down the hall.

Someone cried out.

"Odysseus, come help your son," Hermes said, sending a wild wind to open the heavy door that cut through the inner courtyard.

A charging boar, that's what the king was.

Without delay, Odysseus slammed himself against the suitors piling on the prince. He broke fingers, snapped back elbows, and suffocated another with his large, blood-stained hand. Dare say, Hermes witnessed him bite an ear off.

Telemachus scurried out from the heap, fiddling for the bottom of his spear. The bronze clanged on stone and bone; he groaned, wet palms squeaking on the floor.

Athena...

Ares' grumble rolled in, *Stand by.*

No one would believe such a story, of the entire royal family of Ithaca taking down over a hundred men. Or perhaps they would. The Ithacans were a wild bunch.

Penelope shrieked in her rage, hammering down the axe on the collarbone of the suitor that dared to touch her son. Her hair had fallen in sweat-soaked wisps, clinging to her cheeks. She pulled Telemachus behind her — so much sweat, bile, and blood on the ground, he glided with ease. Her blade nearly hit Hermes, who stuck himself to the high ceiling to avoid the spray of gore.

She followed his glow with her eyes, pupils blown wide enough she would be capable of seeing anything.

But there was no time to dwell on the presence of gods.

The queen and king of Ithaca both had to realize they were in the presence of each other first.

Now, Athena finally spoke to her siblings, her unseen, elongated primordial form retracting to the tall, womanly skin she often wore, *I am done.*

Telemachus sighed before slumping back to the floor.

Penelope's axe whirled over Odysseus' shoulder at a suitor running with the hopes he could sneak off and escape. Blood lined her torn peplos, clinging to her like second skin. Her face was bruised and her lip busted, but despite it all, her energy persisted — animated by Ares' blessing. Odysseus staggered towards her, spear pulled back like a javelin; it whisked by her cheek at another who wished to take Penelope from behind.

Hermes tucked his hands into his hair and pulled at his curls.

This was such a more interesting outcome than he could've hoped!

Without a word, the two took on several more men, finding them with weapons in hand. But raised in Athena's willpower, Odysseus offered no mercy, his mind locked in the heat of battle like he was there, still, in Troy, being attacked on all sides.

And the three gods watched on, certainly not sending dissonant breezes to coax arrow shafts here and spears over there; neither wincing nor gasping when skulls continued to crack and men choked on their teeth. They just admired the additional color to Hermes' cloak as ninety-eight, ninety-nine, one-hundred stars speckled the cloth…

"Hermes," Odysseus spoke as the halls were quieting. Hermes appeared back in the throne room where two young men clung to the king and the tired prince's knees. "Open the door so these bards can wait in the courtyard for me to finish my chores. Telemachus spared them and so, then, will I."

With a small flick of a finger, the great bronze door creaked open, and a warm red glow from a sun finally dawning filled the room. Odysseus let his eyes fall upon the grime and dust, the spilled guts and twitching corpses that laid where thousands of feasts were held in his absence. The sight alone smelled foul and wicked.

No man spoke a word; thus, it seemed, to be over. Vengeance over the suitors was had.

Odysseus' chin tilted as the rush of bare feet approached him, turning with the shield held high at the same time a sword clashed down on the metal with a resounding *clang*. Penelope pulled back, her teeth bared, and struck down again towards the king's legs, forcing him to squat and block. Telemachus retreated five steps to the table, speechless as his mother charged forward with the blade.

She was ruthless and quick. Odysseus parried what he could, taken aback by the woman's ferocity. Had they not just fought as allies? She took hold of the helmet he wore by the faceplate and tore it asunder, for she got too close for him to dare make any return advances. A relentless punch thrown into his cheek — it was the beggar's cheek, rather, sort of. The guise had teetered between forms as the night dragged on for hours on end. Penelope wept, pushing his spear away with her bruised arm and twisted it around her body before turning it back on him.

Odysseus dodged and ducked, gasping at every slight nick to his skin.

"You strung the bow," she said, and Odysseus' heart softened at her voice. "You shot the arrow through my axes?"

"Penelope," Odysseus replied, stepping over bodies as he blocked another advance with his shield.

"All this time, and you didn't say anything to me?" she raged, pushing until his back hit a column and Telemachus cried out in protest from across the room. "Do you realize how *long* it has been? How *long* I have waited! Bearing the strain of being a woman in this world without her husband for twenty years," she dug the spear into the shield at the same spot, "one-hundred-seventeen days," again, "and five hours—! And you limp into my house like this? Endanger your life again before I have the chance to speak? Has your mind weakened? Have you forgotten?" The tip dented through the old armor, speared like a great fish. She hurled the shield away, off Odysseus' mighty arm. It smashed like another bell in the hall as she spun the spearpoint back to his chin. "You are *mine*."

The king of Ithaca fell to his knees.

Athena lowered herself to Hermes' level. *Make him himself, little brother. As you see fit.*

Hermes twirled his head around. He was relishing in the moment. *Really? I get to?*

Try not to overdo it.

Oh, I've been planning this in my head for years, you have no idea.

The smile was contagious, passing his hand over Odysseus. Throwing away the elderly age — *far* away — his tanned, firm but weary skin returned; long, untangled locks of deep, brown hair glowed nearly auburn in the dawn's light. Hermes kept his great grandson true to who he was, adding that keen sparkle back to his grey eyes.

Aha! And his stupid felt cap that delighted Hermes to no end.

Athena squinted and folded her hands behind her back. *You left him naked covered in blood.*

They can wash it off each other, and crown the other in olive branches, Hermes mused, spinning his caduceus. *Mortals find that romantic.*

I find that romantic, Ares nodded along, letting his influence on Penelope fade. He disappeared among the reflections in the blood, off to Olympus, and the poor mortal woman trembled as she held the spear against Odysseus.

"Penelope," breathed Odysseus, letting his throat lean into the point. "There was never any doubt. If you're angry with me, then dispatch me now, for I cannot be as patient as you have been."

"If you are so impatient, sir, then carry down our wedding bed," she quickly replied, trying to blink her tears away. "You've won my challenge, you may taste your victory."

There was a choking grimace from Odysseus — how insane he appeared, nude and caked in blood, shaking his head as his own tears fell. "I cannot carry down our wedding bed, Woman. I built it myself into our olive tree," he cried. Angry, if he were not so pleased to see his wife and spent all of his fury on the bodies that stained his palace. "Tell me it still stands firm — that someone has not chopped it away like carving the beating heart out of my chest! If it hasn't been hauled off, my lady, then I'll carry you there instead, for there's still strength in my arms to hold you, always!"

Penelope sobbed at last, the bronze spear slipping from her white-knuckled grasp. Crumbling to her knees, hoisted by Odysseus' arms as he pulled her in, she kissed his face and tangled herself in his hair, shaking in her tears. He clung to her waist, dragged his hand up her back to feel every part of her — the wife he sacrificed all for, the joy of his life, whose warm breast lit up a fire within him that had been lying dormant for so long.

Hermes settled by Telemachus' side. A gentle nudge and the boy jumped from his skin, raising his eyes to the glowing god.

"Not that a herald *must* declare it, but I think it'd be ill-fitting, dear prince, if you didn't go over to your parents for a brief embrace now that you're all reunited at last. A quick one, certainly. I believe your father will take your mother to delight in that unused bed upstairs. And you may come back here, call upon your loyal servants and women to clean up this mess, and prepare for the day ahead."

"You are Hermes," Telemachus said.

"Aren't you very perceptive," Hermes replied with a grin. But he couldn't keep looking at this boy's face. Leaning down, he took the pale chin in hand and turned it from side to side. Telemachus stood deathly still. "Let me just speed this along, you unfortunate boy. Become a man before the sun rises."

An inkling of stubble appeared along the prince's jaw.

"Go. Embrace so your wise parents can wash and be as a loving couple are when taken to bed."

He pushed Telemachus onward; the young man discarded his armor and fell to his knees by their side. Odysseus grasped him, and with Penelope on one shoulder and Telemachus on the other, enveloped both of them with heart-filled kisses and plenty of tears. Odysseus glanced up toward the other side of the room where Hermes watched, his brows pulled in tight. A short nod was all he needed to give.

Are you crying? Athena asked, poking Hermes' forehead back once she was content with her part of the work.

Hermes' wings pulled over his eyes, wiping his cheeks. *No, it's just all the mortal body fluid that flew around. I have never wept a day in my life.*

She sighed and shook her head. *It is a shame you produce such cunning and tactful progeny. They are all too emotional. I will see you at home, Hermes.*

With her helmet, spear, and shield, she sauntered past the family to the door. When Telemachus raised his eyes to her invisible form, she regarded him in silence and departed.

Odysseus followed his son's gaze and said nothing.

Hermes wanted to stay. He wanted to float along and see how they would go about the day and reveal the surprise to the people of Ithaca. Witness how the old king Laertes would react to seeing his son and grandson alive and well; how Odysseus would live his first real day at home. He wanted to dig both feet into the island's sand a leave his mark.

But there was a tug at Hermes' mind.

A little static tick that flicked him to listen to the beckon of his father king.

No time at all, truly? After all this work... The family just got back to their feet, Father, come now, please. Not even a final embrace, no goodbye —?

Chapter 19

Hermes thought maybe there should be a cushioned landing pad along the edge of Olympus where he would so often fall when discarded on the marble against his will.

Open palms to dry stone, he patted and slapped the ground several times, a slurry of silent cusses propped him up on one knee. Olympus wasn't on fire, there were no tumbled walls or flooding streams, nor lesser gods or nymphs bleeding out in the streets.

But Zeus' palace was aglow in the early morning — the color of a salmon against the pale blue sky, for even the gods were subject to an extended night. The pantheon likely waited up there. Zeus probably had planned a worse punishment at Poseidon's behest: Hermes would be exiled for some time to the plains of Egypt, stuffed in a bird cage. The role of psychopomp would be transferred to someone else who had way too much time on their hands, Artemis or the like… She'd hate the job, too many men would try to touch her and then spirits would arrive in Hades with missing hands by the hundreds. Or if Dionysus took it — who was to say the spirits would reach the Underworld at all? He would gather them together on his fruitful party island and let them enjoy a mindless existence there.

Which, in theory, sounded fun if the souls had any forethought to enjoy things in the Upperworld.

Hermes stood. That was progress towards possible doom.

No use prolonging it. He still had some luck with him! Maybe Zeus, knowing Hermes' fondness for mortals, would send him down to some lord to play as a songbird. There would, at the very least, be drama unfolding around him, people to interact with, a nicer climate to be stuck in a cage for years.

Folding his hands over his staff, he stepped into the air, flying over the palaces and courtyards. Get right to the point. It was mercy enough that Zeus kept his brother stationary instead of raging over Ithaca. With the air so fresh, Hermes' lungs were overwhelmed with how clear they suddenly felt. A good omen, right?

Yet Zeus' inner courtyard was uncomfortably silent. Even on normal gathering days, there was chatter coming from the room. A pin could drop here and erupt in the ears.

He landed without a sound, maybe the *smallest* buzz from his wings fluttering so quickly had betrayed him. It bounced off the bronze columns around him; the vibration sent a distant, thundering echo rolling miles away. No wafting smell of ambrosia or the burning of offerings came from the grand hall. Hermes lifted his foot and gave the wings of his talaria a pensive stroke.

His own challenge, then.

The first he saw in the room was Hera, sitting straight upon her throne; her face always peered down the hall where everyone else arrived. There was a single upright line upon her brow as she tapped a bracelet against her open palm, waiting to lock eyes with Hermes. She sat back with a nod and a whisper to the profile of Zeus in his elevated chair.

Beyond his line of sight, there was a skidding of a heavy throne, followed by a jostle of four others. Hermes wheeled himself into the room — better to see what was coming for him than taking wild guesses.

He almost turned right back around at the sight of Poseidon. The Lord of the Sea stood restrained by Hephaestus and Demeter, his throne toppled. Never had the young god seen his uncle so dilapidated: bandages wrapped around his upper arms and across his chest where a bulk of the Leto twins' arrows had struck him, and the lightning bolt thrown from Athena singed his skin an ashen purple. Less than a week had passed, and Hermes couldn't look the god in the face while Poseidon's head was half-malformed from the blade that was thrown precisely through one eye.

It would heal and grow back with the right care, that wasn't a concern. But it *was* Hermes' blade that did the deed.

Four Olympian gods were at fault for causing harm to one of the three great kings.

Those four gods all had their hands folded behind their backs, waiting for Zeus to say something while Poseidon's temper flooded over his threshold.

"The absolute impudence!" he shouted, yanking his arm from Demeter's hold to thrust his finger at Hermes teetering to his own chair. "I could write a list that covers the sky with the disrespectful actions taken towards Zeus and I — the absolute hubris of one so small to put the life of a conniving mortal, whom I had every right to seek comeuppance for injuring a son of *mine,* over the obedience of his rank in this family. No amount of years in chains would stop this feathered son of a nymph from thinking he could play savior to the damned."

Hermes curled his nails into the skin of his forearms.

Poseidon's lips twitched as he summoned all his anger to the forefront. "Brother, not only did he allow a mortal to use his own sword against me, but he conspired with others in this court with seditious intent. If I were any less powerful, I may have succumbed from the assaults of your *favored* children, Zeus."

Zeus, perched forward in his throne, let his gaze wander over to where Apollo, Artemis, and Athena stood shoulder to shoulder. They bore a hole in the wall across the room like sly, scolded children, patient and resiliently holding their tongues.

Hera tapped her bracelet to the table. "Poseidon, they would not have *killed* you," she said bluntly. "The Fates would give warning if your demise was imminent by the hands of Zeus' bastards. Was the attack over a single human's life necessary? Perhaps not, in my opinion; but then perhaps it was not *just* over one man's life that this act of defiance occurred."

Aphrodite slowly rose from her chair, the pearls in her dark hair clinked together like an announcement chime. "I agree with her Majesty," she said. "There has been some dispute over this mortal — this son of Laertes — for years now. Even though I have had my gripes about his crimes against my favorites in Troy, it *was* said that this man was to return to his home. The love between he and his wife is something that I haven't seen in some time."

"This is not about love," Poseidon spat. "To insinuate that I do not also love my own child who had been humiliated and pleaded for my aid is ludicrous at best. You would put a human's feelings above my own?"

"Of course not," Aphrodite replied, tucking her hair behind her ear. "But you have bountiful offspring who live and perish, reign and suffer daily, my lord. Mortals are soft, fleeting little things, their emotions are *everything* that drive them. The drive in the son of Laertes was worthy of him overcoming you as his last great obstacle."

With a content hum, she sat back down, weaving her fingers through Ares' hand.

Hermes had to puff out his cheeks to keep his snide remarks inside of his mouth. Poseidon's cheeks boiled red.

"It would be foolish to disagree," Athena spoke. Zeus' watchful eye moved to her.

"You, of all of us," Poseidon argued, "surprise me the most with your sudden second thoughts. Having put that man off his path in the first place, sending him towards my islands, knowing fully well his tendencies and cockiness. You, *wise* goddess, who had asked me to show no mercy on your Achaeans before that Ithacan blinded Polyphemus, ransacked his home and property, and called it clemency. I know Hermes here is full of deceit and tricks, but I would not think he had the wit to change *your* resilient mind."

Hermes scratched his elbows as they rested behind his back and glanced at Athena in all her steadfast glory. Her face was softer, chin resting parallel to the floor while she regarded him with the smallest of nods.

"It was more of a change of heart," she said. Her back straightened, and she shrugged her arms, gesturing to Hermes. "Argeiphontes is a fine judge of mortal character; no doubt from all his years spent with Man's righteous and their nefarious. He is of the best among us to decide what to *do* before the Fates declare what is to be *done*. Just as Aphrodite had every right to try and save her kin on the battlefield, so did Hermes with his own."

There was a stinging on the inside of Hermes' face. He wiggled his nose and looked up at the immense looking glass of Zeus' all-seeing-eye as it settled like a distant cloud, overlooking the islands of Ithaca and Same. It was sunny there, as Odysseus often had described it. Hermes wiped his upper cheek with a pinkie, and tucked some curls behind his ear.

Zeus pursed his lips. "And Ares," he said, and the god of war jutted up from his seat.

"Yes, Father?"

"You'd gone down as well to aid in Hermes' pursuit?"

Ares blinked. From Hermes, to Athena, back to their father he turned and nodded. "Yes, Father. I —"

"Interesting," Zeus said, leaning back in his chair. All ten gods raised their brows. "No, no, I may let this revelation sit for a moment while I have a drink. I'm thunderstruck at this affair, truly." A wild chuckle resounded deep from his chest as he picked up his goblet. "Hermes, my boy, I was right about you. I do love being right."

Hermes blew out the air he kept in his cheeks, his wings folding back as tightly to his head as he could manage. "Right about me, Father?" he asked.

Not usually a good thing: Hermes had many contrasting traits.

"Ten years ago, you first crossed the table to sit amongst your siblings who were, for a time, your enemies. I told you that was a sign of good leadership. Now I look among my warring children and they intermingle together like true family — ones who were at each other's throats, now aiding the other against a common enemy."

"Zeus," Poseidon said, pulling himself from Hephaestus' powerful grip. "You cannot be serious."

"I can hardly recall the last time my family united so quickly, and all because of Hermes' attachment to this quaint, royal great grandson of his," Zeus exclaimed. "Poseidon, your wounds will heal. Perhaps in a few years, you'll join me in laughing about what an absolute wreck you look. Do you want some new punishment issued? Fine. Hermes," he curled his finger, "come here."

Oh.

Oh, he was so looking forward to seeing mercy in his father's smile.

Apollo raised his voice from under his helm. "Father, you cannot hurt him — he still carries souls for Hades!"

Flying up to Zeus' throne, Hermes bowed his head and pushed back the cloak that glimmered with the spirits of the damned. His chest was tight, but his mind was clear. Whatever it was Zeus had planned for him, he could bear it.

Zeus leaned next to him and whispered his demands into his ear.

And at first Hermes smiled, for what he heard was good.

Then the stinging returned to his nose and the tightness to his chest. To swallow was a mighty task and to hold his composure was altogether more difficult than having to drag a holy chain around Olympus. What smile he had fell faster than Troy.

"That's generous enough, yes?" Zeus said, moving Hermes' face with his thumb and forefinger to look him in the eye.

"Yes, Father," Hermes whispered through pinched lips. "I am... very grateful for your considerate decisions."

He held his breath as he removed himself from the raised throne, and kept his gaze to the floor as he flew across it. If any one of his brothers or sisters saw his face, no master of deceit could lie his way out of what it was he held back.

Poseidon could not touch him no matter how disorientingly savage his threats were.

All was safe, at least.

With the task given, Hermes was allowed to leave the palace without partaking in the morning feast. There wasn't much to say that would keep him at the table. Besides, over a hundred souls waited to be led to the River Styx. Giving them the luxury of feeling Olympus' presence was too kind for them.

Hermes whisked down the long staircase, catching a breeze at the bottom that carried him through the palace gardens and over much of Olympus' dwelling.

His sandals landed flat again along the scuffed overhang of the mountain just as a choked sob hiccuped its way out of him. He cried briefly into his palms, squishing his face between cold fingers. He had to pull himself together; he slapped his cheeks.

Can't be pathetic in front of everyone.

After everything in the past twenty years, this punishment was the best thing the man could have in the end.

This was mercy.

"Hermes?"

Six feet into the air he leapt, the voice startled him so greatly, he grasped for a blade that no longer existed. A whisper in his head, but not the distant echo of faraway prayers. It was direct, like spoken from behind him.

He looked over his shoulder just to be sure.

"Not available, leave a message," Hermes replied aloud.

There was a short pause and a muffled hum of a chuckle before Odysseus' voice resonated into his ear once more. *"You left."*

"You're home."

Walking to the edge, the snowy breeze that was never allowed into the heavens pushed up against his face and folded back to the earth. Every cloud rolled like the sea, rimmed in gold.

"And you're home too, I take it."

"For now," Hermes said. He tucked his chin into the fabric draped over his shoulders. It still smelled like Ithaca. "I have a lot of baggage to carry; deliveries to make to Hades with your name on them all. It'll be a busy day for both of us."

Odysseus clicked his tongue. *"I have,"* he paused, *"so many families to speak to about the reason for why their sons, fathers, or brothers are dead by my hand. My father is the only one who gets their son, my wife her husband, my boy his father. Ctimene is taking a boat from Same to see me this evening. The time keeps ticking and I haven't thought of the right words for her yet."*

He sat and stretched his feet over the limitless drop below. "You'll find them. You're a clever man." Each foot was large enough to stomp mountains flat from this angle; like he were a Titan. "How're you speaking to me?"

Not the first wonder he had about Odysseus.

"You left your feathers on the arrows here," Odysseus replied. *"I couldn't simply let them be put aside in the storage room, nor for any other man to use in his naivety as you said they'd bring intent to their quarry. So I cut them clean from the shafts. Now they're safe with me, sewn into the tainia my mother left behind. You were my intention. But just in case this wasn't enough, Telemachus and I are sitting in an orchard he said was promised to you for your strawberry trees. We've assembled a modest shrine for your visits."*

Hermes put his face into his hands again and shook his head. His shoulders couldn't stop quaking. This man was impossible.

"I wanted to thank you."

"You've done that plenty, Ody," Hermes whispered. Pinching his nose, he rubbed a thumb under his brow. Staggered steps crunched on the walkway behind him. Athena and Apollo paused where the grass faded away to stone, come to check in on their favorite brother.

"And Athena, of course. Would you tell her that if you see her?"

"Tell Athena you said thank you?" Hermes repeated, glancing over to his eldest sister. "I don't know if she's free; she's always up to something."

"But I swear if she endangers my son before he grows a full beard, I'll put all her statues in that cave and seal it back up."

"Oh, well, I certainly don't think she's free to hear that you'd fight her in hand-to-hand combat if she puts the good prince in harm's way," Hermes said straight to Athena's unfrazzled face.

He won over a smirk, but the corner of her smile waned.

Turning back to the open air, like his progeny was sitting just out of reach, his voice was trying to hide from him. "But Odysseus, I need to speak to you as the herald of Zeus — for his command is law and it affects you specifically."

There was a long pause that chewed on his confidence. Hermes tugged at some curls and opted to continue.

"It's good news! You'll like it," he lied, or maybe he wasn't. He wasn't sure anymore. "The god king declared that no god or goddess has the authority to step foot in the kingdom of Ithaca; it encompasses the region around it as well. You and your family are free from Poseidon's threats and all the dangers we deathless folk wreak. While home, you're safe and sound from the doubts of your people, for Zeus has deemed you their rightful king, and forsaking all others, gives you back an unchallenged life… so long as you remain in your kingdom's boundaries," Hermes relayed. "Now isn't that just wonderful — a tranquil Ithaca, a happy queen, a healthy son…?"

A hot tear fell off the mountain and froze the moment it passed into the mortal realm, whisked away in the breeze.

The silence was eating away at him. They weren't meant to be silent people.

In the depths of the pause, the Ithacan king replied in a quiet breath, *"I'm grateful for you, Hermes. That you've sacrificed even a sliver of your immortal life to be in a large fraction of mine."*

It began to snow over the bottom of the mountain where the town of Litochoro lay as Hermes couldn't stop all the water that poured from his eyes.

"Tonight's first libation is all yours," Odysseus said, *"if you still wish it."*

"Damn your memory," he cursed. Never did he ever come first. "Of course I still wish it. Demand it, even. And when the first strawberry tree blossoms and bears fruit, I want the largest one sliced in half and laid at my shrine. And I want a statue built; one as nice as Athena's. I expect it to be the most accurate to my likeness. You've had enough time to memorize my physique."

"I will see it done before I see you again."

Hermes lifted his chin and wiped his face. "Are my feathers not working properly, you great fool? I cannot visit. I'm not allowed to step foot in your land by my father's orders. This is my punishment. This is the goodbye we have."

There was hardly a time when Hermes was allowed his own choices. Everything he's done was met with punishments and restriction since the day he was born; why should he expect to have this one thing — this one little mortal?

"When I spoke to the prophet," Odysseus said, and his voice was even and slow, *"he told me I had an obligation to find a land where the people don't know of the sea. And there I'm to erect a temple to Poseidon to appease his anger. It's*

the last thing I must do, then I can truly be at peace with my wife and son. That's something I'd like to get done as soon as possible."

A swirling cloud kissed his shins.

"I could use a guide."

The talaria pushed Hermes up to his feet in a single bound before a thought formed in his brain. Cocking his head, he scanned the earth as it curved over the horizon. He knew the paths even in the driest of deserts, every simple civilization on the earth; all of Gaia at his fingertips.

"And if that's not allowed, well... I'll still see you back in my home one day. You have a knack for my beds, and this is one I don't think you'll avoid. When my mind is too weak to command my legs to move and my heart to beat," Odysseus exclaimed, *"when my son is king and I'm in the arms of Penelope, I'll greet you then. The finest, most loyal guide I have ever known; arriving to take me back to those green shores that our lost loves have walked."*

The hundreds of souls pulled his cloak down over the edge, like a typhoon's gale that called to the psychopomp. Hermes balanced on his toes, four wings beating back to keep him upright.

"That's a promise, then," he said, his heart jump-starting, "King Odysseus."

Apollo scoffed behind him. "Oh just go and stay out of trouble, you miscreant," he said with a wave of his hand.

Hermes laughed, letting gravity take hold as he slipped from Mount Olympus and let himself free fall for the several minutes it took for land and sea to open their arms to receive the god of boundaries.

What a couple of rule-breakers they were, snaking around the god king's rules.

"You only need to speak my name and I'll be there. Whenever you are, wherever you are, for whatever you need. I'll appear."

He slipped nimbly above the ocean's bubbly surface, a heavy mist splashing over him as he sped on towards the edges of the world.

And Odysseus, crowned with olive branches and feathers, fated to rule Ithaca for his life, finally laughed with him in earnest, and sighed out a wise, *"I know."*

Epilogue

The dampness of the Underworld was sorely missed, and he didn't realize how much he looked forward to his time there until he set his feet down on his favorite damp rock.

Air in the bloody Ithacan palace was brimming with toxins that needed fumigating; Olympus was too fresh, so clean that it burned his nostrils; but by the Styx? It was like sticking his nose into a cool, moist towel after a hot bath.

Removing his caduceus, the serpents summoned forth the swine of mortals that clogged up his cloak. Out they poured, broken and in pieces, full of holes, guts, and fear. Any spectre, Fury, and Judge would know these hundred men were brutally murdered. Coincidentally, the handful of men on the beaches, still waiting for the ferryman's passage, were also of Ithaca's vast kingdom.

Was it poetic irony? Hermes was still deciding if it warranted a little laugh.

Feet set above the sand, he slapped away any desperate hand that reached out to grab him. They were on the beach, they could figure out where to go from here.

There was one soul he happened to sneak into the drafty tunnels, the only one he was happy to bend rules for. Crouching among the group, Hermes tucked his hands under two long, nipped up arms, and raised the neglected dog to his chest.

"Welcome to the foyer of your new home," he said, drifting down the beach towards the illuminated water's edge. "You're not going to find many dogs here, except one who I think will really like you, but you'll enjoy your company. Everyone down in this kingdom has a riveting personality."

Argos sniffed Hermes' cheek. A tiny blip of a ghostly tongue pressed against his skin.

"No Master, yet. I shoved his soul so deep into his body, I think he has another thirty to forty years left in him unless he does something stupid. Which… he's mine, so I imagine that may be the case. You'll see him *all* the time in your dreams. Souls glimpse into the future so you keep that tail wagging. He's going to be so surprised to see you! Yes! I know he wanted to give you all the pets and all the kisses," Hermes cooed, walking up over the river. "You're such a good dog."

The river rippled from afar, the slow but steady pull of the ferryman's oar bringing the boat into view. Hermes was already several yards over the river, caught like a thief in broad daylight trying to steal as casually as possible. Except this time he was smuggling.

Charon paused his rowing.

Hermes took one more long step.

"Hermes," Charon said.

The young god turned his back to his friend, craning his neck to glance around. "Charon, how lovely it is to see you again! You must've missed me this time! Thinking I keep neglecting my duties, but I would never — there are the new ones, all the same scenario. None have money to pay you, so let them wander the shores for as long as you wish. I'm just stretching my wings a bit, no need to worry about me."

"Woof," Argos agreed.

Charon raised his eyes from beneath his hood. *"A canine?"*

Hermes pouted. "He's just a puppy."

"Old dog."

"Definitely a puppy," Hermes replied, turning himself and Argos around. He raised the dog's head to his cheek. "Oh, come now, Charon, what's one dog in the Elysium Fields? He's just waiting for his master — and he's such a good boy."

Argos' ghost gave his tail the smallest of wags.

Charon shook his head. "No animals with humans."

"Says who? Who wrote that rule? I cannot imagine our good king of the dead would write something like that," Hermes said. "Maybe he has. Maybe he wants to keep all the good dogs to himself."

Sauntering over, he perched on the rim of the boat and lowered Argos to Charon's feet, right in the deepest divot of the craft where Charon's robes bunched up like a perfect blanket.

"Fine, *you* should bring him to Hades and Persephone. He's a loyal guard dog, and I owe the king a gift for coming to my rescue. Consider Argos a present; one I may visit from time to time. Can't go discarding this soul anywhere else, my friend, I'd be terribly upset. And look at that, he already likes you!" He pointed at the sleeping hound at the ferryman's feet, half tucked under the long drab robes.

Charon's discontent bored into Hermes' smile.

"Fine," he muttered.

A tiny dance on the side of the boat, Hermes bent over and kissed the top of the moot god's head. "I always appreciate you, Charon. Just one more task of mine and I'll be back out of your hair. It'll remove one soul from your line that you wouldn't care to carry anyway. See how generous I can be?"

"Do not go over your authority," the ferryman warned, but Hermes waved him on, flying back up to the beach where the spectres of the suitors wailed and gawked at each other, the jagged walls, the endless river…

There he plucked one up, knuckle deep through the base of his hair. The ghost stumbled back as Hermes flew, dragged straight over the river, flailing and kicking his feet. If the hands had any texture, they'd be roughly dragging coarse lines through Hermes' forearms. But they didn't, and so Hermes paid the struggle no mind.

Whisking past Charon towards the tunnel that led deeper into the Underworld, his content smile fell away.

The white and gold exomis that glowed over his chiton clung to the darkness of the cave. Black shadows stained the cloud-like pattern, dragging like ink, as the psychopomp carried this ghost passed the path of the three-headed Cerberus. But the great dog didn't growl, as the serpentine hiss from Hermes' staff lulled the beast to a short sleep.

This task wouldn't take long.

His fingers itched to just let the soul go, to let it be lost in the caverns of Hades for all of eternity, but that was too nice for this one. Hermes' scowl grew as the ghost continued to fight back. Always aggressive in life, and too in death.

Technically he shouldn't know the layouts of every tunnel. As his task usually ended at the beaches, there was no reason for him to venture this far in this direction — the palace of the king and queen was the opposite way, and the three judges who were meant to cast a vote were in their hall several caverns down.

Their vote would be what Hermes' was; he was just expediting the process. Patience wasn't in his domain.

But cleverness was; the labyrinth in the endless hells were etched in his memory. Flying through crude, spear-like rock, it was easier to get in than it was to get out.

Hermes never really stopped by the lower entrance to Tartarus before.

The buzzing hit his ears like a chorus of angry wasps.

"Now, now," he said, pulling Antinous up to his face as he dangled the spectre in the air. "Greedy as you are for your rewards in the land of the living that you'd mock even a god in your midst, I rush you towards your deliverance. Aren't I kind?"

Perhaps the buzzing could be the sound of screams, of dampened power and harsh abuse. Hermes balanced a fresh smile on his face.

"You'll find all those like you here, perhaps you'll even make friends. Or maybe they'll find you weak: a boy worth very little; maybe they'll chop you up into little pieces and sew you back together. I really don't care what they do to you. But as you share the worst with those old rulers of the universe cast down by the Olympians, know that you're not even a fraction as great as they — your body will be dust and your essence will be flayed. If you have anything to say, if you wish to argue against my judgment, then speak now. I shall listen and consider."

The ghost of Antinous wheezed and sputtered through the hole in his throat. It did nothing but make Hermes' lip curl.

"No? Nothing? I'm usually a stickler for a good argument. Some sort of deal. Make me debate my case, second guess my decision," he said, holding him out over the small gaps in the pit. A flimsy leg kicked out again. "Very well, though. If you insist."

Hermes opened his fist.

The bottom of Tartarus was about the height Hermes flew from Olympus to the sea, which if the ghosts were paying attention in his flight, they would know how long it could take in a free fall, but it was too bad they had very little thought at all.

He waited over the barred hole with his hands on his hips just to hear the landing, a sound to satisfy his anger. Tartarus' opening wasn't too large considering the Titans and the immense, damned jailed inside of it. The Furies ran their punishments with passionate grit; goddesses of pain and suffering and everything in between.

Through the deafening buzz, there came an echoing thud and the haunting skitter of abnormal legs and hissing croaks. A strange heat rose from beyond the cage, pushing Hermes' dim cloak in lazy circles while he squinted down into the dark.

The Titan War was fought far before his years, before any of his siblings' existence. He had only heard the stories from Zeus, his mother, and the other Titans allowed to be in the Upperworld in Olympus' service. Six remained imprisoned far under the earth — it was said that Kronos was kept asleep in its deepest chasm.

Hermes didn't hold any real amnesty against the Titans; Atlas was his mother's father. She had told him a thousand and one stories about his resourcefulness, his love in his craft, and how strong he was. And his strength was turned against him: forced to hold up the heavens in the western sky for the past few thousand years.

Thousands of years was a long time for an immortal not even in his fifth century.

Hermes' vexed smirk deflated to a frown. His cloak slowly drifted back down in the gnawing silence and stillness.

Like the lashing of a whip, his whole body slammed against the gridded bars of the cage with a sharp *crack* as his helmet hit the metal.

So small he was that he slipped inside the prison from the great force that guzzled in all the air, as if some monstrously sized creature inhaled and wished to drag him down by the cloak that encircled his neck.

With a panicked gasp, he kicked against the air, flying until he could grasp the bars and pull himself through, shoving an elbow and bicep up and around the iron. The pressure rivaled the force of escaping Poseidon's angriest oceans, panting for breath that was so suddenly stolen from him. As he faced the blackness below, phantom shadows created in his mind swooped across the hole; it was just his imagination, there was nothing to see.

His arms shook as he crawled off the cage and rolled into the muddy dirt that led back to the Acheron River. His heart hammered against his throat, stuck there like a cumbersome stone.

That didn't feel right; *he* didn't feel right, watching all the color fade from his skin. Every creature that posed a threat in the pit was locked far away from its opening.

Hades would know if this was normal behavior for Tartarus, Hermes thought, fisting his tunics as if pulling them away from his skin would allow him breath. He didn't spend so much time in the Underworld on a daily basis; even he must've had his limit; he was no chthonic god after all. It wasn't even his responsibility.

Wobbling to his feet, the talaria thrust him up.

He'd have to mention it casually of course… Not to admit that he was snooping beyond his approved bounds to deliver a mortal to the hells out of spite, but it wouldn't do well to lie to Hades. Maybe after the delivery of the dog. The dog would soften the blow. Who knows, maybe Hades already knew about the vacuum inside the pit. Maybe it was some powerful new punishment far down there. The Underworld was always innovative, the thought wasn't so asinine.

Clearing his throat and replacing the helm over his face, Hermes took a final second to tidy the pleating under his belt.

But as he turned to hasten down the winding caverns to Hades' palace, that blessed, known voice called out to him with a resounding proclamation. An appeal of his name that he could *never* nor want to refuse —

"HERMES!"

— and in his next step, like the feathers from the high mountains prayed to by a longing king, he was gone from the Underworld, skimming past the island borders of Ithaca once more.

About the Author

Native to Rhode Island, Kiley Knott studied Intelligence Analysis and National Security at American University in Washington, DC. but started writing fantasy stories since her 7th grade English class had a lot of creative writing time, and expanded to historical fiction the next year. When she isn't writing, Kiley can easily be found playing Dungeons & Dragons, working on cosplay, or hanging out with friends at reenactment events.

Also by Kiley Knott

The Heart of Lafayette

Based on a true story, two young, French nobles in an arranged marriage must rely on each other to survive through the American and French Revolutions.

www.ingramcontent.com/pod-product-compliance
Lightning Source LLC
Chambersburg PA
CBHW030118010826
48973CB00002B/317